# THE MOSSHEART'S
# PROMISE

# THE MOSSHEART'S
# PROMISE

## REBECCA MIX

BALZER + BRAY

*An Imprint of* HarperCollins*Publishers*

BALZER + BRAY IS AN IMPRINT OF HARPERCOLLINS PUBLISHERS.

THE MOSSHEART'S PROMISE

Copyright © 2023 by Rebecca Mix

Map illustration by Molly Fehr

All rights reserved. Printed in the United States of America. No part
of this book may be used or reproduced in any manner whatsoever
without written permission except in the case of brief quotations
embodied in critical articles and reviews. For information, address
HarperCollins Publishers, 195 Broadway, New York, NY 10007.

www.harpercollinschildrens.com

Library of Congress Control Number: 2023932463

ISBN 978-0-06-325405-3

Typography by Corina Lupp

23 24 25 26 27  LBC  5 4 3 2 1

FIRST EDITION

*For anyone hoping to find the sun.*

*What roots shall bloom,*

*What blooms must die,*

*Beneath this city to which we flee.*

*By the Gardener's hand,*

*A false world spins,*

*But in its dust,*

*We find the key.*

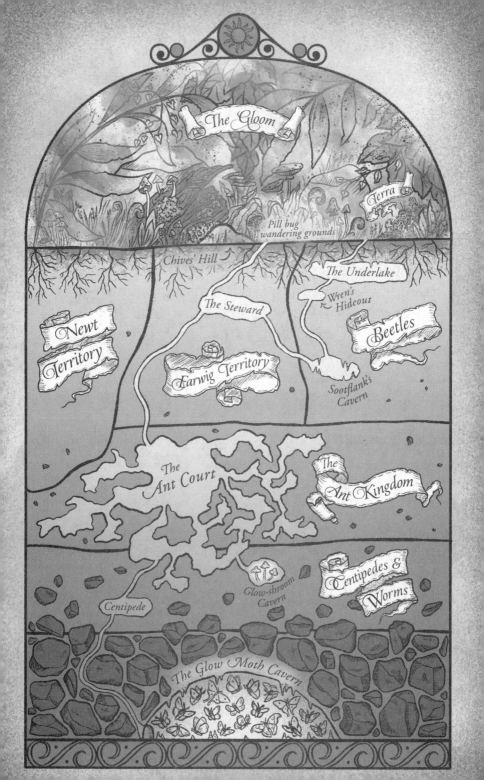

Wouldn't it be strange, she thought, to have a blue sky? But she liked the way it looked. It would be beautiful— a blue sky.

Jeanne DuPrau
*The City of Ember*

# THE TERRARIUM

When the terrarium was freshly planted, the soil damp, the mushrooms not yet sprouted, and the walls free of slime, the gardener held the first fairies of Terra in her palm and told them of their future.

"Someday, the world will be safe again. But for now, you must live in secret. You must hide."

The fairies huddled together and shivered. They would miss the sun. They would miss the rustle of the trees, the dew that gathered in great beads on the grass, the gentle touch of an early dawn breeze.

"How long?" one asked. "How will we know when it's safe to leave?"

The gardener held up a seed. To the fairies, it might as well have been a boulder. Magic crackled in the air.

"One day, when the swamps are filled with frogs again, when the deer return and thistles bristle in the woods, this world will welcome you back. My magic will sustain you for a hundred years—when the century has passed, the flower shall bloom, and its petals will set you free." The gardener's voice grew stern. "You *must* leave when the flower blooms. After a hundred years, the magic will fade—and the terrarium will begin to rot."

They took one last flight around the gardener's cottage and then waved goodbye as she lowered them into their new home. When only a few trustworthy fairies remained, the gardener leaned in, her voice low. "Time dulls even the sharpest memories like water over rock," she warned. "Keep this secret, and keep it close: should the seed fail, seek Atlas. But be warned: freedom will come at a terrible cost."

The fairies promised. The gardener sealed the terrarium, and it was only then that she wept. She had filled the terrarium with the softest moss, the smoothest rocks, the hardiest mushrooms, the gentlest bugs, and the cleanest, clearest water she could find. She'd woven only the most loving magic into every corner of their miniature world.

Still, it did not feel like enough.

The first generation of fairies guarded the seed carefully, as did the second, and the third. But with each year, their memories faded. They stopped telling stories of the sun, the trees, and the breeze. They stopped remembering there had ever been an outside world at all.

And one year, when the remnants of the world were little more than cobwebs clinging in the fairies' minds, the seed was handed down to a young fairy guard.

"One day, this seed will open," the one before her said. "Our home will be destroyed, and we shall be forced to flee."

The young fairy was terrified. She loved their home. She loved the mushroom trees, the moss fields, and the great cold lake. What could be better than the world they already knew? The seed would have to be destroyed.

First she tried to smash it, but it would not break. Then she tried to burn it, but no flame would take. So one night, the fairy carried the seed to the lake and threw it in. The current snatched it up, and away the seed went, past the algae, past the newt caverns, the water beetles, and the bones of fairies long lost. It was still traveling when the fairy turned to leave, a satisfied smile on her lips and a secret in her heart. Down it went, carried by the waters, until it reached the very bottom of the terrarium, where no light reached, and nothing grew.

Years passed. And there the seed waited as the fairies and newts and beetles above it warred and toiled in the ever-constant gloom of their terrarium. Generation after generation, until the magic ran thin and brittle, and the mold crept in.

Until one day, beneath countless layers of soil, bones, and garbage, the flower bloomed—and died.

# 199 YEARS LATER

# ONE

## *A Moth from the Dark*

Ary's wings itched like mad.

She crept forward on her hands and knees, fingers sinking into the soil as her pointed ears twitched. With every movement, her wings rattled and itched something terrible. They were only a few weeks away from bursting free of the pale, papery cocoon that had covered them her entire life. Most of the fairies of Terra grew wings—which was odd, since fairies were not meant to fly. Ary had always known that one day her wings would burst free.

What she *hadn't* known was how itchy they would be, and how *loud*. Even the tiniest twitch caused a ruckus of crinkling and rustling.

And right now they were going to get her caught.

Mushrooms ten times her height surrounded her, their pale brown stalks glistening from another day of mold-scraping. Not that it mattered. Most of them would be covered in mold once more by morning, and the scrapers would return, working as fast as possible yet again to salvage the mushrooms from the creeping rot.

The mushroom field was dark and quieter than a fairy's

prayer, but four months of working as a mold-scraper meant Ary had her route memorized. Ahead of her, in the heart of the field, lay her true prize: half-harvested mushrooms, laid flat to dry before the night patrol came to collect them. *Food*—more than she would get in a year's worth of work rations.

Unguarded and—for now—uncounted.

Ary's stomach rumbled. Mama wouldn't like her stealing, but Mama wasn't here. And though she'd never admit it, Mama was hungry, same as Ary.

A *crunch* came from Ary's left, followed by a low whistle and a wave of pale purple light. Ary flattened herself against one of the giant mushroom stalks, doing everything in her power to keep herself—and her wings—still.

A guard stepped into view, one hand holding a sword, the other holding the leash of a massive moth.

Glow-moths had always been the favored work beasts of the fairies of Terra. They were gentle, hardy, and easy to control. This one was particularly beautiful, with a pearl body and great, powdery pink wings that cast a periwinkle glow over the whole field. Unlike the moths that sometimes drifted over the city, this one's eyes were empty. The moth was enchanted.

"It doesn't hurt them," Mama had said one morning, watching the guard captains sprinkle dust over newly captured glow-moths. "They don't know they're enchanted.

8

Besides, moths can't even talk. For all we know, they can't think."

Still. If the newts and earwigs understood fairies well enough to loathe them, weren't the fairies of Terra borrowing trouble by constantly enchanting one of the few creatures left that *didn't* despise them?

The moth floated forward. Its wings flapped, generating another burst of pastel light that lit up the entire field. Ary's heart seized—but the guard didn't look her way, and the moth's antennae didn't sense her. The pair walked right past, leaving Ary and her itching wings behind.

*Thank the Gardener.* If the guards caught her stealing, they could cut her rations. They could alert the mayor.

Or worse—they could tell Gran.

When the glow-moth's light faded, Ary resumed her creeping toward the harvest pile. She stopped every two seconds to scan the field. With each step, her wings crackled, and though Ary cringed at the sound, she couldn't help but admire them.

What would her wings be like once they unfurled? Would they be soft and opaque, like a moth's, or green, like Mama said hers had once been?

With one trembling hand, Ary reached forward and pulled the tarp free.

Three massive mushrooms lay on their sides, freshly cut into pieces, gleaming with moisture. Ary pulled out her moth-silk bag. Surely no one would notice a few missing chunks.

And even if they *did*, a twelve-year-old mold-scraper would be the last fairy they suspected.

Ary's shoulders drooped. With this much food, maybe Mama would be okay. Maybe she'd build up her strength enough to finally get better.

"That's not a good idea," a voice chirped.

Ary yelped and fell backward.

"Thought you were smarter than that," the voice sang. "Thought wrong."

Ary looked up—and groaned. *"Owl?"*

Owl Diggs peered over the top of the mushroom cap, his wild hair sticking up like fingers, glasses glinting in the dark. Of all the fairies her age, Owl was the most irritating. He was always bothering her, asking her if he could talk to Gran, begging to ask her about the journey that had made Gran famous. He'd finally stopped when Ary yelled at him one day that Gran wouldn't even talk to *her* about it. All Ary had ever learned about Wren Mossheart's famous journey into the Underground was what they'd learned in school— and what Gran blurted out in her nightmares.

Still, a part of Ary felt bad for him. Owl had been born without wings. All fairy magic came from their wings; to keep Terra alive, every fairy had their wings sliced off and ground into a magical dust that grew their crops, healed the sick, enchanted their moths, and kept their fountains flowing. To not have wings that could someday be harvested meant you had no magic. You couldn't do your part in keeping Terra alive.

And yet none of that stopped Owl from being incredibly annoying.

Owl looked pointedly at the mushroom pile. "You realize this is a trap, right?"

Ary scowled. "I was here when they cut them *and* when they covered them. There's no enchantment. I would have seen."

He threw up his hands. "I'm just saying—no one would leave food lying around for no reason. Why are you stealing, anyway? I can give you rations if you need them." He paused, as if for dramatic effect, and added darkly, "Not that it matters. Food is going to be the least of our problems pretty soon."

Ary groaned. She knew how this would play out. Owl was always raving about how Terra was falling apart. He would offer help—*if* Ary was willing to introduce him to Gran. Everything always came back to Gran. Not just with Owl, but with everyone. Ary loved Gran with her whole heart—but being her granddaughter meant that's all Ary would ever be. She was always *just* the granddaughter. Always *just* Wren Mossheart's girl.

A sidenote in Gran's great story.

Owl was still talking. ". . . And the newt attacks have eased off, and the mayor thinks that's a good thing, but why would the newts stop attacking unless they were planning something bad? Plus we haven't heard from the earwigs in months and . . ."

Ary glanced over her shoulder, half expecting to see the light of a glow-moth any moment.

". . . And even the water is getting moldy—"

"Enough!" Ary cried. "No one cares about your ridiculous doomsday predictions, Owl! Least of all my gran!"

"They're not ridiculous," Owl huffed. "There is a very clear multidecade pattern—"

"I don't care! Go home and leave me *alone*!"

The earth beneath Ary's feet gave a tremor, knocking her off balance. When she looked up at Owl, hurt etched every line of his face.

"I was trying to help," he said quietly. "Don't say I didn't warn you."

The boy ducked behind the mushroom and disappeared.

Ary watched the space for a moment, waiting for Owl to pop back up. When a few minutes passed, Ary sighed. "Look, I shouldn't have yelled. I'm sorry."

But no response came. Owl was gone.

Ary rolled her eyes and focused back on the pile. She could worry about Owl later. Right now she needed what she'd come for. She sidled forward, eyes trained on a piece of mushroom the size of her head. Just two pieces would feed her family for a week.

Ary picked up the nearest mushroom piece—and her hand exploded in fire.

The world went white. Blisters burst over her fingers. "Ow! Ow, ow, *ow*!"

Tears flooded her eyes, and she blinked furiously, gasping against the pain. What had she been *thinking*? Of course the pile was going to be enchanted! Owl had been right. They must have done it sneakily, in full view of the mold-scrapers, to find out who had been stealing food. Ary was hardly the only fairy who'd begun pinching extra rations to fill their belly. It seemed like every week more and more guards patrolled the fields.

The heat kept burning, swirling up her wrist. Footsteps thundered toward her. Ary collapsed in a heap, her wings twitching. She needed to run. She needed to get out of here before she got caught for stealing, before they could punish Mama—

Flapping sounded overhead. Ary looked up—

And froze.

One of the glow-moths landed directly in front of her, its eyes starbright and free of enchantment. It seemed to draw Ary forward, drinking her in, until the pain in her hand was only a dull throb. Even as the shouting guards drew closer, the sounds of the world faded away, until it was only her and the moth in the field.

A tired, whispery voice filled her mind as the moth lifted its wings and spoke.

*Wren Mossheart*, the moth said. *Atlas awaits your return.*

Every hair on Ary's body stood on end.

Moths didn't talk. Newts could talk. Earwigs could talk. Even pill bugs *sort of* talked. But a moth? Ary blinked several times, staring at the moth, her heart rate picking up speed as she squinted against the pale pink light.

"What?" Ary whispered. "What did you say?"

A guard picked her up by the wing tip and shook her, and the world crashed back in. Two guards pointed swords at her, spitting words like *thief* and *mayor* and *rations*. One tied her hands behind her back. The other brandished her bag overhead. Ary didn't—couldn't—care, not with how bad her hand hurt.

"It's just some wingling," the first guard snapped.

"Stealing *food*," the second said in disgust. "We're all starving, but instead of getting by on your fair share, you think you can just take extra, eh?"

Ary's hand throbbed. She blinked back tears, suddenly unable to care about getting caught or the hungry pinch in her belly that would only get worse once they surely cut her rations.

"Is this your first time stealing?" the first guard demanded. "Or were you the one pinching carrot rations, too? What's the matter, girl? Mosquito got your tongue?"

Ary shook. "D-did you hear that?"

"Hear what?"

"The moth," Ary rasped. "It just . . . it *spoke* to me."

The guard looked at Ary as though she were speaking gibberish. "Moths don't talk," he said slowly, in the tone of

14

a parent being forced to explain to a particularly dull child that fire was hot and water was wet.

Panic sank icy claws into Ary's heart. He could condescend all he wanted. That moth *had* spoken. Worse, it had called her by her grandmother's name.

Ary had spent her entire life living in her gran's shadow. Being mistaken for her was far, far worse.

Creatures didn't come looking for Gran unless they were fleeing from trouble or bringing it.

"It spoke to me," Ary insisted. "I heard it."

"Sure you did." He turned to the other guard and dropped his voice. "I think that spell might have scrambled her brain. We need a healer."

Ary looked back at the moth, but its eyes were blank again. Enchanted, as if it'd never spoken at all. Nausea swirled in Ary's belly.

Something about this was deeply, terribly wrong.

The second guard peered at her and gasped. "Hang on, I *know* you. You're Wren Mossheart's girl!"

*Oh no.*

"I think we'd better talk to your gran."

The guard grabbed her by her wing tip and marched her forward. But even as they approached Gran's house, all Ary could think about was the moth, and the way its eyes had cleared as it called her Wren.

# TWO

## The Hero in the Fountain

Ary did her best to forget the ominous words of the glow-moth. For the most part, it was easy—between working in the mushroom fields and taking care of Mama and Gran, most days she was so tired that she collapsed into bed and was asleep before her head hit the pillow. But in the quiet moments—when she was cooking dinner, standing in the ration lines, combing the tangles out of Mama's hair—the moth's words came creeping back.

*Wren Mossheart.*

*Atlas awaits your return.*

Ary had searched high and low for the meaning of that strange word—*Atlas*—but neither Gran's books nor the ones in the old library contained a single hint. She'd even snooped through Gran's older diaries—a violation so grave that if Gran found out, she'd be so angry she wouldn't speak to Ary for days—but hadn't found a single reference.

And it wasn't like she was going to ask Gran herself. The old fairy had been furious with Ary when the guards dragged her home. Only Gran's status as the hero of Terra had saved the family from having their rations cut.

"How dare you expose us like that," Gran had snarled once they left. "I don't care if you steal. I care that you got *caught*."

Ary tried to focus on the winding, downhill path to the market. The light was especially poor today, but Mama and Gran needed the lone glow-shroom lamp they had left to light the cottage, so Ary was forced to navigate the dim light alone. Her eyes strained. In Terra, their days were defined by a perpetual twilight. Glowrise came in the morning, when the cliffs that cradled their world brightened and poured watery yellow light across the city. The magical light dimmed throughout the day, until Glowfall came and the cliffs went dark and cold, plunging them back into inky night.

But the worst days in Terra were ones like today, when Glowrise came weakly, or not at all—as if the thing within the cliffs that made the light itself had been dimmed. On those days, the fairies who dared to leave their houses moved about the city with only glow-shroom lamps to light their paths.

On those days, most stayed in their homes, because when the darkness came, so did the attacks from the Gloom.

When she was just a wingling, Ary had asked Mama about the cliffs. How was it possible that the cliffs *made* light? She'd visited them once as a child, had knocked her fists against layers of dried slime long crusted over the rock, and hadn't been able to make sense of it.

"Magic, I suppose." Mama paused, troubled. "They were

17

brighter, though, when I was a girl." As soon as she'd said the words, Mama looked like she regretted them. When Ary pressed her for more answers, Mama had kissed her forehead and told her to leave it alone.

It haunted Ary, even now. Unlike Gran, there were no secrets with Mama. She was honest with Ary always—too honest, sometimes. It felt like a betrayal for her to hold something back.

The chatter of other fairy children floated toward her, breaking her from her thoughts. Once, only adults had gone to market days, exchanging work tokens for meager rations. But as more and more parents got sick, more fairy children took jobs as mold-scrapers and algae-cleaners, and the classrooms grew emptier and emptier. Finally, a year ago, the school closed entirely.

Though the market had just opened, the lines already wound up the road, twisting around the great statue of the Gardener that watched over the market. Ary's eyes lingered. The statue was of a tall, wingless fairy with a smooth face and strange, round ears. In one hand the Gardener held a garden shovel; in the other she balanced a blooming flower.

At the foot of the statue, a few fairies sat cross-legged, tapping the ends of sacred silver shovels together and singing soft prayers about the coming harvest. They called themselves Seedlings and claimed to be the guardians of Terra's history—though Gran liked to sneer and call them the great *liars* of Terra's history. They'd only ever been kind to her, but Ary avoided them all the same.

Now the Seedlings stood in a loose circle, their hands outstretched and wing stubs quivering as they sang the Gardener's Promise, the age-old melody that was imprinted on the heart of every fairy in Terra.

*What roots shall bloom,*
*But what blooms shan't die,*
*Within this city in which we're free.*

One spotted Ary, her brown face breaking into a smile as she lifted a hand.

"Young Mossheart!" she called. "Harvest's blessings on you and the old hero!"

Pretending not to hear, Ary hurried past them. The Seedlings were as bad as Owl when it came to asking questions about her gran and spouting nonsense. And they were a reminder, too, that things seemed to be getting worse. When Ary was tiny, the Seedlings visited the Gardener statue only once a week to sing their prayers—these days, as the mold crept farther and the harvests dwindled, their weekly prayers had become hourly, as if they could sing all of Terra's problems away.

But though there was love in their songs, their eyes were all desperation.

Mama reassured her that eventually, someday, they'd leave her alone, when Ary was older and they realized she wasn't going to be called on some great quest like her gran.

Ary wrapped her fingers around her ration tokens. She'd worked as a mold-scraper every day this month, but now the tiny coins biting in her palm seemed far too small, and far too few. The market sprawled ahead of her.

*Should I join the food line? The medicine line? Oh, the cloth weaver is here today. . . .*

She hesitated. Their cupboard was running low, but the medicine stall might be selling a poultice for Gran's joints, which ached more and more every day. . . . And Ary's shoes were worn so thin her toes now poked out. . . .

Ary's stomach growled. Food it was.

She took her place behind a large fairy man whose wing stubs were bright orange, the scar tissue where they had been sliced off a silvery pink. Fear squeezed her chest. Every fairy of Terra gave up their wings eventually; but now, with her wings only weeks away from unfurling, the sight filled Ary with terror.

*Did it hurt?* she wanted to ask. *Do the stubs still ache, like a bruise that won't heal? Do you miss your wings—or did they cut them so swiftly, you've never even noticed they were gone?*

An old fairy woman with shriveled purple wing stubs got in line behind Ary, wincing as she rubbed her hip. Her hands and legs were twisted with burn marks. Newt scars. Papa had been covered in them. Unlike with the earwigs,

Terra had never been able to drive the newts back into the Underground. And as the rivers ran thinner and the food harvests smaller, the newts only grew more desperate, the fire magic wielded by their generals more vicious as they fought to take what little Terra had.

"Ary!" someone behind her called, breaking her from her thoughts. Tulip and Basil Frostline hurried her way, empty ration bags swinging from their arms. "We knew you'd be here!"

"I'm here every market day."

"That sucks," Basil said. "We don't have to come, but if we stay home, Mama gives us chores. And it's too gloomy today to do anything fun. We can barely *see*."

Ary frowned as they cut in line, glancing at the fairies behind her. "Those people were already waiting."

Tulip snorted. She was a tall, skinny fairy, with fair skin and lovely dark hair. "Does it matter? We're all getting the same gross stuff anyway."

*It matters to whoever is last*, Ary thought. *It matters to whoever gets nothing.*

But she stayed quiet. Why argue? Tulip was going to do what she wanted regardless. Ary looked away. Others joined the line, all marked by Terra's history—missing limbs or eyes, bearing sliced wings and old, aching wounds they'd suffered at the maws of newts and earwigs alike. Ary couldn't meet their eyes. They reminded her too much of Gran—aching, tired, and lonely. She tried to peek around the line, eyeing the meager rations; there were only a few chunks of turnips and carrots. No leafy kale (Gran's favorite) or savory cauliflower (Mama's favorite). Papa had always loved carrots, though Ary couldn't stand them; seeing them now, even wrinkled and withered, made her heart ache.

*I miss you, Papa.*

Ary ran her fingers over the calluses on her palms. She liked to think that he would have been proud of her for being a mold-scraper; that even though it meant missing school, his warm eyes would have shone to know his own daughter was battling to keep Terra fed and strong.

The line shuffled forward again, and the ground beneath Ary's bare feet shifted from dirt to old stones. Tulip and Basil chattered nonstop, not noticing or not caring that Ary barely responded. Ahead of them, the fountain loomed at the very heart of the market. The fountain was a massive collection of wide, shallow pools that fed each other in tiny rivers and glittered day and night. It was a romantic relic of Terra's past, when there had been no mold to fight, and fairies could waste their magical dust on things like fountains and art. Now fairies filled buckets and drank from their palms, picking out clumps of algae and goop, and tossing them aside with hardly a blink.

In the fountain's center, standing proud and eternal, were statues of Terra's three heroes.

The first hero was Monstera Magnos, the founding mayor of Terra, who built their eternal city from scratch. The second was Pothos Petunia, a fairy general who won the first Newt and Fairy War over a hundred years ago.

The third hero, at the center of the fountain, was Gran.

Her statue was newer than the others, built only sixty years ago. It was of Gran as a girl, the famed child of prophecy who'd been born into their world knowing it was hers to save. Gran stood with her face tilted upward, wings flared, hand held high. In her stone palm curled the Sunroot mushroom she'd found in the Underground that had cured Terra's sick and chased away the spotted plague. When Ary was little, she'd thought the statue looked like Mama.

A few years ago, fairies started pointing out that it looked like *her*.

Ary shuddered. The Gran they'd carved into a statue looked fierce and determined—a far cry from the cold hermit who had raised Ary. At her feet was a simple stone placard.

*Wren Mossheart*, it read. *Plaguebreaker.*

There was no mention of the four others who had accompanied Gran on her journey to the Underground. Gran had been the only one to return. The names of her companions, like their lives, had been lost forever.

Ary stared at the statue, her earlier warmth fading.

*What haven't you told us about the Underground, Gran? What happened to your friends? What was so terrible that you've never spoken of them, not once?*

*What happened to you down there that made you so tired and scared?*

23

Behind her, the Seedlings were singing the Gardener's Promise again.

*By the Gardener's hand,*
*The harvest begins,*
*And in Terra's trust,*
*We reap eternity.*

The line moved forward. Tulip and Basil played with their tokens, flipping them in the air and rolling them down their wrists. They had twice as many as Ary did. The Frostline family were the personal guards of the mayor and received the rations to show for it. Tulip and Basil kept chattering, oblivious to the way their clean, fresh-stitched clothes stood out among the rest of the fairies, who stood shoeless and silent, their mouths twisted with hunger.

Tulip kept hopping around, turning this way and that, lifting her dark hair off her neck and dropping it again. When they were halfway to the food stall, Ary couldn't take it any longer. "Something wrong, Tulip?"

Annoyance flashed across Tulip's face. Basil snorted, as if Ary had said one of the most foolish things in the world. It took everything in Ary to keep a kind expression in place.

"Um," Tulip said. She did a weird twist again. Did her neck hurt or something? "Don't you notice anything *different?*" Tulip finally sighed and, in one slow, dramatic motion, spun so her back faced Ary.

"Your wings," Ary gasped. "They've unfurled."

Fresh fairy wings fluttered against Tulip's back. They were quite small, but they *were* beautiful, rounded and lacy blue, with translucent black dots at the tips. Tulip fluffed her hair again. "I bet my wings will make more fairy dust than the next ten combined. They get cut tomorrow."

Ary's stomach did an uncomfortable flip. "You aren't scared?"

"Of course not! What kind of question is that?" Tulip looked down her nose at Ary. "When are *yours* going to unfurl?"

Heat rushed to Ary's face. She was the last of their class to have her wings still growing—but Mama always said good things took time. "Soon, I think. They itch a lot, and they peel more every day, so hopefully—"

"Right," Tulip said, clearly eager to get the conversation back on her. "Well, when *mine* unfurled—"

A commotion came from the front as the vegetable seller clambered onto the top of her stall. Ary's chest squeezed. Was she already out of food? The seller raised her spindly hands, her purple wing stubs twitching. "Attention, everyone! Mayor Nightingale has announced that today the potatoes are ready for harvest—all vegetables are half off!"

Ary's heart leaped. All year, fairy folk toiled in the field, growing massive potatoes, pouring every extra drop of water, fertilizer, and fairy dust they had into their care. Unlike turnips or carrots, which rotted quickly, potatoes lasted forever. Just one potato could feed all of Terra for *months*.

With the potatoes unearthed, there would finally be extra food. Maybe she wouldn't have to be a mold-scraper anymore. Maybe the school would even reopen.

The line moved quickly after that. Instead of worrying over whether they got the best piece of turnip or carrot, fairies gladly took whatever was offered first, knowing fresh potato would be waiting for them soon. Ary didn't even care that her piece was small and hairy.

"Want to climb Giant's Thumb hill and watch the potato unearthing from up high?" she asked.

Interest lit up Basil's and Tulip's eyes. "Don't you usually have to go straight home after market day?"

Ary hesitated. Should she tell Basil and Tulip the truth? That she usually rushed to drop off the food for Mama and Gran because afterward Ary had to go to the mushroom fields to scrape mold until her arms burned?

*We're struggling*, Ary almost said. *We're scared.*

But she was tired of being scared. Her entire life had been plagued by fear. For once Ary wanted to feel *normal*. She wanted to be excited and selfish, the way Tulip and Basil were, with their full bellies and promise of safety. Hadn't she worked hard? Didn't she deserve a few hours of relief?

What was the point of Gran's sacrifice if Ary couldn't have even one day to just enjoy herself with her friends?

"I'm free today," Ary said. "Let's go."

# THREE

## *No Small Potatoes*

Ary, Tulip, and Basil were sweating and puffing by the time they reached the top of the hill overlooking the potato field. Already, a crowd had gathered at the field's edge to witness the harvest. Many of them had poured countless hours into the potatoes—and some had donated their own wings.

From this high, Ary could see most of the city—it looked smaller than she remembered, hundreds of tiny homes packed together, all of them encircled by the massive thorn fence that protected them from the endless Gloom that lurked beyond. From here, she could see the scorched northern gate, where newts had attacked with fire magic only a few months before. Fairies clambered all over the fence, carrying mush-wood to patch it. Glow-shroom lamps flickered like tiny pockets of fire across the city, cutting through the thick midday murkiness thanks to yet another day of low light. Ary eyed the cliffs from the hill.

Once she'd asked Mama if it wasn't the cliffs that made the light, but perhaps something *beyond* them.

Mama had paled. After a long silence, she'd shaken her head and said, "You are too much like your grandmother."

Her words had been like an electric shock to Ary. "What?"

"Too curious," Mama had said with a tight, tired smile. "Nosing for trouble where it doesn't need to be. Look at me, Canary. This world is all we have. It's all we've *ever* had, and all that ever will be. What could be beyond it, when we have all we need right here?"

Ary didn't know. But as she eyed the mostly dead fields and the hungry faces gathered before them, she wasn't sure Terra had everything they needed at all.

"Oh, great," Tulip groaned, snapping Ary from her thoughts. "What is Owl Diggs doing here?"

Ary jolted. Owl sat at the bottom of the hill, his arms wrapped around his legs, alone.

He was always alone.

"Mama said the fairies without wings to give shouldn't get any rations at all," Basil said with a sniff. "All they do is take."

Heat flashed through Ary. If Mama were here, she'd tell Basil she was being unkind, and remind her that Basil hadn't contributed any fairy dust, either. Mama would expect Ary to speak up, to say Owl had offered Ary some of his own rations when he'd realized she was hungry. But . . . it just didn't feel worth it. Being around Tulip and Basil made Ary feel normal for once. Besides, it wasn't like Owl could hear their unkind words.

Basil pulled the turnip chunks from her bag and passed one to Ary.

*I should save this for Mama or Gran*, she thought.

But Ary was up high, her legs outstretched and her friends chattering at her side. Hadn't she worked hard enough, waking at Glowrise repeatedly to scrape mold for hours on end? Didn't she deserve a treat?

Ary bit deep into the turnip and didn't stop until it was gone. Below, the diggers were starting to assemble on the field. Tulip and Basil wriggled in anticipation. They chattered back and forth about rumors of newt attacks and thieves and more ration cuts and—of course—Tulip's new wings. More and more fairies gathered to watch the unearthing.

A cheer sounded in the air, and at long last, Mayor Iris Nightingale walked onto the field.

Ary peered curiously down at her. She'd seen the mayor frequently over the years, but any time she drew near, Ary had always hid, ducking behind doors or mushroom stalks, Gran's furious rants about the mayor ringing in her ears. Every year, Mayor Nightingale sent an invitation to all the notable families to attend the Festival of Terra held at the mayor's mansion.

Every year, Gran tore the invite to shreds and kept Ary home.

Mayor Nightingale raised her hands in welcome. She carried a brand-new, shining glow-shroom lamp with her, and so did every guard in her escort. From far away, it cast the mayor in an ethereal glow, making her silver hair and white robes gleam against the dour, rotting town.

"Folk of Terra!" she called. "This year you all worked harder than ever for our harvest—I am so proud of you, and so thankful for your work. It is you who make Terra strong. It is you who ensure Terra will live forever." The crowd cheered. "Next week's harvest day will mark Terra's *two hundredth* fruitful year. And though our hero is not with us here to celebrate, Wren Mossheart sends her warmest regards."

Ary stiffened. *No she doesn't.* Gran couldn't stand the harvest festival. For as long as Ary could remember, Gran had hidden from every public event. Every year people asked Ary where Gran was—not because they expected her to come, but because they wanted to know why Terra's only living hero wanted nothing to do with them.

A memory flickered behind her eyes; a few years ago, the harvest had been particularly bad. Folk had flooded the mayor's mansion demanding answers. Food theft had sky-rocketed.

That night Mayor Nightingale had visited Gran's house. Ary had held very still, feigning sleep and watching from beneath the blankets. She recalled the way Mayor Nightingale had held herself stiffly and shuddered when Mama offered her tea. She'd refused a chair, and had stood with her arms tightly folded, touching nothing, as though their poverty were an illness she might catch.

The mayor had taken a long, woeful look around their meager cottage and shook her head. "Why do you do this to yourself, Wren? To your family? You could live comfortably, with double rations, if only you'd cooperate."

"Cooperate?" Gran had asked cautiously, coldly, as if she already knew where this was going—as if it was a conversation she and Mayor Nightingale had had a thousand times. And from the way the mayor glared back at her, maybe it was.

Still, Nightingale tried.

"Join me at the festivals," she said. "Walk in the parade. *Celebrate* the harvest. Accompany the city guards on school visits and help explain how vital it is to report when a schoolmate has freshly unfurled wings so they can be cut and harvested as quickly as possible. Help us recruit more soldiers for battles against the newts. People need reassurance, Wren. They need their hero. They need *hope*."

"You want me to lie," Gran said. "My answer is no. I'm not going to smile and pretend everything is perfect when my family is dying from mold and the harvests grow smaller each year. You can spin fantasies all you want, Iris; I'd rather starve."

"Ma," Mama had said in her soft, worried way. "It's not just you starving."

Ary remembered triumph flashing across Nightingale's face, and grief across Gran's.

Gran had looked away. "The answer is still no. Now get out of my house—while I still have it."

Was that why Mayor Nightingale was lying now? To give the people of Terra hope, however she could? It had been a long, hard year. Many had been lost to mold—but something about a two hundredth harvest, and the impending celebration, seemed to fill the air with new energy. Still, it felt wrong to know some of it was built on a lie.

"We face greater challenges than ever," the mayor said. "My scouts have reported record numbers of newts and earwigs lurking in the Gloom beyond the fence—and rumblings from ants deep in the earth, hungry and waiting for Terra to weaken."

Ary shivered. It was a miracle Terra had survived as long as it did. Sometimes it felt like their tiny village of fairies was the only blip of good standing against the monstrousness that lurked in the world beyond. Fear of the newts seemed to creep into every part of life here. But as Ary watched the scared faces around her, it was not Papa she remembered, but Gran.

Gran, turning away as a guard recounted surviving an encounter with a newt that had tried to eat him.

"Liar," she'd muttered bitterly, so soft she could have only spoken to herself. "They've no appetite for us. They only want better. *He* only wanted better."

When Ary had asked who *he* was, Gran had flinched, guilt heavy in her eyes. Instead of answering, she'd ghosted a hand over Ary's hair and squeezed her shoulder tight.

"Remember, Canary, that everything that seems permanent is usually anything but." She'd cast a dark look back at the guard. "And the people who want to convince us otherwise usually have their own agenda."

It had made no sense to Ary then, and it made no sense now as she listened while the mayor somberly listed the names of six fairies lost to the newts that year. A silence descended over the crowd, and the mayor swiped away a tear and lifted her chin.

"Through the harvests they live on," she intoned. "Together, we can face anything. Together, Terra is eternal. Now I'll keep you no longer. Today, we dig. Tomorrow, we feast!"

The diggers leaped to work, grabbing shovels to heave great clumps of dirt over their shoulders. Slowly, the earthy skin of potatoes appeared. Excited chatter rumbled through the crowd as more and more emerged. Finally, after three hours, the diggers sat back and wiped sweating brows as the crowd cheered. The potatoes were *massive*, bigger than last year's harvest, or the year before that. Maybe the biggest ever!

Ary could have wept at the sight. Finally the cupboards would be full. No more hunger pains. No more water-thin soup and choking down hairy turnips. She no longer cared that Mayor Nightingale had lied about Gran. People needed something to hope for. This feeling that bubbled through her right now was why.

When the first of the three great potatoes was unearthed, a long, spindly saw that took ten folk to carry was hauled forward and draped over the top. Ary clenched her fists. This was it. The saw would slice clean through, revealing glistening, pale yellow potato flesh, and all would be well.

The diggers pushed on the saw—and the skin bowed inward.

A nervous titter went up from the crowd. The diggers hesitated. They looked back at Mayor Nightingale, who waved for them to cut again. The diggers pushed once more, and the potato skin bowed farther. The saw seemed to half disappear, like a fingernail sinking into a particularly swollen pimple.

The onlookers shuffled their feet. Were the blades too dull? Were they doing it wrong?

The diggers counted to three, and in one great motion, all shoved as hard as they could. The saw sagged deep into the potato, pushing well into the middle.

And instead of cutting, the potato skin *jiggled*.

The saw wobbled. The diggers gave it one final push. The saw blade sank out of sight. One of the diggers gave a startled shout—and the potato *burst*.

Black liquid exploded everywhere. It rushed over the field, smoke curling into the air where the slime touched the soil. All the diggers cried out in terror and scrambled out of the way. The potato skins came apart and flapped to the ground, revealing undersides coated in a layer of the same thick white mold that crept over the mushroom fields every morning.

The fairies howled as they realized the potatoes they had waited for all year—the potatoes they were depending on to keep them alive—were rotten to their core.

# FOUR

## *The Rot*

For a moment, Ary, Tulip, and Basil didn't move. Startled cries rose into the air, higher and higher, reaching like fingers into the great murky sky. Mayor Nightingale called for calm, but no one listened. The diggers rushed to the second and third potatoes. They heaved the saws over their heads and pulled down.

Both potatoes burst like the first, spilling black slime all over the field, filling the air with the sickly-sweet stench of vegetables left to rot, their skins ruined with mold. Some fairies screamed; others wept. As their cries lifted into the air, the stench of rot overwhelmed the field, and even on the hill the filthy reek of sour compost was so strong Ary's eyes watered.

Tulip and Basil stood slack-jawed, their dark eyes reflecting the ruined earth.

Below, sitting on the hill, Owl Diggs stared up at her, his lips pressed into a flat, knowing line.

"Leave!" Mayor Nightingale shouted furiously. "Get out of the way *now*!"

The slime kept spreading, rushing over the field in thick,

undulating waves. The soil hissed and cracked; the air reeked of rotting flesh.

"Evacuate the area! Return to your homes! And *don't let it touch you!*"

Suddenly what had been a pleasant, excited crowd was now a panicked stampede. Ary tried to swallow the burning wave of fear rising in her chest. That field would never be useful again. Slime like that poisoned soil so thoroughly it would take buckets of fairy dust to reverse the damage. Buckets they didn't have, with fairy wings growing smaller with each generation, and fewer fairies born every year.

"Hey, winglings! *Move!*" a guard below them shouted, gesturing frantically with his sword. Ary, Tulip, and Basil broke into a panicked stumble, letting the crowd sweep them off the hill.

"Someone bring me fairy dust!" Mayor Nightingale bellowed. "Tell the market to evacuate!"

Ary kept running, hot tears threatening to spill down her cheeks. None of this was right. Gran had saved Terra, hadn't she? Wasn't that why Gran was so hollow, and bitter, and distant—because she had given up so much, to give Terra everything?

Gran was a hero. Everyone said so.

So why didn't they have any food?

The market had fallen into chaos. Instead of the calm, orderly lines from this morning, fairies now shoved against each other, their nervous voices filling the air. Someone knocked the food for Mama and Gran from Ary's hands and trampled it before she could snatch it back up. Others knelt in front of the statue of the Gardener, their wing stubs spread wide, their heads tilted to the sky. The Gardener stared back at them, silent as ever. The amassed Seedlings raised their voices in prayer, singing the Gardener's Promise louder than before, as if adding volume to the words would make them true. Other fairies joined in, their voices climbing, climbing, climbing, as though their song might somehow erase the rot now spilling across their field. A few lifted their heads to stare at her, their eyes wide with appeal, holding a question Ary never had the answer for.

*Where is our hero?* their eyes begged. *Why are we still suffering?*

Mayor Nightingale's voice rang through her mind.

*People need reassurance, Wren. They need hope.*

A hand landed on her shoulder. Ary jerked away, fearing it was a Seedling, and instead found herself staring into the frantic eyes of Owl Diggs.

"Do you believe me now?" he demanded. The very ground seemed to rumble as Owl's voice cracked with despair.

Ary cringed away. "Owl, please, now is not a good time—"

"What don't you understand? We're *out* of time! Ary, Terra is dying, and it's getting worse. *Please*, if I could just talk to your gran—"

Ary ripped free of his grasp and broke into a run, blocking out the shouts that followed her.

It always came back to Gran. She was the problem solver, the source of hope, the solution—in theory. They only ever seemed to remember Gran existed when they wanted her to save them all over again.

But Gran had made it clear her days of saving people were behind her.

Terra was on its own.

Ary sped away from Owl. He could have chased her—he was taller than her, and he wasn't weighed down by still-unfurled wings—but instead he let her go. Tears carved paths down Ary's cheeks. When she crested the market road, Ary turned. From here, she could see the field in the distance, the black slime spreading over it like a great, terrible bruise. Mayor Nightingale and two other guards stood with their hands raised, and even from here she could see the shimmer of magic crackling around them as they just barely held the slime from spilling into the market below.

If the slime reached the market, then the fountains and Terra's main water source would be destroyed.

How many more ruined harvests could Terra withstand before they ran out of fairy dust altogether?

In front of the fountains, as still as the old hero statues themselves, Owl Diggs stood alone, hands in his pockets and face tilted to the sky, as panicked fairies streamed by him or fell to their knees in front of the Gardener statue.

Ary jerked away. They'd make it through this—they always did. The folk of Terra were strong. Resilient. They carved out their survival no matter what.

Still, even as she left the market behind, Ary couldn't escape the words that passed from fairy to fairy as news of the ruined harvest spread.

"The rot," every fairy in Terra whispered to the next, "it's everywhere."

"It's here."

# FIVE

## Stories and Dreams

Instead of going home, Ary went to the mushroom fields, rushing to take a spot as a mold-scraper before the panic spread and every fairy who could spare a hand showed up for work. It was past Glowfall by the time she got home. Shadows blanketed the inside of Gran's tiny cottage, broken only by the soft pulse of the glow-shroom lamp that seemed to grow duller each year. Dust had somehow covered every surface again, though Ary had cleaned just that morning. Her heart ached. It hadn't always been like this. When Papa had been alive, even in the hardest days, the walls of their cottage had been filled with light and laughter. Even Gran could be coaxed into smiling.

After he died, the darkness crept in, and it never left.

Now Gran dozed in the corner, her mouth open and her white hair fluffed around her head. She looked softer in her sleep. Where Mama had always been honest and warm, Gran had spent most of Ary's life at a distance, removed and silent. Where Mama gave hugs and laughter freely, Gran served only frowns or quietly murmured rebukes.

Ary tried not to take it personally. Time had softened

Gran, but it had not erased the scars that twisted around her legs like spiderwebs. When Ary was little and she'd asked what had caused the scars, Gran had said she'd gone on a great journey so Ary would never have to find out.

"You must understand," Mama had said once. "People like her, they're different. Heroes give up pieces of themselves to protect the rest of us. Your gran, she loves us in her own way. Even if she can't show it."

"Ary," a voice rasped. "Where is my sweet girl?"

Ary jumped up. "Mama?"

Mama half sat up in bed. The circles beneath her eyes were deeper, her once vibrant skin ashen and covered in sweat, but she was awake. She reached out a hand. Ary scrambled to crouch beside her.

"Ary," Mama sighed, and on her lips, it sounded like a prayer.

Ary's eyes stung. "Hi, Mama."

"Come here—let me look at you." Mama's fingers brushed Ary's cheek. They were warm and dry, but the veins of her arms seemed to bulge more than before. Had she lost more weight?

"How's school? How are your wings? How's Gran?" Mama breathed. Her breath smelled wrong—sickly sweet, like rotting fruit.

"School is good," Ary lied. She didn't have the heart to tell her the school had been closed for ages. "Wings are itchy, Gran is cranky."

Mama laughed, wincing as the laugh became a cough.

*She's getting worse.*

Mama coughed harder. Ary hurried to the other side of the cottage to fetch water, and her heart dropped. The pail she'd brought just yesterday was already cloudy. Tiny clumps of algae bloomed in the center. Ary scooped it out with her fingers, wiped the slime on her pants, and handed green-tinged water to Mama with a wince.

"Would you look at that face—you'd think you found mold in your turnip!" Mama took a sip of stale water and set it aside. She held out her too-skinny arms. "Come here."

And though Ary probably should have gone to fetch clean water—though she should have told her about the potatoes, or gone to bed because tomorrow was another day of mold-scraping—all she could do was clamber into bed alongside Mama. Ary tucked her chin into her mother's shoulder, breathing in deep.

Mama had once smelled like earth and nectar. Now she smelled of sickness and sweat.

"Look at your wings," Mama whispered. She ran her fingers over the itchy, papery cocoon, humming under her breath. "They're going to be beautiful—I just know it. Did I ever tell you what it was like when my wings unfurled?"

"No," Ary lied. She had heard the story a dozen times before—but this was the most Mama had spoken in a week, and Ary would have done anything to keep her talking.

Mama's eyes fluttered closed. "They were beautiful—

43

bright beetle green, with splashes of dark gold. Like your grandfather's wings. I loved them, though I only had them a week. They felt like something I'd been waiting my entire life to meet."

"Did you fly?" Ary asked, like every time before.

"No." Mama looked faintly troubled. "No, silly, fairies don't fly. Besides, they cut them before I had the chance. As soon as my wings dried, they were gone. Just like that. My whole life growing them—years of watching that cocoon get thicker and thicker and dealing with that terrible itching— and then they cut them." Mama forced a tired smile. "Then again, that's why we grow them. They hold the magic that keeps Terra healthy, and we all must do our part."

At the word *healthy*, the image of the ruined potatoes sprang to Ary's mind. Cold crept through her as she remembered the stench in the air, and the way Owl had grabbed her shoulder, desperate to talk to Gran. She swallowed. She wanted so badly to tell Mama about it; to tell her how scared she was, how things were getting worse, that the water was always dirty, and the light kept weakening.

But Mama already looked so tired—and Ary had missed her terribly. So instead, she threaded her arms around Mama's neck and whispered, "Tell me about Papa. Tell me about the day you met."

And Mama did. She held Ary close, her voice low and scratchy as she told Ary of the day she met a fairy boy with brilliant blue wings. She told Ary of the garden they'd planted before a bad harvest poisoned the land and they had to move in with Gran; of the glow-moths that had scattered silver pollen over their wedding. And she told Ary stories about Gran—fierce tales of Gran battling newts as a young fairy, of Gran returning with a rare mushroom that cured their entire city of sickness.

But as Ary drifted to sleep, nestled against her mother's side, the same images kept spinning in the back of her mind—of the water bucket, already choked with algae. Of the potatoes, splitting open and spilling slimy rot across the field. Of the mold that seemed to come back faster and stronger every day.

And of the glow-moth that landed in front of her—and called her Wren.

Ary dreamed of flying.

In the dream, she soared through a strange blue sky. Fairies weren't meant to fly, but fly she did, faster than a lightning bug, smoother than a glow-moth. Papa and Mama flew alongside her, flipping through the air, whooping and laughing.

The dream changed. White mold crept over Papa's wings, and he dropped from the sky. Mama dove to help him, but her wings crumbled to ash. Ary cried out and tried to dive for them, but the wind carried her forward and away. It took her over a great chasm filled with water, and the air clouded with smoke. Terra came into view, overwhelmed by fire-wielding newts, but then the flames vanished, and the newts melted into a wave of black slime. It crept over every house, every cottage, every garden, swallowing all of Terra whole. The slime bubbled and formed a ball. Ary flew closer.

The ball cracked in half—

And inside, coiled tight, was a snake.

It was a writhing silver creature, with milky-white eyes and a pink forked tongue. Mold crept over its tail; slime oozed all around it. Even surrounded by horror, Ary was awed. Snakes were mythical monsters that slithered only within the confines of Seedlings' stories—but here was one, alive and real as the wings on her back. The wind whisked Ary forward, past the burning homes, past the slime. The snake raised its head, and Ary hovered in front of it.

The snake reared up until it towered over Ary. Its scales were dull and cracked. Dust floated into the air as it rearranged its coils, revealing flashes of brown beneath.

It met her eyes.

"Wren Mosssssssheart." Its fangs flashed in the firelight. "You abandoned ussss. You *lied*!"

The snake lunged and swallowed Ary whole.

Ary jolted awake. Sweat covered her body and her wings itched so bad they nearly burned. The last thing she saw was the snake's mouth closing around her, that pink forked tongue pulling her down, down, down.

"It was just a nightmare," she whispered. "Just a nightmare. Go back to sleep."

Beside her, Mama dozed, her mouth open. Ary turned to pull the blanket over her and froze. Even in the half-light, with only a single glow-shroom lamp casting a weak green shadow across the inside of Gran's cottage, Ary could see something . . . odd. Something familiar.

A pit of dread opened in Ary's stomach as she clambered out of bed and unhooked the glow-shroom lamp from the vines strung across Gran's ceiling.

Ary held the lamp over Mama's face. Her cheeks looked swollen, as if she'd just taken a great mouthful of water. With one hand, Ary reached out and gently pried apart Mama's lips—and screamed.

Filling Mama's mouth, coating her tongue and the insides of her cheeks and the back of her throat, was a layer of thick white mold.

# SIX

## *A Good Little Fairy*

The mold was everywhere. It coated Mama's teeth, her tongue, the back of her throat, and blanketed her gums. It grew on her hair, her nails, and fuzzed the soles of her feet. A patch had even grown on Ary's arm where Mama's skin had nestled against hers. Ary screamed again and staggered backward, crashing into the wall, clawing at the mold on her arm so furiously she drew blood. The lamp slipped from her hand and cracked, spilling a few pieces of glow-shroom across the floor. On the bed, Mama began to cough wildly. Her head tilted back at a terrible angle.

Gran's eyes flew open. She half leaped from the rocking chair. Time seemed to slow as Gran followed Ary's horror-stricken eyes to where Mama lay in her bed. Gran moved across the room to peel back Mama's lips just as Ary had, then snatched her hand back as though she'd been burned.

"No," Gran whispered. "Not you, too. Not my girl."

Ary couldn't breathe. Suddenly she was just a wingling again, watching as the mold crept over Papa, peering out from under the bed as the healer pulled Mama and Gran aside and said, "It's time to prepare your goodbyes."

She couldn't lose Mama, too. Not now. Not like this.

Gran was trying to wake Mama. First she shook her gently, calling her name, and then harder. Mama's arms flopped around like a doll's, all limp and wrong, and Gran was shouting at her to wake up. But Mama remained still. Only the slight rise and fall of her chest showed she was still there.

Terror choked Ary's heart. It swept through her body, turning her limbs to ice. Memory flashed behind Ary's eyes. Of Papa, still and silent and filled with mold, lying beside the other two fairies who had fallen ill that same week. They'd been Seedlings, nameless. They were buried in their robes, holding hands, and it had seemed wrong that Papa was alone while the other two got to go together.

It had been a damp, lean year, with less light than usual shining from the slime-slick cliffs cradling their world. But the mold had eventually retreated. It always did.

This time felt different. This time felt like Mama was the beginning of something terrible.

Gran bent over Mama, a low, terrible noise coming from her throat, the same noise Mama had keened over Papa. In the days before Papa had died, when they thought Ary was asleep one night, Mama had pulled Gran aside and asked her if she could find her way back to the Underlake—the magical spring of her youth whose waters were said to heal any and all ailments.

"You know I can't go back there," Gran had argued,

her voice fierce. "Back into the Gloom, and so close to the Underground."

Mama had taken a deep breath. "If you won't go, then I will. I'm a Mossheart. Same as you. If you survived the trip, so can I—"

"*No!*" Gran had sucked on her teeth and finally went limp. "I can't let you go out there—I won't. I'll leave in the morning. And if I don't come back—if Nightingale comes to question you—you never knew a thing about this."

"I would never—"

"Promise me, Robin."

"Okay," Mama had whispered, tears leaking down her cheeks. "I promise."

An hour later, Papa stopped breathing.

*But what if it isn't too late for Mama?*

The water bucket gleamed in the corner.

Ary came shakily to her feet and lifted the pail of filthy spring water. The handle bit into the soft curves of her fingers. Ary's wings itched, itched, itched, and her eyes lingered on Mama. Gran knelt over her, as still as her statue in the town square.

"Gran," Ary whispered, and then louder. "Gran."

Gran raised her head, turned, and froze. Her eyes cleared, as if she were truly seeing Ary for the first time. Instead of speaking, Ary lifted the bucket. Sixty years seemed to pass across Gran's face.

"Canary Mossheart," Gran warned. "Don't you dare."

A chill swept through Ary. "Gran, please. We were too late with Papa, but if the Underlake can save—"

"No."

"The mold is only a day old and maybe—"

"I said *no*."

"If you told me how to get there—"

"The Underlake cannot save her," Gran warned, something bitter in her eyes.

"But that's not what the stories say!" Ary said desperately. "That's not what *you* said. And you've been there before— I know you have. If you just told me where to go—"

"*Enough!*" Gran shouted. She seemed to swell as she stalked toward Ary. "No more, Canary! There is nothing I can do—there is nothing *any* of us can do! What part of this don't you understand?"

"But you're a hero," Ary stammered. "You're *the* hero."

"I *was* a hero!" She'd never yelled like this before. Had never looked so *angry*. It was as if a completely different person wearing Gran's face had stepped into the room. "And now I'm old. And what did I get for it? A broken body covered in scars, a mind plagued with nightmares and guilt, and a world that's still rotting." Her lips trembled, and Gran looked past Ary, as if staring at something only she could see. Her fingers knotted at her sides. "You're just a child," Gran said softly, sadly. "It's not your job to save us, Canary. It's not your job to save *anyone*."

"But you did," Ary whispered.

Gran's eyes were bright and angry. "Adults love to dream that children will fix the messes they were too selfish to take care of. They use it as an excuse, push their problems to the next generation. Do you think I *wanted* to venture into the Underground at your age? I never asked to be born to prophecy, to have the world dumped on my shoulders. I was only a girl. The things I saw . . . the things I *lost* . . ." Gran shuddered. "It shouldn't have happened to me, and I won't let it happen to you. You're staying here. I'm sorry, Canary. Even if the Underlake could help, it's too late for her. My answer is final."

Ary grew still. Her attention drifted past Gran, to the limp form of Mama on the bed, lips covered with mold. The silence blanketing the cottage was so thick Ary could have sliced it with a knife. Her chest threatened to cave in on itself.

"Please," she tried again, tears streaming down her cheeks. "She's my mom."

Gran had never looked more tired. "And she's my daughter."

Cold swept through Ary. It was as if she was finally seeing Gran for the first time. Her whole life, Ary had viewed Gran through the same reverent lens of history as the rest of Terra—but at the end of the day, this was all she was. This was all that was left.

Gran had been a hero once. But now she was a scared

old woman who would let her daughter die for fear of things lurking in the dark. There would be no convincing Gran. No begging.

"Okay," Ary whispered, her voice sounding far away. "I'm sorry."

Gran softened. "I'm sorry, too. I wish—" Her voice caught. "I wish we could help her, truly. But the most we can do now is keep her comfortable. Get some rest."

Ary nodded wordlessly, her body numb. Gran never, ever said she was sorry. If she was saying it now, that meant Mama was truly doomed. Ary climbed into bed and rolled over to face the wall. She lay there for a long time, her eyes closed, her body stiff, mind racing too fast to sleep. At one point, Gran's shadow fell over her, and every part of Ary cried out for Gran to wake her. To say, *I changed my mind. Pack your things. We're going.*

But Gran merely sighed and went back to Mama's bedside. It was hours before she fell asleep, and finally the cottage was still.

Ary counted to ten—and before she knew what she was doing, she slid out of bed, careful to avoid the floorboards she knew to creak even at the slightest touch, and worked her arm into the crook in the wall where she knew Gran kept her journals that Ary was to never, ever touch. Her heart beat so hard her chest hurt. Her fingers skimmed the spines, groping in the dark, and she pulled several free, flipping through them. Gran's journals never made sense to her; they were mostly gibberish scattered across pages filled with sketches. Usually the drawings were of Mama, of Terra, of the mushroom fields or the market stalls.

But there was one person in the pages Ary didn't understand—a beautiful fairy, with wide eyes and shiny dark hair. Ary paused on the drawing of her now, her fingers skimming over the sketch. She'd made the mistake of asking Gran once who the girl was, and Gran had gone white and told her if she ever touched her journals again, Ary would no longer be welcome in her home.

Ary flipped past the girl, searching for the pages she'd read in secret before. Her heart seized.

In sloppy handwriting across the top of the page, the Gran of over forty years ago had written:

*Year 152*

*THE UNDERLAKE*

There was a single entry. It was about her grandpa, Rowan, who'd died long before Ary was born. Gran rarely spoke of him, and when she had, Ary's grandpa had always sounded more like a distant friend. Any hint of him always felt like a gift from the past, a glimmer of family she'd never known. She'd often wondered, if her grandfather were still alive, if he might have loved her in a way Gran never could.

Ary's eyes drank in the words.

*Rowan caught the mold.*

*I thought the Sunroot had wiped it out of Terra along with the spotted plague, but it's come back.*

*He's lucky—I was able to sneak off to the Underlake and bring back a pouch of water to cure him. We agreed to keep the lake a secret, in case Terra needs it someday. But the waters were so low. . . .*

*It still haunts me. It fills my nightmares; it clouds my dreams. Rowan tells me not to fret, that I did my part, and Terra is safe. That a few people sickening was inevitable.*

*But I know in my heart I failed.*

*The mold will come back. It always comes back.*

*And that means this was all for nothing.*

Beneath Gran's dour, worried words, drawn in a scratchy, uncertain hand, was a map.

Ary raised her eyes. Gran had fallen asleep curled beside Mama in her bed. In her sleep, Gran looked smaller. More mortal. It was strange to be near her sometimes, to reconcile this frail, scared old woman with the statue of a brave girl in the center of the fountain. Terra's third and final chosen hero.

Ary was no hero. She was just Wren Mossheart's granddaughter. Just the shadow of a chosen one who'd long hung up her sword.

But she was also Mama's daughter.

And Mama needed her.

So maybe that was why Canary Mossheart—who had always been a good, polite little fairy—looked at her sleeping grandmother in the waning light of their cottage and made a choice that was not polite or good. Maybe that was why, instead of putting her grandmother's journal away, she tucked it in the front of her shirt, unhooked their cracked glow-shroom lamp from the wall, and crept toward the bucket in the corner of the room.

The Underlake existed. It had healed someone before. And by Gran's scribblings, she knew could get there in only two days, so long as she walked the right path.

Ary stole toward the door. She turned and took one last look around the small, dirty cottage where she'd spent her entire life. She looked at Gran, so frail in sleep, and Mama, barely breathing at all.

Once, Gran had given up everything to save Terra. Mama had never been a hero—but she had spent her entire life sacrificing everything for Ary, shielding her, giving up rations and water and hope so Ary could survive. And Mama had loved Ary, fiercely and brilliantly, long after her own reason for loving had disappeared into the dirt beside two nameless Seedlings.

It was time Ary made that love worth it.

"Hold on, Mama," Ary whispered. "I'm going to fix this. I promise."

Ary locked the door behind her and did not look back.

# SEVEN

## *The Fence*

Instead of taking the winding path down to the town market, Ary tied the bucket to her hip and climbed.

She moved north, toward the great spring where the fairies had once collected water before it became so thick with algae and mold that it began to make them sick. The glow-shroom flickered treacherously, and Ary couldn't tell if it was her imagination or the early Glowrise that made it look dimmer than usual. The road grew knotted and uneven. Unlike the dirt paths worn smooth by thousands of fairy feet, the roads of outer Terra saw only the boots of guards and the stray troublemaker.

Signs painted on mushroom-parchment flapped around her.

*Village limits*, they read. *Guard escort only.*

*Do not pass.*

Beyond them, a braided fence of thorns, wicked tips gleaming in the gloom. Three glow-moths perched atop the fence, their great, luminescent wings bathing outer Terra in soft blue and purple. Their eyes were blank, enchanted— empty.

A single guard sat in front of the fence, his back to the gloomy wastes that lay beyond the village.

The guards of Terra were meant to keep the beasts out. The fairies might have won the newt wars, but that didn't stop the creatures from attacking. So why was the guard *facing* Terra? Fairies had no reason to flee Terra—right?

Gran's voice floated through her mind, bitter and clear as day.

*The guards don't protect us. They protect what they can take from us. You try to keep your wings, little one, and see how kind they are then. You try to leave Terra behind, and watch how quickly this paradise becomes a prison.*

Ary sat back on her heels and shoved the lamp under her shirt to dull its glow. Her eyes scanned the thorn fence. It was a twisting, terrible thing that towered well above their tallest building, woven so tightly even the smallest fairy couldn't slip through.

Ary crept closer. The guard didn't budge.

Shouldn't he be patrolling?

Or doing . . . something?

A line of drool ran from his bottom lip as he snored. A sword lay unbuckled in the dirt by his feet. At his hip, sitting half open, was a rucksack of food. Ary's stomach gurgled. She could almost *smell* the vegetable chunks he'd squirreled away. He must be high-ranking to have so much food.

*Or maybe he stole it,* she thought. *But unlike me, he didn't get punished for taking what he needed.*

If she was heading out into the Gloom, she'd need supplies. It hadn't felt right to take food from home when their cupboards were already nearly empty. But surely the guard could get more supplies? Her attention darted from his sword to the food again. Gran would have taken the weapon.

The sword was the smart choice. The hero's choice.

Her stomach rumbled.

Ary took up the rucksack, wrapped a hand around the nearest thorn, and climbed.

It was slow, exhausting work. Every time Ary reached for a new thorn, the papery cocoon covering her wings rustled, and she'd freeze. Sweat crawled down her arms and pooled in the crooks of her elbows. Her shoulders and calves burned. After several minutes of climbing, Ary's fingers ached, and her legs trembled.

*Almost there. Don't look down. Don't look—*

Ary looked down.

The guard from before was no bigger than a child's toy, slumped against the earth, still dozing. A dizzy feeling spiraled from her belly all the way up to her ears. From here, she could see the potato field, the slime-ruined soil bare and charred like a great, terrible scar.

Owl's voice rang through her mind.

*Terra is dying, and it's getting worse.*

Ary shook herself. That problem wasn't hers to solve. She just had to get to the Underlake and back to cure Mama. The mayor and the other adults could figure out how to save their town.

Ary twisted and placed her foot on a branch. Her toes brushed something soft—and she froze.

Flat against the fence, wings cloaked in shadows, the sleeping moth she'd just stepped on was nearly invisible. The great beast stirred. It rustled its wings with a shiver, and its eyes focused on her.

A terrible humming filled the air.

*Brrrrrrzzzzz, brrrrrzzzzz, brrrrzzzzzz.*

The moth shook itself, sending out great pulses of light with its wings.

"No," Ary begged. "No, no, *no, please!*"

It was too late. To her left, another moth stirred, then another.

*Brrrrrrzzzzz, brrrrrzzzzz, brrrrrzzzzz.*

One by one, the glow-moths awoke.

Now, instead of their gentle pastels, their wings flashed bright yellow and vibrant green. They lit up Terra's sky like the heart of a terrible fire. Ary's hands went numb.

In the distance, more beacons leaped to life. Lights flickered on in Terra one by one. At the base of the fence, the guard finally jolted awake.

"It's a wingling!" he shouted. *"Stop!"*

Fear stuttered in Ary's heart. Fleeing Terra was the ultimate offense, especially as someone with wings that hadn't yet been cut. She had spent a life taking from Terra's resources.

Terra would ensure she replenished them, one way or another.

The fence trembled as the guard began to scale it. Ary began climbing as fast as she could now, hands burning, arms straining. She was so close. Gran's journal bumped against her chest, and the bucket rattled against her hip. Ary's hand hit the top of the fence. She grabbed at a branch and vaulted herself over—and froze.

Before her, sprawling into an endless sea of darkness, was the Gloom. Ary swayed on the fence, suddenly overwhelmed by the urge to either laugh or cry. The darkness seemed to have a weight to it—heavy and cold and endless, swallowing up everything beyond Terra's tiny, gleaming heart. How did anything move out there, in the center of their world, where even the watery light from the cliffs didn't reach? How did anything survive at all? It seemed to go on forever. She'd always thought she'd be able to see the cliffs on the other side of the world from up here—but all she saw was an endless, ever-stretching, cold night.

*I am so small,* Ary thought hysterically. *Me, Gran, Mama, all of Terra—compared to this, we are so, so small.*

Terra was a fluke. A blip of light and life thriving in a gloomy, dead land. Who was she, to think she could venture out into that endless stretch of black and return with water to heal Mama? Who was she to think she could find the Underlake with only a tiny lamp and an old journal to guide her?

Was this how Gran had felt when she left Terra? Infinite and tiny all at once?

Ary's hands shook. She pulled Gran's journal from the front of her shirt and flipped it open. Again, the face of the mysterious girl Gran had compulsively drawn stared out at her. Ary flipped past her, fingers shaking as she looked for the map to the Underlake. Washes of blue, green, and yellow light flared across the page. The map swam in front of her eyes; Gran had circled markers such as rocks and old, dried riverbeds, but from up here, Ary could see nothing. She'd have to be on the ground to find any landmarks—

A hand closed around Ary's ankle.

Ary screamed, jerking backward, and the journal spiraled out of her hand.

*"No!"*

With a sad flutter of pages, it plummeted into the dark. That journal was her only map to and from the Underlake. Without it, she'd be navigating mostly off Gran's myths, and what little she remembered from glancing at the pages. If she didn't have it with her—if she didn't know the way back—

"Hey!" a voice barked. "What do you think you're doing?"

The guard tugged sharply on her leg. He'd scaled the fence with frightening speed.

Ary twisted to look at him, and shock washed across his face. "You're the little Mossheart girl. The one they caught stealing."

Numbness swept through her. They might punish Gran and Mama. "No, I'm not—"

"Look," the guard said carefully. "Whatever your reason for leaving is, it's not worth it. Climb down, child. Go home."

And she could. If she waited any longer, the guards would carry her back down the fence themselves. Who was she, to think she was up to this task? Gran would be furious, their rations would be cut, but Ary would be safe from whatever was waiting beyond the fence.

And Mama would die.

The guard tensed. As if in slow motion, Ary watched as he reached for his sword. He meant to slice the fence she was clinging to. It didn't matter if she broke bones during the fall—so long as she had wings, she could give Terra what it needed.

Ary took a breath—and swung her bucket at his head.

The guard cried out and ducked. His grip on her ankle slackened.

Ary jerked her leg free and flung herself over the fence.

For a moment, she hung in empty space. Then she was falling, scrambling for one of the ropes binding the glow-moths. The guard shouted. Her fingers caught a rope and she clung on tight, gasping with pain as it jerked her body upright and sent an ache ripping through her shoulders. Her hands burst with heat. The rope snapped with her weight, tugging the attached moth into the air with Ary. For a terrible moment, Ary wondered if she'd made a mistake.

Then the moth spread its wings wide, casting Ary's world in a hue of soft rose, and they were flying.

Ary dangled helplessly, clinging to the rope for dear life. Behind her, the other guards had climbed Terra's fence. They shouted for her to come back—but they didn't leave the fence to chase her down. They just watched her go.

Ary's hands burned. She was too heavy for the glow-moth to carry for long. They glided downward, until the voices of the guards were muffled, and all Ary could hear was the flapping of the moth's massive wings. Pink light pulsed all around her.

They hit the ground with a crash.

Ary landed on her back, wings flailing awkwardly, and the rope slipped from her grasp. Her world tipped around her with a dizzying frightfulness, and she gasped, struggling to pull air back into her shocked lungs. For several minutes, the sky swam above her, and her head pounded. Tears leaked down her cheeks. Slowly Ary picked herself up. Every part of her ached.

The moth had not fled.

It perched in the dirt, looking sad and out of place. Its

eyes were still blank with enchantment, and though it could have been free, the great, beautiful bug remained on the ground, the rope tied around its middle looking more like a chain.

Ary's heart squeezed. She should have been grateful—but instead it just felt wrong.

If Gran were here, she'd probably take the moth with her—use it to light her path or try to leverage it against whatever beasts lurked in the Gloom. Gran would be brave enough to take what she needed. Tough enough to get the job done.

But Ary wasn't Gran. Terra had spent a lifetime ensuring she never forgot that.

So instead, she reached forward and slipped the rope free.

The moth fluttered backward, as if startled, its eyes passing right over her. And maybe it was a trick of the light, but Ary could have sworn in that moment that its eyes cleared like the one that had spoken to her.

She could have sworn, for the briefest second, the moth looked grateful.

Then the moth gave a great shudder and launched itself into the air.

It floated right up into the sky, pink wings dimming to a soft blush, growing fainter as its wings carried it higher still. Now that it was free of Terra and its enchantments,

Ary wagered it would return to wherever the glow-moths came from before the fairies had caught them and bespelled them.

She hoped the moth could find its family, if moths had families at all.

And she hoped it was smart enough to never come back.

"Good luck," Ary whispered, and then she turned to face the dark.

# EIGHT

## *Into the Gloom*

Ary walked in silence.

She carried her light wrapped beneath her shirt to conceal the glow. The thorn fence, and the safety of Terra's gleaming lights, had disappeared from the horizon. She'd debated going back to hunt for the journal—but it didn't seem worth it. She was already losing time.

Now Ary walked through an endless night, shivering in the cold with nothing but dry dirt and dead bushes for company. The farther she got from Terra, the more desolate the land grew. There were fewer bushes, fewer patches of soft moss or wispy cave ferns. Everywhere she looked, there was mold—coating the rocks, the plants, even empty soil. Always creeping closer. Always taking more.

Yet there was a strange . . . peace to it. All the stories she'd heard of the Gloom made it sound like a land of constant chaos and upheaval. The fairies of Terra were so fearful of the lightless land beyond their fence that they made it sound as if the moment one stepped foot into the Gloom they'd be devoured alive. They'd painted it as a wasteland teeming with monsters, so full of danger that newts and beetles alike tripped over each other as they scuttled over the earth, waiting for a stray fairy to snatch up.

Instead, the Gloom was distant, cold, and entirely empty. It wasn't lying in wait for her. It didn't seem to care about her at all.

Ary found she quite liked that aspect of it.

When Ary was just a wingling, Mama had been fond of a story—about Ary, as a baby, bold even for a fairy toddler. She'd vanished one night into the dark, and soon half of Terra was out hunting for the beloved grandchild of Wren Mossheart. They'd found Ary near dawn, fast asleep in a glow-moth nest, her hair shimmering with phosphorous dust.

"You must have walked right into the dark," Gran had laughed. Ary loved the rare occasion when Gran laughed and her eyes filled with light. "Fearless as a firefly. Right into the pitch black! How you made it into that moth's nest, none of us know."

"Lucky you did," Papa had said with a wink. "Or we never would have found our fearless little hero."

Ary's chest pinched. *Hero.* Everyone but Mama and Gran had joked about Ary being a hero. They'd showered her with the word, said it with full smiles and warm eyes whenever she walked by. They'd brush their fingers over her hair and whisper blessings and look at Ary like she was a cure they'd spent a lifetime waiting for. Even as a child, she'd felt the weight of their expectations.

Gran had been a hero. Mama had been average. But the descendants of the other heroes had gone on to do incredible things—they had become mayors, inventors, fierce warriors. Perhaps the hero gene was late. Perhaps it skipped a generation. Surely the granddaughter would be special? Surely she carried something inside her—something they all needed, living in their tiny, gloomy world that cracked at the edges if you looked a little too close at it?

Then Ary had grown up. And she'd proven to be terribly, disappointedly . . . average. Timid instead of brave, gentle instead of brash. And once Papa died, *worried* about everything and everyone all the time. It seemed like all of Terra came to an agreement: Canary Mossheart was no hero. She was ordinary. And Terra had no need for the ordinary. They had plenty of that already.

Ary hugged her bucket to her chest. She pushed the thought away and instead pictured Mama. The rose of her cheeks, the light in her eyes. The sweetness of her breath when she kissed Ary's forehead good night. Mama had been the only one to ever think of Ary as special. Mama had always seen the extraordinary in a painfully ordinary girl.

Once, when children at school had sneered that Ary was a disappointment, Mama had gathered Ary into her arms with a sigh and kissed the tears from her cheeks.

"They said the same to me," she murmured. "But it's a gift to be no one, Ary Mossheart, because to be no one means you can be *anyone*. No one has chosen your fate. No one has set out a path for you. You get to be exactly and only *you*. And I think who you are is already far more wonderful than anything a prophecy or a legend could predict."

To her surprise, Gran had nodded with a tired frown and looked away. "Trust me, little one. Being no one in a world desperate for a hero is as close to freedom as you can get."

Ary blinked back tears and resisted the urge to hum under her breath to break the silence. How did anything survive out here, when even the softest whisper of wings sounded louder than a scream? Ary swung her light up—and an eye gleamed back at her.

Ary put out her lamp and threw herself to the ground. She clasped her hand over her mouth, straining for any hint of sound, any indication that something was coming closer.

Only silence greeted her.

Ary lay there for a long time, flattened against the ground, eyes trying to adjust to the never-ending dark, terrified of what lay in wait that she could not see. And it was there, lying against the dirt, that Ary realized for the first time that she'd made a terrible mistake.

What had she been *thinking*? Scaling the thorn wall, leaving Terra behind, plunging off into the dark for water from a lake she wasn't sure existed, with no guarantee it'd even help Mama? Tears of frustration burned her eyes, and Ary remained there, trembling and still and waiting. But nothing came. No creature reached for her or flew overhead. Finally, after what felt like a horrible eternity, Ary picked herself back up. She held her breath and swung the glow-shroom lamp in the direction of the eye.

Something gleamed back.

"Hello?" The lamp trembled wildly. The . . . *thing* kept gleaming, but made no movement, and uttered no sound.

*Move in a straight line.* She dared not venture off her path or to the side, because she'd never find her way back.

But whatever was gleaming was so close—and if she didn't investigate it now, the terror of the unknown was going to haunt her until it became unbearable.

"I'll count my paces," Ary said. Ary scuffed her foot extra hard in the dirt to mark her place and then set off in the direction of the thing, counting under her breath. "One, two, three, four . . ." The glow-shroom lamp trembled in her hand, but Ary kept walking, ready to bolt at any moment. ". . . sixteen, seventeen, eighteen."

Ary swung the lamp up to face the eye—

Which was only a garden shovel.

It was a Seedling shovel, one of the flat, hollow instruments they often clanged about when singing prayers to the Gardener. The tool was bent and covered in several layers of dust. Whatever fairy had owned it was long gone.

Ary hesitated. The shovel looked so forlorn and lonely, lying in the dirt. She picked it up and turned it in her palm, running her fingers over the faded shroom-leather handle.

"You're awfully far from home, aren't you?" Ary asked softly. "That makes two of us." Ary tucked the shovel in her waistband. The weight against her hip was oddly comforting. It was hardly a weapon, but it was still *something*. And it reminded her of home.

Ary turned—and walked directly into a boulder.

She bounced backward, her knee smarting where she'd struck the rock. A large, smooth boulder sat directly in her path. One she was almost certain hadn't been there before. The hair on Ary's arms stood on end. She looked at the boulder for a moment longer, and then counted her paces back to her original path before striking out again.

It wasn't long before a snuffling noise sounded.

Ary stopped.

So did the snuffling.

Ary took several steps forward. The snuffling restarted.

She stopped.

It stopped.

*I'm being followed.*

Ary's hands began to shake. Slowly, she drew the shovel from her waistband. The glow-shroom lamp bobbed dangerously, making the gentle glow it cast flicker and jump about. Ary held her breath. She had no armor, and only a shovel to defend herself. Feeling quite foolish, Ary put the bucket on her head, the handle fitting just beneath her chin. It was no helmet—but it was better than nothing.

*Maybe it's just the wind.*

Ary held the shovel out in front of her. A pale, sharp-featured girl wearing a bucket for a hat stared back. Had her cheeks always been that thin? The circles beneath her eyes always that dark? The weariness in them that heavy and deep?

*Maybe Mama isn't the only one who's sick.*

Ary shook herself. She stared at the haunted girl for a moment longer—and then behind her came the snuffling. Breath tickled her shoulder.

Ary's blood ran cold.

With one shaking hand, she turned, angled the shovel past her shoulder—and met the eyes of a massive insect as it reared up behind her, its pincers spread wide.

# NINE

## *Shrimp*

"*Aaaahhh!*" screamed Ary.

"*Aaaahhh!*" screamed the bug.

Before Ary could react, the giant bug tumbled backward, legs flailing—and then it transformed. It bent forward and shrank, body clicking, legs disappearing. The transformation took only a moment. What had previously been a giant bug was now a smooth, hard sphere.

Or a boulder.

"You're a pill bug," Ary said.

Pill bugs were harmless. Most folk had little use for them, thinking the roly-poly critters to be cowardly, dim creatures too weak to choose a side in the age-old war between fairies and newts. They were little more than scavengers, living on the fringes of everyone else's worlds, eking out survival, doing their best to remain unnoticed. They had no organization to them, no village to call home, just their nervous little pods, scuttling for eternity, dozens and dozens of tiny creatures that would likely hurry after each other over a cliff if it meant not breaking from the line.

The often-repeated mantra of the pill bugs was famously, laughably, "We follow."

Ary took a cautious step forward. She touched the shovel to the pill bug's hard shell and gave it a gentle tap. The noise rang out around them in a strangely beautiful, high-pitched melody. A *squeak* came from the ball.

"It's okay," Ary said softly. "I don't want to hurt you—if I'm being honest, you gave *me* quite a fright."

One leg poked out from the ball. Then a second, and a third. Suddenly Ary found herself staring into a pair of round eyes that sat on either side of a wide, flat face. The pill bug peered out at her, ready to snap shut again at any moment. "Really?"

Her heart skipped. He could talk! Unlike the newts and earwigs, which used sound to communicate, most bugs preferred to communicate through scents, which were often difficult to parse for the fairies of Terra and their weak noses. Although judging by the tiny, panicked squeak of the pill bug's voice, Ary wasn't going to get more than one or two shy words out of him at a time.

Ary twisted her hands together and peered at the bug. "So . . . if you're not here to kidnap me or eat me . . . why were you following me?"

The pill bug finally unrolled entirely. He looked pointedly at Ary's rucksack, then pointed to his stomach with one of his many legs. "Hungry."

"Oh," Ary said, heat rushing to her cheeks. "Oh, how rude of me. But of course."

Gran would have her head for entertaining a pill bug, but Mama had taught her to never turn away a hungry mouth.

Then again, Mama had meant other fairies. But this bug seemed harmless enough.

Ary fished a chunk of carrot from her bag and passed it to the pill bug. The bug dropped on top of the carrot chunk, snipping it into tiny pieces with the little pincers that poked from his mouth. The carrot was gone in a matter of seconds, and before Ary could think twice, she was reaching into her bag to offer the bug the loaf of mushroom bread she'd found inside.

The bug made a strange, appreciative *whrrrrrrr*, and gobbled that down, too.

Finally he looked up at Ary with bright eyes. Again came that shy, nervous voice. "More?"

Her heart ached. Ary looked from her bag back to the bug. Even in the soft glow of the glow-shroom lamp, the scratches and nicks in his shell were visible. "You can have one more piece, I suppose." She passed him her last chunk of carrot, and the pill bug immediately began eating. Ary watched him with a funny warmth. Folk always spoke poorly of pill bugs, but this one wasn't so bad.

"I'm Ary, by the way," she said.

What would Gran say if she saw her introducing herself to a pill bug?

"Shrimp," said the bug around a mouthful of carrot.

Ary frowned. Most folk were named after mythical creatures and plants—strange creatures called birds, like canaries, wrens, and larks, or odd plants called tulips, basil, and roses. Things that existed only in legend, and in the heavenly kingdom of the Gardener, where there was no gloom, but an infinite light in the sky.

"What is a . . . shrimp?"

The pill bug was silent for a long moment, then his antennae twitched. "Don't know."

"Oh," Ary said, feeling a little foolish. An awkward silence lapsed between them, and she glanced around. "Where's the rest of your pod?"

Shrimp was quiet for a long moment. "Gone."

"Gone?"

"Lost." Shrimp twitched two antennae back at himself. "Looking."

Ary's heart twinged. "You lost your family? And now you're all by yourself?"

The pill bug's voice was barely audible. "Yes."

Ary sat down hard. She passed Shrimp a chunk of turnip. This time he ate slowly, and the silence between them was a weighted, cold thing.

"I've lost family, too," Ary said. "My papa, he was sick. And now my mama . . ."

"Gone?"

"Not yet." Ary's throat bobbed. She gestured around

them. Even here, in the heart of the Gloom, patches of fuzzy white mold grew in sporadic clumps. There was nothing here for the mold to eat—no shrubs, no mushrooms, no fairies. And yet still it spread. "The mold has gotten out of control. It made her sick."

"Bigger sick," whispered Shrimp. "Every year. Many lost."

So the other creatures suffered from the mold, too. Many folk had long suspected that the mold might also be a threat to the critters that occupied the Gloom, but now, as Ary looked at the pill bug—as she saw the sorrow in his eyes—she knew it to be true.

The mold was waging a war against all of them, and it was winning.

If Shrimp knew of the mold's impact on the Gloom . . . maybe he knew other things, too.

"There's a rumor," Ary said slowly. "About the mold—and what can stop it. My gran said that when she was a girl, there was an underground lake, hidden in the heart of the Gloom, with magical healing waters. It's called the Underlake."

"Cold water. Down deep." A thoughtful light entered Shrimp's eyes. "Heal."

"You know where it is?" Ary asked, so thrilled she thought she'd weep. "That's what I'm looking for—that's what she needs. Can you take me there?"

"Far," the bug said forlornly.

"Please," Ary breathed. Desperation was a claw around her heart. "I'll give you anything—I'll give you all my food!"

He hesitated. ". . . *All?*"

"Yes, all of it! Every last crumb!" Ary emptied the contents of the rucksack in front of him. Soft tuber cheese, two baked mushroom stalks, even a candied root. Her stomach did an uncomfortable flip. The mayor had told everyone they were out of tubers months ago. How, then, had a guard been carrying supplies? All the food she'd dumped out looked uncomfortably, suspiciously fresh—far better than what was sold in the market.

Where had this all come from?

Ary shook the thought away and looked at Shrimp. "If you help me, the fairies of Terra will reward you with all the food you can eat."

She didn't know if the last part was true—but she'd worry about that later. If Shrimp helped Mama, Ary would find a way to ensure Terra repaid him. Somehow.

Shrimp stared at the pile of food for a long time.

As if on cue, Ary's stomach gave a pitiful growl. She ignored it.

"Please," Ary breathed. "She's all I have."

The pill bug met her eyes. "Lost."

"Yes, lost. I would be very, very lost without her. I love her very much. And she's counting on me."

"Okay," said the bug. "Okay."

Finally, Shrimp unrolled to his full length. Now that he was no longer curled into a ball, she was able to count fourteen legs and two sets of long, twitching antennae. The bug hunched down, his old, scratched shell creaking with the effort, and said, "On."

"Pardon?"

"*On*," the bug repeated impatiently, flicking his antennae dismissively at her. "Folk *slow*."

This was ridiculous! Only a day ago, she had been in the mushroom fields, scraping until her palms bled. And now she was—what? Bargaining with a pill bug? One she planned to *ride* to a magical spring no one had visited in decades?

*What would Gran do?*

The answer there was obvious.

Ary steeled herself and clambered up Shrimp's shell. Her wings were heavy and awkward, itching under their thick cocoon, and it took a moment for her to settle her weight.

And then they were moving.

Shrimp took off with a start, his fourteen legs scurrying so quickly Ary's hair snapped against her forehead. The land blurred beneath his feet.

"Shrimp?"

"Yes?"

"Thank you," Ary whispered.

Shrimp didn't say anything. He didn't have to. He just picked up speed, his antennae pointed north, leaving the empty Gloom and the mold that devoured it far behind.

*I'm coming, Mama.*

# TEN

## *Welcome to the Underlake*

On Ary's legs, the Gloom had crawled by at a painfully slow pace. Now it was a blur.

Shrimp never slowed down, and he never seemed to tire. They'd made it only a few minutes before Ary realized it was easier on him if she was flat on her stomach, so now she sprawled with her cheek against Shrimp's shell, head propped on her arm as the world flashed by. The only sounds were the constant drum of Shrimp's feet and *thump* of her pack against her hip. The pill bug had decided to save some of the food Ary had traded him, so now it sat in her rucksack once more, jostling merrily along.

Ary's stomach growled, but she forced her hands to remain still. She wouldn't mess up this bargain. Not when it could save Mama.

Glowrise came in a wash of watery light that leaked through the cliffs. Out here in the Gloom, Ary could see far more of them than she'd been able to in Terra. The cliffs stretched even higher than she'd imagined. Oddly enough, where they weren't covered in as many layers of dirt and grime, the light seemed . . . brighter. The fairies of Terra had long described the Gloom beyond their fence and the Underground far below as a rotting, chaotic place. But so far it seemed mostly empty. Were it not for the mold that blanketed the ground and every scraggly, sad plant that tried to grow out here, it might have even been beautiful. So much of Ary's childhood had been spent fearing the creature-infested lands of the Gloom, but there were no wicked, fire-wielding newts out here, no hungry earwigs or endless jungles of shroom-trees where little fairies too far from home would be forced to wander forever. It was just . . . empty. Just mold and dead plants, echoes of a world once lived in, now abandoned.

Ary's heart squeezed.

Maybe it was true that Terra was dying. But it wasn't because of the Gloom.

The Gloom, it seemed, had died long before Terra started to.

Ary's eyes roved the land around her, taking in the endless dust, the light gleaming above. There was a beauty to the emptiness, a kind of peace even in the wrongness of it all. She wished Mama could see it.

Her stomach flipped.

Mama would be in a panic by now, if she woke at all. And Gran would be furious.

*Or maybe she'd be proud.*

It wasn't that Gran didn't love Ary—she just didn't understand her. Ary had accepted that a long time ago. And could she really blame Gran? Here was a woman who had plunged into the Underground when she was only a few years older than Ary, who had fought giant, folk-eating ear-wigs and battled newts and beetles alike to bring back a cure for the plague that had nearly wiped out the fairies of Terra for good.

And then there was Ary.

Quiet, ordinary Ary, who couldn't even get her wings on time.

Timid, nervous Ary, who had never yearned for adventure, and ran from fights instead of starting them.

Plain, disappointing Ary, who would never be a hero at all.

How was Gran supposed to understand that?

*But maybe she'll understand now.* Ary's fingers tightened on Shrimp's shell. *Maybe she'll be proud.*

Ary could almost see it—the pride in Gran's eyes once she realized Ary had saved Mama. And if the water worked, Ary wouldn't stop there. She'd tell the mayor; they'd lead an expedition to the Underlake to cure the rest of their sick. She'd cure them all.

*And maybe . . .*

Her fingers tightened.

If the water worked on people . . . who was to say it wouldn't work on crops, too? Ary ran a thumb over the thick blisters that calloused her palms. After months of mushroom-scraping, her hands were rough to touch.

Gran had cured a city—but what if Ary cured an entire *world*?

Heat flooded into her cheeks. It was foolish to think like that. Even if she *could* be a hero, what would she get for it? Another sad statue in the fountain? An honorary place in a lifetime's worth of dull parades and lukewarm dinners with the mayor?

No, that wasn't for her.

Still—if Gran were proud of her? That would be worth it. That would be enough. That would be—

"Burn," Shrimp whimpered. "Bad."

Shrimp slowed his run to a careful trot. Ary looked up—and all the blood drained from her face.

Every fairy child in Terra knew to fear the newts—of all the creatures, they and the fairies were the only two that could work magic. But where fairies wielded magic to grow crops and bring light, the water-loving newts had chosen a particularly cruel outlet for their magic: fire.

Ary had spent a lifetime wondering what the monsters she'd learned to fear looked like. The newt before her was a massive, hulking beast, with a flat, cruel mouth, and soulless, empty eyes.

And it was dead.

From the look of it, the newt had been dead for weeks. Mold covered half its body, and what the mold had not taken was already shriveled and dried.

Ary went limp with relief. But even in death, the sight

of the newt sent cold spiraling through her. So much of Terra bore the scars of the newt attacks—ash marks on the great outer fence, sections of field still scorched black from the wars fifteen years past. Fairies missing limbs or sporting nasty burn scars, the warning about the cruelty of the newts branded to their very bodies. Families of folk long lost carried the same warnings in their hearts.

Papa had never spoken of what he'd witnessed when he had been sent to fight the newts—not once—but the haunted look in his eyes had always been answer enough. It had been the only subject Papa and Gran refused to speak on. For all her faults, Gran had seemed to genuinely like Ary's father, had grown soft and patient with him when the night terrors began.

But on the subject of the newts, they'd never agreed. Papa had suffered too much—and Gran would never explain *why* she refused to hate them. The old hero would merely turn away, muttering something about old mistakes causing new pain, and refuse to discuss the subject further.

Shrimp shivered and pointed with a shaking antenna. There was another creature there, rotting beneath the mold-covered newt—an earwig, burned to a crisp. The long, flat-bodied insect had died midtwist, its many legs stretched at crooked angles, the long, wicked pincers that protruded from its rear end spread wide as if it had been preparing for a fight before it had fallen still for good.

That didn't seem right. The newts and earwigs were

allies; they hated the folk equally and had long attacked Terra in coordinated pairs.

So why had the earwig been set aflame?

And why had the two creatures died out here, alone, only a day's walk from Terra?

"I don't like this," Ary said. For the first time, she wished Gran were here. She would have known what to do. Gran had fought earwigs and newts alike on her famous journey— she was one of the few folk to face the monstrous critters and live.

"Come on, Shrimp," Ary said. "Let's keep going."

The bug resumed his running, and they left the dead newt and earwig far behind. Ary's body grew heavy and tired, lulled by the constant rhythm of Shrimp's running. Yet even as Shrimp's feet pattered on, all Ary could think of was the newt's corpse—and that, in the end, even the newts could not outrun the mold.

"Wake," a voice murmured.

Ary jerked her head up and shivered. The air was colder here. The hair on her arms stood on end, and while the world around her was still nothing more than an endless stretch of darkness, it felt . . . different.

It felt alive.

Shrimp slowed his run to a steady trot, his feet drumming quietly in the dust. Ary rubbed her eyes. It was still a marvel to her that Shrimp could run with barely any light at all. No wonder the pill bugs had thrived on the edges of the world even when the newts had chased them from their lands.

Ary drew the glow-shroom lamp from her bag. It came to life with a gentle tap, illuminating the world around them, and Ary went still.

She didn't know what she'd expected—a sign, maybe? Some grand entrance? But where some great marker might have once waited was now little more than a collection of tumbled rocks with a gaping black hole that drank up the lamplight. And yet something about it seemed different. Something about it seemed like it was . . . watching.

Ary slipped from Shrimp's back and raised the lamp higher, but still the light did not break the swath of darkness. Was it dimmer than before? Something crunched beneath her foot, and Ary drew back.

An old garden shovel, frail and rusted, lay half buried in the dirt. Ary knew it was a Seedling shovel before she even knelt to inspect it. Something in her warmed. The shovel couldn't have been here by accident; maybe other fairies had walked here before her—a long, long time ago, before Gran had plunged into the tunnels beneath Terra to save them all.

Maybe, in another lifetime, the Gloom had been a place that welcomed the folk of Terra, instead of a nightmare they were desperate to avoid. She had no need for the shovel—not when she'd already found one—but it felt almost like it had been waiting for her. Ary tucked it into her belt.

She glanced back at Shrimp. "You're sure this is the place?"

"Down," Shrimp whisper-insisted.

*I'm coming, Mama.*

With her heart in her throat, Ary lifted the lamp and descended into the dark.

The ground sloped down.

Even though she could barely see, Ary could *feel* the sharp slant the floor was angled at. The air grew colder and drier with every step. There was no sound except for Ary's breathing, and the scuttle of Shrimp's feet behind her. She hadn't asked him to follow; he simply had, and she was grateful for it.

She could have laughed. What a wild thing! She had woken up yesterday morning as Ary Mossheart, mold-scraper and disappointing granddaughter. Now she was descending into the dark to find a magical lake she still wasn't certain existed, armed with only a bucket, a lamp, and two old shovels, accompanied by her sole companion, Shrimp the giant—and very shy—pill bug.

Gran would hardly believe it when Ary told her.

Ary's calves burned from walking down the steep slope.

It was hard to keep her balance, and her wing tips brushed the tunnel walls, their papery cocoon crackling as bits of it snagged on the rock. She walked until her feet ached, and after what felt like a lifetime, the barest flicker stirred ahead. *A light*. Her heart leaped. She picked up her pace, leaning into the cold air that rushed toward her. The light grew brighter.

The bucket creaked, and Ary put it back on her head. She took one step forward, then another. The air grew colder, carrying a tinge of salt, of rust, and old things long lost.

*Soon*. She would get the water and then return to Terra immediately. Mama would be fine.

*And the mold?* a voice inside her that sounded far too much like Owl's asked. *The potatoes? The rot? What then, Ary? What next?*

Ary pushed the thought away. Mold and missing food and rot that crept into the heart of everything—that wasn't her responsibility. She'd leave that up to people like Gran and Mayor Nightingale. She was just a kid. She was already doing more than she should have had to. Once the mayor knew about the Underlake, she'd use it to save the rest of Terra, and someday the mold would be nothing but a distant memory.

The tunnel curved sharply to the left. More light flooded around the corner. Ary dimmed her lamp, then tapped it off entirely. She hooked it to her belt and froze.

What if she wasn't alone?

After all, if Shrimp knew where the Underlake was, surely other creatures did, too?

She pulled the Seedling shovels from her hip. A tiny laugh squeaked out of her. The shovels would be near useless against anything more dangerous than a moth—but still, it was comforting to have the weight of them in her hand. A piece of home when she was so very far away. Maybe that was enough.

Ary drew in a deep breath.

*Okay. I'm ready. And then it's back to Mama.*

*Back to normal.*

Ary turned the corner and froze.

"Hello, Canary," said Gran. "A little far from home, aren't we?"

The feeling drained from Ary. Both shovels clattered from her hands, and she blinked furiously, trying to clear her eyes. Was this some kind of dream? Surely her mind was playing tricks on her—

"Canary," Gran said, her face strangely worried. She took a careful step forward. Gran was *never* worried. Why did she look so worried? "Listen to me, child. Had I known—"

Ary blinked, but Gran was still there. She was definitely real. How she'd gotten here so fast, how she'd known Ary was gone at all, Ary had no clue. And she might have asked her—except in that moment, Ary spotted something behind Gran and could think of nothing at all.

"Is this it?" Ary asked. Her voice came from far, far away, as though someone were speaking for her. "The Underlake?"

"Canary," Gran said tightly.

"Tell me the truth, Gran," Ary said, her voice edging on hysterics. "Is this the Underlake or not?"

Gran closed her eyes. "I'm sorry, child."

Ary's legs buckled. She didn't hear what Gran said next.

Behind Gran, instead of a vast, glittering pool of crystal-clean groundwater was . . . nothing. Just a deep stone basin, lightly ridged around the sides from centuries of water eating away at the rock, its walls long lined with dust.

The Underlake was completely dry.

# ELEVEN

## *The Gardener's Promise*

*It's empty.*

*It's all just . . . gone.*

Ary took an unsteady step forward. She looked right past Gran, to the gaping hole of stone that used to be the Underlake. Once, it must have been a sight to behold: a behemoth of icy, healing water, waiting in darkness to help those brave enough to find it. A miracle hidden beneath the Gloom, capable of saving anyone and anything.

Now it was nothing.

*Mama.*

Ary had known the Underlake was a slim chance at best—but she had believed, like a fool. She had *hoped*. And now she would return with nothing.

*What if Mama is already—*

"Canary. Look at me."

Gran touched her shoulder. Ary jerked back as if she'd been shocked. A part of her had been half convinced this was a dream—but Gran's hand on her shoulder meant it was all horribly, painfully real. She couldn't remember the last time Gran had placed a comforting hand on her, let alone hugged her. For Gran to reach for her now felt less like comfort, and more like they were actors in some strange play.

Reality slowly seeped in. Gran was here. *Here.* At the Underlake, in the heart of the Gloom—and she wasn't alone.

Off to the side, hands awkwardly tucked into his pockets, was Owl.

Ary's mouth dropped open. *"You."*

"Um," Owl said. "Hi, Ary."

"Why are you here, Owl?"

"Why is he here?" Gran barked. She dropped her hand, any trace of gentleness gone. "Why are *you* here? You should be thanking the boy, not scowling at him. I nearly had a heart attack when he woke me and told me he saw my granddaughter *scale the thorn wall and disappear into the Gloom!*"

Ary glared at Owl. He looked back, a strangely stubborn glint in his eye. An unfamiliar, sour taste flooded Ary's mouth. This had to be Owl's dream—all his life, the paranoid little fairy had been aching for a way to get closer to Gran. By sneaking out of Terra, Ary had given him the perfect chance. She didn't even want to know how they'd gotten here so quickly. Gran had her tricks—she always did—and it stung even worse that she'd shared them with Owl to chase after Ary instead of offering up a path in the first place.

Gran was still talking. "Honestly, Canary—what were you thinking? Sneaking out into the Gloom *alone*? Evading the guards? Leaving in the middle of the night? Do you know how terrified I was? I had to use some of my last reserves of fairy dust to get us here and—"

"Mama," Ary interrupted urgently. "Who is with Mama?"

"Tulip and Basil's mother is watching over her for now," Gran snapped. "Honestly, Canary, I cannot believe you would be so *selfish* . . ."

Panic bubbled up in Ary's chest. This couldn't be it. She hadn't come this far to fail.

". . . you are lucky that boy saw you leaving and came to get me. How did you even think you'd get back alive—" Gran's face went blank. ". . . What . . . is . . . *that?*"

Shrimp crept forward. He looked massive compared to Gran and Owl, his dark, beady eyes revealing nothing. A low rumble coming from his chest, the bug drew himself up into a seated position and waved with an antenna.

"That's Shrimp," Ary said, as if being followed by a massive fourteen-legged pill bug was nothing new. Her eyes were still on the lake. "He's a friend."

"Why . . . ? Never mind." Gran pinched her nose, exhaustion lining her face. "It can't come home with us."

"Home?" Ary jerked back to reality. "I just got here! I'm not going *home*!"

"Is that so? And where do you plan to go, exactly?"

"Mama is *sick*!" Ary hadn't meant to shout, but now the words burst from her. "Mama needs me, Gran. She's counting

94

on me. There has to be some water here—there has to be *something*."

"Canary," Gran tried again, her voice an edge softer. "Listen—"

"No!" Ary shoved past her, her wings flopping awkwardly, and went to stand at the edge of the Underlake. She couldn't lose Mama. Not like she'd lost Papa. There had to be *something* she could do. Her eyes roved over the gaping maw of the lake. "What if it's not completely dry?"

*"Enough."* Gran reached out and gripped her shoulders. Ary tried to jerk away from her, but Gran was surprisingly strong for an old woman. *"Canary Mossheart, look at me.* There is no water here. There was before, yes, but that was decades ago, and even then the lake was losing water—for all we know, it dried up the day I came back to the surface. There is no cure here, child."

"Then find one," Ary begged. Her body wouldn't stop shaking. She didn't know if she wanted to scream or cry. "You were—*are*—a hero, Gran! Isn't that why you have the statue? The parades? You're the chosen one, the plague-breaker, the third hero chosen by the Gardener to fix Terra's problems. *So fix this.*"

Gran stared at her for a long time. For a brief moment, Ary thought she saw the girl her grandmother had once been peering back at her from Gran's wide, dark eyes, a flicker of the child who had plunged into the Underground with her close friends and emerged alone with a cure for an entire city. Then it vanished, and Gran looked away. "I can't."

"Then what good are you?" Ary whispered.

Gran flinched and dropped her hands.

Ary's heart twinged with regret, but she shoved the feeling down. She turned away from Gran. Her legs moved as if on their own accord, as if someone had tied an invisible string around her waist and *pulled*. Endless darkness yawned before her; for all she knew, the lake could go on forever. It could be an endless pit that went to the very bottom of their world—or a short drop that ended in pointed, jagged rocks.

*No.*

She hadn't come all this way for nothing.

There had to be something here.

Her heart began to pound.

"Canary." Gran raised her voice in warning. "Get away from there—"

Ary closed her eyes.

*Gardener guide my light.*

And Ary jumped.

# TWELVE

## *The Warning at the Bottom*

The walls of the lake were steep. Ary slid on her bottom down the walls, wings splayed awkwardly to slow her descent. Stones cut her palms and sliced her clothes. Cold air whipped at her cheeks and chapped her lips. Above her, Gran was shouting, but her voice was far away and muffled. Ary could see nothing but darkness, hear nothing but the wind. For a terrible moment, she wondered if she'd made a mistake. Maybe the Underlake *did* go on forever. Or maybe she was truly about to smash into a bunch of pointy rocks.

Then the ground leveled out, and Ary stopped sliding.

She had reached the bottom.

It was all darkness. Ary waved a hand in front of her face and saw only black. She craned her neck and looked up. Far, *far* above came the faintest glow at the top of the lake. That had to be Gran with the lamp.

Even if there *was* water down here, she had no idea how she was going to get out.

Ary shook herself. She'd figure that out later. She'd come here searching for water. Now it was time to find her answer. She didn't need to be able to *see* to feel something wet.

Ary steeled herself and began to crawl.

It was strange, to crawl through a world where she could see nothing. Even as Ary moved forward, she could tell she was still heading downward, the gentle tilt of the stone lake bed guiding her toward the center. Her fingers passed through layers of dust; this lake had been empty for quite some time.

What did it mean for a world when even its sacred waters had long run dry?

There had to be something left. A puddle, a few drops. Just enough to make a difference.

"Come on," Ary whispered, crawling faster, even as her palms and knees began to ache from the freezing stone. "Come *on*."

There had to be something left—it couldn't all be gone—

Her fingers touched something hard and cold.

"Canary!"

Gran's voice echoed from high above. There was a shuffling, and then a tiny beam of light flared overhead as Gran and Owl began to slide down the Underlake basin with the glow-shroom lamp, shouting her name all the while.

"*Canary, Canary, Canary . . .*"

Ary ran her fingers over the bottom of the lake. Her fingers dipped, slipping into strange, looping crevices. Almost as if the lake had cracked. Or as if something had been . . . carved? Whatever she was touching wasn't lake rock—it was too smooth. She knocked her knuckles against it, and a hollow echo bounced back to her. *What the . . . ?*

"Over here!" Ary called. "I think I found something."

Light fell across her from behind, and Ary didn't look up as Owl and Gran came to stand beside her. Owl raised the lamp, and the three of them sucked in a collective breath.

"Gardener's light," Gran whispered.

Before them, sprawling across the stone, ten fairies tall and three wings wide, was a beautiful, ornate circle.

It was massive—a great circle of raised rock, its center marked by a carving of a Seedling shovel. A fat-petaled flower bloomed behind the tool, cradling a strange, shallow indent at its very center. Ary knew that sigil; every fairy of Terra did. It was the sacred sigil of the Gardener, crafted on the day she had built their world from nothing and formed the folk from the very soil.

Except the flower was wrong—the sigil that decorated Terra's streets and flags was ever-blooming.

And this one was dying.

"Look," Owl whispered. "The Gardener's Promise."

Just like the Gardener's sigil that decorated Terra, there was a brief, seven-line poem curling around the emblem of the image. But while it had the same cadence, the lines were all wrong.

Owl held the lamp higher and read.

*What roots shall bloom,*
*And what blooms must die,*
*Beneath this city to which we flee.*
*By the Gardener's hand,*
*A false world spins,*
*But in its dust,*
*We find the key.*

Cold crept into Ary's heart. It was the Gardener's Promise, but it was all wrong. The Gardener's Promise that had been printed into the very heart of the folk of Terra was one of eternal life, of a world that would never die.

But this? A false world? Keys among dust, dying blooms, and a city they had to flee?

Ary turned to Gran, but the old woman's face was blank.

"The indent," Owl said, his dark eyebrows furrowing. "It's a Seedling shovel."

Ary's fingers twitched to the shovels at her hip.

"Why go through all this effort?" Owl asked. "Why hide something like this in the Gloom—at the bottom of the Underlake, no less?"

Ary moved forward to stand beside Owl. The boy stared at the sigil with an odd expression on his face. He had the air of someone who had bit deep into an apple only to find it teeming with worms. "There's more."

Beneath the sigil, in messy, small scratches, someone had hurriedly carved their own message.

Ary went cold.

*Atlas.*

Ary remembered the glow-moth, the strange clarity in its gaze as it told her Atlas awaited Wren Mossheart's return. This entire time, Gran had been silent. Ary turned to her, dread sitting like a stone in her throat. "Gran—what is Atlas?"

All the color drained from Gran's face. She looked away. "I don't know."

A cold feeling swept through Ary. All her life, Gran had hidden things from her. She had tweaked, twisted, and watered down the truth enough times for Ary to know when she was lying. And Gran was lying now. Suddenly it felt as though Ary was no longer in control of her body—she had the sense that she was watching herself from far away. Like the girl who now occupied her flesh and bones was some entirely new, different Ary.

That Ary held still for a moment—and then she turned to the indents in the sigil and knelt. They were the exact size and width of a Seedling shovel. She had seen enough in her lifetime to know at a glance.

"Canary," Gran said. "Look at me."

Ary pulled the shovel from her hip. An odd feeling burned through her, from her toes to the tips of her still-growing wings. She had the sense of standing on the edge of something very tall and preparing to jump. That by placing the shovel here, she was going to begin something that could not be un-begun. But she had come here for a reason, hadn't she? What if this was her answer? What if the water that could cure Mama was beneath this, and the Seedlings had hidden it because they knew it was special?

Or—she almost didn't dare to hope—what if it was something more?

"Ary," Gran said. Gran had never called her Ary. Not once. It had always felt like an extra layer of formality in the softest, cruelest way. "Don't."

Ary pressed the shovel into the rock.

For a moment, nothing happened.

The shovel fit snugly, as if it had been crafted solely to be placed in the middle of a sigil at the bottom of a magical lake, but nothing changed. There was no movement. No lights. No healing waters bubbled up; no creatures came to attack. Ary touched it again, as if to be sure, but the shovel remained.

Owl reached forward.

There was an odd look on the boy's face—as though he had the same cliff feeling Ary did. He hesitated, his eyes flicking to hers, asking for permission. Ary nodded.

Owl placed his hand over hers and pushed.

The shovel sank deeper and made a soft *click*. Dust puffed up from the crevice, as if the earth were letting out a sigh, and Owl snatched his hand back.

And then the ground began to tremble.

"Watch out!"

Ary and Owl scrambled backward. Behind them, Gran watched, white-faced and silent. Shrimp whimpered and retracted into his shell. The stone *crack*ed with a terrible, ear-splitting noise, so loud it shook the walls of the Underlake.

The carving was *moving*.

The ancient stone groaned as it turned in a slow circle. The petals of the flower separated as the sigil broke into pieces, sliding across the floor of the lake, until a great, gaping hole was revealed. Cold air and dust whooshed out, filling the bottom of the Underlake, and Ary could only stare, slack-jawed.

Owl jumped up.

He scrambled toward the hole in the ground and flopped to his belly to peer over the edge. Before Ary could think to tell him to be careful, Owl swung the glow-shroom lamp into the pit of darkness—and disappeared.

"Owl!" Ary cried. She raced forward.

Owl was several feet below, standing in a *room*.

Old shelves sagged under countless books, and a table and a ladder were tucked into the corner, covered by decades' worth of dust, all of them fairy-sized. An old glow-shroom lamp flickered dully on its edge, and Owl stood in its dim glow, his back to Ary, holding an old, battered book in his hands. There was no image on the cover, no words. Owl flipped it to the first page and went completely rigid.

"Owl?" The hair on Ary's arms stood on end at his expression. "What is it? What's wrong?"

For a moment, he said nothing. Then he stepped closer to the glow of the glow-shroom lamp and read.

*"If you're reading this, then the terrarium is dying, and it's time to leave."* The boy blinked slowly, as if waking from a long sleep. He looked at Ary, and his eyes seemed to hold the weight of a hundred years. *"If you're reading this, then I am so sorry, because that means Wren Mossheart has failed us all."*

# THIRTEEN

## Wren

*Wren Mossheart has failed us all.*

Before she knew what she was doing, Ary snatched up
the shovel from the carving and leaped down into the hole.
More of the tiny room swam into view: a chair in the corner,
an old mug filled with dust. There were more books, some
of them far, far older than the one Owl held in his hands
now. Someone had lived here, once. Someone had spent
months—maybe years—beneath a wide, cold lake, all alone.

Someone who knew her gran.

Against the far wall stood a simple wooden door.

Ary turned to where Owl was holding the journal,
frozen, his face stricken with horror. She leaned over his
shoulder and began to read.

> *If things have gone as planned—and Gardener*
> *help us all, I hope they have—then you're probably*
> *a Seedling, like me. And you're prepared. But if they*
> *haven't . . . if my worst nightmare has come true . . . if*
> *Wren and the others never told the rest what we found*
> *deep within the Underground . . . well, maybe you don't*

*know who I am. Maybe you don't know what must happen next.*

*And if that's the case—I'm sorry. I will do what I can to prepare you. But it could never be enough.*

Ary read faster. The handwriting grew quick and sloppy, as though whoever had scribbled in these pages had done so in a hurry. Her people's own history was recounted back to her, but it was tilted at a terrifying, incorrect angle. Terra's heroes, the first mayor of Terra and the fairy general Pothos Petunia, were in this version of history, too—but in this one, they were selfish, scheming bullies who hoarded glory and peddled lies.

Owl's voice was the only thing alive in that cold, cold dark.

*I hope I'm wrong about Wren. I hope she saves us all. But if I'm right—if we have failed you—then there are three things you must know:*

*Terra is dying, and Terra is not a world at all. We live inside a strange contraption called a terrarium— a tiny, enclosed world that's actually part of a much bigger one. And we have overstayed our welcome.*

*If you've found this journal—if even the Underlake has dried up like we feared—well, I hope it's not too late. Because it's up to you to reach Atlas and find the way to leave this place.*

*But you must do it before Terra's two hundredth harvest day.*

*Because after two hundred years, Atlas will disappear—and we'll be trapped forever.*

Ary stared at the pages.

That couldn't be right.

It didn't—it didn't make sense.

*Terra is dying.*

The blood roared in Ary's ears.

*Before Terra's two hundredth harvest.*

That was only a week from now.

A world couldn't die . . . could it?

*But the mold,* a tiny voice in her whispered. *The shriveling magic, the shrinking wings, and all the rot.*

They'd learned in school that Terra had once been a land of abundance, a city of endless harvest and perfect health. There had been no mold, no food shortages, no ruined crops or creeping rot. Just endless magic and life. But the Terra they were taught about in school and the Terra they saw every day were very different. Even Mama, whose calm optimism had long kept Ary afloat, had grown wan and worried in recent years.

A light appeared overhead. Time seemed to slow as Gran lowered herself into the hole. She approached Owl as if in a trance, her lips pressed into a thin line.

"May I see that?" the old hero whispered. When Owl

didn't budge, Gran gave a long, slow blink and added, "Please?"

Reluctantly, Owl handed over the book. Gran turned it over in her hands, flipping to the first page. Inside the cover was a single name.

## DRACAENA

It meant nothing to Ary, but Gran's head dropped to her chest, and the breath whooshed out of her.

"So she lived," Gran murmured, trailing her fingers over the cover of the book. Her hand shook. Were those tears in Gran's eyes, or just a trick of the light? "She just never came home."

Ary's heart threatened to pound out of her chest. "Gran? What's going on? Who was Dracaena and why—why is she saying you failed us?" She couldn't even get the next words out. "What did she mean by—?"

*What did she mean by "Terra is dying"?*

Gran looked as though she had aged a thousand years in only a few minutes.

"She's saying that because I did," Gran finally said, her voice far away. "I failed."

Ary whipped her head to look at her. "What?"

The old woman lowered herself to the ground, as though her legs could no longer bear her. "When I was a girl—when

I went into the Underground—I . . . learned things. Saw things. There was a message I was supposed to bring back to Terra. A problem I was supposed to solve." Her voice caught. Gran dropped her face into her hands. "But I couldn't pay the price I was supposed to. I wouldn't—couldn't—I wasn't strong enough. I hoped if I ignored it—I hoped if enough time went by—maybe the warning wouldn't come true." Her voice was weak. "Or maybe I would die before it did."

The blood roared in Ary's ears.

It was Owl who spoke. "What was the price?"

Gran seemed to look right through them. She opened her mouth to speak—and then Shrimp came barreling into the hole at full speed.

"*Fire!*" cried Shrimp. "*Flee!*"

The pill bug careened upward, his entire body trembling, his antennae twitching like mad as he slammed right into a shelf.

"Shrimp!" Ary scrambled over the fallen books. "Shrimp, calm down! What is it? What's wrong?"

"Bad," Shrimp whimpered. The words seemed to tumble out of him in a hurried, garbled heap. "*Fire.*" Ary stared at him, not understanding, but Owl shot past her. The glowshroom lamp hooked around his wrist, he half scaled the wall of the hole—and froze.

"Um, guys." His voice squeaked, jumping two octaves. "I think someone heard us, uh, break the Underlake."

Crawling down the walls of the now-empty Underlake, their wicked pincers gleaming in the weak light, were five massive earwigs, their legs carrying them at a frightening speed.

And at their lead, tail thrashing, dark eyes wide as it smiled in a wicked, cruel grin, was a newt.

# FOURTEEN

## *What Once Was*

"How did they find us?" Gran demanded. "We didn't bring any food—I made sure of it."

Ary's heart sank. "I did."

*"What?"*

"I didn't know!" Ary cried. "I—I didn't know how far the Underlake would be, or how long of a journey. I didn't think I'd run into any newts or—"

Her words fell silent at the sight of Gran's face. In her twelve years, Ary had seen many, many emotions on her gran's lined face—but fear had never been one of them.

Newts and earwigs were not supposed to work together. They both antagonized Terra, yes, but they'd been enemies of each other, too. Papa had said even the newts had disdain for the fairy-eating earwigs. But that was years ago, long before the food rationing, when the mold had seemed like a distant nuisance instead of a problem so massive even children were expected to leave school to fight it.

If the mold had affected the food within Terra's walls, leaving folk hungry and eager for any morsel they could find, who was to say it hadn't ruined the Gloom long before?

The newts could hate the earwigs all they wanted—but hunger was something every creature understood. And trapped in the Gloom, maybe they had decided it was better to work together if it meant beating starvation by taking down their common enemy: the folk of Terra.

For a moment, Gran seemed frozen. The newt and the earwigs drew closer. Gran lifted her eyes from Ary's face to the critters bearing down on them—and then, suddenly, Gran transformed.

Gran always had been strong, even as she'd aged and her bones had ached. But there had always been a kind of ever-constant weight to her—a melancholy that clung to her skin, a sadness pooling in her gaze. Yet here, standing amid books and secrets, with earwigs and newts bearing down on them, an eerie calm seemed to descend over her. Gran took one last look at the approaching critters, then dropped back to the floor, spinning at lightning speed to point at a still-cowering Shrimp. "You there—bug. Can you run?"

Shrimp hesitated, and squeaked, "Yes."

"Good. Owl, hand me the lamp." Gran hurried around the room, knocking books off the shelves, kicking them into a great pile in the center of the floor. Overheard, the skittering of insect feet and the clicking of pincers drew closer.

"Gran, what are you—?"

"Quiet." Gran put a finger to her lips. Her black eyes darted about as she snatched the ladder off the wall. "Ary, open the door."

"What?" Ary squeaked. "But we don't know what—"

"It unlocks from inside and leads into the Underground tunnels; we're in beetle domain right now, which isn't ideal, but it could be worse. Owl, follow Ary. Both of you get on the bug and get ready to run."

Ary stumbled to the door. Just as Gran had said, the door unlocked from the inside with a simple latch. Ary pulled it free and pushed at the door. It didn't budge. She tried again. Nothing. Behind her, Gran was tossing more books into the pile.

"Canary, into the tunnels *now*!"

Ary turned herself sideways and threw her shoulder against the door.

It groaned—and swung open.

Ary tumbled through the opening. Cold air and dust greeted her; the tunnel was like the one she had taken to the Underlake, but wider and taller. The dirt at her feet was worn smooth and hard, but unlike the well-trodden footpaths of Terra, where hundreds of fairy feet had left smooth indents in rock and earth, these indents were long and sloping.

Because whatever thousands of creatures moved through these tunnels did not walk—they crawled.

"Ary, Owl, get on the bug!"

Owl shot out into the tunnel, a terrified-looking Shrimp close on his heels. It was her fault Shrimp was in this mess. He'd only wanted some extra food; now he was running for his life. She swung herself up onto Shrimp's back behind Owl, her heart pounding. Owl hunched forward oddly, his shirt bulging with awkward, square shapes.

"You're bringing *books*?" Ary demanded.

"*Shhh.*" Owl shot her a dark look. He had three, maybe four journals shoved under the hem of his shirt. "I was right about something being wrong with Terra. Everyone thought I was crazy—*including you*. But I was wrong about your gran. If we can't get the truth from her, maybe we'll find it here instead."

Ary swallowed. Owl had spent his entire life begging Ary for a few meetings with her gran. In some ways, Gran's reveal as a failure had to be more unnerving to Owl than it was to Ary. Owl had seen her as a hero, just like everyone else had.

Ary turned, and her heart stopped.

Gran knelt before a pile of books and broken wood. In front of her was a glow-shroom lamp, cracked open so the enchanted fungus was strewn over the books and the floor. Gran shoved a hand in her pocket and withdrew a tiny silk satchel. The scent of new earth and reaching roots filled the air, of clean air and a bright, warm light Ary had only ever seen in her dreams.

Only the mayor was supposed to have access to fairy dust.

Gran drew out the smallest pinch. Magic shimmered brilliant pink and gold beneath her fingers, waiting to be cast, molded, shaped. The sheer power pulsed through the room. The screeches of the earwigs came closer.

Ary had only ever watched magic once, from a distance, when Mayor Nightingale blessed the fields.

A pair of pincers appeared in the space over Gran's head.

"*Gran!*" Ary shouted. "*Watch out!*"

Gran opened her palm over the books and whispered a single word.

"*Ignite.*"

And then there was fire.

It was everywhere—racing over the books, eating up the floor. Thick, black smoke billowed into the air. The earwig that had crested the lip of the hole reared back with a hiss, and Gran was already on her feet, turning toward Ary and the rest. For a breath, she seemed frozen there, outlined in flames, and in that moment, Ary understood that she had only ever seen one part of her grandmother. That this woman who stood backed by fire and who handled magic was not her gran, but Wren Mossheart herself. Terra's third and final hero. This was the girl in the fountain, the one they whispered about in the market, the child who had disappeared into the Gloom with a band of companions and had been the only one to return alive.

Gran stood there like some kind of vengeful goddess, her fingers still shimmering with magic, her eyes bright and brave with the kind of anger only heroes and fools could summon, and for the first time, Ary understood why other folk had followed her grandmother to their doom all those years ago.

Then the moment shattered, and Gran was sprinting for the door, an old, rickety ladder tucked under her arm. She burst into the tunnel and kicked the door shut, jamming the ladder up against the handle. She spun, her eyes wild, and leaped onto Shrimp's back. Shrimp squeaked under the sudden weight but didn't complain.

"*Run*," Gran urged. "Once's the fire's out, that ladder won't hold them for long—*go*!"

Shrimp lurched forward, moving surprisingly quickly for a bug with three folk on his back. "Where?" he called, voice tight with fear. Gran rose up on her knees, the white wisps of her hair whipping around her face as she took in the tunnel. Her mouth settled into a grim line.

"South," she said, her voice low. "I know someplace we can go where we'll be safe. Not welcome, exactly. But safe."

Ary opened her mouth, but there was nothing in Gran's eyes that invited questions. The woman who sat astride the pill bug might have been a stranger, the way she looked forward with hard, angry eyes and a dangerous set to her jaw.

"Left," Gran ordered quietly as a fork in the tunnels appeared ahead. "Faster." Shrimp obeyed without a word, as if he was too terrified to question her. Gran kept her eyes ahead; she didn't look to Ary or Owl once to check on them and make sure they weren't injured. It was as if they weren't even there.

Behind them, far down the tunnels, came screeches.

"*Faster*," Gran said. "If the earwigs catch us, they'll eat you first, bug."

Shrimp made a terrified noise and put on an extra burst of speed.

Ary sat rigidly, her entire body numb.

As the Underlake faded into the distance behind them, all she could think was that for the first time in her life, she had truly met Wren Mossheart—and she wasn't all that sure she liked her.

# FIFTEEN

## *Into the Underground*

No one said anything as Shrimp carried them through the dark with only Gran's soft, whispered directions to guide them. The air grew damp, and the stench of mold far worse. Several times they heard a noise far behind them, but whether it was the pursuing earwigs or newts or just a passing critter, there was no way to know. Ary had half expected the Underground to explode with the writhing bodies of hungry earwigs—but like the Gloom above it, it seemed mostly abandoned. Though the well-worn tunnels spoke of many lives passing over this very ground, dust gathered on the walls, broken up only by mold. The fairies of Terra made it sound like the Underground teemed with millions of creatures waiting to rip them limb from limb—instead, they were strangely alone.

Many times Ary sat upright, questions bubbling in her chest, prepared to demand answers from Gran—only to meet the cold, focused eyes of the old woman guiding them, and shrink. Owl was surly and silent, curled protectively over the stolen journals as though he feared Gran might rip them from his hands and cast them into the dark if she noticed he'd stolen a piece of history to bring with them.

And Ary, remembering the flames, remembering the woman who had stared at them like a warrior out of a painting, that ache in her eyes when she'd read Dracaena's name, thought it was probably for the best that Owl had hidden them. The Gran she'd come to know wouldn't have ripped journals from a boy's hands and burned them—but this woman just might.

Ary's legs were beginning to ache from gripping Shrimp's shell when Gran finally whispered, "All right, slow down."

The pill bug obliged, his antennae drooping with exhaustion as his panicked run slowed to a painful trot. Ary's heart twinged. *Poor Shrimp.* She had dragged him into this, and for what? All he had wanted was some food.

"Left," Gran murmured, her eyes scanning the walls. She sat up straight, passing a wrinkled hand over her face. "It should be here . . . if my memory hasn't failed me. . . . We should see it soon. Ah, yes! Stop!"

Shrimp stopped abruptly. Ary pitched forward, her chin knocking into Owl's back. The boy grunted and said nothing.

Gran had stopped them, it seemed, in the middle of an empty tunnel.

The old woman slid from Shrimp's shell, her hip making an audible *pop* as she landed. Gran winced, braced a hand against her lower back, and limped toward the far wall, her fingers skimming over the handpicked earth. Here, in the eerie darkness of the tunnel, she looked like Gran again—old, tired, and a little bit sad.

Was it strange for her to return here, to the testing grounds of her youth, with a body that now ached and creaked? Was it terrifying?

"This way," Gran said, gesturing to a smaller, crooked tunnel branching off from the main one. It had an uneven, rocky floor, and had Gran not stopped them in time, anyone hurrying by would have missed it entirely. "You two will have to walk—I don't know if the bug will fit."

"His name is Shrimp," Ary said, a little louder than necessary.

"Excuse me?"

"His. Name. Is. *Shrimp*." She pointed at the pill bug in question, her hand trembling in an embarrassing way. Ary tried to make her voice braver. "Not Bug. Not *the Bug*. Shrimp. Otherwise known as the pill bug that just saved our lives. *Shrimp*."

Gran's eyes narrowed. She glared at Ary, lips twitching as if she wanted to say something—then she turned away, plunging into the tunnel without a light. Owl cast a raised eyebrow at Ary and followed. After a long moment of skin-crawling unease, Ary followed, too, with Shrimp bringing up the rear. It wasn't until they were entirely enveloped in darkness that the pill bug brushed an antenna over her shoulder and whispered, "Thank you."

They heard water long before they saw it.

In the beginning, it was soft—just the barest trickle, a whisper of water hitting stone. But as they moved through the tunnel, the trickle became a roar. The floor beneath Ary's feet began to vibrate. Soon they were stepping over puddles, and the ceiling began to drip.

All the while, Gran said nothing, leading the way with a straight back and a lifted chin. And all the while, a sense of disquiet built in Ary.

*I don't know this woman*, she kept thinking, over and over again. *I have never known her.*

If this was truly her gran—if this was who Gran *became* when everything else unraveled—then who was the quiet, frowning old lady who had raised Ary? Why had Wren Mossheart spent so long hiding? And was it her fault—or Ary's?

They turned the corner—and were greeted by a wall of cold, clear water.

It poured straight down in an ear-aching roar, slicing through sheer rock. The water fell at such a sharp angle that, had it frozen, it would have made a perfect wall. Streams rushed away on either side, disappearing under more ledges of stone. Ary dipped in a hand and immediately snatched it back, gasping as cold burned her fingers. The few fairy-carved streams that ran through the City of Terra were slow, shallow, and warm. But this water was a wild beast, cold and unrelenting. Ary could feel its rumble in her bones, in the beat of her heart and the quiver of her breath.

Tears pricked her eyes. Memories danced in her mind—of Mama, patiently straining algae from their drinking water, murmuring stories to Ary about how things had been different when she was a girl.

"When I was your age, some of the water was still clean," Mama had said. "It was so clear, Ary, it tasted like nothing."

"Maybe it'll be clean again someday," said Ary.

Mama's smile had faltered for only a moment. "Maybe so, sweet one. Maybe so."

Years had passed, and Ary accepted their world had long run out of water that wasn't tinged green and filled with muck. That clean, pure water was a thing only in her dreams. But here was a *force* of it, rushing so fast nothing could bloom, so cold nothing could grow.

Mama would have loved it.

"It's called a waterfall," Gran said, an odd wistfulness in her eyes. "Remarkable, isn't it?"

"I wish Mama were here to see it." The words were out of her mouth before Ary realized what she'd said.

The light in Gran's eyes dimmed. "Me too."

The weight of it seemed to settle between them—Mama

was still home. Mama was still sick, filled with mold, with probably only days left to live.

Gran's face darkened and her eyes snapped ahead as she turned to address Owl and Shrimp, seemingly determined not to meet Ary's stare. "We'll be safe on the other side," she shouted. Though she was yelling at full volume, they could barely hear her over the roar of the water. "Follow me—and step *exactly* where I do, unless you want to be swept away and drown."

Owl and Ary balked. *"What?"*

Gran stepped into the waterfall—and disappeared.

# SIXTEEN

## *An Old Friend*

"*Gran!*" Ary cried. She scrambled forward, her heart pounding against her ribs. Gran was gone. One moment she had been there, alive and breathing, and the next there was just water, racing past Ary, flecking the rocks as it rushed to some distant place far, far below. A burning panic swept up from Ary's belly. How could Gran have been so foolish? Could she have—

A shadow appeared, then Gran stepped through the curtain of water.

She was soaked to the bone, but otherwise all right. Her dark eyes bright, the old woman smirked and lifted her chin. "Well, come on. We don't have all day." Only the amusement in her voice betrayed her. The old hero beckoned at them and disappeared into the water once more. Ary had the faintest sense that someone had played this same trick on her once.

Silence lapsed in the cavern. Ary turned to look at Owl and Shrimp, who stared at the water with the same bewildered expression Ary was sure she had on her own face. Owl scrunched up his nose and shook his head, muttering something about "crazy old lady," and wrapped his arms protectively around the journals under his shirt.

"Owl," Ary blurted. "Wait."

Owl turned to her, a suspicious look on his face. Could she blame him? She hadn't exactly been kind to him . . . well, ever. And she certainly didn't *like* him. Still, a part of her felt bad. Because now instead of looking at Gran with shining, awestruck eyes, he stared at her with the same look Ary knew she'd carried her entire life—a little disappointed, a little betrayed, and a little scared.

It didn't make it all right that he'd only ever pretended to care about Ary because he wanted to use her to get close to Gran. And it didn't make him any less annoying.

But right now, they were on the same side.

Ary held out the rucksack she'd stolen from the guard.

Owl stared at it blankly.

"For the journals," Ary clarified, her cheeks flushing with heat. "So they don't get ruined." She had spied him reading in secret as Shrimp carried them through the tunnels. She didn't dare say what she wanted to aloud: that she was grateful that Owl was digging into Gran's past. That it made her feel less alone for someone else to have the crushing realization Wren Mossheart wasn't as heroic and perfect as everyone wanted her to be.

Owl stared at the bag a moment longer, as if convinced it might be a trap. "Thanks," he said, finally taking it, his eyes lingering on her face. He dropped the journals into the bag, shoved it under his shirt, and turned away, as if fearing she might change her mind. The boy stared at the waterfall, shuddered, and stepped through.

And then Ary and Shrimp were alone.

"All right, Shrimp," Ary said. "Let's go."

"No," Shrimp said softly, his dark, beady eyes taking in the water.

"You'll be okay. Just hold my hand."

Shrimp didn't budge. *"No."*

Ary chewed on her lip. "I don't want to leave you out here by yourself. What if those earwigs come back? Or the newt?" The Underlake was the closest she'd ever been to a newt before, but the sight of it had chilled her to the bone. Some folk were convinced that the mold was their work, that the newts had designed it to kill off the folk.

Remembering the look in the newt's eyes—the empty, bright hatred—Ary wondered if that might be closer to the truth than she'd initially suspected.

"Shrimp," Ary tried again. "It'll be okay."

"*No*," the bug said resolutely.

Ary's shoulders sagged. What was she going to do? Drag him? She pinched her nose. "Okay, fine. You can stay out here—but you have to hide."

The bug bobbed his antennae up and down in agreement. He scuttled to the wall of the cave and immediately rolled himself into a ball, wobbling for a few seconds before settling in among the rocks. Slime and patches of mold grew in sad, dispersed clumps throughout the tunnel—but covered in dust as he was, Shrimp blended right in. So long as no one looked too closely, he could have just been another boulder. Ary pressed a kiss to the pill bug's shell and leaned her forehead against him.

"Be careful, okay? And if you need us—just call, and I'll come running."

"Yes," Shrimp squeaked from inside his ball.

Ary turned to face the waterfall alone. Owl and Gran had not returned—which meant they'd either made it through or had been swept away entirely. She tried not to think about what waited on the other side of the waterfall, or what Gran had meant by "safe, but not welcome."

Ary squared her shoulders, took a deep breath—and stepped inside.

And then her entire world was water.

It roared all around her, flattening her hair to her cheeks, weighing down her wings and howling in her ears and rattling her bones. It punched the breath from her lungs and tried to drag her to her knees. Fear blossomed in her chest, and she was alone in the wide, wet dark, and she was *afraid*. She had always been so afraid. That was the difference between her and Gran, really. Gran had been born brave, and Ary had been born terrified. Fear had driven her all her life, and it drove her now, as the waterfall threatened to sweep her away. It wasn't bravery or heroism or even her desire to save anyone that drove Ary forward; it was terror, the sheer need to live, to keep *moving*. The water thundered around her, and Ary slid a foot forward, unable to hear or see a thing. She took another step, and then another, her lungs burning and her body aching as thousands of bucketfuls of water rushed over her—and then air hit her face.

Ary fell to her hands and knees, coughing and gasping for air. Her wings flopped to the ground with a wet *slap*, the papery covering soaked through. She was drenched, but safe. The water she'd walked through was no thicker than the length of her hand—from this side, she could just barely make out Shrimp, tucked against a wall. The other side of the waterfall was pitch black, roaring so loudly she could barely hear herself think.

Ahead of her, Gran and Owl waited.

"About time," Gran shouted. That strange light was back in her eyes—as if she was enjoying this.

As if she'd *missed* it.

Owl said nothing, looking miserable and damp, his arms protectively curled around the rucksack. Ary staggered to her feet and hurried after them, navigating her way over the slippery rocks, her wings heavy and dripping in the dark.

Ahead of them, a second curtain of water roared. Gran drew up to it—and hesitated. Something strange seemed to come over her. For the first time she looked . . . almost timid? She glanced back at them and opened her mouth, and then an odd look crossed her face, as though she thought better of it. In the end, all she said was, "Stay behind me."

Gran squared her shoulders and stepped through to the other side of the waterfall. Ary and Owl took a deep breath and followed suit. For a horrible moment, Ary was back in that awful, roaring world of water again—and then they were through, dripping and cold but otherwise unharmed. Ary opened her eyes and gasped.

Light was everywhere.

The tunnel had opened into a giant, sloping cavern. Water gathered in a deep, clear lake in the center of the cavern, fed by three different waterfalls that roared out of the rock, crashing over rocks and ledges to feed the endless pool below. Dozens of tiny streams broke off from the main pool, racing in different directions and vanishing again to the rest of the Underground. And illuminating the cavern, growing in great bunches on the floor, climbing up the walls, even growing in patches on the ceiling, were glow-shrooms. There had to be thousands of them, all giving off brilliant, soft blue light. Some had been half consumed by mold, but others glimmered fiercely, alive and shining despite the decay threatening them. A single glow-shroom could make twenty lamps; they were worth their weight in fairy dust, and more, back in Terra. And they were always the first to die when the mold crept back. This year's crop had already been completely obliterated, promising a long, dark year until the new spores could grow.

Tears blurred Ary's eyes. The fairies of Terra had long described the entire Underground as a place that held nothing but death and chaos, but to see the glow-shrooms here—wild and thriving, even as her city and the world around it choked on mold—felt like hope.

"Ary," Gran said, her voice soft but strangely tense. "You and Owl stay hidden, and don't come out until I tell you to."

Ary blinked. "What? Gran, why?"

"Don't argue. Just hide." The old hero limped forward into the cavern. A strange stillness had washed over Gran. She stood rigidly, her hands squeezed into white fists. Even her wing stubs were frozen. The old woman took a long, deep breath—and put up her hands as if in surrender. "I know you're there."

Ary went rigid, and then she heard it—a shuffle in the dark, an intake of breath, and a deep, throaty chuckle. Ary went stiff, from her toes to the tips of her wings. They were not alone here. Ary's mind leaped to the face of the woman in Gran's journal. Her words rang through Ary's mind. Was it her? Was it Dracaena?

"Well, well, well," a new voice said, too deep and booming to be a fairy. "Am I having another nightmare—or is that Mossheart?"

"We bring no harm," Gran said, her voice low.

"Please, Wren," the voice said. "Harm is all you've ever brought."

A *hiss* sounded, and a spark flared—and then there was fire, leaping to several torches around the room that formed a loose circle.

Curled in their center, poisonous tail flicking lazily, was one of the largest newts Ary had ever seen.

# SEVENTEEN

## *Sootflank*

The newt was a terrible sight to behold. Instead of the bright orange or dull red of the newt from the Underlake, this one's orange skin was broken up by dark clouds that splashed over its slick, poisonous body. Smoke drifted from his tail, from which the newt had summoned fire only moments before. His eyes were wide, unblinking, and devoid of all light.

The newt's entire body was covered in scars.

All the feeling drained from Ary's body. Owl went rigid beside her.

Standing before that newt, alone and unarmed, Gran had never looked smaller.

"After all these years, you're bold to show your face in the Underground at all, Wren." The newt flicked its tail. "Or perhaps you have a death wish."

"Perhaps," Gran said slowly. "It's good to see you, Sootflank."

"Oh, no need to lie," the newt, Sootflank, sighed. "And what's this—you've brought friends?"

"We ran into some trouble. We need shelter—just for the night—and then it's back to Terra for us."

*Back to Terra?* After everything they'd learned? Mama was sick, but she wasn't the first, and she wouldn't be the last. What about Dracaena's warning? They were only six days away from the two hundredth harvest, which was supposedly the end of their chance to find Atlas. And what about all that nonsense about Terra being stuck inside a *terrarium*—whatever that was?

Gran had told Owl and Ary nothing after they'd found the journal, but one didn't have to have a brilliant mind to understand what came next. There was less food every year. Less light, less water, less air that didn't reek of rot. Owl had been right all along—Terra was dying. And it was going to take the fairies with it. And if Dracaena was to be believed, that ending could be as close as six days away.

Unless they stopped it and found this mysterious Atlas that would—well, Ary didn't know—do *something* to fix it— they were all as good as doomed.

The newt, Sootflank, gave a long, low laugh. "After all these years . . ." His great head swung from side to side, his dark eyes blinking. "You truly are something, Wren. After what you did—after the way you left us. Now you dare return, sixty years later, and ask for *shelter*?"

"I wouldn't have come if I weren't desperate."

Sootflank seemed to weigh this for a long time, then gave a long, slow blink. "My answer is no. Leave."

"There are children with me." Gran's voice cracked. "My granddaughter and her friend. They are young—the girl has not even earned her wings. If the Underground catches them—"

"And what does the fate of two folk pups have to do with me?" The anger had left the newt's voice—now he merely sounded bored. His eyes began to close. "Leave, Wren, back the way you came. Before I make you."

Gran stood there, her arms limp at her sides. "You gave us shelter once, when Dracaena and I—"

"You are not Dracaena," Sootflank snapped. "*You* are the one who left her behind."

Ary's blood roared in her ears.

*He knew Dracaena?*

At the mention of Dracaena, Gran seemed to grow smaller. She shook her head and murmured something bitter, then turned to walk back to Ary and Owl.

Was Gran truly going to give up that easily?

Ary couldn't take her eyes off Sootflank. If this newt knew Dracaena—and if Dracaena had known something vital about their dying world—if Dracaena had known about *Atlas*—

"Go on," Sootflank drawled. "I know you're there. Leave the way you came, little folk."

They hadn't come this far for nothing.

"Ary," Owl whispered furiously. "*Don't.*"

But Ary's legs seemed to move of their own accord, and suddenly she was stumbling forward, out of the tunnel and into the cavern.

Gran's face went white.

Folk were raised to fear and hate the newts. The closer she got, the bigger Sootflank seemed, and the more wicked the scars on his body appeared.

Ary stood even with Gran. Her hands trembled, but somehow her voice emerged steady. "Wait—Mr. Newt, sir. If you'd just listen to me—please."

Sootflank's eyes remained closed. "Your youth need better manners, Wren."

Ary swallowed.

Her entire life, she'd lived in Gran's shadow because she'd assumed Gran had done the bold thing. The noble thing. Gran was old and cranky, sure, but she was a hero, a legend, one of the few folk who had secured Terra's future with their sacrifices. But if what that journal said was true . . .

Ary took another step forward. "We're not going back to Terra."

Sootflank snorted.

"We need your help."

His eyes did not open. "I am no longer in the business of helping fairies—you might ask your grandmother why that is."

"What if you weren't helping fairies? What if you were helping yourself?"

"Wren." A warning growl reverberated low in the newt's chest. "Silence this pup—"

"Can you help us find Atlas?" Ary blurted.

Silence crept across the cavern. Sootflank said nothing. The tip of his tail twitched again, and the old, powerful newt held terribly still.

"Canary," Gran hissed under her breath. She reached for Ary—and Ary ducked away from her hand.

She took a step forward, then another, until she was only several paces from the newt. Fear made every part of her jitter. This close, she could see the painful curves of the scars rippling over his lanky form—years, maybe even decades, of wounds that had healed into permanent echoes of hurt.

Sootflank opened his eyes.

The weight of his gaze felt like the falls, but a thousand times heavier—where Sootflank's body was a swirl of orange and gray, his eyes were pure black, deeper than night, colder than the darkest waters, more endless than the Gloom itself.

"I trusted a young fairy who came seeking Atlas once," Sootflank said, his voice soft and dangerous. "And I was a fool for it."

*Gran?* Ary wondered. *Or Dracaena?*

"So you do know of Atlas?" she asked.

Sootflank's tail quivered. For a moment, there was a spark in his eyes—but then it vanished, and the old newt's eyes began to drift closed a second time. When he spoke, it was in the voice of one quickly losing their patience. "I am old, and I am tired. I do not wish to be bothered by enemies who ought to be long dead, nor by their meddling offspring. Go away, little girl. *Now.*"

"Please," said Ary. "The mold is everywhere, and we only have six days."

"I want you gone."

"If what Dracaena said was right—"

"*Leave!*" Sootflank bellowed.

His eyes flew open—and the newt lunged.

# EIGHTEEN

## *The Newt's Condition*

Time slowed down. Ary could only watch as the newt's mouth opened to swallow her whole. Sparks danced around his poisonous tail. Magic crackled in the air, burning her lips, itching her skin, making her hair stand on end. This was not the gentle magic of the folk that grew weaker with each generation, ground from their precious wings, sprinkled over fields to coax dead seeds to life. This was the wild magic of the earth, of crawling things and critters down deep. This was magic that burned.

Sootflank's mouth snapped shut right in front of her, so close that the air made her eyelashes stir.

Time resumed. The newt had moved so fast Ary hadn't had time to blink. For a moment, she was face-to-face with him, standing before his great black eyes that shimmered with anger and hurt.

"*Leave*," the newt snarled, his breath wet and rank on her face. "While you still can."

Adrenaline kicked in. Tears pricked her eyes, and her knees buckled.

She could have died. Had this been anything but a threat,

she would have been gone, swallowed whole or burned in only a moment.

What had she been thinking? What was *wrong* with her?

A hand landed on her shoulder. It was Gran, wide-eyed and furious. She spun Ary around as if to rebuke her.

"Come on." Gran put a strong arm around her and tugged her forward quickly. "Let's go."

"I'm s-sorry," Ary stammered. "I was t-trying to help. I'm sorry. I—"

"Shhh." Gran smoothed a hand over her hair, her touch so like Mama's but not. "Shh, little one. It's okay. I know, I know."

"He almost ate me," Ary babbled. "He was so fast— I didn't think—"

Behind them, Sootflank said nothing. He didn't need to—the newt had made his point. Gran and Ary stumbled away from him, both shaking, tears leaking down Ary's cheeks as her mind replayed the image of the newt's mouth snapping closed in front of her over and over again. She would have been gone. With one terrible snap of his jaws, everything would have ended.

What had she been *thinking*?

"I'm sorry," Ary whispered.

"It's okay. It's my fault. I shouldn't have let the boy read that journal—I should have known he'd see something written about Atlas."

"He didn't read about it in the journal," Ary said numbly. "A glow-moth told me about it."

"That's—"

"What did you say?"

Ary and Gran both froze.

Behind them, Sootflank had raised his head from the cavern floor.

"I'm sorry," Gran said. "She's just—"

"Not you," the newt said flatly. He looked at Ary, the full weight of his gaze bearing down on her. "What do you mean, a glow-moth told you of Atlas?"

Ary swallowed, numb with terror. Her voice felt faraway. "A few days ago, I was out late in the mushroom fields. I was, uh, stealing." Heat crept to her cheeks. "Or trying to. The guards caught me—but one of their glow-moths talked to me. It looked at me—really *looked* at me, not that empty-eyed stare they usually have—and it spoke."

A strange hunger burned in the old newt's eyes. "What did it say?"

"It called me Wren Mossheart," Ary said. "And it told me, 'Atlas awaits.'"

Gran shot her a furious, horrified look, but Ary avoided her gaze. She'd never told Gran. But now, seeing the way Sootflank regarded Ary as if she were a ghost made flesh, she wondered if she should have.

"There are old stories," Sootflank said finally, his words careful and slow. "Of the Gardener, when she made our world. She built in safeguards. Protections. Guards designed to rise up if those who lived here failed. One of them was

140

the glow-moths. Only they have access to Atlas. They are born there, and some are chosen to guard its secrets. If one approached you, then it was one of those guards. And it came bearing the truth."

Ary felt faint. Sootflank kept talking.

"This world is dying—we have known it for some time now. We were *meant* to do something about it years ago." His eyes cut briefly to Gran, and the disdain there was enough to make even the proudest fairy shrivel. "I had long accepted that our battle for life was lost—but if Atlas is real—if the glow-moths have come seeking a fairy to unlock its secrets—then there is hope."

Ary swayed. A thousand emotions clashed in her—shock, terror, hope, all swirling together. If Atlas was real, then maybe Mama still had a chance. Maybe they all did. If anyone could fix things, it was Gran. Surely that was why the glow-moths had come to Ary—they'd been trying to find Wren after all. Now Ary had brought her here. Now Gran would save the world once again.

"Atlas," Ary said, her head spinning, "you can find it?"

"No." Sootflank shook his head. "Even the moths would not guide us. They are its messengers only. But if any creature knows where we should start, it will be the Steward."

"The Steward?"

"The keeper of this world's history. If anyone will know where to find Atlas, it will be him." He paused. "The Steward lives deep within earwig territory. You will need a guide."

Ary could hardly breathe. With a newt at their side, one old and powerful enough that it could wield fire magic, they'd be unstoppable.

"I will help you—on one condition."

"Anything," said Ary.

The newt inclined his head to the side, as if savoring the moment, and then his dark eyes settled on Gran. "I meant what I said—Wren Mossheart is no longer wanted, nor welcome, in the Underground." He turned his eyes to Ary. "I will guide you—and you only. If you wish to seek Atlas, little fairy, you will do it without your traitor of a grandmother by your side."

# NINETEEN

## *A Hero No More*

*What?*

For a moment, the offer didn't quite sink in. Ary stared at Sootflank, heart pounding, head spinning. His words rang around her.

*You will do it without your traitor of a grandmother by your side.*

And then Gran's voice shattered the air.

"Absolutely not."

Ary turned. Gran jolted forward, her entire body quivering with rage, nostrils flared and wing stubs twitching. She snaked out a hand and grabbed Ary's wrist, shooting a nasty, furious look at Sootflank.

"I am sorry for disturbing you," she snapped in a tone that suggested she was not sorry at all. "I should have known better than to count on your kindness. You'd just as soon betray us to the earwigs. We'll seek shelter elsewhere. Goodbye, Sootflank."

Gran turned to leave, her small, warm hand still encircling Ary's wrist—and Ary stayed put.

Gran nearly toppled forward. The old fairy's arm jerked back, and she spun, shock lighting up her eyes as she stared at her granddaughter.

Ary didn't budge.

"Let's go," Gran ordered.

"We have six days, Gran," said Ary. "Six days until Terra's two hundredth year."

"That's just an old myth—"

Ary shook her head. "Mama is sick."

"I know, Canary, but—"

"But what? We're going to go back to Terra and let her—let her—" She couldn't say it. Didn't dare to breathe it into the air and tempt whatever ear of fate might be turned their way.

*Let her die like Papa.*

Ary had been small when Papa died. A child, too young to quite understand. She was twelve now, still small, still a child, but she wasn't as helpless as before. The cavern seemed to shrink around her; she could feel the weight of Sootflank's patient stare, of Owl's nervous eyes peering from the tunnel in which he still hid. They had come so very far, and already Ary had a thousand questions. Why had Gran lied? Who was Dracaena? Why had Gran reacted with so much pain when she'd heard Dracaena's name?

And why—if what Dracaena had said was true—were they in the terrarium to begin with?

Ary might have been able to walk away from those questions, too, if it wasn't for a single image playing in her mind repeatedly.

Mama, growing sicker and weaker over the last few years.

Mama, who had always been gentle when Gran had been cold, who had never made Ary feel lesser for not being the kind of hero that would honor Gran's legacy.

Mama, filled with mold.

"Canary," Gran said, her voice soft. Dangerous. "We're going home."

Ary licked her lips. "No."

Gran's eyebrows lifted. "Excuse me?"

"*No.*" Ary turned, her chest rising and falling frantically as she whirled to look at Sootflank. "This Atlas—could it have a cure for us? A way to stop the mold?"

Sootflank had curled back into a ball, his eyes half lidded, as though he intended to fall asleep, but his attention had never left Ary. "I don't know. But if anything will have a cure, it will be Atlas." His eyes shot to Gran. "We were meant to find that *anything* sixty years ago."

Gran's fingers curled into fists, and she said nothing.

Ary's heart beat harder. She could almost see it—a path forward. Even if the moths wanted Gran, not Ary, surely it didn't matter so long as *someone* went? "If my gran leaves, you'll help us find Atlas? You swear?"

"I don't know where Atlas is. No one does. But I will

do everything in my power to guide you, while there is still time." Sootflank gave a long, slow blink. "Time we are quickly running out of."

It was like someone else were speaking through her body when she turned to Gran. Ary had always followed the rules, had always been a respectful, good little fairy, content to stay quiet and live on the sidelines. She'd comforted herself with her own fear, assured herself it didn't matter if she was small, quiet, and weak, so long as the heroic Wren Mossheart was there to pick up the pieces.

Ary had always been no one. She'd never asked questions, never chased down trouble.

She had always trusted Gran to save them in the end.

But now, as Ary looked at her gran, her voice came from far away. "Go home, Gran."

Gran's eyes widened. She looked at Ary as if she didn't recognize her. In the dreamy glow of the mushrooms, she looked like some ghastly figure from an old workers' tale. "Excuse me?"

Ary had not come here to save Terra. She'd not come seeking a cure for a dying world, a solution to the mold that had already taken so much. But saving Mama now meant saving Terra. It seemed she could not have one without the other. It felt too big, too much, for a girl of only twelve whose wings had not yet unfurled.

But there was no one else.

"Finding Atlas is Mama's only chance," Ary said slowly.

"Whether the myth is true or not . . . our world is sick. There must be something we can do. And if Sootflank will lead me, I'd be a fool to turn him down." She exhaled a shaky breath and did her best to keep her voice from cracking. "Go back to Terra, Gran. Please."

Gran's voice emerged quiet and cold. "You have no training. No magic, no preparation. You have always been gentle, Canary, and I have been patient with your weakness and your fantasies until now. But this is where I draw the line. The Underground is cruel to even the strongest of folk. The things I saw—the things I suffered—you are not ready for them. You are too *young*—"

"You weren't much older than me when you entered the Underground," Ary said quietly. "What you mean is that you think I'm too weak. I am not a hero like you." Her voice quivered. "But it sounds like you weren't much of a hero, either."

Gran reacted as if she'd been slapped. "I was ready for it. You are not."

"You don't know that!" Ary burst out. "You don't know a thing about me, Gran! I was always the disappointment, too timid, too shy for you to notice. Too plain to carry on your legacy. Did you know I skipped school long before it closed to work the mushroom fields and keep us fed? Did you know I regularly stole us food tokens?" Her heart pounded. "Maybe I'm not a hero like you. Maybe I'm not chosen. But I've had to be tough, even when I was scared. I had to be strong, even when I was all alone. I've had to fight and scrape and *survive*. And you saw *none of it*."

Heat rushed to Ary's face, and now she was trembling not with fear, but with anger. A lifetime of feeling too small, too timid, too *weak* rushed through her. Her entire life, she had kept Gran on a pedestal, forgiving her faults, thinking her wise and right, because she was the hero who had saved Terra.

But Gran had known this world was dying. She had turned away from it, deeming the problem too big to fix.

Gran had failed them all.

"You may have a statue in the town square, but ever since Mama got sick, *I've* been the protector of our family. I've been keeping us safe. Not you." Ary's voice softened, but the fury in it cut like a knife. "You don't get to tell me about being brave."

Gran stared at her, eyes glistening, mouth working furiously as she chewed on bitter words she was only just holding back. The silence between them was thick and painful. Around them, the waterfalls continued to roar.

Ary swayed slightly. Where had that come from? The urge to apologize and take it all back rose, but something in her whispered *no*. It had been the truth. Sometimes the truth was ugly; sometimes it hurt. But it was a truth twelve years coming, and it was one Gran needed to hear.

Gran closed her eyes. "Very well. You want to throw your

life away? Be my guest." Her eyes snapped open, pinning Ary to where she stood. "But when you emerge with scars and night terrors, haunted by the ones you leave behind who you could not save, the folk you left to rot, do not expect me to pity you. I was forced by the threads of fate to throw away my innocence and enter the Underground; you are choosing to do so. We are not the same."

"No," Ary said quietly. "We're not."

They stared at each other. The waterfalls roared around them, broken only by the sound of both of them breathing. Sootflank was silent, but Ary could feel his stare burning with interest.

"Shrimp can guide you back," Ary said gently.

Gran's voice was flat. "I can find my own way home."

Ary nodded. If she was being honest, she didn't really want Gran alone with Shrimp. Gran had shown no kindness toward the roly-poly even though he'd saved their lives. Ary much preferred the idea of him remaining with her until she could find somewhere safe for them to part ways.

Ary folded her arms. Her earlier boldness was fading; now she felt more like an awkward, scorned child, squirming under her grandmother's disappointed gaze. Even now, after everything, all she wanted was to reach her arms out to Gran for a hug. To fold into her, and know that they were okay, that Gran could love and forgive her, even when Ary didn't do what she wanted.

Gran only stared. She didn't soften—she never did. Any soft parts of her had been hardened and made sharp long, long ago.

"Have a safe journey back to Terra, Gran." Ary's voice hitched. "If Mama wakes up—tell her I'll be back soon?"

Gran cast her eyes upward, as if appealing to some invisible force for help, then shook her head. "The Underground took everything from me," she said tiredly. "Take care that it doesn't take everything from you, too."

And then she was gone, hobbling out of Sootflank's cavern and up to the tunnels, where she would disappear through the waterfalls and return to Terra alone. She was a pitiful sight—a single old fairy, her wing stubs shriveled, her steps slow and uneven as she lurched over the rocky cave floor. Every part of Ary cried out to follow her.

That was so like Gran—no well-wishes, no hug or *I love you*, knowing she might never see her granddaughter again. Just an argument, and nothing more.

Ary cast a quick prayer to the Gardener.

*Guide her back, please. Take her home safe. Give her the strength to care for Mama while I'm gone.*

Ary had broken something between her and Gran that had long been fraying.

Now she had to make it worth it.

# TWENTY

## *No Turning Back*

"Well," Sootflank drawled. "That was dramatic."

Ary's head spun. Had she really just done that? Stood up to Gran and sent her back to Terra? Ary turned, a nervous shiver rising in her. She stared into the newt's wide, dark gaze, crossed her arms, and tried to force herself to at least *look* braver than she felt. From the wry glimmer in Soot-flank's eyes, she wasn't successful.

"I have a feeling I'm going to regret this." The old newt sighed. "Oh well. We leave in a few hours—I would recommend you sleep while you can. The two of us have a—"

"Wait!" Owl stumbled out of the tunnel, the stolen journals bumping awkwardly under his shirt. He leaped over the river winding across the floor and nearly crashed into Ary before coming to a halt in front of Sootflank.

"I'm Owl," he gasped. "I'm coming, too."

Sootflank's tail gave an irritated twitch. "I did not agree to guide *two* little folk."

"Well, we're a package deal." Owl looped his arm through Ary's so hard he nearly yanked her off her feet. "Isn't that right, Ary?"

Ary blinked. "Um."

He glared at her. There was a wild light in Owl's eyes. To see him so bursting with energy and purpose now was unnerving—but it was clear she wasn't going to get rid of him.

And though she hated to admit it, she was grateful she wouldn't be heading deeper into the Underground alone.

"That's right," Ary said unconvincingly. "Where I go, Owl goes."

"Oh, and Shrimp," Owl added. "Shrimp has to come. I can go get him. He's probably still pretending to be a rock."

"Who is—" Sootflank gave a long, slow blink. "Do I even want to know?"

"Probably not," Owl said. He cocked his head to the side. "Sootflank, right? It's nice to meet you. You know, I've never met a newt, except for the one that tried to murder us a few hours ago, but I've heard stories. I mean, we all have. Bad ones—no offense. Say, does it hurt when you make fire? How does that even work—"

"*Enough.*" An annoyed growl rumbled from Sootflank's chest, and Owl's mouth clicked shut. "You may come along if you are *silent*."

Owl opened his mouth, closed it, and opened it again. A long, awkward beat passed, and he frowned. "How silent is silent?"

Sootflank looked like he wanted to eat him.

Owl, to his credit, did not shrink under the newt's furious glare. Sootflank shook his head and muttered something under his breath about getting soft in his old age. Then, instead of answering, he turned away from them, lumbering toward one of the great, wide pools.

"We leave in the morning," Sootflank snapped. He disappeared into the water without a sound, only the barest of ripples stirring on the surface, and sank out of view.

And then it was just them—Ary and Owl, alone in the great, glowing mushroom cavern. Ary had never felt smaller. She looked around, her stomach flipping and her ears ringing from the waterfalls. They were truly meant to sleep here? Her eyes scanned the cavern, darting back to the water where Sootflank had disappeared, and landing finally on Owl, who was staring at her like she'd just sprouted turnips from her ears. "What?"

Owl's eyes practically bugged out of his head. "What do you mean, *what*? Ary, that was *bonkers*! You stood up to Sootflank, and you stood up to your *gran*, and now we're going on an adventure and—"

Already regretting the fact that she'd let him stay, Ary tuned him out and wandered away. She was too tired to be annoyed with Owl. She just wanted to *sleep*.

"He can summon fire, Ary! *Fire!* And now we're off to find the Steward, which sounds terrifying, and we might absolutely die, and these journals are absolutely wacky, everything we've been taught in school was all wrong . . ."

Ary's head pounded. If he was going to keep babbling all night, she was going to have to sleep underwater with

Sootflank. The cave did not look welcoming. Half of it was ruined by damp—but against the far wall, patches of moss and lichen grew among a few stray mushrooms. Behind her, Owl had blessedly fallen silent. Ary knelt before one of the mushrooms, whispered an apology, and snapped the cap off at the stem. It was hardly her bed at home—but it was better than nothing.

She lay down—and found Owl staring at her.

Irritation prickled through her. "Can I help you?"

The boy had one of the journals open again.

He looked at her, his eyes bright and bursting with a thousand questions. "Dracaena is *from Terra*. Did your gran ever mention her?"

"No," Ary snapped, sharper than she'd meant to. She looked away, embarrassed by the bite in her voice. "There's a lot Gran forgot to mention."

Owl wilted a little. He looked like he wanted to say more—but instead, the boy slowly closed the journal and tucked it into his waistband. For the first time, his words came out slow and shy, instead of in a panicked, excited rush. "I guess I should go get Shrimp, huh?"

"I guess." Ary turned so she was facing the wall.

Owl lingered. "Hey—are you okay?"

Ary closed her eyes. Even if she wasn't, did it matter? It wasn't like he actually cared. Knowing him and his Gran-obsession, he probably just wanted to pry her for more facts. She knew better than to think he was coming along because he wanted to help her. This was just to prove his doomsday theories right. Owl Diggs had been born dying for an adventure; now he'd gotten one.

But it didn't make him her friend.

He was just using her, like he always had.

"I'm fine," Ary muttered.

Her head sank into the mushroom cap, muffling half the sound in the cavern. If Owl had more questions for her, he kept them to himself. After another long moment, the fairy boy padded away, scrambling back up into the tunnel to retrieve Shrimp from the other side of the waterfalls. Ary stared at the wall long after they'd returned, after Shrimp curled up beside her and pressed his shell against her back with a comforting weight, after Owl made his moss bed annoyingly close to hers. Both of them fell asleep, and yet Ary remained awake, her eyes tracing the wall, remembering the exhaustion in Gran's eyes, that *look* on her face that was so familiar.

It was the way Gran had looked at Mama, knowing she was doomed.

*The Underground took everything from me. Take care that it doesn't take everything from you, too.*

What had she gotten herself into?

# TWENTY-ONE

## *The Gardener's Warning*

It was dark when Sootflank woke them—but, Ary realized blearily, they were in the Underground now. It would always be dark.

"Get up," the newt said quietly. "We have a long way to go, and the Steward is deep within earwig territory. We will need to be swift and silent."

Ary and Owl rose groggily. Ary picked one of the glow-shrooms from a nearby wall. She packed it into her lantern, comforted by the light, and looked up to find Sootflank watching her with a funny expression.

"What?" Ary said defensively.

"The glow-shrooms have long been rumored to be tied to the magic that powers Atlas." He gave them a pointed look. "They've gotten a lot dimmer lately."

He turned away before Ary could react. Dread made her clutch the lantern closer. Stretching the sleep from her limbs, she clambered onto Shrimp's back alongside Owl, and they left the cavern behind.

If Sootflank was glad to be helping them, the newt was doing a good job hiding it. For someone who supposedly believed in an apocalypse that was only five days away, he didn't seem to feel that strongly about *anything* besides his hatred for Gran. He ignored them, pausing only to bark instructions—*quiet down, move faster, breathe softer, speed up.* The latter was directed at Shrimp, and it took everything in Ary not to snap at Sootflank. Shrimp was doing his best. He was clearly nervous around the newt, but when Ary had tried talking him out of coming before they'd left, the giant roly-poly had simply shaken his head and touched Ary's shoulder gently with an antenna.

"No," the bug said softly, firmly. "Together."

"You could get hurt," Ary had protested.

Shrimp shrugged.

He would not be leaving her side—and she wouldn't leave his.

It was more than Gran had been willing to do, in the end.

Now the Underground sped past them. Unlike the wide, sweeping tunnels they had taken from the Underlake, these were more cramped. Yet even down here, the mold was taking over everything—twice they turned down a tunnel to find the mouth completely choked in a wall of hungry white fuzz. The stench of it was so thick it made Ary gag. Even Sootflank, for all his sour moods, seemed to shrink at the sight of the devastation the mold was wreaking on his land.

How long had it been like this?

How had anything lived down here at all?

They kept going. Sometimes Sootflank walked ahead of

them, and sometimes the newt disappeared, his lithe form sliding through the rivers that crisscrossed Terra's underbelly. It was far more peaceful without him; the hulking form of the newt took up the entire tunnel, and he insisted they travel in the dark.

Again, Ary noticed uneasily how *empty* the Underground seemed. Someone had carved these tunnels, after all. From the way they looped and curved, they'd seen regular use. The fairies of Terra had made it sound like the fence was holding back millions of starving, fairy-hungry critters lurking beyond their walls.

But the most abundant thing in the Underground wasn't vicious earwigs or hungry beetles—it was just mold.

Where *was* everyone?

Sootflank vanished ahead of them, and Ary withdrew the glow-shroom lamp. Its gentle, pastel glow had grown dimmer, and it didn't reach much farther than a few paces ahead of Shrimp's antennae, but it made the darkness feel a lot less suffocating.

Owl squirmed behind her. The fairy boy froze and smiled awkwardly. One of Dracaena's journals was splayed across his lap, the letters barely legible in the dim light.

"Sorry," Owl said, all too quickly. "If it bothers you—"

Ary's throat tightened. Within those pages were words that undid everything she knew about Gran. Words that had tilted her world upside down already.

Words that were the truth.

"Of course not," Ary said with some effort. She'd spent most of her life hating Owl because he had only ever treated her like a means to get to her gran. But he seemed *worried* about her. He'd stuck with her when Gran had abandoned her so easily. He was here now, and he was trying to help.

That was worth something—right?

Ary looked out at the endless dark of the Underground. "I didn't expect it to be so . . . empty."

Owl raised his head. "What?"

"The Underground," she elaborated, gesturing. "The mayor and everyone else made it sound like this place would be a giant nightmare. Instead, it feels . . ."

"Abandoned?"

"Yeah," Ary said softly. "It feels like instead of being chased by insects down here, we're being chased by ghosts."

Owl licked his lips. His words came back to her—his insistence that the world was dying, that something was deeply wrong. He was kind enough not to say *I told you so*, but the anguish in his eyes said he was far less surprised by the desolation of the Underground than she was.

He was trying to help—she ought to be kinder to him. She cleared her throat and changed the subject. "Have you learned anything about Atlas?"

Owl lit up and shook his head. "No. This Dracaena girl— she jumps all over the place. One minute she's talking about growing up in Terra, and the next she's talking about waiting for your gran to come back." He frowned. "Your gran never mentioned her? Not once?"

Ary's chest tightened. Her eyes traced the lines of the journal.

> *Wren was everything to me, our entire lives. When she was chosen to find a cure, there was no question—of course I would follow her. I would have followed her to the ends of this world and back if only to keep her close to me. I thought she felt the same.*
>
> *I guess I was wrong.*

"No," Ary said, her throat tight. "She didn't."

Her fingers skimmed over the pages. Years of pent-up feelings swept beneath her touch. Owl had been right; the journal was horribly jumbled, the words scribbled at a messy slant. It was as if Dracaena had written in a panic, trying to cram in as much as she could. Her thoughts constantly leaped back and forth through time, spinning from anecdotes about her childhood to memories of the Underground, to entire pages musing and worrying about what would become of the world if Wren never came back.

Who was this girl who had cared so much for Gran? Why had Ary never known she existed? She recalled the girl Gran had drawn repeatedly in her journal, the loving care with which she'd rendered every line of her face. If it was Dracaena who Gran had been drawing, why had she never mentioned her? Why hadn't she even bothered to write down her name?

Owl turned the page. More scribbles filled the old paper. Ary was bored after only a minute of looking at them, but Owl seemed mesmerized. He turned another page.

"Ary," he said. "*Look*. It's the poems."

In huge, dark letters, Dracaena had transcribed the Gardener's Promise—and the odd, twisted poem they'd found at the bottom of the Underlake.

*What roots shall bloom,*
*But what blooms shan't die,*
*Within this city in which we're free.*
*By the Gardener's hand,*
*The harvest begins,*
*And in Terra's trust,*
*We reap eternity.*
*What roots shall bloom,*
*And what blooms must die,*
*Beneath this city to which we flee.*
*By the Gardener's hand,*
*A false world spins,*
*But in its dust,*
*We find the key.*

Covering the page, written at wild angles in a dozen different inks and smudged at the corners, were fragmented, incoherent rants.

*Why are some lines left the same?*
*What is the key? What dust makes a key?*

"I think she was trying to solve it," Owl said. "That weird, cryptic poem we found—she must not have been the one who put it there."

Ary swallowed. Somehow that was worse. If everything odd could be chalked up to *just* Dracaena, that was one thing. But if there was something larger at play?

Something older, that reached past even Gran's time?

A wave of terror rose in Ary.

That made this problem much, much larger than it had been before.

Her eyes scanned the page. Dozens of musings pondering the meaning of the poems were crammed into the margins—each of them more frustrated than the last.

*Terra = city flee??????*
*??? What bloom died?*

"Ary," Owl said, his voice heavy with dread. "Look."

Slashing across the bottom of the page, cutting through Dracaena's own pondering, in furious letters:

*WHO / WHAT / WHERE IS ATLAS?*
*WHAT.*
*DID.*
*WREN.*
*SEE?!?!*

Ary closed her eyes.

*What did you get us into, Gran? What mess did you leave me to clean up?*

Owl stared at the pages a moment longer, then snapped the journal shut with a frustrated huff. "It just doesn't make sense. If it's this important, why make it so cryptic? 'A false world spins.' That's Terra. But the rest of it—'in its dust we find the key'? I'm just as confused as she was."

"Maybe the Steward will know," Ary said.

Owl looked doubtful. "Maybe."

Ary wrapped her arms around herself and shivered. The air was tepid here, but she felt a chill all the same. The tunnel sloped sharply downward; still, there was no sign of Sootflank. An awkward silence lapsed between them.

"Owl?" Ary asked. "Why were you always so obsessed with my gran?"

His head snapped up. "What?"

"My whole life," Ary said slowly. "You treated her like a god. You never talked to me except to beg for a chance to talk to her. You were obsessed with her. *Why?*"

His eyes searched her face, as if he was expecting a trick.

Something sad and tired blossomed in his gaze—a hint of something more, beyond the excited, all-over-the-place persona she'd come to know. His throat bobbed nervously, and he looked away. "Because my parents were."

Ary's heart skipped a beat. "Were?"

Owl looked away. "They died, the same year your papa did. From the mold."

"I . . . I didn't know. I'm sorry."

Owl cleared his throat. "They had the, uh, same burial day as him."

Horror froze her in place. "Oh."

"Yeah."

Ary's head spun. She hardly remembered the details of Papa's burial day; only after, once the guards had lowered him into the field, when she hadn't been able to tell his plot from the dozen others, and it had sent panic spiking through her to think about him lost for good.

She hadn't even noticed Owl that day.

But he'd clearly noticed her.

Suddenly Ary was grateful for the dark, if only so Owl couldn't see her tears. Shrimp kept moving. He was listening—she could tell by the way he walked more quietly now, his antennae pricked, but he didn't interrupt. Something told her he didn't need to. That Shrimp, like her and Owl, also understood loss.

Guilt prickled through her. She'd noticed before that Owl was always alone—that no one came to his school visits or escorted him to the market. But he was annoying, and excitable, and only ever pestered her about her gran. So she'd never put much thought into it. The year Papa had gotten sick had been the beginning of the end; everything after had been a terrible fog, an endless fight to survive. She'd never considered she might not have been the only one fighting.

Owl picked at a cuticle. "My dad was a Seedling. And when he was a baby, he got sick from the plague. Real sick. If your gran hadn't returned with the Sunroot, he would have died. He always told me that everything we owed, we owed to Wren Mossheart. That we had failed her—and your family—by not telling her story right." His lips quivered. "My parents knew something was wrong with this world. They always talked about how Terra had lost its way, how even the Seedlings had failed in their duty."

Ary recalled the Seedling shovels scattered through the Gloom and the indent at the bottom of the Underlake, the cryptic warning swirling above, painstakingly etched into stone by fairies long lost. The Seedlings she knew were little more than nuisances, constantly singing the Gardener's Promise and clanging about with their shovels. Thoughtless and silly. But there had been nothing thoughtless or silly about that carving in the lake.

"They said they felt the world dying. But no one listened to them. No one understood. Except me. And after they were gone, no one would listen to me, either."

"And you thought my gran would," Ary said softly.

"Yeah." Owl stared at the journal, something hard and angry in his eyes. "I thought she would."

The last few years replayed through Ary's head, recast in a terrible light. Suddenly, Owl wasn't a selfish boy drunk on hero worship—he was just terrified.

Just an orphan, trying to get hold of the one person he thought could fix the problem.

"I don't know what I'm doing here," Owl admitted. "But . . . I'd like to think my parents would be proud. And even if you don't believe it, Ary—I think you're our best chance."

She looked at him, surprised. He still wasn't looking at her. A faint blush touched his cheeks. She didn't know how to tell him she didn't want to be anyone's best chance but Mama's. That the moth had come seeking Wren Mossheart, not Canary Mossheart, and she was no hero, and had no idea how to *be* one.

But maybe this was how the journey of every hero started—not with a grand prophecy, but a few scared people realizing it was time to do the right thing, not because they wanted to, not because they were ready, but because no one else would.

One thing still didn't make sense, though. Ary scanned the darkness flashing by them, her brow wrinkled. "You said your parents knew something was wrong—and so did you.

But how? We all know things weren't *good*, obviously. But you've always been so convinced the world was ending."

Owl looked at her, surprised. He opened his mouth and closed it again, then looked away. "We just . . . knew." He cleared his throat. "I don't know how to explain it. It's just a feeling, I guess. A strong one—like a toothache, or a dream you can't remember but you still know you had. Every part of Terra felt sick where we touched it and we just . . . knew."

It sounded like gibberish. Ary eyed him warily. He was holding back. Hiding something from her. Could she really blame him? She'd spent their whole lives pushing him away. It wasn't like one moment was going to have him divulging his secrets.

But maybe Ary could start to make up for how she'd treated him in the past. Before she could change her mind, she shoved the glow-shroom lamp into his hands, her face burning. "Since you're the one doing the reading. No sense straining your eyes."

Owl took the lamp slowly, as if fearing it might bite him. "Thanks."

The two them sat awkwardly, the light bobbing between them. Ary half expected him to say something more, but Owl's attention was already drifting back to the journal, to the page filled with Dracaena's ranting, his brow furrowed.

"Owl," Ary said softly.

He looked up. "Yeah?"

"Thank you for coming with me. For not . . . abandoning me to figure this all out on my own."

He gave her a tight smile. "I couldn't let you have all the fun."

She returned his smile, which only made guilt squeeze her throat. She had been so unkind to him, and now he was here, risking his life, for . . . what, exactly? She wasn't sure. None of them were. They had so little to go on. Even Soot-flank seemed uncertain and anxious.

Five days. That was all they had to find Atlas—five days, before their one chance at saving Mama, and their whole world, disappeared entirely.

Ary's attention lingered on the second poem. The Gardener's Promise had always been a comfort—the Seedlings had long claimed it'd been written by the Gardener herself, passed down from generation to generation to remind them of how she had built Terra for them by hand. Crafted an eternal world where fairies could always thrive.

But the second, twisted version read less like a promise and more like an omen.

As the tunnel flashed by around them, Ary couldn't shake the feeling that a warning was exactly what the second poem had been—one that the people of Terra hadn't heeded until far, far too late, if any of them had ever listened at all.

# TWENTY-TWO

## *The Steward*

"*I said no light!*" a voice boomed.

Ary cried out, nearly toppling off Shrimp. One moment they had been alone, riding comfortably through the Underground tunnels as darkness pressed around them, then suddenly Sootflank was there, blocking their path, dripping and furious.

"Have you lost your minds?" the newt thundered. "Carrying *light* through the Underground?"

"We can't see," Ary said hotly. "And *you* left us."

"I didn't leave you," Sootflank snapped. "I was scouting. And I could hear you and smell you the entire time from the rivers. Really, do they teach you folk nothing?" The old newt made a noise of disgust. His tail cut through the air, lightning fast, and knocked the glow-shroom lamp from Owl's hands. Owl yelped in dismay as it tumbled down the tunnel and winked out in the dark.

Ary held carefully still, trying to quell the panic that threatened to overwhelm her at the sight of their sole light disappearing.

"We are nearly in earwig territory." Sootflank glared at

her. "They are drawn to light. If we are lucky, your foolishness did not give us away. But if it did—do not speak to them. Do not *look* at them. As far as they know, you are a prisoner of the newts."

Ary's skin crawled. It didn't feel too far off. Sootflank had said he would guide them—but what reason did they even have to trust him? She didn't know a thing about him. And so far it was clear the newt wasn't interested in being their friend.

But he *was* guiding them, even if it was only for selfish reasons. It was hard to look at Sootflank and not hear Papa's haunted voice as he recalled battling the newts, to not see the scars that twisted the bodies of so many folk in Terra. But Gran had left and Sootflank had stayed, and if she could not trust him, maybe she *could* trust his determination to find Atlas.

Maybe that was enough.

Ary eyed the space where the glow-shroom lamp had vanished. "How far into earwig territory is the Steward?"

Sootflank gave her an annoyed look, as if Ary was being insolent for asking. "Not far. He lived there before they claimed that land—they leave him well enough alone." He paused, the very tip of his tail twitching in that way Ary had already learned meant he was trying to keep his temper in check. And she'd thought Gran was cranky! "I mean it, little folk. I expect you to follow my instructions *exactly as I say them* from now on. If you put me at risk—if we end up in danger—I will not hesitate to abandon you. I am not risking my life for a Mossheart again."

A sour taste flooded Ary's mouth. So they were back to Gran. None of this felt entirely fair. Until yesterday, she hadn't even *known* the Underground hated Gran! And other than keeping the secret about the terrarium—which, granted, was a very big secret indeed—she wasn't certain what else Gran had done, because no one would tell her.

Yet Sootflank seemed content to punish her all the same.

At their silence, Sootflank drew closer. Shrimp whined low in his belly but didn't flinch as the newt lifted his head so that his wide, dark eyes were level with Ary's, glittering with a quiet warning. "Do you understand?"

Ary put a comforting hand on Shrimp's shell and glared back at Sootflank. "Perfectly."

The sooner they found Atlas and got rid of Sootflank, the better.

From the look on his face, it was clear the feeling was mutual.

"You should walk," Sootflank said flatly, casting them the barest glance. "Prisoners wouldn't be given the luxury of a ride."

And though Ary hated to agree with Sootflank about anything, Shrimp *did* seem exhausted. Silently, she slid off the roly-poly's back. Owl followed suit. The two of them exchanged a long, slow look as Sootflank turned around and slipped back into the dark.

After nearly an hour of walking in the dark, Sootflank said, "Wait."

Ary stopped so suddenly that Owl crashed into her, the two of them collapsing in a tangle of limbs and wings. Ary pushed Owl off her with a grunt, too tired to be polite. Her head hurt, and her feet ached terribly. Ary and Owl were constantly tripping over rocks and fumbling in the dark. If she didn't get a scrap of light soon, she was going to scream.

Sootflank's voice floated around them.

"We're close." He paused. "The Steward is very old and easily startled. Be silent and walk lightly."

Ary blinked, though it did nothing to clear the darkness in front of her eyes. *Walk lightly?* What did that even mean?

"One problem with that—Ary and I can't see," Owl said dryly. "Maybe some light would help?"

Ary didn't have to see Sootflank to know from the rumble in his chest that he was annoyed. But instead of ignoring them, the newt snapped his tail twice in the air. White-hot sparks flew around them for a moment before dying, but in their wake they left Sootflank's tail glowing a soft ember orange. Even from a distance, Ary could feel the heat rippling off it, and she shuddered.

*He's on our side*, she reminded herself. *He's just some old newt, and he's on our side.*

Still, all she could think of was how Sootflank's tail would surely singe anything it touched; all she could remember were the burn scars far too many folk wore like permanent nightmares on their skin.

Scars Papa himself had carried.

"This way," Sootflank said.

A strange mound of earth reared before them. It was unlike anything Ary had ever seen, bubbling upward like a giant burial mound. At the very foot of it was a yawning dark hole. They drew nearer, and a musty smell wafted out. It didn't reek of insects or newts; it almost smelled like wet, dirty fairy hair.

The tunnel sloped sharply downward. But unlike the wider tunnels that carved through the Underground, which had been worn flat by thousands of insects, this one was made of soft, mushy earth that sucked at their feet and made it hard to walk. Strange, long gashes were carved along the tunnel walls. *Claw marks?* Ary wrapped her arms around herself. Just what kind of creature was this Steward?

The odd, hairy scent grew stronger the farther they walked. Ary gagged, and Owl tore strips of cloth off his shirt and shoved them up his nose. After a few minutes, Ary copied him. Down, down, down the tunnel sloped. All the while Sootflank was silent, pausing only to summon more sparks and reignite the fiery glow of his tail that cast the entire tunnel in a strange, eerie orange haze.

Though he was old, it was clear the newt was strong.

Fire magic even among newts was rare. Usually newts that could summon flames became generals in their constant war against the folk.

So what was Sootflank doing off on his own?

"We're here," Sootflank said quietly. "Remember to be quiet—and don't panic."

Owl straightened. "*Panic?* Why would we panic?"

The ground began to tremble.

Ary and Owl jumped back and collided with Sootflank, and Ary could only watch as massive claws broke through the earth, and from the ground climbed one of the strangest, ugliest creatures she had ever seen.

# TWENTY-THREE

## Chives

The creature was three times the size of a newt, and twice as terrifying. The ground quaked as the beast scrambled forward on great, scraping claws. But the most curious part was its nose—instead of a round button nose like Ary's or a snout like Sootflank's, the tip of this creature's nose ended in writhing pink tentacles. And instead of scales or skin, the beast was covered in what looked like . . . *hair?* Flat brown hair, almost like fairy hair, but far thicker. She'd never seen anything like it. It looked like something out of one of Mama's stories.

The creature hesitated and took a long, slow sniff. Ary's entire body turned to ice. This was it. Sootflank had tricked them after all. He had clearly brought them here as a sacrifice, and she should have listened to Gran, because now this monstrous creature was going to—

"Oh!" gasped the creature in a high-pitched squeal. "Visitors! It's been so long since I've had *visitors!*" It turned its head, still sniffing, and fixed one dark, beady eye on them. "*Sootflank?* Is that your cranky stench I detect? What

175

a delight! It's been *years*, hasn't it? Oh, you smell terrible as ever!"

"Hello, Chives," Sootflank sighed.

The creature, Chives, sat back on his haunches with a chortle. His lips peeled back in a smile, revealing strange, sharp teeth. "Truly, Sootflank, I'm just tickled to see you. To what do I owe the pleasure?"

Ary couldn't stop staring. *This* was the Steward? The ancient guardian of Terra's history? The one that was supposed to know how they could find Atlas and save everyone? The animal they were relying on to save the world was a big, hairy creature named *Chives*?

Sootflank inclined his head to the side. "We seek Atlas."

And just like that, Chives' friendly demeanor vanished. He grew still. Only the very tips of his pink tentacle nose twitched. When he spoke, his voice came out slow and wary. "For as old as you are, Sootflank, I see you are still a fool." The creature linked his claws together. "Did you not learn your lesson with the Mossheart pup?"

Instead of answering, Sootflank stepped aside so Chives could see Ary in full. "I suppose not."

A pin could have dropped in the silence that followed. Chives turned his head slowly to one side and fixed her with one beady eye before turning back, his tentacles twitching furiously. Instead of addressing Ary, he turned back toward Sootflank. "Is this some cruel joke?"

"Unfortunately not."

"Then have you lost your mind?"

"I seem to still have my sanity." Sootflank sighed. "Unfortunately."

Chives looked at her again, and the anger that crackled off him was so startling she took a step backward. She had thought Sootflank had been nursing a decades-old wound, but this creature was positively furious. His strange mouth worked over and over again, sharp teeth glinting as though a thousand cruel words were bubbling behind them that it took everything in him not to say.

Finally, Chives shuddered and turned away. "I think it best you leave."

"I was afraid you might say that." Sootflank closed his eyes. "Chives, please. Hear us out. You know the myth as well as I do. If it's true we only have five days—"

Chives slammed his claws down on the soil, hard enough to make them all jump. "Don't you dare recite the old myths back to me, Sootflank! You think I don't know what's at stake? You think I haven't lived my entire life in fear, in *dread*, knowing I am the last Steward of a dying world?"

Sootflank, to his credit, was unfazed. "I had given up, too. But please—hear what the girl has to say."

"I listened to a Mossheart once," Chives said coldly. "And we all paid the price. I'd think you, of all creatures, would know better than to make that mistake again."

Sootflank said nothing. Ary watched the exchange between them, her heart beating so hard it hurt. Was he truly going to turn them away? They had no one else. Nowhere to go. If he did not help them, then Mama was already dead.

She'd thought before that Gran had simply failed the Underground by not telling everyone about the terrarium—but it was clear something worse had happened. Something deeply painful that had cost the Underground far more dearly than it had ever cost Terra. Her head spun.

*What did you do, Gran?*

*What kind of villain were you?*

"Please." Chives' voice was barely audible. "I cannot help you. Please, just go."

Ary's legs buckled. If Gran were here, she would argue with Chives, with that sharp tongue and dry wit of hers. Gran had always been able to force her will when she wanted to.

Well, not always.

But Ary didn't want to be like Gran—brash and cold, sharp-tongued, bitter, and alone. So instead, she looked Chives square in the eye and tried to be proud of her voice even when it came out scared and small, because it was a miracle Ary the nobody was using her voice at all.

"I'm Ary," she began nervously. "I—I'm Wren Mossheart's granddaughter. You knew that, obviously. That's why you want us to leave. That's why you don't want to help us."

"Not a single Undergrounder could blame me, child."

"I know," Ary said quickly. "Gran let you all down. And from the way everyone reacts, she must have done other terrible things—though no one has *told me what*." She cut a glare at Sootflank.

The newt blinked back at her, his wide, dark eyes impossible to read.

"Look," Ary said, turning back to Chives. "I'm not my gran. I'm not some chosen one Terra has sent to steal the secrets of the Underground. I'm just some girl, okay? I didn't even want to come here." Her voice grew small. "I just want to help my mom."

Her voice broke on the last word. Memories flashed behind her eyes: Mama flush-faced and smiling, teaching her to weave dried moss into cloth. Mama pulling her close when Ary woke sweating and screaming from nightmares, kissing the tears from her cheeks and promising she was safe, she'd always be safe, so long as they had each other.

And Mama, so many times over the years, telling Ary that she was brave and brilliant *because* she was ordinary, not despite it.

If Gran were here, she'd probably have talked about fate. About saving the world. About making the hard, bold choice for the good of all. But Ary had never been cut from the cloth of bravery the way Gran had. Ary hadn't been born with her name written in prophecies, raised to be a hero, showered in the knowledge that she would be special, chosen, and precious.

And Ary didn't *want* to be responsible for the good of all people.

Just one.

"She's sick, and I have to save her," Ary whispered. "I don't know about prophecies, or warnings or promises, or whatever it was Gran found and lied about. I don't know if the world will really end in five days or if it's true that I can't save Mama without saving everyone else. I don't *care*. I just—" Her voice caught. "No one else wanted to do anything. Even Gran was just going to let her die. So if finding Atlas will help her—I have to do it. I have to try."

Suddenly she was just a little wingling again, eavesdropping as Mama argued with Gran, begging her to set out in search of Underlake water that might save Papa's life. Mama had never forgiven Gran for not leaving right away—and now Ary knew, with the hollowest ache in her bones, that even if Gran had left the instant Papa had fallen ill, it wouldn't have mattered.

The Underlake had been dry long before mold grew in Papa's lungs.

An awkward silence stretched through the air. Sootflank watched her oddly, and Chives stood very, very still.

Owl edged forward to stand beside her. He lifted his chin and raised an awkward hand. "I'm Owl. Um. I'm not here to save anyone. I'm just tagging along."

Ary shot Owl a glare. *How was that supposed to help?*

Owl looked back at her, shrugged, and shoved his hands in his pockets.

But Chives gave Owl an appraising look. "You have no wings."

Owl straightened. "Um, yes, sir."

"Are you a Seedling, too, then?" There was a weight to Chives' voice—something hidden there. A test.

"Um, no, sir. But my parents were." Owl's cheeks turned pink. "I'm just here to help Ary."

"And so history repeats." Chives let out a heavy sigh. "I'm sorry about your mother, little Mossheart. Truly. But Atlas is a precious secret with a terrible price. You mean for me to believe that after all these years, Wren Mossheart is going to let her own granddaughter pay a price she herself refused?"

"My gran has nothing to do with this," Ary said bitterly. She could have laughed at the irony. Chives didn't trust her because he thought Gran cared about what happened to her. As if Gran hadn't just cast her into the Underground with some cryptic warning about becoming a fairy left to rot in the dark.

"Tell him, little folk," Sootflank said, his voice surprisingly gentle. "Tell him why I helped you."

"Tell me what?"

Ary's heart sank. She was already so tired of this part of the story. Of admitting that her role in all this was an accident.

"A glow-moth came to me," Ary said finally, numbly. "I had never even heard the name Atlas before, and a few days ago, a moth came to me out of nowhere in the mushroom fields. It called me Wren and told me 'Atlas awaits your return.' It meant . . . nothing to me. I never even brought it up to Gran. I thought it was nonsense." A bitter taste flooded her mouth. "Obviously, it's not."

"They said those exact words?" Chives asked, his tentacle nose twitching. "You're not mistaken?"

"I couldn't forget them if I wanted to."

Chives sat up straighter now, every part of him gone still as he considered her in a new light. A chill swept through Ary. That look on his face—it was the same way Sootflank had looked at her when she'd confessed back in his cave.

It was a look she was already learning to dread because it said: *You're special. You're different.*

It was the way people still looked at Gran.

Ary's throat bobbed. If Chives was going to help her, she didn't want it to be because of some blasted moth. She didn't want it to be for any reason other than it was the right thing to do.

And she wanted him to stop looking at her like that.

"Look," Ary said weakly. "Whatever your feelings are about my gran, I'm not here for her. I'm here for my mom. She's depending on me. And if I can find Atlas, and then go back and get Mama—"

Chives looked sharply at Sootflank. "You haven't told her?"

Sootflank avoided looking at Ary. "Didn't seem necessary to scare the girl until we knew whether or not you'd help."

"How kind," Chives drawled. "Leaving me to do the honor."

"Told me what?" Ary's heart pounded. "What are you talking about?"

For a long, terrible moment, no one said a word. Chives and Sootflank almost looked guilty.

And then Chives spoke.

"You say you don't know why we all loathe Wren Moss-heart." He paused. "Some of it is not my story to tell—some of it, you will learn in time."

Chives' voice came slowly, softly, and it was the pity in his eyes more than anything that struck a chord of fear deep in Ary's heart.

"None of us know who, or what, or entirely *where* Atlas is. All we know is that it's sealed away—and anyone who seeks it must pay a terrible toll. The price is too high for many. It was certainly too high for your gran."

Ary's voice came from far away. "What is the price?"

"Your life," Chives said gently. "If you seek Atlas, little folk, and you find it—you will have to pay with your life."

# TWENTY-FOUR

## *You'll Never Be Her*

Ary dreamed of Gran.

In the dream, Gran was no longer the bitter, world-weary old woman Ary had known for most of her life. She was a girl again—the fierce-eyed girl in the fountain, who returned from the Underground to cure a plague and save Terra.

Supposedly.

In the dream, they wove through a field of mist, Gran's dark silk hair bobbing behind her, wings flared delicately as Ary struggled to keep up. There were others with them—young, like Gran, with bright eyes and wary smiles.

*The other heroes.* Because while Gran had returned from the Underground alone, she had not *entered* it alone. Their names, like their lives, had been lost to history; now only this fragment remained.

One of the heroes walked closest to Gran. She was young like Gran, beautiful and smiling. Cold rocketed through Ary. It was the girl from Gran's journals—the girl Gran had drawn obsessively, compulsively, for the rest of her life. She was here, she was *real*, laughing and tossing her hair, blushing at something Gran whispered to her, gesturing wildly at the vast reach of the Underground before them.

And she was a *Seedling*. The brown robes that marked the folk who worshipped the Gardener swirled around her ankles. In one hand, she held a shovel.

Her other hand held Gran's.

Ary hurried after them. "Wait for me!"

They were always just out of reach, laughter pealing through the air like the dew-bells that used to call the fairy children to school before it closed. A hulking mountain rose above them; the stone was sloping and strange, crafted of smooth, patterned rock that shimmered a beautiful silver. Gran and her friends began to climb, hopping from stone to stone, their wings catching the currents of air and guiding them upward with ease.

"Wait for me!" Ary cried again. The air grew colder; the light faded. One by one, the other heroes winked out of sight, until only Gran and the girl from her journals remained.

Ahead came something like muffled sobs.

"Gran, wait!" Ary cried. *"Wren!"*

Ary kept climbing. Her fingers and hands slipped on the odd, silvery rock. When she lifted them, her skin was coated in shimmering, iridescent dust.

Whispery voices swirled around Ary, chanting a familiar phrase on an endless loop.

Overhead, Gran was nothing more than a blur. There

was no more laughter in the air now, only the scrape of nails on rock. Panic thrummed through Ary.

On the horizon, she smelled smoke.

The voices grew louder. Gran grew farther away.

*Flee* . . .

*Spins* . . .

*Dust* . . .

Ary reached the top of the mountain.

Gran was gone.

In her place was the Seedling girl from before. But she was older now, the shadows beneath her eyes darker, her Seedling shovel dented and scratched. Tears streaked her cheeks as she rocked in place, lattice wings flared behind her. Around her neck, she wore an odd charm—a flower, half wilted, carved from old wood.

In her hands, she gripped a journal.

"She'll come back," she whispered. "Wren always comes back."

The voices kept whispering.

Ary inched forward. "Hello?"

The girl didn't budge. She rocked harder, gripping the journal, her eyes squeezed shut. "Wren always comes back. *Wren always comes back.*"

Ary took in the sight of her—the Seedling robes, the shovel, the odd wood necklace, the journal.

"Dracaena?" Ary whispered.

The girl whipped her face up. Her eyes widened, and brilliant joy crashed over her features like the warmest light. *"Wren."* She leaped to her feet and threw her arms around Ary. "Oh, *Wren.* I knew you'd come back. I knew you wouldn't leave me behind."

Ary drew back, her body trembling. "I'm not—"

The girl cupped Ary's cheeks in her hands. "Why did you lie to me, Wren?"

"I'm not Wren," Ary whispered. "Wren is my—"

The girl squeezed Ary's face until it hurt. *"Why did you lie?"*

The voices reciting the Gardener's Warning rose to a shout.

*FLEE! SPINS! DUST!*

"Stop it," Ary said desperately, trying to break free of the girl's grip. "You're hurting me—"

"You *lied*, Wren," the girl said. Her mouth parted as though she was in pain. It was filled with mold. Ary screamed. Slime poured from the girl's mouth; it oozed from her eyes, dripped from her nose, ran from her ears.

*"Wren,"* she moaned. "You lied. *You left."* The mold crept over her hands and onto Ary's skin. It swept over her, suffocating her, rotting her wings, wrapping her in that deathly white cocoon. "Why did you leave us, Wren? *Why?"*

"I'm not her! I'm not Wren," Ary screamed. *"I am not*

187

*Wren Mossheart!* My name is Ary! *Ary! My name is Canary Mossheart!*"

The mold stopped. Suddenly the girl was returned to normal; the voices vanished.

The girl let go. She took a step back and frowned at Ary, perturbed. "Who are you?"

Ary reeled back, gasping.

"You're not her." The girl shook her head, painful disappointment flitting across her face. "You could never be her."

And then she vanished in a whorl of smoke, leaving only the journal and the shovel behind. Ary trembled wildly. Echoes of those voices screaming the Gardener's Warning rang all around her.

The shovel glinted in front of her.

Ary took a step forward—and the mountain *lurched*.

She toppled backward. The ground shifted, uncoiling, rising, tilting, and Ary fell to her hands and knees as she struggled to hold on. Iridescent powder swirled in the air, coating her lashes, her lips, her tongue. It tasted of mold and rot but also something brighter, warmer. Something she'd known only in her dreams.

A massive shadow fell over her.

Ary looked up and found herself meeting the milky eyes of a massive silver snake.

"Little Mosssssssheart. Little *liar*."

Tears dripped down Ary's chin. "Please. I don't know who you are, or what you want—"

"The cossssst," the snake hissed, "issss your *life!*"

The snake lunged down and swallowed Ary whole.

Ary woke with a gasp. Dark lingered all around her; for a moment, she forgot where she was, her memories still filled with Gran, of the girl who had clearly been Dracaena weeping in her Seedling robes, and the snake that had swallowed Ary whole yet again. Slowly her senses returned to her body, and her heart slowed. She felt the hard-packed dirt floor beneath her, the warm current of air flowing over her. They were in Chives' house—if it could be called that. After he'd confessed the price for seeking Atlas, he'd ushered them inside, and disappeared down a tunnel with Sootflank. Reeling and exhausted, Ary had fallen asleep sitting up.

Now her companions dozed all around her. To her left, Sootflank slept silently in a coiled heap of scars and smooth muscle. Even when lost to the realm of dreams, he was a terrifying sight. She knew he was hiding something from her.

And yet it was already a comfort to have him near.

Maybe she was a fool to trust him. But she'd trusted Gran, and it wasn't Gran who now slept a few feet away, preparing to lead her through the dark to find a cure for Mama.

At the other end of the cave, Owl slept next to Shrimp. The pill bug was curled protectively around him, and the fairy boy dozed with his mouth open. Ary's heart sank.

Two more souls pulled into this mess by Gran's lies. Two more who could get hurt.

Ary didn't know if it made her brave or a coward that she was glad to have them with her all the same.

In sleep, Owl looked younger. Ary lingered for a moment, studying him. He slept with one of Dracaena's journals clutched to his chest, face faintly troubled even while dreaming.

*I'd like to think my parents would be proud. And even if you don't believe it, Ary—I think you're our best chance.*

Memories flashed behind her eyes: Owl, pleading for a chance to talk to Gran, insisting their world was doomed and dying for *years*. Owl, getting laughed at in school, having things thrown at him for being the weird doomsday boy.

Ary had stood by and let it happen.

She was no better than Gran.

Their journey had just begun, and she had already done so, so many things wrong.

"Can't sleep?"

Chives lurked behind her. For a hulking beast, he moved with an eerie silence.

Ary wrapped her arms around herself. "Nightmares."

"Ah." His strange nose wiggled. "Humor an old mole

and walk with me, little Mossheart. There's something you ought to see."

Chives turned away, waddling awkwardly out of the burrow he spent his days in. Memories of mold and snakes still swirling in her mind, Ary cast one glance back at Owl, Sootflank, and Shrimp sleeping, and tried to ignore the feeling that something bad was coming for them all—and Ary wouldn't be able to protect them.

# TWENTY-FIVE

## *Sun*

Chives led her out, and up.

They climbed in silence. The ground here was so steep she had to crawl on her hands and knees, but thankfully it was dirt her fingers sank into, not silver scales. Soon Ary was sweating and panting, struggling to climb as her wings splayed awkwardly behind her. She swore they got heavier and more ungainly by the day. If her other classmates were any indicator, she had maybe a week before they unfurled.

Once, they'd been her greatest dream. Now she couldn't even muster a flicker of joy, knowing what lay ahead.

They kept climbing. Chives rarely spoke, pausing only to tell her that beneath this hill was where every Steward had lived since the very beginning of the terrarium's days.

*Terrarium.* The word rattled around in Ary's head. It didn't feel real. Some faint part of her was still hoping it was all a lie, a grand joke. That she'd be able to return home and forget any mention of a world trapped within a world.

Currents stirred around Ary, and the world lightened. They had entered the Gloom that hung over the Underground like an old, damp cloak; even though the world was still dark, she could tell from the scent in the air as it shifted from that of dirt and insect shells to mold and mushrooms. Finally they reached the top of the hill and stopped.

"Welcome," Chives said softly, "to the highest point of the Underground—the only place where our world touches yours."

An endless expanse of darkness sprawled all around them. Ary could see nothing when she looked down the hill, though she knew that far, far below, Sootflank, Owl, and Shrimp slumbered. She'd long thought the soil beneath Terra to be empty, but how wrong she was. There was an entire world living beneath her feet—one the folk had ignored completely. So much of what she'd been told about the Underground had been a great lie. So much had simply been left out.

There, on the horizon, flickering faintly, was a tiny pinprick of light. A single beacon, cutting through an endless swath of darkness.

*Terra.*

Tears sprang to her eyes.

Was Gran back home already? Was she caring for Mama? Was Mama even still . . . ?

*No.* She couldn't let herself think about that. Mama was alive. Ary would have known if something had happened to her. Would have *felt* it.

But she was running out of time.

Chives sat with a great *thwump*. It was plain he was

not made for climbing; he belonged within the hill they'd scaled, deep in the Underground. He patted the ground next to him with a claw, and, exhausted, Ary moved to sit beside him, her eyes never leaving that faint glimmer in the dark. High above, other lights bobbed—glow-moths, riding the currents, their shimmering iridescence a defiant light in a dark, dark world.

"You still hope to return home," Chives said finally. "You don't believe it, then. That this world is not a world at all."

The mole—that was what he had called himself earlier, though the name sounded like nonsense—watched her with a heavy sadness.

Ary picked her at her cuticle.

"I don't know," she said honestly. "It's . . . a lot."

"It's against everything you know," Chives said, not unkindly. "And every belief you were raised to protect."

Ary nodded.

Her entire life, she'd been raised to believe one truth above all: that Terra was all they had. Their village was the only haven in a dark, mold-filled world. Everything they suffered and endured had purpose, because Terra was it. The fairy folk of Terra had only each other, faults and all. There were no other villages, no other chances. Nestled against the cliffs that created magical, lifesaving light, her home was sacred ground, blessed by the Gardener herself.

But what Dracaena said in those journals . . . what Chives was asking her to believe now . . .

If Terra wasn't all there ever had been—if there was something beyond it, something *more*—then it made all the mold, all the death, all the wings sliced from fairies' backs and the folk lost to wars with newts and earwigs completely, utterly, horrifyingly *pointless*. Every terrible sacrifice; every family gone hungry and every child orphaned; every rotten harvest and fairy stricken with mold. Every pain, worry, and hurt the folk of Terra had swallowed would no longer be for some great, noble cause, to protect the only village that ever existed.

It would have been for nothing.

A terrible price, paid across generations, for a mistake.

And *that* terrified her.

Chives closed his eyes. "Long have I carried the stories passed down to me by my father, and his father. The folk were meant to have their own storytellers, guardians of memories from the world we fled. Seedlings, entrusted to cherish flowers of truth that bloomed on the vines of history. Tell me, little folk. What stories have you been told of the world beyond? Of thunderstorms that shake the earth, of birds that glide forever on a summer's breeze, of the warmth of the sun and constellations of stars shining eternal across time?"

Ary said nothing. The old stories describing the Gardener's heavenly kingdom were little more than fragments, washed gray by decades of being passed between the lips of fairies who'd never know anything but an endless gloom.

Yet even then, the few stories she'd heard glittered with promise—of plants she'd never seen or tasted, or creatures whose complexity and beauty were beyond comprehension.

So many of the words he said meant nothing to her—*stars* and *sun* and *thunderstorms*. They sounded like something out of a story. They sounded like lies.

"Tell me this, Ary Mossheart: When you dream of the sky, does it ever burn blue?"

Tears pricked Ary's eyes. Something aching and lost opened in her chest—because she had, and it did. And that was ridiculous, because the sky was never anything but endless shadow. It held no color, no life, no light. But in her dreams—in the dreams where she flew, though fairies weren't meant to fly—her wings carried her on an endless breeze, through rays of golden light, and the sky she soared through was not the deep, bruised gray of Terra's perpetual night, but an endless, soft, impossibly beautiful blue.

But it was a dream. A fantasy. And the old stories were just that—*stories*. Right?

"I'm sorry," Ary said. "I'm trying to understand, truly. To listen. But what you're asking of me—"

"I am not asking you to listen, little Mossheart." Chives turned his gaze to the horizon. "I am asking you to *look*."

There, in the darkness, came a light.

Ary had long grown used to Glowrise, that precious hour when the total darkness of night shifted to the gentle gloom of day, where fairies only needed a few lanterns to light their path. All the light in their world was generated by the cliffs Terra had been built against, made possible by leftover magic, a gift from the Gardener herself.

But now, sitting on the hill, watching as light crept up the base of the cliffs, a chill settled over Ary.

Because it didn't look like the light was shining from the cliffs—but rather *through* them.

And for that to be the case, that had to mean there was something *beyond* them.

The light kept climbing. Slowly, it inched up the cliffs that had long cradled Ary's world, illuminating everything in a gentle, eerie glow. She'd never questioned it in Terra, but here, watching from the hill, she could see where certain patches were brighter. Light shone through some parts of the cliffs, the brighter rays carrying the faintest golden hue. As if the cliffs were not cliffs at all—but something clear, long covered by filth and time.

"That light," Ary whispered. "What is that?"

"Sunlight," Chives said, so reverently the word might have been a prayer.

She'd heard that word before: *sun*. It had crept into so many precious names, it seemed. *Sunroot* had been the name for the cure that chased the plague away. *Sunsongs* were what Seedlings called their most revered prayers. Surely the word was no accident. Surely it had been sacred once.

Ary's voice came out in a whisper. "What is a . . . sun?"

"I don't know," the old mole said, looking faintly troubled.

"All I know is that it shines from the world beyond. One we were meant to return to long ago."

And though she didn't want to—though it was terrible, and terrifying, and made everything that would come next all the more inevitable—Ary knew he was telling the truth.

From the hill, staring into the sunlight that shone from beyond the cliffs enclosing her world, Ary could *see* the way they curved—not endlessly, in a formidable wall of rock, but in a massive circle.

"You have inherited a terrible burden," Chives said gently. "I am sure you feel, right now, that this is all very unfair. That you're not certain what you are fighting for. So look, Canary Mossheart, and look hard. *That* is what you're fighting for. A new life, a new world, not just for your mother's sake, or your friends'—but for every creature that still breathes in this dying, mold-ridden land. If any of us are to survive, that light is our only chance."

Ary's hands began to shake.

Because, finally, she understood.

Once, maybe the fairies of Terra had remembered the world beyond theirs. But the stories had warped with time as memories became myths. Hadn't Ary herself been per-plexed by the cliffs, bothered by the concept of the great walls making light from magic alone? Hadn't she, like so many others, noticed the cracks in the stories about their world, but had never dared to prod at them, lest reality splinter and break?

Well, reality had been broken now. Because here was painful, undeniable proof, shining gold and eternal from the highest parts of the "cliffs" where the mold had not yet crawled.

Her home—her entire world—was one great lie. It was not a world at all, but a *bubble*. A self-contained ecosystem, closing them all in, separating them from whatever lay beyond.

A terrarium.

And now—if there was any hope, for her, for Mama, for *any* of them—Ary had only four days to find a way to leave it behind for good.

# TWENTY-SIX

## This Tired, Old World

For a long while, Chives and Ary did not speak of missions, prophecies, or Atlas. They only sat on the hill and watched the sunlight climb higher, shining through in gold patches wherever the slime, moss, and mold had not formed a layer too thick for light to puncture, illuminating the terrarium in its faint glow. Terra's own shimmer dimmed with Glowrise; the mold-scrapers would have already headed to the fields for battle, precious glow-shroom lamps snuffed out.

It had been Ary's entire world. But now, sitting up here, it looked so . . . fragile.

Leaving Terra was forbidden for a reason. Owl had not been the first to insist something in their world was broken. But everyone who tried to speak of any faults in Terra had been punished, scorned, and painted as mad.

Even from the hill, it might have been easy to convince herself of what she now knew to be untrue—that this was all that could ever and would ever exist. That they were simply a small world, existing in a pocket of life amid a great stretch of nothingness. Even now, seeing the light, seeing the way the terrarium curved, she could have convinced herself. Could have believed it.

Except for the light. Except for the patches of cliffs where it shone brighter, stronger, with a hue of gold unlike anything Ary had ever seen before. And except for the dreams of an endless blue sky.

"Chives," Ary said faintly. "I don't want to die."

Chives kept his beady eyes fixed on the horizon.

"If there is anything I've learned," he said slowly, "it is that prophecies and old promises are never what they seem. It's true that the myths surrounding Atlas call for a life most loved, freely given, but none of us truly know how that toll will be paid, or when. Maybe a life is needed in that moment; maybe fifty years beyond. I'm sorry I don't have more for you, little folk. But no one can blame you for not wanting to walk toward death."

Ary looked at her hands. "It's not just that. Everyone is so set on me finding Atlas. On saving everyone. But if my gran couldn't do it—"

"Your gran was a different girl, with different goals."

"And she was a hero," Ary argued. "Gran grew up *knowing* she was the girl of a prophecy. She had training. Resources. I haven't even earned my wings! I'm not a hero. Or a chosen one. The glow-moth was looking for my *gran*. I can't—I'm not—"

"You are not Wren Mossheart," Chives said gently.

"And whether you believe it or not—there is strength in that."

Ary fell silent. It was hard for her to wrap her head around it; for all her faults and failures, Gran *had* still saved Terra. She had altered the course of history, left her mark on this world so strongly they'd found it only right to erect a statue in her honor.

And Ary? Ary was no one. Ary was the girl who stole mushrooms to feed her family. Ary was afraid. And Ary did not want this.

Why didn't that matter? Where was the mayor, the guards, the adults of Terra who were surely more equipped for a dangerous journey than a twelve-year-old girl who hadn't even finished school?

*Where*, Ary thought furiously, her eyes threatening hot tears, *is my gran?*

"Why put us here?" Ary asked, forcing her attention back to that light, back to Chives. "If—if everything Dracaena is saying, if everything you're saying is true, why lock us away, in a world destined to die?"

"Maybe the Gardener did it to save us. Maybe she did it to punish us. And maybe she had no reason at all." He gave her a sad smile. "I'm afraid even I don't have all the answers."

Ary nodded. She wrapped her arms around herself. The dream lingered at the back of her mind. The voices that had been chanting a melody like Seedlings singing their Gardener's prayer.

*Flee . . .*

*Spins . . .*

*Dust . . .*

"I keep having these . . . nightmares. Before I left Terra, I dreamed of mold—of everything rotting apart. And then at the end there's a massive beast, pure silver and covered in dust. It calls me Wren and tells me I lied. And then it eats me alive." She looked out across the terrarium and shivered. "It feels . . . real."

Chives looked troubled. He was silent for a long beat, the pink tentacles on his nose twitching in time with the air currents that swirled up from the Underground. "It could be the fears of a tired mind. Or it could be more."

"More?"

"The closer you get to the bottom of the terrarium, where fewer souls wander, the thicker the magic keeping this world alive grows." The old Steward closed his eyes. "Someone—or something—could be calling out to you. If the moths came to you . . . I would not be surprised if there was another out there, reaching out."

"Well, I wish they'd find a nicer way to go about it."

"Niceness may not be their goal." He paused. "The wing-less boy—has he said the same?"

"Owl? I don't know. Why?"

Chives' expression was thoughtful. "None of the first Seedlings had wings. Did you know that?"

Ary jerked to look at him. "What? No."

"Talk to your friend," Chives suggested. "The Seedlings were once entrusted with Terra's history for a reason. You may find that the earth's magic that only whispers to you speaks to him in more of a shout."

Ary recalled the odd look on Owl's face, the surety with which he spoke of things sometimes, though he clearly had no real evidence to back it up. "Owl can't have magic without wings."

Chives looked at her, faintly amused. "And who told you that? The same fairies who told you this world was the only one that ever was?"

Ary opened her mouth and closed it again. She liked Chives, though half the things out of his mouth sounded like gibberish. She leaned forward, her heart beating painfully in her chest. "Chives?"

"Yes, little Mossheart."

"What did my gran do that was so awful everyone hates me as soon as they see me?"

Pain flashed in Chives' eyes, as bright and alive as Sootflank's flame. The old mole sighed. "It is . . . a long story, and not all of it is mine to tell. I saw Wren in you, and only Wren. There will be others like me, with long memories and wounded hearts, and they will not be so gentle or quick to forgive."

"But *why*?"

"Because Wren Mossheart came to the Underground,

and we trusted her to face Atlas and set us free. Because we all suffered the plague the same as Terra—but when she found the Sunroot, she left us to die while her own people recovered."

Ary's heart pounded. She'd known Gran had balked in front of Atlas, but no one had ever said anything about the plague affecting *other creatures*. The plague had nearly wiped the fairies from existence. If it could sicken the newts, the earwigs, the beetles, and the worms—the havoc it must have wreaked—the deaths that must have piled up—

The horror of it dawned on her.

The empty tunnels . . . the dust on the walls . . . the *rage* with which every creature now regarded the fairies . . .

"Chives," Ary said slowly, her voice quivering. "Was the Underground always this . . . empty?"

The old mole's face clouded with pain, and it told her all she needed to know.

*Oh, Gran. What have you done?*

Tears pooled in her eyes. Shrimp said he'd lost his pod. She had no idea how old he was, or how long he'd wandered. But what if he hadn't been separated from them? What if they'd gotten sick?

How many creatures down here had lost entire families to the plague and remembered the Mossheart name, and the fairy who had come seeking a cure and stole it instead?

"That's why no one trusts me," Ary said hollowly. "The

205

plague is gone, but now mold threatens us. The creatures that managed to survive think even if I find a cure, even if I face Atlas, I'll keep it to myself."

Chives watched her with sad, tired eyes. "Could you blame us?"

She couldn't. Still, something gnawed at her. There was a ghost of horror here that didn't make sense, a personal anger in both Chives' and Sootflank's eyes when they spoke of Gran that she couldn't place.

"Chives," Ary said slowly. "What else did Gran lie about? What aren't you telling me?"

The old mole looked away. His great back shuddered; his hair stood on end. He spoke slowly, as if the memory pained him. "The rest of the story . . . is not mine to tell. But you will learn the truth soon enough. Even with all we've lost, the folk have left their mark here, and you'll learn how deep that scar runs soon enough."

More nonsense. More riddles.

Ary looked out at Terra glimmering in the distance. If what Chives said was true, she would never see it again—never walk the winding paths to the market, never curl up in the bed she shared with Mama, never stalk the mushroom fields late at night in search of scraps to boil down into a soup to ease the ache in her belly.

*Four days.* She only needed to pretend to be a hero for four days. She could handle that, right?

"This tired, old world was never meant to last," Chives

said, and there was true mourning in his eyes. "We have wrung everything we can from it. The mold grows stronger each day. The last shreds of magic are dwindling. Even the Stewards are coming to an end—I am old, with no children of my own. The last stories of the world beyond ours will die with me. And in four days, when the two hundredth harvest comes, Atlas will vanish. You may not feel ready, Ary Mossheart, and you may not want it. You may not be chosen or foretold—but the moths came to you, and you alone. No one else will seek Atlas. No one else will give us this one last chance. And for that reason, I will entrust you with a secret—the last one I have to give."

Finally Chives turned to her.

"There were once many maps to Atlas—now there is only one. It lives in the Ant Court, deep below our feet, jealously guarded by their queen. It's there you will find the answers you seek—and it's there you will have to answer for your grandmother's crimes against the Underground and the ones who loved her, little Mossheart, if you are to have any hope of finding Atlas at all."

# TWENTY-SEVEN

## *We Follow*

It was late morning by the time Ary and Chives returned, though it made little difference in the perpetual darkness. The image of that golden light peeking through the high point of the cliffs—if that's what they even were—lingered in Ary's mind.

"Sootflank," Ary asked Chives as they descended. "Can we trust him?"

Every time she looked at Sootflank, she saw the scars that warped the fairies of Terra, the burn marks that had taken Papa from a captain to a shell of who he had been before.

And yet she *liked* him. And she was terrified she might be proven a fool for it.

"Sootflank is . . . an odd creature. And he has suffered, more than most. He wears his harshness like a shield, but you have seen his scars," Chives said, his voice soft. "Those are not the only wounds he carries. They're merely the ones we can see. You are not the only one who has lost family. He's been alone for many years now. He is . . . difficult. But

208

he has his honor, if nothing else. If he has sworn to fight with you, you can trust that."

*That.* Not *him.* Not Sootflank himself, simply his cause.

Exhaustion thrummed through Ary.

So many secrets. So many lies. All of it too much for her, who had never wanted anything more than Mama's health and a full belly.

They stepped back into Chives' burrow. The others were already awake; Owl jerked upright, concern washing across his face when he saw the exhaustion lining Ary's. Shrimp let out a soft trill in greeting. Sootflank watched her silently, as impossible to read as ever.

Ary cleared her throat and tried to resist the urge to shrink. "The map to Atlas lies in the Ant Court. That's our next move."

Sootflank sagged. Ary watched him closely.

*He wasn't sure Chives would confide in me.*

She didn't know why that rankled her. Why *would* Sootflank have any faith in her, anyway? Why would anyone? She'd done nothing to prove herself useful so far. All she had was an accidental vote of confidence from a moth and a famous last name. It wasn't much to go on. And yet it stung.

"The ants live several layers down," Sootflank said. "Beneath the beetles, the earwigs, and the worms, above the caverns where the centipedes once crawled. We will need to travel quickly. It would take me only a half day alone to get there through the riverways, but with you both riding the pill bug, it might take us a day and a half, if we're lucky."

*A day and a half.* That would only leave them two days to actually *get* to Atlas. Ary's heart fluttered.

"Chives—you're certain our next step is with the ants?"

He didn't say what they all knew—that if this was a dead end, they were all doomed.

"There were many maps to Atlas once." There was something there, in his gaze, in the way he looked at Sootflank, that spoke of a painful secret. "Now there is only one."

Ary recalled the weary sadness in Chives' eyes when he'd asked what Gran had done.

*It is not my story to tell.*

She had the uncomfortable feeling she was about to find out.

"Well," Sootflank said flatly. "I could have happily lived the rest of my lifetime without seeing ants again. But to the Ant Court we go, I suppose."

What if Chives was wrong? What if the ants had nothing? Or what if he was right, but they refused to help her?

Ary had told him only half the truth. It was true that dying scared her. What scared her more, though, was the realization that she could be leading them all to their doom.

"Wait," Ary blurted. "Before we go."

Everyone turned to her. Ary took a long, uncertain breath.

"I'm not my gran," Ary said softly. "I didn't train for any of this. I'm terrified. I need you all to know that—that I'm terrified. That I don't know what to do, or how any of this will work out. None of you signed up for this. If any of you want to go home, I understand. I won't hold it against you."

Sootflank was the first to speak. "And what am I going to do—go home, curl up, and die?"

"I was just—"

"Enough with the theatrics. We are losing time." He swept past her, tail brushing the burrow floor, and vanished into the Underground beyond. Ary watched him go, a funny warmth prickling her. Was it her imagination, or had there been a light of challenge in Sootflank's eyes, as if his fierceness were something he hoped Ary might catch? It was the kind of look Gran might have given her. Wren Mossheart was not one for warm, coddling words—but she could make her loyalty known with a single pointed stare. If Gran had faith in you, it was a faith that was earned.

Sometimes Sootflank reminded Ary so much of Gran it stung. It seemed she'd traded one impossible-to-please old hero for another.

*Did you?* a tiny part of her whispered. *Or did the hero you thought you could count on abandon you?*

Ary shook the thought away and turned to find Owl staring at her.

He shifted his weight from foot to foot, holding tightly

to the journals as always. "I don't have anywhere else to go. So. Yeah. Ominous world-saving adventure it is. Plus . . . it wouldn't be terrible to have time to finish the journals."

Ary smiled at him, weary and grateful. After an awkward pause, Owl shyly smiled back. There was a kind of tentative understanding between them now. Gran had lied to the entire world; she'd failed them both. Now they were united in picking up the pieces.

Ary was glad to have his company, even if she didn't deserve it.

That left only Shrimp.

Ary turned to the pill bug. "This is already so much more than you bargained for. I won't ask you to travel to the end of the world with me if it's the last days this world has left. You can turn back, and no one would think less of you because of it."

Shrimp was quiet for a long moment. She could see in his eyes that he was considering her words with careful thought. The pill bug made a series of humming noises, then curled his antennae forward.

His voice emerged in a soft, shy whisper as it always did—but this time, there was a hardness to it that Ary had never heard before. A strength rippling through his barely audible words. "World's dying." Deep sadness flickered in his eyes. "Shrimp's been alone for . . . many, many years. No family. No home. No hope."

The pill bug settled an antenna on Ary's shoulder.

"New family. New hope." He dipped his head. "We follow."

Ary swayed, her eyes burning with tears. His words rang in her ears. *We follow.* She recalled how the fairies of Terra had mocked the pill bugs for their common refrain, how even when she'd met Shrimp, she hadn't understood it. So many saw it as a mark of cowardice, of weakness.

Ary knew better now.

To follow was to trust, and to follow was to hope.

She didn't deserve it—this unwavering faith. This willingness to stick by her. And though they veiled it in sarcasm, hadn't Owl and Sootflank expressed the same?

A new, terrible weight seemed to settle on her. Gran had long said that leadership was like a suit of armor: glimmering and beautiful to everyone around you, something to envy and covet—but unbearably heavy to the wearer, so overwhelming in its weight, it threatened to crush you more with every breath.

Ary was starting to understand.

"Thank you, friend," Ary whispered. Shrimp dipped his head, and Ary knew he would follow her to the end of this world and the next. She was no hero, but she would try to be worthy of that if she could.

Ary swiped at her eyes and forced herself to straighten. "Sootflank is right—we haven't any time to lose. To the ants we go."

# TWENTY-EIGHT

## *The General*

They left Chives and took off toward the ant kingdom with a new vigor. The Underground pressed around Ary. She and Owl rode on Shrimp's back again, clinging to the pill bug's shell as he and Sootflank wound their way down, down, down. The air grew colder and damper, and the scent changed too—less like earth, and more like dust and old, dying things. Yet even here, the mold flourished.

Ary shivered. Everywhere they looked, it was clear this land was holding on by the barest thread.

There was a tenseness in Sootflank that unnerved Ary; he was grouchier than usual, snapping at them every time they made the slightest noise, urging them to move even faster, though Shrimp was plainly exhausted.

The land grew sicker as they descended. The mold here bloomed in columns and had taken on a horrid, sickly yellow color. The water, too, though it ran cold and swift, had accumulated too much rot to stay clean. Half the time Sootflank emerged from the water he was covered in a thick, rank slime that soured the air so terribly they gagged. Though he would never complain, Ary could tell by the way the newt shuddered that it sickened him, too.

They saw very few other creatures—only a few small, sleek beetles that scuttled away as soon as they spotted them. Sootflank snarled under his breath every time it happened, muttering something about spies, but seemed too tired to give chase.

Chives' voice returned, haunting Ary as they descended through tunnels that felt more like a graveyard. She'd thought Terra was in rough shape—but the Underground had begun to die out long before potatoes burst with slime and fairies sliced off their wings to grow what little produce they could. There were so many echoes of past lives here—burrows left empty, tunnels lined with dust. Strangely enough, some of the once-traveled paths were smaller, almost fairy-sized, and twice she could have sworn they passed flights of stairs carved into the dirt. It was a pretty, silly dream—that maybe before the mold had ruined everything, fairies had been welcome here, that the Underground had been their world, too. But whether it was her imagination or a relic of a long-lost past, it didn't matter. Whatever—or *whoever*—had once lived here was long gone.

No one spoke. Owl rode in front, hunched over Dracaena's journals. Chives had given him a tiny glow-shroom lamp before they'd left, and whispered something to Owl that made the color drain from his face. Ary recalled the old mole's amusement when Ary insisted only fairies with wings had any kind of magic.

But whatever Chives had shared with Owl, the fairy boy seemed keen to keep to himself.

After a few hours, Shrimp grew tired, and Owl and Ary slid from his back to give him a break. Owl regretfully put out the glow-shroom lamp to save its dwindling light. Walking in total darkness on a steep decline forced Ary and Owl to trek single file, arms splayed for balance, while Sootflank grumbled about their lack of speed. Several times Ary's wings snagged on the uneven cave walls. The itching had only grown worse, morphing from a nuisance to a near-constant burning, creeping, and crawling, as if millions of tiny creatures were skittering over her back. She wanted to scream. If they didn't unfurl soon, she was going to rip them open herself.

From behind them, deep within the tunnels, came a hiss.

Ary's toes snagged on a rock. She stumbled, and Owl crashed into her wings with a yelp. They both toppled to the tunnel floor, and Ary braced herself for the impact of sharp rocks—but instead they fell into a pit of something furry and soft. She relaxed—and the stench of rot filled her world.

They'd fallen directly into a giant clump of mold.

Ary let out a horrified cry and scrambled upright. Owl flicked on the glow-shroom lamp. He was clean, because he'd fallen on top of her—but giant patches of mold now covered her own skin and clothes. Worse, some of it *was on her wings*.

Ary's voice climbed, breaking in hysterics. "Get it off me. *Get it off me!*" She scrubbed frantically, trying not to think about what had been big enough to rot here that so much mold had accumulated. Panic bubbled up in her; Owl came to help, gagging as he picked bits of mold from her wings. Shrimp whirred anxiously in the background.

Sootflank spun around. "You two are going to get us caught."

"We can't *see* anything," Owl snapped, but he clicked the glow-shroom lamp off all the same.

And then Ary heard it—a shuffling noise in the dark, a snapping of pincers, a rustle of shells. Hisses swirled all around them, and icy fear plunged through Ary as a new voice greeted them.

"And what is this?" said a flat, monotone voice void of all emotion. "Trespassers, with fairies among them?"

Terror turned every part of Ary cold.

*Earwigs.*

Suddenly Ary was glad she couldn't see anything. There was little possibility of fighting off an earwig horde; one simply had to hope they couldn't smell you and would pass you by.

Now they were all around her.

"Move along, pincers," Sootflank said in his patented

combination of bored and annoyed. "These are property of the newts."

"And yet you bring them through our land," a different, emotionless voice said somewhere behind them. "If the fairies are not our business, then why do you trespass on earwig grounds, newt?"

"They are my prisoners." A note of danger crept into Sootflank's voice.

"We received no word of a prisoner transport."

"Perhaps you forget our agreement. The newts may travel wherever they please."

"Newts, yes. But not little folk."

"Perhaps we won't let you pass," a different voice said. "We are so very hungry these days."

Something touched Ary's arm. She flinched, pressing closer to Owl. Behind them, Shrimp trembled. Something told Ary the earwigs weren't any kinder to pill bugs than they were to the folk who lived safely behind Terra's thorny walls.

"Enough," Sootflank snapped. Ary couldn't see him, but she felt his massive form lumber closer to them, shoving some of the earwigs out of the way. "We have business below. Let us pass, or your prince will hear of it."

"Just give us one of them. Just a taste."

"I said *move*."

"We do not follow your orders," one earwig said in that

flat, cold tone, void of all emotion or warmth. "Quickspark gave her blessing to target any and all folk."

Sootflank fell silent.

Who was Quickspark? Why had that name quieted him in a way Ary didn't know was possible?

The earwigs pressed closer still, murmuring to themselves about little folk, about hunger and a prince who lurked in the dark. Sootflank hissed for them to stay back, but they were beyond listening. Their voices held no feeling, no emotion, just cold, cruel hunger. Ary trembled. Sootflank would protect them. Sootflank would keep them safe.

Bodies rustled all around her. She remembered fairies returning home with pieces missing, or worse, the ones who had returned home *in* pieces, carried in moth-silk bags so their families could bury what remained in the mushroom fields, and set them to rest.

"This one is so young," a voice dangerously close to Ary rasped. "Its fear smells so very sweet."

Something snagged Ary's wing and *tugged*.

"Sootflank!" Ary screamed.

"*Enough*," Sootflank boomed.

And then, from the dark, came fire.

One moment they were wrapped in shadows; the next, Sootflank's tail was alight, sparks flying all around them. Flames illuminated Sootflank's entire body, snapping over his sleek, poisonous form in cruel ribbons of blue and orange, lighting up the scars and cords of muscle that marked him out as someone who had suffered, and caused suffering in turn. Sparks flew in the air, dancing like fireflies, and the earwigs cried out in terror, scrambling away from the threat of his fire.

Sootflank stalked forward, his tail snapping, so effortlessly conjuring the flames that fairies had long feared, and so few newts were able to master.

"*You will let us pass*," Sootflank snarled.

And though Ary knew that Sootflank was on her side, and she was his best shot at rescuing a world that had only four days left, the sight of him struck a cold chord of fear in her. With this magic, it was no wonder the newts had long terrified the fairy folk of Terra. It was no wonder they'd been nearly wiped from existence, and Papa had been plagued with nightmares of them for the rest of his life.

The newts were pure, unrivaled destruction.

The earwigs fell back together, curling their long bodies up, their pincers quivering. They might have been allies of the newts, but it was clear they knew the dangers of their fire, too. "We apologize, General. Please—put out the flames. *Please*."

Ary flinched. *General?*

"*Move*," Sootflank hissed, his tail still sparking. The earwigs scrambled away, keening in fear, and though Ary loathed them, a part of her felt bad.

Beside her, Owl and Shrimp looked on in horror, the

flames making long, warped shadows dance across their faces. The fire dimmed, and then there was silence, broken only by the frenzied scuttle of the earwigs fleeing from Sootflank's flames. In the dark, his tail still glowed, fading from bright white to soft orange as it cooled. It was beautiful. And it would have seared Ary's skin in an instant had she touched it.

"Let's go," Sootflank said roughly. "We want to be halfway there by the day's end."

He set off without them again, his still-burning tail bobbing down the tunnel like a lantern.

Ary watched him go, gooseflesh rising on her arms.

Papa had given everything to the war against the newts. So many of the folk of Terra had. Ary had long wondered what she would do if she'd met one of the monsters that had stolen Papa's will to live and left him a shell of himself.

Now, as Sootflank lumbered away, all she saw was Papa's haunted face.

All she heard was one word, ringing through her head on a terrible, cruel loop.

*General.*

# TWENTY-NINE

## *Who We Leave Behind*

*General.*

For hours, the word marched a drumbeat through Ary's head. Dread made her steps heavy as they followed Soot-flank across tepid, algae-choked streams and through giant swaths of mold. But something else sparked low in her belly, lighting up her nerves, making her quiver from her toes to the tips of her still-unfurled wings.

Anger.

Why hadn't he told them, knowing the history of the folk and the newts? Why would he *hide* it? Ary had been nothing but honest with Sootflank. He knew more about her history than she did. Yet she knew *nothing* about him. And now she was meant to follow him to the end of their world?

"Ary?" Owl whispered at some point. "Are you okay?"

"I'm fine," Ary said flatly.

"You don't look fine," Owl muttered, but he dropped it.

Owl had barely spoken to her since the earwigs; now he read as he walked, nose buried in Dracaena's journal. Every now and then, he'd squeak in surprise, or puff out a frustrated breath, but when Ary questioned him he waved her away.

Owl reminded her of Mama in that way: so absorbed in the journal, he'd been pulled into another world entirely. But he was doing them both a favor by being the one to parse through the journals, and Ary knew it. Though she ached to understand what Gran had lied about, it was too painful to read about the history of Wren Mossheart through the eyes of someone who'd also been hurt by her.

But now, instead of reading peacefully, Owl kept *glancing* at her. Every few minutes he'd look at her all funny, like she had food on her face.

"What?" Ary snapped finally, and then winced. "Sorry— why do you keep staring at me?"

Owl chewed on his lips, his eyes darting back and forth. "I have . . . kind of a weird question for you."

"Okay . . . ?"

"It's, uh." Owl hopped from foot to foot. "Well, it's kind of a lot. Don't freak out."

Ary frowned. They had just learned Sootflank was a newt general; earlier, Ary had been shown strange, golden light by a giant furry animal named Chives, confirming the existence of a world beyond theirs, one Ary needed to find a way to in four days before they were all doomed. Ary doubted there was very little he could say that would make her freak out, considering how the past day had gone. "What'd you find?"

Owl lit up, nearly bouncing with excitement, and flipped open one of the journals. "So Chives mentioned *people*. But we've only heard about Dracaena being left behind."

"So?" Ary asked wearily. "Is now really the best time for this?"

"I think there were others down here. Other fairies."

Ary jerked to look at him. *"What?"*

"Yeah. She mentions them sometimes—but only in passing. But it makes sense, doesn't it? Otherwise, how could she have survived on her own?" He frowned. "Plus . . . did you see those stairs earlier? And some of the tunnels don't look built for bugs. I think there were folk here, Ary. A lot of them."

Ary recalled the funny way Chives had looked at her when he spoke of those who had suffered from Gran's betrayal. She'd assumed he meant other creatures, but had there been folk living in the Underground? Truly living here, existing outside Terra?

Owl licked his lips. "I think Dracaena isn't telling the whole story in the journals. I thought it was just information she was holding back before, but I don't think it's on purpose. I think her priorities were muddled." Owl had a thoughtful, almost sad look on his face. "Ary . . . your gran. She ended up choosing a partner eventually, right?"

"Yes . . . why?"

"Did she ever mention loving someone else?"

Ary stopped walking. "Excuse me?"

Owl scratched awkwardly at the back of his neck. "I think Dracaena's hurt feelings got in the way of her telling the whole story, which is why she mentions important things in passing instead of focusing on them. All she talks about is your gran, even when it doesn't make sense. Everything comes back to her. And the way your gran reacted to news about her—it seemed extremely personal."

Ary recalled the obsessive drawings in Gran's notebooks, the dream that had felt so real, she could have sworn she'd slipped back through time. The way Dracaena had blushed so often when she looked at young Wren Mossheart, their fingers permanently intertwined. "What are you saying, Owl?"

"Two things." Owl took a deep breath. "One, I think everything that happened was bigger than simply your gran lying or being too selfish to save everyone or . . . whatever. In those pages, Dracaena is *mourning*. And she blames herself. She beats herself up for still caring about your gran. I think there was something even bigger they *both* found down here. Dracaena stayed behind, expecting your gran to come back and . . . I don't know. Change her mind? Complete the mission? But she didn't. And it ruined Dracaena's life."

"Okay . . ." Ary said slowly, watching Owl with a sense of unease rising in her. "But what does that have to do with feelings?"

"Because I think your gran hurt Dracaena way worse than we thought." Owl's throat bobbed nervously. "Ary, I think Dracaena expected Wren Mossheart to come back for her because they were in love."

# THIRTY

## *Monsters Alike*

*They were in love.*

"*In love?*" Ary demanded.

"The way Dracaena talks about her—the way your gran *reacted*—the way they both kept their secrets forever . . ." Owl chewed on his lip. "Your gran never said anything about her? Not a word?"

"No," Ary said sharply, her head spinning. The dark swam around her, cluttered with memories of Gran saying Ary's grandpa was her best friend. They had always seemed more like companions than people in love when Gran told stories of him, but Ary had thought that was just how old people were.

More images, more memories. Gran, always looking mournful and lost at weddings, sometimes watching the way Mama and Papa giggled in the corner with an ache in her eyes. Always seeming like she was missing something essential, plagued by a constant air of regret. Ary had long chalked it up to her being a tired, old woman wounded by the world. A hero who had fulfilled her purpose as a child and then was promptly forgotten, left to spend the rest of her days with scars she didn't know how to heal.

Gran had also always been so *haunted* by the Underground. Ary had thought it was because of what had happened there.

What if it was because of what she'd left behind?

Another memory flickered behind her eyes: of Ary, only ten, with her first crush, on a rosy-cheeked fairy girl named Daisy. Of Mama teasing her that she'd always had a weakness for pretty things; of Gran, *smiling*, for once, as though Ary were a mirror she saw herself in . . .

"Ary?" Owl asked quietly, still watching her with worry on his face. "If Dracaena's story is muddled by heartbreak . . ."

"Then her journals aren't telling the whole truth," Ary said thickly.

The look on Owl's face confirmed it. Ary's legs threatened to buckle.

How did this only get messier? How did it keep getting *worse*?

Owl looked grave. "We need answers from someone else. If Dracaena's journals are warped because of your gran, she can't be objective. She's going to be leaving things out, unintentionally exaggerating others. And with only four days left—"

"I can't talk about this right now," Ary blurted, and she spun away from him before Owl could say more. Her wings itched like mad; she reached back absentmindedly, scratching furiously at the hard, papery cocoon, walking away as quickly as she could.

*Could Gran have really . . . ?*

*No.*

Gran had her faults. Even stealing the Sunroot cure was bad enough, but Ary could see it, knowing how cold Gran was, how clinical. But leaving behind someone she loved? Someone who *loved her back*?

It was too much. Too unforgivable. It seemed like ever since Ary had stepped into the Underground, everything she'd learned about Gran made her worse.

But Gran had also protected Ary. Gran had done her best to shield her and Mama from the ways Terra sought to use them. She'd always done what she could for the people she loved in her own distant, cold way.

Or so Ary had thought.

What kind of person left the love of their life behind to die in a mold-filled, ever-dark Underground?

*Probably the same kind of person that lets their only granddaughter go on a doomed mission in that same mold-filled, ever-dark Underground.*

Ary kept walking, her eyes scanning the tunnel around her, looking for any distraction. Ahead of her, Sootflank lumbered alone.

Gran hadn't been the only one keeping secrets.

*General.*

Fury bubbled in her chest. Ary had never been an angry child. It had always felt too dangerous and unwieldy. Even when she left school to work as a mold-scraper, even when her friends mocked her about her wings. Even when Papa died. She had never been angry—only sad. And her entire life, she'd told herself that was a good thing. Safer. Anger was dangerous. Anger was explosive and hot and could cut like a knife.

She'd seen how anger had burned Gran out, leaving only the cold ashes of resentment in its place. Ary had promised herself she would never give in to anger. She didn't want to end up like Gran. But right now it felt a lot easier to fixate on anger than the ache that had long haunted Gran's eyes or the journals Owl carried in his arms.

They'd just rounded a corner when Sootflank finally stopped short and spun around to face her. "I can *feel* you glaring at me. What do you want?"

Ary didn't have it in her to be polite. "Why didn't you tell me that you're not just some newt—that you're a *general*?"

"Was," Sootflank corrected quietly, "a general."

"Oh, like there's a difference—"

"There is"—Sootflank's eyes were cold—"a difference."

His eyes sparked with an anger Ary didn't—couldn't—understand.

"Newt generals serve until they die," Sootflank continued bitterly. "They never leave their position. Ever."

Something in Ary whispered for her to pull back. To let

it drop. The anger and grief in Sootflank's eyes were unlike anything she'd ever seen.

Instead she said, "So?"

"*So,*" Sootflank spat. "I am no longer a general because I am a traitor. I betrayed my people to help Wren Mossheart seek Atlas. I betrayed my family. And then I betrayed them again, tenfold, by protecting the ones she left behind. I was stripped of my title, my rank, and my home. Left to spend the rest of my days in exile." He made a disgusted noise. "I tried to do the right thing, the brave thing, by helping Wren and then Dracaena. And I was repaid by losing everything. I have lived my life alone, scorned by a mate who has long passed, hated by a daughter who still lives, and what has it gotten me? A chance to betray them all a third time, as the apocalypse edges near, to ferry two ungrateful, snot-nosed fairy pups toward a myth I'm not certain they're ready to face."

Ary pulled back, reeling from the grief and rage that crackled in Sootflank's voice. She hadn't questioned it before—why he hadn't been in newt territory when they'd found him, but instead had been resting in the odd, secluded cave. Something told Ary it had been a precious place, once. Gran had known a creature like Sootflank would seek refuge there.

And that meant Gran had known, on some level, that he had suffered after she left the Underground behind.

He'd had a family. A partner, a *daughter*, and he'd lost

them all when he'd agreed to help Wren. It was no wonder he'd been so furious when he'd first met Ary—when he'd realized Wren Mossheart's life had continued on while his had remained frozen in place.

Sootflank's voice floated around her.

"Do I shock you?" he asked quietly, his voice dripping with scorn. "Are you suddenly reminded of what your grandmother did? What she is? What *you're* forced to ally with to clean up her mistakes? You may think me a monster all you want, little folk. But given the name you carry, you're in no place to cast judgment on those who were forced to choose cruelty to survive."

Ary would not cry in front of him. She refused. "I'm sorry," she stammered. "I was just surprised, and the newts are a sore subject because Papa—"

"I'm sorry," Sootflank drawled. "Did I give the impression I care?"

Ary went cold.

It was like every bit of camaraderie that had tentatively blossomed between them withered in a blink. Now a chasm roared before them, cold and unyielding. Sootflank stepped forward. Instinctively, Ary took a step back.

The same fear she'd felt toward him in the cave returned, drip by terrible drip.

The fury in Sootflank's eyes could have set all of Terra aflame.

"You seem confused, little fairy, so let me make something

painfully, abundantly clear," Sootflank said, his voice low and deadly. "I am not helping the spoiled, sniveling spawn of Wren Mossheart seek Atlas out of any act of charity. I do not care about you, your wretched city, your grandmother, or your precious papa. I am not your friend. I am hardly your ally. What I am is *desperate*. I've spent far too long suffering on the behalf of this ungrateful world; I am only interested in helping myself now. I had given up all hope of finding a way to utilize Atlas. Then you and your wretched traitor of a grandmother stumbled into my cave, and suddenly a path opened up. And despite my old age, I am not quite yet ready to die. Once we have the exit, I will be the first to leave."

"I suppose I shouldn't be surprised," Ary said, struggling to quell the tremor in her. "You're a newt general, after all. I shouldn't expect you to be anything but a monster."

"And you are the granddaughter of Wren Mossheart," Sootflank said softly. "I suppose that makes us equal."

It was plain from the way he towered over her that Soot-flank expected her to back away. But instead Ary remained, anger and shame and grief pounding through her, meeting the endless dark of the old newt's eyes. Gran had not been willing to face the hurt she'd caused Sootflank or anyone else in the Underground. Ary could not rewind time; she could not bring back his mate or his daughter. But she could face his anger and pain. And weren't they alike? Both betrayed by Wren Mossheart in the end?

Sootflank glared, and Ary held his gaze all the while. The silence was so thick it was suffocating.

And then, from the ceiling, something *clicked*.

Ary blinked. She turned to look at Shrimp, but the pill bug looked just as puzzled as her. She wheeled around, and Sootflank's eyes had narrowed. "What—"

Owl clicked on the glow-shroom lamp and squeaked in terror. "Oh boy."

Covering the walls, clinging to the ceilings, slipping from around corners, were hundreds upon hundreds of ants.

# THIRTY-ONE

## *We Had a Deal*

The ants came from every direction imaginable. They scuttled from the ceilings, swarmed up from the floor. Unlike the earwigs, whose rustling and messy ranks betrayed them long before they arrived, the ants moved with terrifying silence. One moment they hadn't been there; now they surrounded them, their shiny carapaces winking in the soft glow of the glow-shroom lamp, lining up in rank after silent rank like perfectly trained soldiers until they were eerily still.

For a moment, no one moved. Even Sootflank seemed a bit alarmed—which, given the recent revelation that he was a literal fire-wielding newt general, was *not* comforting.

A single ant broke away from the pack.

It was the same size as the others, indistinguishable from the rest. The ant drew closer, beady eyes revealing nothing. It stopped and let out a long series of strange clicks and hisses.

"Oh, good," Sootflank said dryly. "I have no idea what it's saying."

They all looked at Shrimp, who wordlessly shook his head. Whatever the clicks and hisses of the ants meant, they didn't translate to the soft trills of pill bugs, either. The ants edged closer.

"Well," Ary said. "Now what?"

"Don't ask me. You're Terra's chosen hero."

Ary bristled. "For the last time, I'm *not* a hero."

"Obviously," said Sootflank.

"Um, guys," Owl said. "I don't think they like us."

The lead ant let out another long string of clicks, and the ranks of soldier ants rippled.

"Maybe we can just . . . keep walking?" Owl suggested hopefully. He took a step forward—and the ants immediately started hissing. One snapped its pincers furiously, and Owl yelped and jumped back. "Can't keep walking! Can't keep walking!"

All the ants began to gnash their pincers. They inched closer, the light winking off their hard shells, and fear scuttled through Ary. She had been raised to loathe the newts, to fear the earwigs. But ants? They rarely broke the surface of the Underground, and the folk had seldom dealt with them, if they ever had at all. She knew nothing of them, of their land, of who they fought for or what they wanted.

The ants pressed closer. One darted forward, snapping its pincers in the air, and Ary scrambled backward. Her wings collided with something sturdy and cool; Ary looked up and realized she'd backed right into Sootflank's chest.

The old newt was holding very, very still.

"Little Mossheart," Sootflank said, an unusually serious

note in his voice. "If you have anything planned—now is a good time."

Ary's throat bobbed. Ever since this had started, she'd been nothing but a burden. She had no magic; she couldn't even fight.

*And?* a voice like Gran's demanded. *You're a Mossheart, aren't you?*

She recalled how on the day of Papa's burial, the light had been particularly poor. Huddled together in the cold, the three of them had watched as Papa was lowered into the field. Mama, for once, had been listless and silent. That had terrified Ary more than anything—to see the hope dead in Mama's eyes. Gran had silently towed them back to the cottage, and then gripped Mama by her shoulders.

"Listen to me, Robin," she'd said firmly. "We'll be okay."

"How?" Mama had whispered, tears spilling down her cheeks.

"We're Mosshearts," Gran said bluntly, as if that explained everything. "We figure it out and survive. We always do."

Ary had thought Gran callous in that moment. That had been her refrain for everything—they were Mosshearts, and so they'd endure. So they'd go on, and be brave, and face whatever horror came next.

But maybe there was a strength in that—in being brave, even when you had no reason to.

Ary took a deep breath. She'd led them all down here— and it was up to her to get them out safely. Maybe she didn't know how to fight, but she had sat through lessons in school as they taught about the famed journey of Terra's heroes. She might not have had Gran's training, but she had her knowledge. She had her blood, and her name.

She was a Mossheart. That had to mean something—right?

Ary forced herself to take a step forward and spread her hands in greeting.

"We come as allies. My name is Ary Mossheart. Granddaughter of Wren Mossheart. I am the"—her voice faltered—"*fourth* hero of Terra."

Behind her, Sootflank choked on a laugh.

Ary fought the urge to scowl and steadied herself, focusing her attention back on the ants. "We come seeking Atlas, sent by the Steward, and we bring the blessing of the glowmoths. Please—we mean you no harm. We just need to speak to the queen."

The lead ant tilted its head backward. A slow ripple moved through the amassed crowd. One by one, the ants started to shiver. Ary's own words rang in her ears.

*My name is Ary Mossheart.*

*The fourth hero of Terra.*

She'd spent her life wondering if she'd ever get to claim that title. All of Terra had wondered the same.

And now that she'd spoken the words, they felt like a lie.

As the ants rumbled and relaxed their antennae, the words opened an uncomfortable pit in her stomach. Her skin felt too tight and hot. She was trying so hard to do this right—to be a leader, to take up the mantle of chosen one, but the title of *hero* felt so wrong. Even the glow-moths hadn't come seeking *her*. They'd come to find Gran. Some foolish part of her had thought this would get easier, that something in her would wake up and realize she was a hero after all, that she was meant for this, that her name belonged to legends of greatness as much as Gran's had.

Instead, she wanted to take the words back. She wanted to say: *I'm not a hero. There aren't any heroes anymore. I'm just a kid trying to fix the mess the adults left behind. I never wanted any part of this, and I still don't. But I'm all Mama's got, so here I am.*

What was wrong with her?

The lead ant gave a long, screeching trill—and every single ant went still.

One moment they had been shivering and clicking, and now they were silent again, so perfectly immobile they might have all been carved from stone. Unblinking and rigid, an endless sea of perfectly silent soldiers. Ary's heart pounded in her chest.

Had it . . . worked?

Behind her, Sootflank straightened.

"Ary," Owl whispered. "That was extremely cool."

Giddy relief flooded through her. Maybe that was the trick to this—maybe she didn't actually have to be a hero. She just had to convince everyone else she was one. "The fourth hero of Terra" *did* have a nice ring to it, even if it was a complete and utter lie.

"Okay," Ary said shakily. "Good. Now that we're all on the same page, if you could take us to your qu—"

The lead ant lunged.

It was so fast even Sootflank didn't have time to react. One moment the ant had been there; the next it was on them, pincers snapping. A faint pinprick of pain flared on Ary's arm. When she looked down, a long, slender cut welled with blood on her wrist. Ary flung out her hand—but instead it flopped to her side, tingling and useless.

*What?*

Her leg buckled, then her other one, and then Ary collapsed.

Behind her, Owl crumpled in a heap. Poor Shrimp slumped to the ground, half curled into a ball, his wide eyes bright with terror as he, too, found himself unable to move. The ant drew back, waiting expectantly, as the three of them collapsed, paralyzed. Ary couldn't move, but her mind whirred in a panic. She'd never even heard of ants interacting with fairies. How had they known how to attack them so perfectly?

Only Sootflank remained. His back leg sagged; Sootflank snarled, leaning his weight on his front. He stepped backwards. The tip of his tail twitched like mad; the scent of something burning stirred in the air.

He was trying to summon magic.

Ary's heart pounded. If he summoned flames, this was all over. The ants had paralyzed them—but what if they weren't totally their enemies? What if they'd done it as a precaution?

Sparks flashed in the air.

"Sootflank," Ary yelped. "Don't!"

The tip of his tail began to glow. The newt took another step back, and then another. The blood roared in Ary's ears.

*Surely he wouldn't—*

The lead ant darted forward and cut Sootflank again. The newt gasped and lurched backward. His entire body trembled. His eyes drooped closed.

Yet still he remained standing.

Veins bulged on Sootflank's legs. The ants crept closer. Sootflank snarled.

And this time the fire caught.

It flared in the air, small but brilliant, swirling around him in crackling ribbons of orange. Immediately, the ants cringed away. A dim victory sparked in Sootflank's eyes. The massive insects hung back, as fearful of the flames as any fairy would be. But his fire wouldn't last forever—it was so much weaker than the last flame he'd summoned, and it was clear from Sootflank's labored breath that he didn't have long before he gave in to the venom. His eyes darted around, something like anguish on his face—and then they went cold, all emotion wiped away.

Gooseflesh rose on Ary's arms as Sootflank took a step backward.

*No.*

He wouldn't. Not after everything they'd been through. Not with the very end of the world at stake.

"Ary," Owl whispered.

The newt took another step back.

Betrayal throbbed in Ary like an open wound. It shouldn't have mattered. He hated the folk, and her gran especially. He'd never been kind to her, and she'd found him intolerable.

And yet something in Ary tore as the newt took one step back, then another, his eyes stone-cold, his flames flickering weakly but never going out.

"Sootflank!" Ary cried. "We had a *deal*!"

Without the newt, they were doomed. They would have no protection, no guide, no way of finding Atlas without being totally at the whim of the Underground. He knew that. Even if they survived the ants—even if by some miracle the queen agreed to help them, their mission was as good as dead.

For the first time, Sootflank looked at her. Something strange flashed in his eyes; Ary thought it looked like regret. She had seen that look in Gran's eyes before. It seemed she'd been right to find them similar. Sootflank, just like Gran, was going to choose himself in the end.

He was going to leave her behind.

"Sootflank," Ary begged. "*Please.* If you leave us, we won't find Atlas. Everyone will die!"

Sootflank's head dipped.

"I know," he said.

And then he kept going.

Step by terrible step, Sootflank put more distance between them. He never once looked back at her after that; his eyes were only on the ants, fury-bright as his body fought off the venom racing through his blood. His legs trembled like mad. Several times he stumbled, but he never fell.

Ary could only watch as the old newt general disappeared around the bend and left them behind.

# THIRTY-TWO

## Down, Down, Down

The ants wasted no time. As soon as Sootflank vanished, they lurched forward and hoisted Ary, Owl, and Shrimp into the air. Frozen as they were, there was nothing the three of them could do but close their eyes as the ants lifted them high and carried them away.

Betrayal pulsed in her like a fresh burn as the ants whisked them away.

Sootflank had left them so easily.

The old newt's voice rang through her mind.

*I am only interested in helping myself now.*

How could she have been so foolish? The newt had flat-out told her he cared only for himself. The Atlas mission was important, yes, but not if it would cost him his life. He had allied with Ary *only* under the agreement that they were trying to leave the terrarium. But Ary herself meant nothing to him. And if she failed, and the world was going to end regardless, then Sootflank would rather spend his final days in peace, in his cave, than meeting whatever gruesome end the ants had in mind.

243

Her eyes smarted. Gran had tried to warn her, hadn't she? And Ary had trusted him anyway.

The Underground raced by around them, and the pressure built in Ary's ears as the ants took them down, down, down. The only comfort was that they were still alive; surely if the ants intended to eat them, they would have already done so.

As they continued their descent, some of the feeling trickled back into Ary's limbs. First she could twitch her toes; then she was able to wiggle her thumbs. Her heart picked up speed. She forced herself to stay limp, even as the feeling returned to her bit by bit. The tunnels kept flashing by, an endless pit of dark. Her wings crackled as the ants jostled her.

Only the soft patter of ant feet drumming against earth broke the silence; if Owl or Shrimp was nearby, she had no way to tell. No way to ask them if they were getting their feeling back, too.

Which begged the question: Should Ary try to escape— or stay?

Sootflank would have escaped. Gran would have escaped.

The feeling returned to her hands, her legs, her arms. Minutes inched by; now, Ary could move half her body. She craned her neck, hopelessly scanning the endless dark, praying to catch a whisper from Owl, a whimper from Shrimp.

*Jump*, a voice in her willed. It sounded like Gran's. *Save yourself.*

Her ears popped again. The air smelled only of clay and

mold. If Ary abandoned Owl and Shrimp now and managed to escape, she'd never see them again.

But she had good reason to, didn't she? An entire world over two souls.

*Atlas. All of Terra. Mama, back home.*

Was it even fair, or right, to weigh Owl and Shrimp against that many lives? Was she weak for hesitating to abandon them even now? Gran had left Dracaena behind to bring the cure back to Terra. All the other heroes had surely made similar sacrifices.

If there was one lesson Gran had taught her above all, it was that being a hero was a terribly lonely thing.

*I am the fourth hero of Terra.*

She'd said the words. Tried to believe them. But now, racing through the dark, as Ary's feeling returned to her body, a new paralysis gripped her. She could not—*would* not—leave her friends behind. Even though it made sense. Even though doing so might have enabled her to continue her mission to find Atlas.

So instead of escaping, Ary Mossheart lay in the dark, un-heroic and afraid, and hoped against all hope that wherever the ants were taking them, it was somewhere she, Owl, and Shrimp would at least be together to face whatever came next.

Light flickered overhead. The ants swept them forward, and Ary saw them: glow-shrooms.

They were the same ones that had grown in abundance back in Sootflank's cave, the same ones that were more precious to the folk of Terra than food or water, because they were their main source of light to cut through the long, dark night. The mushrooms grew high, high above in small, bulbous crops, clinging to the walls, unbothered by the affairs of ants and newts. Mold sprouted on some of them and slicked up the walls, but most of the glow-shrooms seemed unscathed.

Even here, hundreds of paces below the surface, as the whole world rotted above, they thrived.

Cold air hit her in a blast, so sudden it made her wings ache. Ary twisted, scanning the writhing bodies of the ants in the dim light, and—there! Not too far behind her, Owl bobbed helplessly as the ants carried him along. He looked at her with a sheepish smile and raised a hand. Gripped to his chest, of course, was the rucksack containing the journals. Far behind him, Shrimp was curled in a tight, nervous ball, held aloft by an indifferent ant.

Ary's eyes watered. They both had regained feeling, then, too.

And they hadn't abandoned her.

Clicking filled the air again, and the ants came to a halt in perfect sync. They were almost directly beneath the glow-shrooms now, and though Ary knew the lights were so far above, a part of her almost believed she could reach out and touch them. Ary held her breath. Maybe the ants didn't want to hurt them. Maybe this was where the queen lived, and Ary and her friends would be safe after all.

One of the ants began to click with rapid-fire noises, and an ant carrying Owl broke away from the pack to march forward. Owl lifted an eyebrow at Ary as if to ask, *What's going on?* Ary shook her head, careful to keep the rest of her body still. There was no telling what the ants would do if they knew they could move again. Owl must have gotten her hint, because he remained limp as the ant carried him several paces and stopped. Now the ant with Shrimp approached, coming to stand beside Owl.

Finally the ant carrying Ary marched forward. A gust of air rushed against her cheeks. It was cold. *Damper.* As if there was some kind of sharp decline ahead of them.

The ant holding Owl clicked once, twice—and Ary understood.

She jerked upright, her suspicion morphing into horror. Before them yawned a massive, dark pit, so deep even the glow of the mushrooms above could not puncture the shadows. The ants had carried them to its very edge. She twisted, a cry leaving her lips, but she was too late.

She could only watch as the ant holding Owl flung him forward—and he disappeared into the dark.

"*Owl!*" Ary shrieked.

And then the ant holding her seized her by her calf and flung her forward, too.

Time slowed. For a long, perilous moment, Ary hung

in the air, her unfurled wings splayed uselessly behind her. Ahead of her, she could just make out the rows upon rows of silent soldier ants. Above her, the glow-shrooms continued to pulse, bathing the cavern in their soft, eerie light.

Below her was a wide, gaping maw of nothingness.

Time resumed.

And then she was falling.

# THIRTY-THREE

## The Map to Atlas

In the dark, flightless and alone, Ary fell.

The air roared around her, ice cold, chapping her skin and slicing at her wings. Ary screamed, but the wind swallowed that, too. She could see nothing, feel nothing, *hear* nothing beyond the air rushing by. All she knew was that she was falling, and she was falling fast.

She flipped helplessly, her body twisting like a broken doll. Desperately, she tried to flare her wings, but wrapped in their papery cocoon they were as unhelpful as her arms or her legs. All her life, Ary had dreamed of flying; finally, here was a moment where she needed her wings—and all they could do was weigh her down.

There was no way out of this. There was only gravity, pulling her toward a swift demise.

Was this how it would end, then?

Alone in the dark, with no one to tell Mama what had happened?

And then—a familiar weight on her wrist.

A long, multi-jointed leg pulling her close.

And a voice whispering in her ear.

"Ary," said Shrimp. "Hold tight."

Ary's eyes stung. Shrimp curled around her, flexing the bands of his shell as far as he could, and she clung to his belly for dear life, her useless, papered wings pulled tightly against her back. The irony of it was so terrible, she didn't know whether to laugh or cry.

Here they were, falling. She was the one with wings— and she was unable to help them at all.

"Owl," Ary gasped. They were still falling. "Shrimp, we have to find Owl—"

They kept falling, kept tumbling, with Ary still curled protectively into Shrimp's belly. And then—a familiar, panicked yelping came from their left.

"Owl!" Ary shouted.

"*Ary!*" Owl screeched back. *"We're gonna diiieeee!"*

Ary was too terrified to be annoyed. When Shrimp grabbed him and thumped him against Ary's back, she could have wept with relief. Owl made a terrified sobbing noise and buried his face in her hair, and when he wrapped his arms around her middle and squeezed tight, Ary threaded her shaking fingers through his own.

"Hold," Shrimp warned. *"Tight."*

The pill bug closed his body around them—and they plummeted like a stone.

*WHAM!*

Shrimp's tightly coiled body hit the ground—and then they were flying *upward* again.

"Hold," Shrimp grunted. He sounded like he was in pain.

The impact of hitting the ground nearly knocked Ary's teeth out. Owl's chin slammed into the back of her head. He grunted and clung to Ary's back, squishing himself against her useless, papered wings. They went up, up, up—and then down again.

*WHAM!*

This time, they flew up less high than before. Shrimp let out a painful wheeze.

How much of this could he take?

*WHAM!*

"*Ready*," Shrimp gasped.

They flew up again—and this time, Shrimp unrolled and let them go.

Ary and Owl flew backward, still clinging to each other. They flipped in the air, Ary's wings splaying awkwardly, Owl screaming, and then tumbled several paces to crash into the dirt with a giant *thump*. They hit the ground in a heap of fairy limbs, grunting and groaning, and a painful twinge rocketed through Ary's left wing from where she'd landed oddly on it. Somewhere ahead, Shrimp landed again, much lighter than before, and scuttled toward them. Not a scrap of light broke the unrelenting darkness. Ary swayed, grasping for something, anything. Her fingers touched something soft and squeezed.

"Um," said Owl. "That's my ear."

Ary snatched her hand away, face burning. "Sorry."

She untangled herself from him and scrambled backward. Behind her, Shrimp settled and touched her shoulder with an antenna to let her know he was there. Ary rubbed her hands over her face. "Is everyone okay?"

"Am I okay?" Owl repeated slowly. "Well, let me think. A giant mole said our world is fake, we're all actually trapped in a massive bubble that we were supposed to leave a century ago, and your gran knew this, and lied, and left the girl she loved behind in the Underground to—die, or something, that part was unclear—so we allied with a giant fire-wielding newt, who I'm pretty sure is a war criminal, to go find some magical Atlas thingy that no one is sure even exists, were *betrayed* by said newt when he let a bunch of ants paralyze and kidnap us, and then were promptly flung to our deaths into a giant pit—and you want to know if I'm *okay*?"

"I meant physically," Ary snapped. "Is anything broken?"

"Oh," Owl said. "No."

"Good." Ary rubbed her forehead. "That was an impressive recap, though."

"Thank you. I'm very clearheaded in a crisis."

Ary snorted. "Shrimp? You all right?"

"Okay," Shrimp squeaked. And then, as if it wasn't obvious, "Ouch."

*Ouch* indeed. Ary's heart ached. She reached for him in the dark, her fingers ghosting over his shell. "How bad is it?"

Shrimp's shell creaked painfully as he shrugged. "Had worse."

He was clearly hurting. Guilt made Ary's limbs heavy. "I'm so sorry. All this is so much more than you bargained for."

"Family," Shrimp said firmly, softly, repeating his promise from earlier. "We follow."

Yet again, Ary was grateful for the never-ending dark of the Underground, if only because it hid her tears.

"Well . . ." said Owl. "What now?"

Shrimp made a thoughtful noise that seemed to echo Owl's sentiment.

Ary blinked. And then she realized, with a panicked jolt, they were asking *her*.

All along she'd been counting on following Sootflank through this. But now he was gone—probably back to his cave, to live out his days in private while the rest of their world crumbled. That left just her. The useless granddaughter of Wren Mossheart who had no wings, no magic, and no training.

And it was there, surrounded by nothing but pure darkness, sitting at the bottom of a giant hole with the pill bug and a fairy boy who were there because of her, that the weight of what this meant finally settled on Ary.

This was up to her now.

Ary leaned forward and put her head on her knees. She drew in several steady breaths, inhaling through her nose, holding, and exhaling just like Mama had taught her, until some of the panic left her. She was not the fourth hero of Terra; the ants had made that painfully, abundantly clear.

And would it have mattered even if she was? No amount of training could have prepared her for this. Nothing in the old stories and legends had prepared her for how endlessly dark, how massive, how *terrifying* the Underground was.

Was this how Gran had felt, too?

Frozen in place, knowing if she failed, the ones she loved would pay with their lives?

Ary took a deep breath. Gran's voice rippled through her mind.

*We're Mosshearts. We figure it out, and we survive. We always do.*

Ary wasn't a chosen one or someone predicted by a prophecy. She was just a girl who had gotten her friends into an extremely big mess.

And she was all they had.

"Okay," Ary said with more confidence than she felt. "We're all unhurt. That's good. So—what do we know?"

"Sootflank is a lying traitor and fire is terrifying," Owl offered unhelpfully. "Also, moles exist, apparently?"

Ary threw a punch toward what she hoped was his shoulder.

He grunted. "Sorry."

Shrimp rustled behind her. "Alive."

"We are alive," Ary agreed wearily. She dragged a finger-nail in the dirt, racking her brain. Something about this wasn't right. "The ants knew who we were."

"All right," Owl said slowly, clearly not following.

"They were looking for us." Ary chewed her lip. "Chives was confident they have the map. Which means the ants wanted to—what? Stop us from getting to Atlas?"

"Maybe they don't know the world is dying?"

Ary opened her mouth to correct him—and closed it. It sounded ridiculous. And yet—

The ants lived *incredibly* far down. They rarely had contact with the newts, and never with the folk. Even the cavern above them had been sparse with mold compared to the world above. If the ants lived even deeper down, they might not have felt the full force of the chaos the rot was wreaking above. And if the ants had something precious, something they knew might lead to the end of this world . . .

"Okay," Ary said slowly. "Maybe that's true."

"Or maybe we're prisoners," Owl said helpfully. "Maybe they just want everyone else to die out and leave the world for them to use."

"That could also be true," Ary said. "And is . . . extremely depressing. But we'd have no reason to be their prisoners."

"Actually," a new voice said. "He's right. You're definitely prisoners."

Overhead, a light flared. A glow-shroom lamp sputtered to life. It bathed the pit in an eerie, pale blue light that washed over them in gentle waves.

Sitting on a ledge, arms crossed, nose wrinkled and eyes glinting, was a fairy.

She couldn't have been much older than Ary. Like many

of the folk of Terra, she had wide, big eyes that had long adjusted to the dark, and ears that ended in fine, tiny points.

But this fairy had wings—real, unfurled, *working* wings, which was less of a shock than seeing her here at all. They fluttered absentmindedly behind her, the color of an ember about to go out, rippling and uncut and *real*. Tears pricked Ary's eyes.

They were so, so beautiful.

The newcomer glared down at them as though they'd done something to personally offend her. She was a stranger. Which wasn't possible, because she was clearly a fairy, and all fairies lived in Terra, and Ary had met everyone in Terra. Yet here was this girl, long-limbed and scowling down at them, as mysterious to Ary as the strange, warm light that had blazed through the cliffs and lit their world with a golden glow.

A complete and utter stranger.

And a terribly pretty stranger, at that.

Ary blinked. Why was she thinking about that? That didn't matter!

The girl was staring at Ary, and only Ary, with such intensity that it felt like they'd met before. But, no—Ary was certain. She would have remembered this girl, more than anyone else. She would have seen those fury-bright eyes in her dreams.

"Um," Ary said, feeling quite foolish. "Hello?"

"Hello indeed." The fairy girl kicked her legs and tilted her head to the side, something dark flashing in her eyes. Around her neck, she wore an odd charm—a flower, half wilted, carved from old shroom-wood. It sparked a memory in Ary, but she couldn't place where she'd seen it before. The fairy girl lifted a brow. "Surprised to see me?"

Owl blinked up at her, clearly as confused as Ary was. "I think the safe answer is yes."

The girl tossed her head back and laughed. "Of course you are. *Of course*. They taught you nothing!" She made a disgusted noise and shook her head with a sneer. "Quickspark warned me you'd be unprepared, but this is pathetic."

*Quickspark*. That name again, spat like a curse. The earwigs had referenced her before, and even Sootflank had flinched. Whoever Quickspark was, the fact that she wanted Ary and Owl here couldn't be good.

Maybe the fairy could be reasoned with? Ary climbed to her feet. "Who—"

"Who am I?" the girl cut her off.

Ary nodded. The familiar ache was still there. She recognized this girl—she was certain. But that wasn't possible. So why did her face, her glares, even the melody of her voice seem so familiar?

"Who am *I*?" The fairy girl leaped to her feet and clasped her hands dramatically in front of her. "Such an interesting question. I suppose it depends on who you ask. My mama called me Briar. Her friends called me *little Sunleaf*. The ants call me *that creature*. Is it starting to click together, little hero of Terra, or do I need to spell it out for you?"

"I'm sorry," Ary said faintly, more and more bewildered by the moment. "Do I know you?"

"Oh, no. You don't know me—but I know *you*, Ary Mossheart."

Ary's entire body turned to ice. "How do you know my name?"

The fairy girl, Briar, bared her teeth in a sharp, humorless smile. "Because *I'm* what you need. I'm the map to Atlas. And *you* are the granddaughter of the traitor who left *my* grandmother behind."

# THIRTY-FOUR

## *Like Grandmother, like Granddaughter*

For a breath, Briar's words rippled in the air.

*The traitor who left my grandmother behind.*

*Grandmother.*

Horror crashed over Ary in an icy wave. "You're . . ."

She couldn't say it. Couldn't get the words out. Of all the horrid things Gran had done, every terrible fate she'd imagined for Dracaena, this was beyond what she could have feared. It hadn't just been one girl Gran had doomed to a lifetime of mold-filled darkness—

It had been *generations.*

"Briar Sunleaf," the fairy girl finished bitterly. "Daughter of Nettle. Granddaughter of Dracaena. The latest—and last— map to Atlas."

All this time, they'd assumed the map to Atlas would be just that—something physical, something to guard, something to *hold.*

But wasn't a map just memories made permanent?

What better way to protect Atlas than to ensure only a select few could ever find it?

"I don't suppose you're here to help us?" Owl asked weakly.

Briar gave him a dull look. "Certainly not."

Ary could see the resemblance to Dracaena now—Briar had her grandmother's same round chin, her dark eyes and dancer's frame.

*Oh, Gran. What have you done?*

"Briar," Ary began carefully. "I know you don't know me."

"Oh, here we go. This ought to be good."

"I know you have no reason to trust us. But you don't understand—"

"*I* don't understand?" Briar's laugh was sharp and unkind. "Let me make something clear, Mossheart. *I* grew up understanding. *I* understand more than anyone. I understand so well that I already know what you're going to say: you want to tell me that we're all stuck in a terrarium. That we're doomed to die here without Atlas, that our world is ending, and for some rotting reason I'm supposed to trust *you* to save it."

The fight drained out of Ary, and uncertainty swept in. "Well, yes . . ."

"Let me guess," Briar mocked. "You're *different.* You're no hero. You're just trying to do the right thing. You didn't ask for any of this—but someone has to do something. Someone has to step up."

Dread turned every part of Ary's body to stone. Because there was no way Briar knew that this was what Ary had said earlier, both to her friends and to herself. Which meant it wasn't the words of *this* Mossheart she was echoing.

It was the promise of a different Mossheart, in a different time.

Briar met her stare, and for the first time Ary saw what lay behind the anger in her eyes.

It was loss.

And what could Ary say in the face of that? She had only just met this girl, had only known her for a few seconds, and yet Ary had also spent a lifetime learning to cope with that sting of betrayed grief shining in Briar's eyes. Wren Mossheart had left her scars on Briar without ever setting foot in the same room as her.

Who was Ary, to try to recruit this girl who had lost so much to a fight she'd never asked for?

A fight Ary herself hardly wanted?

"What happens now, then?" Ary didn't bother to hide the tremor in her voice, the scratch in her throat. Faking bravery was what had gotten her into this mess, after all. "We're stuck here as prisoners to . . . what? Waste away, until the mold takes us all?"

"The ants have sent word to the earwigs," Briar said bitterly. "That was what I came here to tell you—not to rehash history. The earwigs will be here tomorrow to collect you. After that? You belong to the newts. Whatever plans they have for your city are no concern of mine."

Ary went cold as she recalled the hunger of the earwigs,

the pull of their pincers on her wings. The newts would surely kill Ary and her friends if they made it to their kingdom anyway—but something told Ary that left in the pincers of hungry earwigs, it would be all too easy for their prisoners to disappear on the journey.

"Bad," whined Shrimp, folding himself against Ary's back.

"My friends," Ary said desperately, half rising. "This was all my idea. They had nothing to do with it—"

"And why would I help you?" Briar gestured angrily. "I don't know you. I don't care about you or your friends. All I know is that *your* gran is the reason I lost *mine*."

Ary faltered.

"Grandma spent a lifetime waiting for Wren Mossheart to come back to her," she whispered. "She gave Wren her trust, and worse—she gave Wren Mossheart her heart. A Sunleaf has already been betrayed by one Mossheart's promise. Forgive me if I'm not eager to do the same."

"Briar, wait, *please*—"

"Goodbye, Ary Mossheart," Briar said bitterly, and then she was gone, and it was only Ary and her friends in the wide, empty dark.

# THIRTY-FIVE

## *Hope with Claws*

Ary didn't know how long they waited. In the pit the ants had thrown them into, there was no light. No sound. No life. There was only blackness, and the strange, spongy earth beneath them, coupled with a sickly-sweet smell she couldn't quite put her finger on.

After what felt like far too long, Owl's hand found hers. "Hey," the fairy boy whispered. "Are you okay?"

Ary didn't know whether to laugh or cry. "Am I *okay*?"

"Fair enough."

"She hates me," Ary whispered. "We've never met, and I can't even blame her. I'd hate me, too."

"I'm shrugging," said Owl. "I know you can't see me, but you need to know it was a very helpless shrug."

"Me too," Ary said wearily. Her shoulders didn't move. It was the thought that counted.

Ary heard the faint rustle of pages, the scratch of fingers on moss paper as Owl thumbed through the journals he could no longer read. But instead of talking about Dracaena, or Gran, or even the girl who had appeared hours before

263

and upended their entire world, Owl whispered, "Ary, I'm scared."

Ary whipped to look at him, though she saw only darkness. How strange, to be this close to Owl, and were it not for the weight of his hand in hers, he might not have been there at all. She waited, let the silence stretch, to see if Owl would fill it.

"I've always felt so . . . useless." His words came out slow and unsure, dripping like root sap. "When my parents were alive, it was a little different—they believed in the old ways, that the Seedlings were one half of some greater whole, not just shovel-clanging fools who sang a bunch of silly songs on market day. And I thought . . . I don't know." His voice caught. "I spent my whole life sure something was wrong with Terra. When I saw you scale the thorn fence, and I went and told your gran I thought—I don't know. I didn't really care about Terra being saved. I just wanted something to *happen*. I wanted to be a part of something that mattered, and I wanted it to matter that I had spent my entire life afraid. And now we're here . . . and my parents are gone . . . and it's not like I have anyone who will miss me. It's not like I have anyone who will care, but . . ."

"What?" Ary asked weakly. "You don't want to be eaten by a bunch of feral earwigs? Wow. You're supposed to be the adventurous one."

Owl sniffled. "Well, I'm certainly still the funny one."

Ary laughed, though the threat of tears ached in her throat. It seemed like she was always crying lately. She leaned against him, comforted by his weight, by the press of Shrimp against their backs. And strangely, somehow, Ary almost felt . . . happy. Her entire life she had tied herself into knots trying to fit the mold Gran and Terra had cast for her. She'd not had a family since Papa had died, not truly.

How strange that it felt like she had one now.

Ary frowned. There was something that had been bothering her this entire time. "How did you know Terra was dying?"

*Talk to your friend*, Chives had urged. *You may find that the earth's magic that can only whisper to you speaks to him in more of a shout.*

Owl hesitated, his voice reluctant. "What?"

"How did you know?" Ary pressed. "You knew about the mold, about the creatures disappearing—*how?*"

"I . . . feel things," Owl admitted. She couldn't see him, but from the embarrassment in his voice, she could only imagine how pink his cheeks were. "And I hear things, in my dreams. It's like . . . I don't know. Sometimes it seems like the earth is trying to tell me something, but what it says doesn't make any sense."

"What does it say?"

"Reach," said Owl. "It's just the same word over and over again, and it keeps saying, 'Reach.'"

She waited for him to elaborate—but it was clear Owl was as lost as she was. Ary slumped. How was it that things only got more confusing?

"I'm sorry," Owl said suddenly. "That's what I keep wanting to say. If I hadn't gone for your gran—if I hadn't pushed that shovel into the Underlake—"

"What? Owl, no, stop."

"You would have turned around." Owl was crying in full now, his voice breaking, his whole body shaking. "You'd be *home*, Ary, and so would I, and at least we wouldn't be here."

"Owl."

"I don't know what I was thinking—why I couldn't ignore the stupid nightmares—"

"*Owl.*" Ary reached in the dark and caught her friend's shoulders. "Look at me."

"I can't see you." Owl hiccuped. "We're at the bottom of a pit."

Ary rolled her eyes. She loosened her grip but didn't let go.

"Listen to me. I don't care who opened the seal. Who went for Gran. *I* scaled the thorn fence. *I* jumped into the Underlake. *I* made the deal with Sootflank. If this is anyone's fault, it's mine. If it's anyone's fault, it's *Gran's*, okay?" Ary's voice trembled. "I'm sorry you're here—I am so, so sorry. But I am glad you're here, too."

Ary sucked in a shaky breath, startled by just how true

it was. She'd been so annoyed at Owl at first. But he'd stuck by her.

It was more than most would have done.

It was more than Gran had done.

Ary blinked furiously. She'd spent her whole life looking for love, surviving on the scraps Mama could give her, on the memories of Papa that swirled like smoke, desperate for the rare times that approval lit Gran's eyes. But she'd never had anyone beyond her family. Tulip and Basil had never *seen* her, not really. Terra had tried to mold her the same way they'd molded Gran. Terra had never been on her side.

But Owl?

"About before," said Ary, her cheeks hot with shame. "I was so mean to you. I'm really sorry."

"You—"

"Please don't say I wasn't mean," Ary blurted. "I was, and . . . I looked away when others were even meaner. I could have stopped them, or said something, but I didn't. And I'm sorry."

"I wasn't going to say you weren't mean," Owl said dryly. He squeezed her hand in the dark. "But you were scared, like me. And . . . I don't know, Ary. I guess sometimes we aren't our best selves when we're scared." He paused. "Although, since we're reflecting on how mean you were, there's something I've been meaning to say."

Ary braced herself. He hated her. "Okay."

"*I. Told. You. So.*" Owl tapped his knuckles against her

forehead with each word. "We wouldn't be in this pit if you had just listened to me about not touching that mushroom pile. But *nooo*, you had to try to and steal the obviously enchanted mushrooms, scale the thorn fence like some kind of criminal, and strike a deal with that grumpy old lizard."

"Sootflank is a newt," laughed Ary, her limbs wobbly with relief. Owl had not exactly forgiven her, and Ary didn't really want him to—a few days of friendship did not make up for the years she'd shut him out. Mama had always said kindness was its own kind of bravery, and when it had come to Owl, Ary had been a coward when it mattered most. But this felt like a start.

"Thank you for everything, Owl," Ary whispered. "I couldn't do this alone. I . . . I don't think I've ever had a real friend before, not really. Not until I met you."

"That's embarrassing." Owl sniffled, but the weight of his shoulder on hers told her everything he could not say.

Silence stretched between them, thick in the black of the ant pit. Behind her, Shrimp made a faint snuffling noise. Owl began to shake again, and the earth groaned as it, too, began to tremble alongside him. Ary remembered the way he had clung to the glow-shroom lamp, his insistence that he always have light. It had been under the guise of trying to understand Dracaena's ramblings, but Ary had never seen Owl in the mushroom fields, though she was certain no one needed ration tokens more than him. *You're afraid of the dark.* She almost said the words—but what good would they do? She'd had smaller fears, sillier fears. They'd frozen her all the same.

All her life Ary had fled the shadows of their world, the uncertainty that lurked within them.

Now she was drowning in them. Now she was nothing.

Maybe there was power in that. Maybe, down here, she didn't have to be Ary Mossheart. There were no heroes, no Gran, no fairies raised in the dark or warnings and promises written in stone.

She was just a girl in the dark, holding the hand of her friend who was scared.

And they had a pit to escape.

"Owl."

No answer.

"*Owl.*" Ary squeezed his hand.

The earth ceased its trembling. Ary wondered again about the voices she had been hearing, and the voices Owl said he'd heard his entire life. Chives had said the magic of their world would grow stronger as they drew closer to Atlas. Was that what this was—or something more? She wanted to ask Owl about the voices, and if he'd also had dreams filled with mold and monstrous snakes, but something told her it would only scare him further.

The dreams—this mission—was her problem to solve.

Right now, Owl didn't need reminders of magic or strange legacy. He needed his friend.

"I'm going to get us out of here." Her voice came out

calmer than she felt. "I don't know how. I don't know when. But I am going to get us out of this pit, and we are going to make it to Atlas, and then . . ." She licked her lips, memory taking her to a different patch of darkness, a different voice among the shadows as light spilled all around her. "Then, Owl, we are going to find the sun."

Finally, Owl answered, his voice reluctant and weak. "What is a . . . sun?"

Ary blinked against a new kind of grief as Chives' words flooded her. She knew from her nose to her wing tips she would never see the Steward again. That should they leave the terrarium, Chives would not join them when they left this land of mold for whatever lay beyond. A part of her suspected Chives had been relieved to find Ary on his doorstep. That he had hung on, alone in the dark, carrying that last mythos of Atlas for someone who cared enough to seek the ending of this world so that they might find the next.

And Ary did—care, that is. She wasn't a hero, didn't have training or a plan or even a sword, but she cared. She cared so much it *hurt*. She cared so deeply, and wildly, and constantly, that she was determined to see this through, no matter the cost. That had to mean something, right?

"I don't know," Ary whispered. "But we're going to find out."

Slowly, softly, Ary told him of what she had seen on the hill with Chives. She told Owl of the way the light had spilled above the cliffs, golden and brilliant where the mold and slime had not yet climbed, and she told him of the fragments of stories Chives had carried. There, in the dark, Ary admitted to Owl what she'd refused to admit to herself—that the light had proven the seemingly un-provable. That their terrarium was *small*, and this tired, old world of theirs was never meant to last.

Because somewhere, somehow, out there was *more*.

As the hours crept by, Ary held tight to Owl's hand. And when her fear rose bearing claws, she welcomed it, letting hope flood into the gashes fear carved in her heart. Hope, and belief—that this pit would not be the end.

*Forget heroes*, she thought furiously. *Forget glow-moths and Atlas and prophecies.* It didn't matter that she hadn't wanted any of this—didn't matter that she wasn't ready. She had started this journey to save her family, and Shrimp and Owl were family now, too. She didn't need to be the fourth hero of Terra to protect the ones she loved. She didn't need to be any kind of hero at all to get them out of this.

They would face the earwigs. They would make it to Atlas. They would save Mama.

Somehow, in three days, they *would* leave the terrarium. And then?

"Then," Ary whispered as Owl slipped into sleep beside her, "then we find the sun."

# THIRTY-SIX

## *The Life Required*

Ary dreamed of flying.

In the dream, like all the others, she soared above Terra. But there was no Mama or Papa beside her this time, no beautiful fields fighting off impending rot. For the briefest flicker, Ary pulled back, fearing another vision of slime and ruin that would sweep over everything she loved—but instead Terra was still.

Something tugged Ary down. Where fear should have lived, a kind of numb curiosity rested instead. She flew closer, marveling at the strength of her wings, and hovered over a strange heap. It was little more than rubble, a home now reduced to upturned stones and rotting mush-wood. Ary's heart skipped a beat. She knew this plot of land, knew the road that cradled it, and the hills beyond.

This was Gran's house.

Well, *had* been Gran's house.

But whatever chaos had finally come for Wren Mossheart had long left. There was no slime, no blood, no newt-fire cracking the air. Just dust, and mold growing in the spaces fairies had left behind. Ruin had long come for

Terra, it seemed, leaving only dust and decay as footprints. All of Terra was gone; all of Terra was quiet.

And it was strangely . . . peaceful.

Ary moved on.

The rest of Terra had suffered the same fate. Every home was in a state of slow collapse, doors hanging ajar, windows blown open. The hair on her arms stood on end. Clothes that were now threadbare hung from drying lines strung between homes. An old picnic blanket was spread out next to one of the roads, the plates still set in place, the food long reduced to dust. There were no bodies, no reek of death in the air. It was as if the fairies of Terra had all simply gotten up and left—but not an hour ago, not a day ago. Ary studied the gray film covering everything in sight.

No one had been here for *years*.

Ary kept flying, following the roads toward the market. More evidence of Terra's abandonment was all around her: Seedling shovels rusting atop knolls, children's toys scattered in the road. The fields where Ary had worked were now abandoned, carefully curated rows of mushrooms long withered and dead, the soil bare and covered in dust.

Where was everyone?

Ary's wings carried her to the market. The great fountains were cracked and dry, the basins filled with that strange, silvery dust. Two of the hero statues had toppled over; only Gran's remained. Ary landed before it, a shiver passing through her.

There was so much she'd never known to ask Gran. So much she wanted to know and still didn't know how to ask even now.

Ary reached for the statue and touched her fingers to Gran's stone cheek. The statue groaned—and cracked. Where Ary had touched it, the stone began to crumble, not in a violent, roaring tumble, but quietly, with a whimper, crumbling to dust before her until only rubble lay at her feet. Silver-gray dust plumed in the air, coating Ary's hair, her skin, her wings. She sneezed, and when she wiped her face clean, the dust smelled strangely sweet.

The world around her shifted.

A cold breeze slipped past, rustling her wings, stirring the dust at her feet. Ary turned and found herself in a village she'd never seen before. Fairies had clearly lived here—but unlike Terra, everything was carved from dirt and stone, clustered together in a great Underground cavern. If she strained, she could almost hear voices pitched in song, the gentle hymns of Seedlings past swirling around her.

She kept walking, her sense of unease growing, fed by the sense that she was not quite here, but she was not quite elsewhere, either. Ary took one step forward, then another. Mold coated everything—the stone-carved homes, the fire-pits, the gouges in the rock where rivers had once run. Was this where Dracaena had lived? Ary remembered the tunnels she and Owl had seen, the hints that some folk had once existed outside Terra's walls. Once this had been a village of its own, filled with families and love and laughter.

Now it was empty, its residents all gone save for one.

*Briar.* A life in the dark, her family vanishing one by one, haunted by the specter of Wren Mossheart on which she could place all her blame. How had she coped? How had she survived at all?

The world grew dark at the edges. Chives' voice wrapped around her, warm in its surety, waking a throb of grief for someone she'd not yet lost.

Was it him that a part of her heart already knew to mourn—or someone else?

*The closer you get to the bottom of the terrarium, where fewer souls wander, the thicker the magic keeping this world alive grows.*

*Someone—or something—could be calling out to you.*

"Hello?" Ary whispered. "I can feel you calling. I think I felt you before I even entered the Underground. I am trying to understand."

The dreams. The voices. They'd all started when that glow-moth had found her.

Faces began to swim before her: Owl, Mama, Gran, Sootflank, and Shrimp. And Briar, her eyes blazing bright with grief and loss, her beautiful face carved into a sneer far too old for the roundness of her cheeks.

"I'm trying to save them," Ary whispered. "And I don't know how. I know . . . what I have to give."

*From the dust.*

"The life required—I know it has to be me."

*We find the key.*

Ary faltered. She thought of Owl, his hand trembling in the dark, of everything in the Underground that had suffered. Of the golden light beyond the walls.

Maybe there was something wrong with her, that all she wanted was to go home. That even here, in the dream, she wished the moth had visited anyone else that day.

"But," Ary whispered, "I am afraid."

Ary took a step forward—and a scream split the air.

"*No!*"

Gran stood before her, trembling like a leaf, her hands balled into fists.

No—not Gran.

Wren.

"No," said Wren Mossheart, once more a girl only a few years older than Ary. "This wasn't—this wasn't how it was supposed to be."

Wren fell to her knees, the heels of her hands ground into her eyes, her entire body shaking as she muttered to herself.

Ary took a breath and moved toward Wren, curiosity slinking in where fear shivered in her heart. Though she didn't bother to lighten her tread, her steps made no sound; the dust no longer stirred wherever she walked. Here, she was only a ghost.

"That was what the mole said," Wren said furiously. She cocked her head as though she was listening to something— or someone. "That was what he *said*! No, that can't be how it works—*no*."

In a jerking, panicked movement, Wren leaped to her feet. She paced in a circle like a newt in a cage, her chest rising and falling, her hands buried in her hair. Ary watched her with a strange numbness. This felt different from before, when she'd seen Wren with her friends, entering the Underground with their confident laughter ringing in the air. She knew from her school lessons that Wren's journey had only taken two weeks.

But Wren, it seemed, had aged years.

Her hair was shorn short, her skin a mess of scratches and wounds. But worse than anything else were her eyes—gone was the confident light of Terra's chosen hero, the easiness of a girl with a whole life ahead of her, the sharpness of a child who knew far more than she ought to.

Her eyes were tired and angry.

They were the very ones Ary had gazed into her entire life.

Wren reached into her backpack and ripped something free, hurled it to the ground, her face twisted into a pained, feral thing. "Is this what you want? Is this enough? *Take it*. I don't want it, not like this, not for this price."

The feeling left Ary's body. Because what Wren had pulled from her bag—what she had tossed forward as though it were mere garbage—was a small, fire-colored mushroom. Ary had never seen one in person, but she didn't need to. She had grown up surrounded by stories of it, had seen it depicted in paintings and murals.

She'd spent her whole life gazing upon its stone twin, outstretched in Gran's hand.

*Sunroot.*

The mushroom that had cured Terra's plague.

The mushroom that *could* have saved the Underground—had Gran not kept it to herself.

Somewhere in the strands of time, someone must have answered Wren, because her face went white, and she *screamed*.

"Then let them die!" she cried. "If I am not enough, then they'll have *no one*. Why do you need more? Why do you need her?"

Panic began to rise in Ary. The wheels of her mind turned, but too slow, as though they were churning through thick mud. This was all wrong. Gran had saved Terra with the Sunroot. She'd chosen it over the Underground, over *Dracaena*, had lied to the world about the fate of the terrarium because—Ary thought—her finding of the Sunroot was a hero's quest she could achieve. She had left the Underground to die, entire species eaten by mold, because she had not been up to the task of freeing them all.

But Wren wasn't stealing anything.

She was trying to give the Sunroot *back*.

Wren dropped to her knees, the fight seemly gone out of her body. Ary inched toward her.

"I made a promise," Wren whispered. Tears dripped down her chin. "A promise on my honor, a promise on my name. It was supposed to be *me*."

Silence followed. Ary strained to listen, inching so close that she could have touched Wren, but all she heard was the panicked breath rattling from Wren's lungs.

"I can give you so many things. But not that." Wren shook her head. "There has to be another way."

And for the first time, a voice answered.

"I may hold up the world, little folk. But even I cannot make an exception. Even if I wanted to—the key would not let me." Gooseflesh rose on Ary's arms. The voice was old, deep and tired, a timeless voice with a familiar echo she could not yet place. And it was so *loud*—booming all around her, making her teeth ache as it echoed through her bones. The dust surrounding them kicked up into whirlwinds.

"Forget the key, then," Wren whispered. "Forget the warning. Take my life and be done with it. I'm ready. I *promised*."

Ary inched forward, her heart pounding, straining in the dark, straining to see, straining to understand.

Ice crept through Ary's veins.

*We have it wrong*, she realized with horror. *We all have it wrong.*

Gran hadn't just abandoned the Underground. It had

been messier than that—she had failed, yes, and she had *lied*. But Sootflank had thought Wren Mossheart had chosen her own life over theirs. Atlas had demanded a life most loved, freely given, and Wren had been ready to do what Ary feared she could not. She had been ready to give up all of her, so everyone else might live.

So why hadn't she?

Ary was nearly upon Wren now. The dream swirled all around her; the echoes of the voices she'd been hearing raked against her bones. Whatever had happened here sixty years ago had set all of this in motion—had thrust Ary and her friends into the ill-fitting role of desperate heroes.

*Someone* wanted her to see this. *Something* wanted her to understand.

*I am trying*, Ary thought wildly. *Help me.*

Her heart beat so hard it threatened to make her sick. Sweat beaded on her palms. It would change nothing, save no one, but it *mattered* that Gran had failed the world to save someone else.

"Please," Wren begged. "Please, don't ask this of me. Don't make me choose."

Who was out there?

"Take the cure, child," the voice said, and it sounded almost sorry. "It cannot cure any creature but the folk. Fix what you can now. Let another carry the burden."

Who'd swayed her from saving the terrarium to passing the problem to the next generation?

"There are no more heroes," Wren whispered, tears dripping down her cheeks. "There is only me."

Who had fated Gran to become a false hero?

"Oh, Wren," said the voice, not unkindly. "There are alwaysss more."

Who was Gran talking to?

"Atlas," Wren whispered. *"Please."*

Ary's entire body went cold.

"Go, while you can," said Atlas from somewhere beyond, somewhere in the wide, dusty dark that only Wren could see. "Goodbye, little hero."

"*No*," cried Ary, lunging forward.

She leaped right through Wren, the specter of the girl her gran had once been passing through her in a shock of cold air. Ary crashed to her knees, scanning the endless, dust-specked darkness for Atlas, and found . . . nothing. Her heart railed against her ribs, and fury mounted in her. The past few days crashed through her in a terrible wave—Mama, the mold racking her body. Sootflank, his eyes lit with pain as he recounted how helping Wren Mossheart had cost him everything. Chives, speaking of sunlight, the lonely ache in his voice as he admitted he was the last of his kind, and that for better or worse, the terrarium would be the only world he ever knew. Owl and Shrimp, trapped in that pit with her, terrified and alone. Briar, doomed to a life in the Underground. Papa, ruined by the newt wars, dead long before the mold took him. So many had suffered, so many had been lost, and Mama had only a few days left and Atlas was their only chance and now it was *gone*.

Ary bunched her hands into fists and screamed. The nothingness shook; the dust danced. Why give her these dreams, these voices, these visions if they weren't going to show her anything useful? If the magic tied to Atlas was truly calling out to her, why did it only ever leave her more confused than before?

A strange, prickling pain danced across her back. Ary twisted and watched in horror as her wings curled, graying at the edges—and then they began to turn to dust, too, the same dust that surrounded them, the same dust Gran's statue had collapsed into.

"I'm sorry," a familiar voice whispered.

Wren Mossheart stood over her.

"I'm sorry," Wren whispered. She was crumbling at the edges, fading into nothingness, the colors leaking away from her until she was nothing more than a ghost of a girl, the truth of her and what had happened here lost to time. "I was ready for it to be me. Not her—anyone but her. I'm so, so sorry."

And then she was gone in a whirl of smoke, leaving only dust behind.

# THIRTY-SEVEN

## *For What It's Worth*

Ary woke to two feelings—the wetness of tears on her cheeks, and something . . . nudging her shoulder? Her eyes opened. A fairy girl leaned over her, face creased with worry, wings flared wide as she held a sputtering glow-shroom lamp over Ary and poked her with her foot. For a brief, wonderful moment, Ary had no idea where she was. Something about this girl was familiar, from the furrow between her dark brows to the pout of her lips—though Ary couldn't place her finger on why, which didn't seem right. Surely she'd have remembered any fairy who still had their wings. Especially one so terribly pretty.

"You were crying," the fairy said, "in your sleep."

The world rushed back in. Gran, Briar, the pit she and her friends were trapped in, the terrarium—and *Atlas*, voice ringing in the dark, telling Gran to take the Sunroot, telling her it could only cure the folk from the plague that had wiped out so many in the Underground long before the mold finished the job, telling her that her life was not the price required. More pieces of a puzzle Ary didn't yet understand. Ary gasped and jerked upright, and Briar flinched, a cold mask sweeping away the soft concern that had lit her face only a moment before.

Ary didn't know why that disappointed her. Didn't know why she wanted Briar to look at her softly, if she looked at her at all.

Maybe she really did have mold poisoning.

Ary swiped at her face, her cheeks heating. "Sorry. Had a weird dream."

"You screamed," Briar said quietly. "Like something was hurting you."

*Something is*, Ary wanted to say. She swallowed and turned her face away. An awkward silence stretched between them, and Ary didn't know what to do, or what to say, her head muddled with sleep, her mind still ringing with Gran's voice.

*Please, don't ask this of me. Don't make me choose.*

"Anyway, the earwigs need you alive. That's the only reason I came to check." Briar had a funny look on her face— like she was angry with herself for something. She turned on her heel. "They'll be here in the morning. Probably to eat you."

"Wait," said Ary. "Briar."

There were so many things Ary wanted to say, wanted to *ask*. Were Gran here, she might have appealed to Briar's larger duty to the world, would have made the terrarium her priority. She'd have breezed right past the pain and grief in Briar's eyes, because what was the pain of one girl against the lives of the world? If what Briar said was true, she was the map to Atlas, the sole descendant of Dracaena, the keeper of secrets that could save them and the key to their salvation. There was no time for feelings, no time for questions or apologies, no time for *Briar*.

Gran would have looked at Briar and seen an opportunity.

Ary looked at Briar and saw another girl who'd been left behind.

So even though the world was ending, and Ary still had no clue how she was going to save Mama or her friends, Ary looked at Briar and said what she wished she'd heard years ago, from anyone at all.

"Briar," said Ary. "For what it's worth, I'm sorry."

Briar whipped to look at her.

"I know you don't know me. I know you don't care. But it's wrong, what happened to your grandmother. What happened to your family. And you deserve to hear that—that it was wrong, and it shouldn't have happened, and I am so, so sorry."

What had Dracaena been to the Underground? Had she been their own kind of hero, foretold to protect them all, unwittingly giving her children and her children's children the burden of picking up that mantle, too? When Briar had been small, what had others seen when they looked at her? A little fairy too far from home, or legacy surely soon to bloom?

How quickly had Briar's world also become a question not of *Will she save us?* but a simple *When?*

It wasn't right. *None* of this was right. And though Ary was loath to admit it—it wasn't fair to Gran and Dracaena, either. Gran had not been much older than Ary when she'd entered the Underground alongside the girl she'd loved.

And she had been afraid, too.

Briar didn't look at her. "All these years I wondered what I'd do if I ever met a Mossheart—all the dreaming I did, after watching the way Grandmother withered—and now . . ." Her laugh was flat. "Look at you. Just some lost little girl. You really have no idea what you've stumbled into, have you?"

"No," Ary said honestly. "I don't. I never wanted any of this."

Surprise and understanding flashed across Briar's face, and Ary wondered if in another life they might have liked each other, these two girls carrying the burden of their grandmother's failed fate.

She wondered if they might have been friends.

Behind her, Owl and Shrimp slept, fairy boy and pill bug snuggled against each other. Even in sleep, Owl's face was lined with worry.

Ary looked at Briar and made a plea in the dark. "My friends. If there is any way you can help them—"

"I can't."

"But if there *is*." Ary clenched her fists. "The Underground is angry at Wren Mossheart. They look at me and see her. They want a price paid, so, fine, I'll pay it. But Owl and Shrimp didn't ask for any of this. They followed me down here to try to help—"

"I can't help you," Briar snapped. "And even if I could—why would I? I've had enough trouble in my life thanks to the Mosshearts."

Ary deflated. She would have to try to bargain with the Ant Queen—and if that didn't work, when the earwigs took them, then Ary would simply stay behind when her friends tried to escape.

It was probably for the best that she and Briar weren't friends. If they were, this was the fate she'd have. Doomed for an ending in the dark, battling creatures and parsing through old legends in journals that hardly made sense.

*The journals.*

"Briar," Ary said suddenly. "Wait."

"Um, I haven't moved?"

Ary rolled her eyes. Okay, she definitely did not want to be friends with Briar. She was *annoying*.

Ary jumped up, creeping toward the bag of journals Owl had carried throughout the Underground. She hesitated, hand hovering over them. He cared about the journals—they'd become a comfort to him, a way to help, and a kind of reckoning, she supposed, against the hero he'd idolized, the world he'd known. But the journals had never belonged to him or Ary.

She hoped he would understand.

Ary picked up the bag that carried Dracaena's last words and offered them to her granddaughter. "For you."

Briar stared at the bag as though Ary had just offered her a moldy turnip. "No thanks."

Ary made an annoyed noise and shook the bag. "The day we entered the Underground, we found these in a locked room." She hesitated. "They belonged to your grandmother."

Surprise washed across Briar's face. Her throat bobbed, and Ary thought of Papa, of how she would have given anything to find something new of him at all.

"There were more," Ary apologized. "But they burned when the earwigs came for us. It's all in here—why Dracaena entered the Underground. How she felt after my gran left."

Ary set the bag on the ground and immediately moved back.

Briar looked at Ary, her eyes searching her face, her expression raw. Slowly, she knelt and pulled the journals from the bag. Tears welled in her eyes as she touched a shaking hand to Dracaena Sunleaf's writing. "Why give these to me? You don't know me. Why are you being kind to me when you have no reason to?"

"Because Wren Mossheart hurt me, too," said Ary. "I didn't know about Dracaena, Briar. I swear. None of us did. When we found these, I just wanted to understand what made my gran do the things she did."

The dream pulsed all around Ary—Gran on her knees,

pleading, *begging* Atlas to take her life—for what? Gran had been so close. She had been ready to pay the price—a life most loved, given freely.

And Atlas had turned her away.

"I know you won't help us find Atlas. I know you hate me, because of what my gran did to yours." She hesitated. "But you deserve her words, if anyone does."

Briar said nothing. Tears dripped down her chin as she gripped the journals, her eyes flying back and forth from Ary to the words that looped between them.

"Besides," Ary added, "if the earwigs *do* eat us, I don't think they'll have any use for these. I'm pretty sure earwigs can't read."

Briar stared at her uncomfortably.

"That was supposed to be funny," Ary said weakly.

Briar frowned. "You're . . . not good at funny."

Ary sighed. "I know."

They both hesitated, Briar gripping the journals and Ary standing with her hands in her pockets as her friends slept on.

"For what it's worth," Ary said softly, "I don't think any of us have the story right. I think something else happened down there—I think, maybe, both our grans were just kids who weren't ready for any of this. I didn't find the answers about my gran that I needed, but . . . I hope you will."

Briar cleared her throat. Cleared it again. She turned a page of one of the journals, face crumpling as she read.

When she looked at Ary, some of the softness returned to her eyes. Somewhere deep inside Ary, hope stirred dusty wings.

Maybe all was not lost. Maybe Briar would help them yet. Maybe they could repair what their grandmothers had broken and find a way to save this world together. It would have been a pretty tale. Two girls trapped in different threads of fate; the second chance their grandmothers never had. A Sunleaf and a Mossheart, allies again.

It was the kind of story Mama would have told her, once, to chase away the worry that swept in with the dark. A story fit for heroes.

Briar's eyes searched Ary's face, her brows knitting together—and she froze.

From above, in a long, rolling wave, came a series of clicks and hisses.

The blood drained from Ary's face. Dirt sprinkled down on their heads as something descended the walls, and from above came voices—voices she'd heard before, voices that filled her with fear. Clinical, cold, carrying only hunger.

Their time was up.

The earwigs had arrived.

# THIRTY-EIGHT

## *Reach*

The ants carried them up.

They didn't bother to paralyze Ary and her friends this time—it was as if the ants could sense the finality in the air, and that even if Ary, Owl, and Shrimp wanted to run, it wouldn't do them any good. Cold air whistled by Ary's cheeks. The glow-shrooms flickered above, dimmer than before, and then came the rustle of voices, the shuffle of many feet, and the snap of pincers.

*I'm going to get us out of here*, Ary had promised Owl.

She just . . . wasn't sure how.

The ants carried them in a different direction than they'd come before. Tunnels flashed by Ary, and it took everything in her to hold still. Only the pulse of the glow-shrooms above brought comfort, a flicker of hope in that endless, reaching dark.

As quickly as they came, the ants stopped.

Ary looked up—and forgot to breathe.

A cavern unlike anything she had ever seen sprawled before her, so massive it could have fit several of Terra's mushroom fields and the market thrice over. Looping tunnels and pathways danced across the floors and up the walls. Far, far above, glow-shrooms flourished, their light amplified tenfold by crystals that grew in great, clear clusters, refracting the light into a thousand broken rainbows. In some of the cavern pockets, ants slumbered in tiny nests. In others, larvae wriggled, their fleshy white bodies twitching as workers bustled past to check on them. It was an entire kingdom laid before her eyes, thriving far below the soil upon which folk had long walked. It was massive. It was beautiful.

A smell stirred in the air—one she knew all too well—and finally Ary understood why something had smelled sickly sweet ever since she'd entered the ant kingdom.

In front of them, a platform of crystals held a hulking ant Ary knew could only be the Ant Queen herself. She was ten times the size of other ants, the beating heart of the colony around her.

And she was covered in mold.

The Ant Queen was barely moving, her great, shiny carapace spotted with the fuzzy white fungus that had invaded Ary's own mother. She didn't raise her head to look at Ary, Shrimp, and Owl when they entered—instead, the queen lumbered across the platform, moving sluggishly as though she were in pain, to one of the pockets that held the larvae. She crawled in among them and lay down.

Horror coursed through Ary.

The mold was *everywhere*—but not in the way it had been in Terra, creeping upon fields in the night to claim mushrooms and folk alike. The mold was on the ants, it was *in* the ants. All around the cavern, ants slumped against the ground, clung to walls or poised over crystals, their bodies immobile, some of them so covered in decay they were barely recognizable. To her left, a pocket of ant larvae lay entirely still, their nursery bubble completely smoothed over by that familiar stretch of fuzzy white.

Ary began to shake.

She had thought the mold wasn't as bad deeper in the Underground, that surely it was the aboveground it sought, devouring the folk and their fields with eagerness. All this time, she'd held out some faint hope that it was fixable. Maybe only *parts* of their world were lost. Maybe somewhere deeper could be safe.

Maybe, if she failed, it could somehow still be okay.

But the ants were one of the deepest kingdoms of the Underground—and as far as Ary could tell, they had suffered much, much longer than the folk of Terra.

It was wrong. It didn't matter that the ants were about to trade them to the earwigs, that they had never been an ally of the fairies. No one deserved to suffer like this. No one deserved to lose their family.

In the far corner of the cavern, a convoy of earwigs waited. Before them was an utterly pitiful pile of food—little more than tubers and some half-shriveled woody shrooms, from what Ary could see. But the ants approached the food as if the Gardener herself had descended and offered up a blessing. The earwigs rustled, swinging their gazes toward Ary, Shrimp, and Owl, their pincers snipping together with eagerness.

A hollow exhaustion pounded through Ary.

Could she even blame them?

Everyone was desperate.

And everyone was so, so hungry.

The ants deposited them on the ground with an uncharitable thud. The room seemed to narrow as a familiar face approached. Briar walked rigidly, her narrow chin lifted, making a point not to look Ary in the eye as she came to stand in front of her.

"The ants and earwigs have come to an agreement," Briar said mechanically. "You, in exchange for the food. The earwigs will transport you to the newt kingdom."

"What do the newts want with us?"

"I don't know," Briar said. She was clearly lying.

The gears in Ary's mind spun. There had to be some way out of this—some way to save her friends.

"So this is it, then?" Ary asked, searching Briar's face. "What kind of life will you have here, if we never find Atlas?" She gestured around them. "The ants are dying, Briar. I know you see it—and I think you're just as much a prisoner as we are."

Briar looked away. "I already told you, Mossheart. I can't help you."

"I know," Ary said softly. "But I wish I could help *you*."

Briar looked at her, startled, but Ary was staring beyond her now. There was movement in the tunnel the earwigs had come from. A familiar glow she recognized but didn't understand. Her heart began to beat.

"Ary," Owl whispered behind her.

*It couldn't be . . .*

Treacherous hope rooted in Ary. She took one step forward, then another.

Was that smoke she smelled?

"*Ary*," Owl whispered again. She turned, and the fear on Owl's voice froze her in place. "Something feels . . . wrong."

A new voice cracked in the air.

"So this is them, then?"

A newt stood at the mouth of the tunnel.

At first glance, it could have been Sootflank—but, no, this newt was younger, its body sporting fewer scars, and the brightness in its eyes held cruelty where Sootflank's had always burned with tired mirth. The newt took one long, loping step forward and then another. The earwigs practically tripped over themselves to get out of its way, parting like water to tremble themselves against the sides of the tunnel mouth.

Behind Ary, Shrimp let loose a long, uneasy whine.

"All this trouble for a few folk pups," the newt sneered. This newt was smaller than Sootflank, their flanks carrying a strange orange mottling, and the embers that danced across their tail seemed wilder, sharper, and less controlled. "And *that* one must be the Mossheart whelp. I have to say—I expected . . . more."

The newt paused, then continued, "We'll take the other folk too."

Beside Ary, Briar stiffened. "What?"

The newt's smile was sharp and mean. "What good will you do the ants? Look at them—they rot where they stand, and they don't even know it. But our ranks always have need for more fairy dust."

Briar took a step back—and found herself greeted by the pincers of a worker ant who stood behind her. Muttering eagerly, the earwigs clicked among themselves and inched forward.

"Wait," Briar stammered. "There has to be some kind of mistake." She wheeled to look at the sickly Ant Queen, fury and fear warring on her face. "We had a deal!"

"And we made a new one," the newt drawled.

"Fairy dust does not require a living fairy," an earwig said coolly. "May we have that one, Quickspark?"

Ary jolted. *That name.*

The newt's tail gave a lazy slash. Embers scattered everywhere. One of the mold patches struck by an ember sent up a dark plume of smoke. "I hardly care. The newts want the Mossheart pup—do what you will with the other two."

Ary's eyes jumped from the burning mold to the earwigs.

There were only three of them—four, counting Briar, though Ary wasn't sure if she could count Briar just yet—and many, many bugs. But if they could somehow knock them off balance . . . if they could just distract them . . .

The beginnings of a plan clicked together in Ary's mind. It was probably stupid, would almost definitely get them killed, and was *distinctly* un-heroic—

But it was all she had.

"Owl," said Ary. "I want you to reach."

He whipped to look at her. "What?"

Ary turned to him. "The feeling you've always had, the feeling that's only gotten stronger—reach, Owl. Reach for it and *pull*."

Fear washed across his face, and Ary understood. She was maybe the only person who *could* have understood. Because it wasn't confusion that struck terror through Owl; it was clarity. In that moment, Owl Diggs was faced with a choice. He could tell her no; he could continue to ignore the whispers he'd been hearing his whole life and shy away from the inheritance of power Chives had whispered of, ignoring the way the earth shivered when he was filled with fear, forgetting the whispers that once, fairies without wings had been powerful wielders in their own right. He could stay small, and stay the same, and there was a safety in that—a security in being no one. Ary understood that temptation better than anyone.

Or he could reach.

An earwig leaped for Briar. Ary cried out and dove, shoving the other girl out of the way. The earwig crashed against the wall. Below them, Quickspark barked out orders, and the earwigs moved as one, surging toward Ary and her friends in a terrible wave of hungry eyes and snapping pincers.

"*Owl*," cried Ary.

Owl stood with his hands outstretched, his eyes wide, and Ary wondered if he was remembering his parents when they'd been alive and listening to the whispers that so many folk had been unable to hear. Had others once heard those voices? Had they felt that urge to reach back for the thing that had been tugging at their senses their entire life, that pressure in the mind and on the skin and against their lungs that forced them to notice the way the mold grew worse every year, the crops smaller, the fairies sicker?

"I can't do it," Owl said, shaking his head. "I can't—I'm *scared*, Ary."

Ary's throat bobbed. She slid her hand into his and squeezed tight. She couldn't promise Owl safety or wonders or a miracle.

She could only hold his hand and whisper, "I'm scared, too."

*Don't leave*, the squeeze of his fingers seemed to ask.

*Never*, Ary answered with her own grip.

Owl shivered, his head cocked as though he were listening to something only he could hear, the gesture strangely reminiscent of when Gran had spoken to Atlas in Ary's dream. An earwig leaped across the ground, pincers flashing in the watery glow-shroom light.

Owl stretched his free hand toward the dirt.

The earth *groaned*.

Everyone in the cavern paused—the earwigs, Quickspark, even the worker ants that had been pressing them forward. The hair on Ary's arms stood on end.

"I hear you," Owl whispered. "I hear you. I've always heard you, but I'm listening now. We're coming, I promise. So help us—*please*."

And finally, after twelve years of hiding, of turning away from the whispers of the earth, of shying away from murmured warnings of ruin and the constant, prying, desperate *pull* of the ground dying beneath his feet—Owl Diggs reached for the magic in the earth that others had long forgotten. He stretched his fingers the way a drowning fairy would splay out their hand to the precious surface, head cocked to the side, eyes wide as he listened. His pupils dilated.

Across the cavern, Quickspark's fire went out.

"*Stop him*," she bellowed. "*The runt, stop him, before he—*"

"Ary," whispered Owl. "Hold on."

Owl made a fist.

And the earth exploded.

# THIRTY-NINE

## Love, Shouting Louder

As a tiny wingling, Ary had always loved stories about the Gardener's kingdom—a seemingly impossible place where the sky burned blue and strange plants called grass grew in soft, sweeping meadows. But some of the stories had carried darkness, too: stories of fires started not by newts, but strikes of power from the sky. Tales of floods and storms of ice that frosted the world in a frigid, heavy coat.

Stories of a strange thing called an *earthquake*.

Stories Ary now understood.

The ground was bubbling. Everywhere Ary looked, bits of earth bucked and heaved. Ants and earwigs went flying alike as the cavern groaned. Overhead, a great *crack* snapped through the air as the stone ceiling rent in half. A patch of glow-shrooms tumbled through the air before splattering on the ground, their precious, lifesaving phosphorus leaking over the stone.

Owl's hand went limp in Ary's. Her wings flared awkwardly behind her, knocking her off balance as she tried to keep him from collapsing.

"Owl?" she demanded. "Owl, are you okay? *Owl?*"

"Ary?" Owl was very, very pale. "I . . . don't feel so good."

"It's okay. You're going to be okay." Ary's heart was beating too hard. *Shrimp!*

In a heartbeat, Shrimp was there—shaking with terror, beady eyes wide, but there all the same.

Ary's body seemed to move on its own accord, her earlier fatigue vanishing as adrenaline pumped through her. She pointed to Owl, and Shrimp leaped, scooping up the fairy boy with a flick of his legs. An earwig snapped to their left, and Ary yelped, swinging out blindly with her Seedling shovel. It cracked against the earwig's shell, and the massive bug staggered back with a whine. She'd snapped its antenna.

Ary whirled. Briar was standing behind her, staring at Ary and Owl with her mouth hanging open as though she'd seen a ghost.

"Briar!" Ary shouted. "Get on Shrimp!"

It was the wrong thing to say. Instead of moving, Briar put her fists on her hips. "And why would I go with you? What makes you think—"

Ary did not have time for this.

"Gardener help me, never mind!" Ary shouted. "Get eaten for all I care!"

If Briar didn't want to listen to her, *fine.* Thanks to Owl's temporary distraction, the cavern was in chaos. Ants scurried to and fro, fussing over the queen and ferrying larvae to safety. Earwigs screamed in fury, flipped over on their backs, pincers snapping and legs whirling as they tried to right themselves. Her eyes swept the cavern.

Quickspark hadn't moved.

The newt stood patiently, blocking the tunnel through which she'd arrived. The pieces of Ary's absolutely terrible plan swirled through her mind. That tunnel was the exit. It had to be.

As if sensing Ary's eyes on her, Quickspark lifted her head, her stare meeting Ary's. Her mouth curled in the coldest of smiles.

"Shrimp," said Ary. "When I tell you to, run through that tunnel as fast as you can."

"Burn," protested Shrimp in a panicked whine. *"Bad."*

"It'll be okay, I promise." Her throat bobbed. "I'm going to clear the way."

"What?" Briar yelped. She hadn't left—but she hadn't gotten on Shrimp, either. She'd remained where she was, the stubborn look on her face giving way to concern. "Are you absolutely nuts?"

Ary ignored her. "When I draw her away—you take Owl and Briar, and you *run*, okay, Shrimp? You run as fast as you can, and you don't stop."

"Mossheart," Briar hissed. "You can't—"

"I can," Ary said, and for some reason, she believed it. She turned toward the tunnel where Quickspark waited, her heart threatening to pound out of her chest. As the earwigs approached, she remembered how she had felt in the Underlake. So small, so useless.

And she remembered Gran.

Had it really only been a few days ago? Ary recalled the way Gran had frozen, small and old and weaponless as the rest of them, the shudder that had passed through her, and then what came after, when Gran fell away and Wren Moss-heart returned, calmly calling flames from fairy dust and leading them to safety. It had been Wren who saved them, steady in the face of danger, not an ounce of fear in her as she faced down fire and earwigs alike.

Or so Ary had thought.

All this time, she'd thought Wren and her gran were two different people. The fearless girl hero, and the bitter former hero who Terra had forgotten. But what if they were the same?

Gran had moved as though her frail body alone could shield Ary from the earwigs. Ary remembered the way Gran had looked at her, jaw rigid and eyes steely, as she ordered her to run. Ary hadn't understood the look in her eyes then, the hard resolve coupled with fierce determination.

It had been love.

What if Gran had never stopped being afraid, and she had tried to protect her friends anyway?

What if that was what bravery was—not a lack of fear, but just love shouting louder?

Ary looked back at her friends. A tremor rolled through her. Her hands ghosted the bucket she'd taken to wearing on her head, the Seedling shovels she'd carried in place of weapons.

Ary didn't know if she could find Atlas. She didn't know if she could be what Terra needed—and she didn't care. Because hero or no hero, Atlas or no Atlas, she was Ary Mossheart.

And Ary Mossheart was going to protect her friends.

"All right," Ary whispered to no one at all. "I get it now. All right."

The earwigs had begun to right themselves. They drew back, watching warily, but Ary paid them no mind. It was Quickspark's attention she wanted. Her eyes darted from the newt to the mold patch that was still smoldering. She recalled the way Sootflank had lit up the dark—his flames hadn't burned as hot as Quickspark's, but they had been just as bright. They'd been *controlled*.

And it was control that Quickspark seemed to lack.

"Shrimp," Ary said. "Get ready."

Behind her, Shrimp whined.

"Mossheart!" Briar shouted, her wings flared wide as she stood amid the chaos.

Ary looked back at her, again gripped by a grief she didn't quite understand. It was a shame she'd probably never see Briar again. She was frustrating—but so was Owl. It disturbed Ary how badly she wanted that friendship with Briar.

That quiet understanding, a loyalty built on love, the choice to stay because you wanted to, not because it was required or foretold or *expected*.

Friendship, a family, a home. So many things she'd never quite had—so many things she probably never would.

"Mossheart," Briar demanded again. "What are you planning?"

"Something really, really stupid," Ary said wearily.

And then Ary turned and began to run.

# FORTY

## *A Very Bad Plan*

The earwigs sent up a collective *hiss* as she raced forward, bucket clanking noisily on her head, Seedling shovels bouncing on her hip. Ary kept her eyes locked on Quickspark. When she drew near enough, Ary plucked a shovel from her hip, wound up, and *threw*.

The shovel sailed through the air, a creaky, rusty beacon of hope—and plonked Quickspark directly on the head.

The newt snarled as she jumped backward. Embers flared around her, catching another patch of mold on the walls. Hazy smoke wound through the air. Quickspark pinned her burning gaze on Ary.

"And what," she said scathingly, "did you expect *that* to do?"

Ary gulped. She knelt and closed her fingers around a chunk of crystal that had broken when Owl had done . . . well, whatever had just happened. She still wasn't sure. Ary looked at the orange mottling Quickspark's skin, the sparks that flared around her, and remembered the pain in Sootflank's eyes when the earwigs had spoken, the way he had spoken of losing family, too.

Of losing a daughter.

Ary didn't know whether to laugh or cry. How fitting that Sootflank had betrayed them, and now the daughter he'd betrayed had returned to punish Ary twice over. A funny kind of grief strangled Ary. Here she was at the end of the world, facing down death and fire, and all she wanted to do was look at Quickspark and say, *He left me, too.*

Ary forced herself to meet Quickspark's stare, recalling Sootflank's terrible temper.

"I'll give you one chance, newt," Ary proclaimed, pitching her voice to a false bravado she hoped would irritate Quickspark, though her hands shook like mad. "Let my friends go."

"Let them *go?*" Quickspark snorted. "And why would I do that?"

Ary shrugged. "Probably easier than getting beaten by a fairy. But I understand if you're scared."

*"Scared?"* The flames around Quickspark's tail snapped out, catching another patch of mold. The earwigs closest to her gave panicked whines and skittered away. "I'll show you scared. When I'm through with you, little folk, the only thing you'll know is *fear.*"

"Well," Ary yelped. "You'll have to catch me first!"

And then Ary wound her arm and threw the crystal as hard as she could.

Unlike the Seedling shovel, which was little more than a rusty, light piece of metal, the crystal was heavy, and it was *sharp*. It hit Quickspark with a *crack*, and the newt let loose a cry that sounded a little too like pain for Ary's comfort. When Quickspark raised her head, her left eye was bloody.

"Shrimp!" Ary cried. "Run!"

The pill bug gave a terrified whine and leaped forward—and Ary took off in the opposite direction. The worker ants all around them scattered, confused and scared of the upheaval in their midst. Smoke writhed in the air, and the scent of burning mold lingered. Ary pulled her shirt over her nose and mouth.

Behind her came a furious roar—and then fire swept through the cavern as Quickspark gave chase.

All of Ary's thoughts drained away. There was only the crackle of fire behind her, and the ground ahead of her. She ran as fast as she could, barreling back in the direction they'd come, legs pumping, arms flailing, wings crackling uselessly as the paper covering them dragged against the air.

Ary dove sideways, whirling.

"You're *slow* for a newt," she gasped. "Sootflank was as cranky as you, but at least he was fast."

The mention of Sootflank seemed to enrage Quickspark even more than being hit in the face with a rock.

"*How*," seethed the newt, the flames swirling around her spiking wider, higher, hotter. "*Dare. You.*"

"Now that I think about it," Ary chattered. "Your flames look so wimpy. Sootflank's were so much *hotter*."

"You little brat," Quickspark screamed, her tail lashing.

Ribbons of flame spiraled around and away from her. One of them slammed right into a pack of earwigs that were waiting against the wall. They scattered, crying out and hissing as they fled the embers clinging to their shells. She leaped for Ary, and Ary scrambled away. Sweat beaded down her skin and lined her palms. Her lungs burned, and a dizzy feeling pounded through her head.

*The mold,* she realized dizzily. *The mold is turning into toxic gas.*

But ahead of her—a familiar gust of cold air, a sense of yawning nothingness. Ary turned her face toward that breeze and gulped it in.

Behind her came another flash of heat, the snarl of flames growing ever closer.

Ary turned.

The entire Ant Court was in chaos.

Fire roared everywhere, sweeping over mold-stricken ants and healthy ones alike. The earwigs had scattered, some of them running in circles with flames licking up their shells, some of them staggering, their bodies twitching as they inhaled the burning mold fumes.

*Part one of the worst plan I've ever had: complete.*

It was part two that Ary was worried about.

A shadow fell across her.

Ary looked up and forced herself to smile. She remembered the way Gran had almost looked as though she was *enjoying* facing off with the earwigs—the strange exhilaration that had filled her, the wild confidence of standing against something impossible and still trying to win.

She was starting to understand.

"I might have given you a quick death," Quickspark snarled, stalking forward. Her tail whipped, and a ribbon of flame snapped directly toward Ary. Ary scrambled sideways, gasping as heat singed her wings. The smell of smoke curled around her. "But now I'll take my time. I am going to enjoy this."

The air ahead of her grew colder.

*Just a little bit closer.*

Ary danced sideways again, spun, and fixed Quickspark with her best imitation of Owl's most annoying smile. "I don't know why, but I thought you'd be stronger than Soot-flank!"

Fire ripped through the world.

It came for Ary too quickly this time—an endless rolling wave of inferno intent on devouring everything in its path. Time slowed. Ary's body seemed to move of its own accord, her muscles acting on what her mind had been too scared to promise. As Quickspark leaped, fire swirled around her, embers snapping from her tail and white-hot flames licking around her body. And instead of leaping forward, or sideways, Ary leaped *back*.

Her feet met only air.

As soon as she jumped, Ary flared her wings—her useless, bound, papery wings. They caught on the current of upward air for the breath of a second, just long enough for Ary to fish her remaining Seedling shovel from her hip.

And this time when she plummeted, she was ready.

Ary twisted, smoke flashing by as she fell. She swung out with the shovel and struck earth. The shovel bit into the cavern wall. From above and behind her came a roar and a flash of heat as Quickspark leaped into the ant pit—and fell.

Ary clung to the wall, her heart hammering against her ribs. From below, after what seemed far too long, came a heavy *thud*. Sweat beaded down her neck and lined her palm. She needed to climb back up—it was only a few feet, and she didn't know how long the shovel would hold her weight. Ignoring the way stones cut into her hands, she dug her free hand into the dirt, and dug her toes in, too.

And yet still she waited.

*What is wrong with me?*

Quickspark had just tried to *set her on fire*. She'd been ready to feed Owl and Briar to a bunch of earwigs. And yet—

*Gardener curse me.*

"Hey," Ary called into the dark. "You alive?"

A screech came below—followed by a flash of fire. For a brief, perilous second, Ary could see Quickspark where she crouched at the bottom of the pit Ary had slept in only a few hours prior. She was spitting mad, but otherwise unharmed.

Ary felt foolish for being relieved.

"Okay," Ary called. "Well, since you're not dead—I'm going to, um, leave."

"Where is Sootflank?" Quickspark shouted. Some of the mean edge had left her voice.

Ary winced and kept climbing.

"What did he say? Is he helping you?"

*Don't*, Ary told herself.

*"Where is my father?"*

Ary froze. She turned, looking down into the endless stretch of dark. Could Quickspark see her, or was she also looking into the shadows, waiting for a stranger to give her answers about her family?

"Gone," Ary whispered. "If it makes you feel better, he betrayed me, too."

Only silence answered her.

A part of her almost felt bad for Quickspark. Ary knew nothing about newt lives—if, like beetles, their life span was only a flicker compared to the life of the folk, or if they were like the glow-moths, seemingly immortal with their long lives. But Wren Mossheart had entered the Underground sixty years ago. Quickspark *had* to have been young when her father betrayed everything she'd ever known to help a stranger who repaid him with her own betrayal.

"Mossheart," Quickspark murmured from somewhere down in the deep, deep dark. "I will get out of this pit. I will find you. And when I do, I will burn everything you love to ashes."

Ary didn't have it in her to be angry. She only felt tired.

There was nothing she could say to Quickspark to ease the bite of her pain or the burn of her hatred.

And she had a terrarium to break out of. Somehow.

"I'm sorry," Ary told the newt, and she meant it. "I'm sorry for all of it."

And then Ary pulled herself out of the pit and left Soot-flank's daughter behind.

# FORTY-ONE

## *Maybe a Fool*

The entire cavern burned.

Fire was everywhere—racing over the floor, licking up the walls, consuming all the bugs left behind. A few ants scurried past, frantically carrying larvae down the side tunnels, away from the flames quickly overtaking the court they'd called home. Ary didn't see the queen—whether she had escaped or burned, she didn't know. Shrimp and Owl were nowhere to be found, and Ary's shoulders drooped in relief. At least they had made it. No matter what happened, Owl knew about Atlas.

*I'm sorry*, Ary wanted to say to every ant scurrying past her. *You were all just trying to survive, like us. I'm so sorry.*

She'd never understood why Gran had seemed so haunted. So *bitter*. In school, they'd been taught about the fearsome creatures Gran had battled, the earwigs, spiders, and giant fairy-eating ground worms she'd defeated. It had sounded glorious and brilliant.

But there was nothing glorious about this. Even though the ants were technically her enemy, Ary had won nothing here. She'd merely ensured that any ant that *did* survive had yet another reason to hate the Mossheart name.

Fumes of mold-infested smoke curled on the floor. Ary pulled her shirt back up over her mouth and nose, breathing as shallowly as she could. She couldn't think about the mold spores that were landing on her, slipping up her nose, filling her lungs the same way they had Mama's—

*No*, a familiar voice whispered. *Pull yourself together, Canary. You're a Mossheart. Act like it.*

Ary blinked several times to clear the smoke from her eyes, dropped down, and began to crawl across the cavern floor. The stone bit into her palms and cut her knees. A dizzy feeling pounded in her head, and nausea swept through her. She was so tired. She just wanted to lie down.

*No.*

Ary kept crawling. She couldn't see anything. An ant bumped against her, legs skittering across the floor, antennae twitching as it raced through the cavern. Another nearly trampled her. Ary crawled faster. Was she even headed in the right direction anymore? She couldn't see anything, couldn't *think*. The fire was all around her; the fire was inside her. Her skin chafed, and her wings ached, their delicate, papery covering curling in the heat. Overhead, a collection of glow-shrooms burst into flames and plummeted. They slammed to the floor right in front of Ary, and she flinched. Cinders sparked against her skin.

And then her wings were on fire.

It happened in a flash—one moment her wings had been fine, and then the fire caught. Ary screamed and threw herself to the ground, ants and fumes and Quickspark forgotten as she rolled frantically on the stone floor. The flames were out almost instantly; but the terror of the sight of her wings on fire kept her frozen. Ary lay on the cavern floor, fear and exhaustion pounding through her, and for a brief moment, she wondered what would happen if she didn't move.

Maybe Owl could be what Atlas needed.

Maybe someone else could fix it.

And then that voice returned—not her own, not Atlas', not Mama's. The voice she had heard her entire life, the voice she'd loved and loathed and resented and longed for.

Gran.

Not Wren. Not the girl of her memories, the hero, bold and brilliant, but *Gran*, her gran, tired and cranky and faulty and *hers*.

*Canary Mossheart*, Gran's voice demanded. *Get. Up.*

Ary's hands found purchase on the stone floor. She forced herself forward, fumbling uselessly in the smoke and the fumes. She coughed violently, her throat burning. But Gran's voice was there, clear as day, as if she were actually with Ary.

As if somewhere, somehow, she knew what was happening.

*Move*, Gran demanded. *Don't slow down—don't look ahead. Don't think about breathing. Just move. One hand in front of the other. Forward, Canary.*

Tears dripped down Ary's chin.

*Forward.*

The fire was behind her; the fire was all around. She had no way of knowing if her wings were safe, and maybe it was for the best that the smoke was too thick for her to look back and see just how badly they'd been burned.

*Forward, little one.*

*Always.*

Her hand bumped into an ant. No, not an ant—something with skin. A girl, a *fairy*, curled in a ball.

Briar lay on the cavern floor, her hands knotted tightly into fists, her beautiful wings furled against her body in a protective shield. She wasn't moving. Ary put a shaking hand to Briar's throat. Her pulse thumped, barely there.

Ary gripped Briar's shoulder and shook her.

"Briar," she rasped.

Her head lolled.

"Briar, *wake up*."

Her eyes fluttered briefly. Briar looked at Ary with a foggy gaze—and then she was gone again, slipping back into unconsciousness.

*"Briar!"*

Panic stuttered through Ary. There was no way she could

move Briar on her own, and it was clear the fairy wasn't waking up anytime soon. Heat pressed in on her from all sides, and Ary knew that if she didn't do something soon, the fire would catch her, and it'd be over.

But it would require leaving Briar behind.

Ary hovered over the other fairy. She had no reason to save her. She barely *knew* the girl. It was the smart move to abandon her. It wasn't even selfish, because staying with Briar meant risking her life, and the entire terrarium was at stake.

What was the life of one person against everyone else's?

Ary's blood ran cold.

She could no longer feel the heat of the flames, the burn of the smoke. The thought rattled around in her brain, foreign and unwanted and feeling terrible, achingly—heroic.

One life, for the future of many.

One person, against the world.

It was the choice Gran had made, was it not?

Ary hovered over Briar; the flames cracked louder. She had the dizzying sense she was about to fall, as though she was poised atop the thorn fence that encircled Terra once more, one foot dangling in the world beyond, one foot dangling in the village where she'd lived her entire life. One small tip to the left, and Ary's world had changed forever.

That was how she felt now, staring at Briar, fire and smoke and the promise of escape slipping by her.

*Leave her*, something in her willed. *For everyone else.*

But Ary had not come to the Underground to save the terrarium.

She had not come here to save every fairy in Terra.

She'd only come here to save one.

Gran had declared Mama a lost cause. Terra had abandoned Papa when he was at his worst. The village had let Gran suffer in squalor despite the sacrifices she'd made for them. Ary's entire life had been an endless cycle of the sacrifice of one for the benefit of many.

All along, she had been trying to be the hero. To be the next Mossheart savior, a fairy worthy of inheriting Gran's legacy. But Gran's legacy had been a *lie*, and even Terra's former heroes had walked the line between hero and villain more than anyone cared to admit.

Being a hero meant letting Briar die.

It meant letting *Mama* die.

And if that was what being a hero was—Ary didn't want it.

So Ary Mossheart dropped to her knees, wrapped her arms around the granddaughter of the woman *her* grandmother had betrayed, and gave her a great, desperate shake.

"Briar Sunleaf," Ary said furiously. "You will *not* die."

Smoke pressed in all around them, and the fires raged, and Ary did not leave Briar behind. Instead, she dragged her across the cavern floor, walking backward through the soot and the smoke, until her foot dipped lower and she found what she sought. One of the larvae nurseries, long empty, carved deep into the floors of the Ant Court. Ary stumbled and dragged Briar down into the pit with her, careful not to scratch her wings against the stone floors. It wasn't nearly as deep as the pit she'd tricked Quickspark into leaping inside—but maybe it would be enough.

*And maybe I'm a fool. Maybe I'll burn alongside her and the rest of the ants.*

Smoke writhed above, and Ary's head throbbed. The fires crackled closer. They reached the bottom of the pit, and her foot struck something soft and wet. Revulsion shuddered through her, but still Ary kept moving, dragging Briar down, until they were both nearly submerged in the thick, wet mold that blanketed the bottom of the pit. Ary's stomach flipped at the disgusting irony, her skin crawling as she forced herself to be still, the feathery, sticky texture of the mold clinging to every part of her. Briar's head bobbed, and Ary wrapped her arms around Briar's waist, folding herself against the soft lattice of her wings. She smelled of smoke and earth and something sweet—something Ary had known, once, but couldn't remember.

Something that smelled not quite like home, but the memory of one.

As the fires raged on, and the Ant Court burned, darkness crept over Ary while the smoke took its toll. She pressed her back against the wall, wrapping her arms around Briar and holding her from behind, lest she tip over.

"Live," Ary whispered. Spots swam in front of her eyes. Gran's voice was long gone now; it was just her, Briar, and the fires above. "Live, Briar Sunleaf, so we can fix what our grandmothers broke. Not because we're heroes. Not because we're chosen. But because we're all they've got."

# FORTY-TWO

## *Fine!*

Ary woke to ash.

It coated her hair, her skin, even her eyelashes. For a dizzying, terrifying moment, when she inhaled, only ash met her lungs. She coughed violently, gasping as she drank in clean air. Her eyes stung, filled with cold grit. Beside her, someone else began to stir. The world crept back in—the Ant Court, Quickspark, Shrimp and Owl disappearing . . .

"*You*," a familiar voice snarled.

Exhaustion thrummed through Ary as she opened her eyes. "Hello, Briar."

Briar and Ary were submerged up to their waists in a disgusting mixture of mold and soot. Briar looked around wildly, her chest heaving, wings flared. "Where am I? What's going on? What did you—" Her face fell, and she looked up at Ary, her nose scrunching in an expression that, in any other circumstances, would have been irritatingly cute. "The last thing I remember is an ant colliding with me, and falling. I hit my head, then . . ." Her voice trailed away. "What *happened*?"

Ary's throat ached. "Shrimp and Owl escaped—I think.

I . . . lured Quickspark away and, uh, tricked her into jumping into that pit the ants threw us in."

"Good," snorted Briar.

Ary fought off a smile. "When I tried to run, the entire cavern was up in flames—and I found you."

"You let your friends escape." Briar's brow furrowed. "And you stayed behind to save me."

"I guess." Ary was growing more uncomfortable by the second.

Briar looked at her, her gaze pinning Ary to where she sat. Even though Briar was singed and covered in soot, her piercing stare was brighter than a thousand glow-shroom lamps. "Why?"

Why indeed? There was a good chance Ary had jeopardized everything. She had no clue how long they had been asleep or if she would find Shrimp and Owl again. Maybe they were already dead, and this was some strange purgatory.

"Because you needed help," Ary said quietly. "And it was the right thing to do."

Briar blinked. She opened her mouth, paused, and closed it again. Something Ary didn't understand flashed across Briar's face as she peered at her, eyes narrowed, lips quirking. She stared at Ary for so long that it was beginning to veer out of the territory of uncomfortable into downright *weird* when Briar rolled her eyes, slammed her fists onto her knees, and jumped up.

"*Ugh!*" Briar snapped. "Fine! You win."

Ary stared at Briar, bewildered. The fairy girl flapped her wings, sending ash clouding through the air, and then scrambled out of the pit. For the briefest moment, Ary thought Briar had gone.

Briar's face poked over the edge as she scowled. "Well, what are you waiting for? Let's go."

"I'm sorry," Ary said dumbly. "What is happening?"

Briar made a noise of utter contempt. "What do you think is happening? You help me, I help you."

Ary's heart began to pound. "You don't mean—"

"Yes," Briar said grimly. "I'm going to lead you to Atlas."

Ary said nothing. She was too afraid that if she spoke, Briar would change her mind.

So instead, Wren Mossheart's granddaughter reached up her hand—and with a scowl, the granddaughter of the girl Wren had left behind pulled her up into the light.

They left the Ant Court in silence.

Nothing remained for them in the cavern where Briar had spent the last few years of her life, and with only two days to reach Atlas, there was no point in lingering. A part of Ary had hoped Shrimp and Owl would return—but the Ant Court stayed empty. After Briar collected Ary's cracked glow-shroom lamp from where the ants had dropped it, Ary had crept back to the pit she'd tricked Quickspark into

324

leaping down, and found it empty save for her Seedling shovel winking in the wall. Ary had wriggled it free, her eyes on the blank pit floor. Sootflank's daughter had escaped, and Ary knew with an uneasy flip of her stomach it wasn't the last time they would see her. Something still didn't sit right. Why *did* the newts want to prevent them from reaching Atlas so badly?

With a stony expression, Briar led Ary away from the Ant Court and down.

They walked in silence, a strange, amicable quiet stretching between them. She and Briar were not friends, not by a long shot, but there seemed to be a mutual understanding as they wove through the abandoned tunnels of the Underground that for now, they were on the same side.

The ground sloped sharply downhill as they walked, and soon Ary's calves began to burn as she was forced to walk leaning back, lest she topple forward. Her wings ached and itched something terrible, but every time she scratched them, it only made it worse. And it was so *loud*.

Briar eyed her with a knowing expression. "They must be close."

"I've been hearing that for a year now." Ary's face flushed. It was strange to speak in the never-ending gloom that stretched before them, their voices warped and made tinny by the curve of the long, dirt tunnels. "What's it like? Having wings?"

"Like breathing," Briar said instantly. "It feels right. Grandmother once told me . . . she told me what they do to fairies back in Terra." Her throat bobbed. "Is it true?"

Memories flashed in Ary's mind, of the shriveled wing stubs that clung to the shoulders of every folk in Terra. Of fairies younger than her, showing up to school to flaunt their wings, only to return a few days later, bearing bandaged stubs and red-rimmed eyes. It always seemed like a light had been stolen from any folk who'd had their wings cut—their personalities seemed subdued, their smiles duller. Even their hair seemed to lose its shine. As if when they lost their wings—and with it, their magic—they'd lost a piece of their souls, too.

"Yes," whispered Ary. "They cut our wings as soon as they unfurl."

"Why?"

Ary blinked several times. "To survive, I guess. We use the fairy dust from ground-up wings for well . . . everything. Our crops, our medicines, our water."

"Did it work?" Briar asked. "You lose your wings, but you stop the mold?"

The potatoes rotting in the field. The mold. The folk they'd lost, the critters in the Underground who'd died. All this pain, all this suffering, and for what—a lie? To ensure that folk older than her didn't have to live differently, didn't have to struggle, didn't have to *try*? Ary's generation had inherited a dying world long past saving.

She wondered, faintly, what might have happened had someone even before Gran found Atlas.

Had the folk headed Underground the moment the mold appeared, instead of brushing it away as a problem for the future, for a fairy not yet born.

"No," whispered Ary. "No, it didn't work. Everything is still dying—and all we have to show for it are a bunch of wing stubs and mold."

She and Briar did not speak for a long, long time.

# FORTY-THREE

## *What Lives Below*

In the dark, Ary lost all track of time.

Here, in the Underground, without Owl's cheery updates or Shrimp's murmured counting of the hours, she had no sense of what day it was, or how many hours they had left. Several times, she had the terrifying thought that they were too late, but then she pushed it away. Surely they would know. Surely they would *feel* it.

Or maybe that was how a world died—not in a massive, dramatic moment, but quietly, softly, fading out like a light, so that once people realized it was gone, it was too late.

Her only solace was the glow-shroom lamp. It had grown so, so dim, faltering as the magic linked to their world also faded. Every time it sputtered, they put on an extra burst of speed.

Ary walked, and Briar led.

She didn't ask the fairy girl how she knew where Atlas was; something told her even Briar wasn't certain. Every once in a while Briar stopped, her beautiful wings fluttering behind her, head cocked to the side as she tried to remember the way. The mold faded as they continued on, until the great patches were little more than blips of white, and then nothing at all. Briar hummed a song under her breath as she navigated, arms swinging loosely by her sides.

After a few hours, Ary realized with a jolt where she'd heard it before.

*What roots shall bloom,*
*And what blooms must die,*
*Beneath this city to which we flee.*
*By the Gardener's hand,*
*A false world spins,*
*But in its dust,*
*We find the key.*

Briar was humming the Gardener's Warning.

"Did your grandmother teach you that?" Ary asked, her heart fit to pound out of her chest as her next question crouched behind her teeth. *Did she ever figure out what it means?*

Briar hesitated for a long, reluctant moment. "No. But I did learn it from her."

Understanding blossomed in the cracks Briar's words left. Briar stiffened, as if waiting for Ary to pry, to demand, but Ary knew better than anyone what it meant to live in the shadow of a hero haunted by legacy. Whether Briar had learned the melody from Dracaena's mumbled nightmares, from eavesdropping, or from her journals themselves—it didn't matter.

Briar gave Ary that funny look again and, for the first time, dropped back to walk alongside her.

The outright hostility between them had eased—but there was still a strange, electric tension crackling in the air every time she neared Ary. But instead of a sharp quip, Briar simply walked beside her, sighing occasionally, fisting and unfisting her hands. After the fourth dramatic sigh, Ary couldn't take it anymore.

"What is it?" she demanded.

Briar worried her lip with her teeth. "You mentioned someone named Sootflank."

Ary blinked.

"I started reading the journals," Briar added reluctantly. "And I think he and my grandmother were . . . friends." A muscle in her jaw twitched. "She never told me."

Ary's heart did a painful little squeeze. She forced herself to keep her eyes fixed ahead, her hands knotted into fists.

"There's a lot my gran never told me," Ary said quietly. "A lot she never told anyone, apparently."

She didn't quite know where this confession had come from. Maybe it was a bid for peace—maybe it was something more selfish. But every time she looked at Briar, she found herself bursting with questions. The strange history stretched behind them was a confusing, muddy thing, but it was shared, in its own confounding way. They were total strangers; they had only known each other for two days.

Yet something about Briar made Ary feel like they'd already shared a lifetime.

As they descended, the silence between Ary and Briar warmed, then broke entirely. Quietly, Briar began to tell Ary of the life she'd live in the Underground—first with Dracaena and the folk who'd lived outside of Terra's walls, and then, the last few years, alone. Mold had wiped out their small encampment, striking with a ferocity only now reaching Terra. The ants had kidnapped Briar when she'd headed deeper Underground in search of food, and it had been easier to live with the enemy she knew than to face the unknown.

Ary thought of the mold-stricken encampment she'd seen in her dream, and her heart squeezed. She had been so terrified facing the mold these last few years—but at least she had Mama. At least she had Shrimp, and Owl, and Sootflank. Even Tulip and Basil in all their selfishness. Briar had been alone for so long. Could Ary blame her for being mistrustful?

Her heart squeezed, picturing Shrimp's gentle worry, and Owl's excited face. She hoped they would be okay. There had been so much fire, and what if the earwigs had followed them—

*Don't think about that*, she told herself fiercely. Of course they'd be okay. If there was anything she knew about Owl, it was that he knew how to survive. He and Shrimp would protect each other. She'd find them again.

She had to.

The farther they walked, the more Ary understood. Briar was not just prickly—she was lonely and grieving a grandmother who she was just learning she'd barely known.

Ary might not have lived her last few years alone in the Underground, but she knew what it meant to realize someone you loved had been hiding a piece of themselves your entire life. She knew, more than anyone, how badly it stung.

Briar turned a corner. "When you gave me the journals . . . I started to skim some of them. They . . ." Her voice fell away, and Ary wondered if Briar was replaying her memories of her grandmother in a new light, the way she had. Had her grandmother carried a quiet, unrelenting grief? A distance time had never allowed her to shake? Had Briar chalked it up to her also being a tired old hero, long wounded by war? Maybe Dracaena had loved Briar from behind the same glass wall from which Gran had tried to love Ary, and it had been a false comfort, to reason that it was a price to be paid across generations for the acts of a hero.

"They loved each other," Briar said finally. "Our grandmothers."

"They did," said Ary, and knew it was the truth.

"So why leave her behind?" Briar blurted, the strained

note on her voice edging toward desperation. "Why leave *her*, out of everyone, and never come back?"

"I don't know," Ary admitted. "But . . . I had this dream— Briar, my gran found Atlas. She was willing to give her life, and Atlas *sent her away*." She took a shuddering breath. "I know it doesn't change anything. I know it doesn't erase any of the pain, and it definitely doesn't make it right. But it matters, I think, that she tried. I think there's something we're all missing. That it wasn't as simple as my gran leaving yours behind."

Briar looked down the tunnel. "I think you're right."

Ary nearly face-planted.

She was so startled she tripped over a rock. Briar grabbed her arm and jerked her upright. Ary spun, and they were nearly nose-to-nose, Briar's chest heaving, her fingers strangely warm on Ary's skin.

"Careful," Briar deadpanned. "You can't die. Yet."

Ary jumped away as though Briar had burned her.

If Briar noticed Ary's odd reaction, she didn't comment. She scuffed a patch of dirt and nodded ahead. The tunnels ahead were far narrower, twisting and sloping in odd directions, as if they'd been carved by worms. All of the mold had vanished, too; now it was only empty earth and old dust. After a lifetime of being plagued by the ever-growing fungus, its absence almost felt foreboding.

"Those tunnels mean we're almost in centipede territory,"

said Briar. "Don't look at me like that. They all died out decades ago. Come on—Atlas isn't much farther."

Ary followed her in a daze.

*I think you're right.*

Such simple words, yet they meant everything. Ary had spent her entire life confused by the coldness Gran wielded like a weapon, confounded by the almost godlike pedestal Terra placed her on. But something about the cruelty of leaving the Underworld to die just because she *could* had been too much. It was one thing for Gran to have failed; it was another for her to have chosen that failure without a scrap of remorse.

*Does it even matter, if she tried, and she's sorry?* a voice in her pushed back. *She lied. She failed. You walk through the graveyard whose plots she dug all the same.*

Ary didn't know. All she knew was that she loved Gran and hated her. All she knew was that the woman whose shadow she'd been raised in had failed her in a thousand tiny ways, but she had tried, too.

And that mattered.

They looked at each other, Mossheart and Sunleaf, each of them a living, breathing mirror of a different woman's past. All around them was nothing but an endless expanse of dirt, the caverns carving through the underbelly of this world long abandoned. Their footprints had left a trail in the dust behind them, two tiny sets in a wide, empty world as they made their way down through the dark.

Ary had a feeling she knew exactly who had last walked these tunnels, and why.

"Briar," Ary said urgently. "We're going to figure it out, okay? I know we're not friends—"

"I literally do not know you," Briar said. "And even if I did, we would not be friends. You're annoying."

Ary glared at her.

"Okay, okay." Briar put her hands up in mock surrender, softening. "I'm sorry. I don't know how to deal with . . . all this."

Ary wasn't sure if she meant the terrarium, Atlas, their grandmothers, all of it, or none. She didn't ask. It hardly mattered.

Ary kicked a rock down the tunnel. "If it helps, I also think you're annoying."

Briar rolled her eyes. "Whatever, Mossheart." She turned away with a huff, her wings shuddering—and stiffened. *"Look out!"*

The wall immediately to Ary's left groaned as something heavy slammed into it from the other side. Dirt flew in every direction, stones raining down, and then the earth *cracked* as a creature forced its way through. Ary lost her balance as the very ground tilted beneath her. Dust filled the air, turning the tunnel into an impassable haze of brown.

Ary looked up, and her eyes met a set of mandibles as a massive centipede reared over her and lunged.

# FORTY-FOUR

*Don't. Move.*

*"Centipede!"* Briar cried. *"Run!"*

The tunnel was chaos.

Ary threw herself sideways right as the centipede crashed into the earth. A terrible, pungent smell filled the air, and something deep and primal in her understood instantly, shrinking away in terror. *Venom.*

It was like the smoke that had plagued the Ant Court, but worse—heavy and cloying, filling her eyes and mouth with grit. Ary crawled on her hands and knees, panic lighting up every part of her body. A *whoosh* of air passed right over her. She had heard legends of the centipedes that lurked deep, deep in the Underground, preying only on stray ants and bugs that skittered toward the bottom of their world. No one actually thought they were real. The folk had been so preoccupied by their fight with the newts and the ear-wigs, their scorn for pill bugs and moths, their indifference to the lone trapdoor spider or wandering beetle, that the hundred-legged monsters of myth had felt just like that. A *myth.*

Until now.

"Ary!" Briar cried, somewhere to her left. "Where are you?"

"Here!" Ary cried. She kept crawling, her wings flapping uselessly in the dust, weighing her down. Her fingers struck something hard and cool. *Shrimp?* Her heart leaped. He was okay! Surely that meant Owl was, too—

A beady-eyed head swiveled around to face her, mandibles flashing as it sized her up and *hissed.*

*Not Shrimp.*

Ary cried out and rolled away. The centipede struck out at her, missing by barely an inch. It hit the wall instead, and Ary scrambled away, crawling on her hands and knees as fast as she could. She could hear Briar shouting, but she couldn't *see* anything—

The ground beneath her shuddered. Different, this time—not the tremor of many approaching feet or the groan of wild magic buried deep in the earth when someone who cared to listen finally called back. The walls shuddered, the ground tilted, and Ary realized a second too late what was about to happen.

"The tunnel!" she cried. "It's going to—"

With a groan, the ceiling collapsed.

Dirt rained down from every angle. Ary cried out, rolling away from earth and rocks falling in an endless, heavy avalanche. A rock bounced off her shoulder, sending a bright spark of pain crackling down her arm. A clump of dirt crashed into her, and the world went dark. Ary gasped but inhaled only earth, her fingers scrabbling for purchase. Something grabbed the back of her shirt and jerked her free, and Ary shrieked, kicking out.

"It's me!" Briar gasped. "Stop, Mossheart, it's me!"

She spun. Briar panted over her in the dust cloud, her eyes wild and bright with fear. Her wings flared behind her, beating a steady rhythm that pressed the dust away from them. Envy streaked through Ary.

"Briar, what's happening?"

"I don't know!" Briar grabbed Ary by the hand and pulled her up. "This is technically still Ant Court territory. No one has even *seen* a centipede in decades! They never used to pick sides. They wouldn't be attacking us unless—"

*Unless they also don't want us to reach Atlas.*

*Unless the newts got to them, too.*

*Unless somehow, the Underground knows a piece of the puzzle Dracaena and Gran both left out.*

The multisegmented body of the centipede slammed to the ground close to them. Briar stiffened, her hand still squeezing Ary's. The creature was twice Sootflank's height and three times as long. It skittered toward them and reared up, swinging its head back and forth, pincers flashing. Beside her, Briar tensed her legs as she prepared to leap.

The centipede wasn't attacking them. It just kept swinging its head back and forth, up and down, and Ary was reminded of a different creature, only days ago, who'd had far more use for his nose than his eyes.

*It can't see us*, she realized. The centipede had eyes, but Ary recalled how reliant the ants had been on smell, pausing to feel the tremors in the earth.

Ary gripped Briar's hand in a death grip and squeezed twice.

The fairy looked at her sidelong. Not even daring to exhale, Ary's lips formed the words:

*Don't.*

*Move.*

Terror flashed across Briar's face. Ary let her eyes scan the tunnel, wings aching as she kept them aloft, regretting with every passing second that she hadn't folded them against her back.

The centipede lowered the front half of its body to the earth. This close, Ary could see the wicked scars that wrapped its body, long, sweeping marks likely from the pincers of another bug—but burn marks, too. It scuttled even closer to them, and Briar's hand tightened on Ary's. Only the tremor in her hand gave her away.

How she envied Briar, with her unfurled wings that could fan behind her lighter than a feather, instead of the useless, clumpy paper cocoons Ary was now holding aloft.

The centipede jerked. It lifted its head, legs twitching, tasting the air again—and then fanned itself across the ground. Horror shivered through Ary. It was trying to *feel* them, legs and belly flattened to the dirt as it waited for them. The centipede shuddered, and a long, cold hiss filled the room.

"Ssssmell you," it whispered. "Sssssssomewhere."

Sweat crawled a trail down Ary's spine.

She wasn't going to be able to hold her wings up for-ever. Already there was a burning in her shoulders, lines of fire shooting down her spine. She squeezed Briar's hand once, twice. Saw the fairy glance at her from the corner of her eye.

*Wings*, Ary mouthed, again holding her breath, letting only the smallest bit of air leave her nose lest the centipede smell her breath. *Heavy*.

Beside her, Briar gulped.

Maybe she could lower her wings quietly—maybe if she was careful—

She dropped them a hair.

The centipede froze.

"There you are," it hissed, and lunged.

Ary and Briar cried out and dove apart, each running in opposite directions. The centipede swiveled its head, legs flaring, and Ary danced sideways, her wings rustling as she backtracked around the cavern, eyeing the centipede, searching desperately for any kind of exit—but they were trapped. Any tunnel they might have fled from was gone, sealed off from the dirt of the avalanche. The centipede snarled and lunged toward Briar, missing at the last second. Its venomous mandibles sank into the wall.

Ary's mind spun frantically. They couldn't keep moving forever, not when the centipede was nearly ten times their size. The bucket rattled on her head, and Ary ripped it off, wincing at the way it creaked.

"Briar!" cried Ary. The fairy looked to her—and so did the centipede. Ary hefted the bucket and threw it against the far wall as hard as she could. The bucket hit the earth with a *clang*, and Ary dropped into a sitting position. The bucket clattered to the ground. The centipede lunged for it with a hiss, and Ary winced as its fangs punctured easily through the metal. Venom dripped down the inside, pooling on the earth.

Across the cavern, Briar was also sitting stone still, her chest heaving and her eyes wide.

The centipede tugged its mandibles free of the bucket with a hiss, then crushed it with its legs. Grief pulsed through Ary. The bucket was hardly a shield or a sword—but it was a piece of home, and it had protected her.

"Ssssneaky trick," the centipede hissed. It wove its head through the air, legs tapping the earth, but with Ary and Briar frozen in place, it couldn't find them—yet. "Where are you, little folksssss."

The massive creature moved in a slow, languid movement as it circled the cave, legs skirting over the ground, flipping over rocks, poking into the earth. It drew closer to Briar, head swinging this way and that as it scented the air, searching for them in the gloom of the cavern, feet tapping continuously as it hunted for the tiniest rhythm. Briar looked as if she was about to faint dead away as it passed only a few feet from her, worming its way across the floor toward Ary.

"I know you're sssssssomewhere," the centipede sang.

It drew so close to Ary that she could have reached out and touched it. This close, she could see the scars that looped over the centipede's eyes. Old blood crusted in dark flecks along its mandibles. Some of its legs were covered in strange substances—spiderwebs and odd goop. Others were covered in worn, thin fabric.

It was clothing.

It was long faded by time, turned gray and old from years of being dragged through the dirt, but it was unmistakably cloth, likely spun in Terra's very marketplace. Once the fabric might have made up a dress, some trousers, a shirt. Now they were just scraps of garbage, snagged against the sharp hooks that made up the centipede's legs.

No one knew how the other heroes who had accompanied Wren to the Underground had died.

Only that they'd never made it back.

"If I do not find you, the earwigsssss will." The centipede let loose a low, cruel chuckle. "And even if they do not— I will feasssssst on whatever Atlasssss leaves behind."

The centipede's head was only a handspan away from Ary. It hovered in front of her, unseeing eyes staring straight into hers. A scream built in Ary's throat as it reached one leg forward, skittering over the dirt.

It brushed the bottom of her foot.

From across the cavern came a clatter.

The centipede whipped around, scuttling toward the rock Briar had thrown against a wall. Briar crept across the cavern to Ary and sat quickly beside her while the creature was distracted. Ary trembled so hard she thought she was going to be sick. She needed to stop shaking, needed to calm down, but the centipede had been so *close* and it had nearly found her and now she knew how the other heroes had died. It hadn't been an accident; they hadn't simply disappeared. How had this world become so grim?

How had saving it been left to a bunch of *kids*?

The centipede cracked the stone Briar had thrown between its mandibles and let loose a heavy sigh.

"Very well," the centipede hissed. "I will sssssimply wait."

The massive creature writhed, its body tightening into coils as it lay flat on the ground in the very center of the cavern. As the centipede curled up to sleep, it gave one long look around the cavern.

The glow-shroom lamp flickered pitifully. Ary willed it to stay alight. Atlas was so close. She could still do this—she could get them out—

"You cannot sssstay sssstill forever," the centipede hissed.

And as the centipede lay curled between them, no exit in sight, Ary could only watch as the glow-shroom lamp tied to the magic of their world—tied to Atlas itself—finally flickered, wobbled, and died.

And then there was only darkness.

# FORTY-FIVE

## *The First Who Suffered*

When Ary was small, she'd had terrible night terrors—visions of massive monsters and her wings bursting into flames, of earthquakes burying her home and great floods sweeping it away entirely. She'd wake screaming in the night, sweat drenching her body, and it had thrown Mama and Papa for a loss. They didn't know how to help her, their tiny daughter who battled monsters in her sleep. It had been before Papa had been hurt, before they'd moved in with Gran, when they'd had their own tiny cottage on the knoll where cave ferns flowered in cool thickets.

One night, when Ary woke screaming and kicking, it was not Mama who put a cool hand to her forehead, but Gran.

Ary had woken the same as always—tangled in thin sheets pasted to her skin with sweat, heart pounding, stomach flipping. But instead of wrapping her in a hug or kissing the tears from her cheeks, Gran watched her intently.

"What did you see?"

Thrown, Ary had answered, recounting stories of impossible beasts, of hungry flames and mold and avalanches.

344

Gran listened as though they were discussing the weather. Then she had taken Ary's hand, her scarred, wrinkled fingers dwarfing her granddaughter's. She had not seemed surprised by Ary's nightmares.

If anything, it'd seemed like she understood.

"Listen to me, Canary. It doesn't matter if those things are real or not, because the fear is real. But fear is just a feeling, and feelings can be wielded the same as a sword." In the dark, as Gran held her hand, the lack of sympathy in her scratchy voice was somehow more a comfort than Mama's kisses or Papa's promises to vanquish any monsters that emerged. "The next time fear comes for you, Canary Mossheart, welcome it—and wield it."

"How?" Ary whispered.

Gran had given one of her rare, crooked smiles, and smoothed the hair from Ary's face. "Ask it what it wants."

It had sounded like nonsense—but it had helped. Ary's night terrors didn't go away, but when she woke screaming, she'd learned to ask her fear what it wanted—a walk in the dark, a sip of root broth, another layer of blankets to press her into the bed. She'd learned to count to impossible numbers like Gran had taught her, to focus on other senses, twitching her toes one by one, then her fingers, then her thumbs.

But she'd never learned how to *wield* fear, at least not the way Gran had said.

But now Ary sat in the dark, and fear was all around her, fear was threatening to drown her, and she had nothing else she could wield.

So Ary leaned into the fear and listened.

Here was what she knew: She was trapped in a cavern where she could see nothing, with a centipede determined to kill her, and Briar. She was definitely terrified, and it was definitely Ary's fault.

And time to reach Atlas was running out.

Ary stared out into the cavern, her eyes wide and unseeing. The centipede had burst through the wall easily—maybe the earth was weaker down here, where dozens of tunnels had not been traveled by critters for centuries. And maybe it was the terrarium itself, brittle with age, running dry of the magic that had sustained it. Ary recalled Sootflank's scorn for the fairies, the way he'd mocked her fear of the dark.

*One day you won't have a light, little folk.*

*The dark will be all you have left.*

*Best learn to use it.*

In the dark, Ary found Briar's hand. She moved slowly, touching her finger to the back of Briar's hand with the softest brush of her index finger. She felt Briar stiffen and then wait. With every ounce of her effort focused on not making a sound, Ary began to write, drawing out the letters as slowly as she could against the skin of Briar's hand.

*T . . . R . . . U . . . S . . . T . . . M . . . E . . .*

A pause, and then Briar's finger flitted along Ary's palm. O . . . K . . .

Ary steeled herself. She stared out into the dark. She could *feel* the centipede waiting, even if she couldn't see anything, even if she couldn't hear anything. She needed to get away from Briar—if this went wrong, one of them had to make it to Atlas.

One of them had to try.

Ary stood, and this time, she didn't care to be quiet. She scurried sideways, keeping her back to the wall, as far from Briar as she could manage.

"You there," she called. "Centipede. What's your name?"

"It ssssspeaks," the centipede sneered.

"My name is Ary—"

"I know who you are, little Mossssheart."

"Good." Ary's throat bobbed. "I'd like to make a trade. You can have my life—but let my friend go."

"What?" Briar yelped. "Ary, no!"

Ary craned her head. She could hear the centipede coiling in the dark, the slither of its multisegmented body and its legs scurried over the earth, growing closer, growing louder.

"I don't sssstrike dealsssss with dessssperate folk."

"Oh," said Ary. "But *I* am not desperate. *You* are."

A pause.

Ary steeled her nerves and gambled.

"You must be lonely," she said softly. "Living down here for decades, all alone. And *hungry*, with only stray ants for

347

food. I'm sure it sounds wonderful for creatures to be forced into the Underground. Or . . . maybe not. Maybe while the rest of us suffered, you finally learned to thrive." Ary paused. "When did you figure out you could infect the ants?"

A furious hiss filled the cavern, and grim satisfaction rippled through Ary. She hadn't understood why the mold had vanished as they approached centipede territory—but it made sense, didn't it? There had to be *some* creature the mold benefited. Something that could eat it, something that was seemingly immune. Pill bugs were known to eat the trash discarded from Terra, sorting merrily through leaf litter. Newts ate other bugs and vegetables alike. But the centipedes had seemingly vanished when the mold exploded. She recalled the Ant Court, the way they had been dying from within. There was only one kingdom that lay beneath them.

"But you're all alone," Ary whispered. "Aren't you? The rest of you died out before there was enough mold to live off of. So you traded starving for solitude. And you'd sooner let the rest of us die."

"Insssssssolent folk," the centipede roared. "What did you ever do for us? What did the antsss? We died *firsssst* in the plague. We *sssssuffered* when every critter turned away!"

Ary braced herself, conjuring Sootflank in her mind's eye, the way he had moved so effortlessly through the dark.

"I can't fix what happened to you," whispered Ary. "But I can't let you punish the rest of us, either. The mold isn't your fault—but this world of ours was never meant to last.

It's time we leave. It's time we *all* leave. So I'm giving you one chance, bug. Let us go. Let us find Atlas, and you can rule the ruins left behind."

The centipede let loose a terrible scream.

Ary flung herself sideways in the dark. Air whistled past her, and she was reminded of Quickspark, made sloppy by her rage, unsure what to do in the face of a fairy who didn't fight *or* flee. The earth trembled around them; dirt rained down on her head.

*Good*, Ary thought grimly. She hoped Briar had had the sense to hide—to scale a wall in the commotion or bury herself in a divot in the floor. Ary skipped backward, her papery, scratchy wings suddenly a blessing in their noisiness. At least it would provide cover for Briar.

"It wasn't Atlas who killed Wren Mossheart's allies or the others who set out in search of it," Ary accused the dark. "It was *you*. And when the ants acquired the map to Atlas, you poisoned them, too. Because, finally, here was some power you had. Here was something you *ruled*. I may not be a hero—but you're a coward."

"I lossst my family," the centipede snarled. "My friendssss. My *children*. No critter cared. No folk wept. The antssss celebrated our demisssse. Why sssshouldn't the rest of you ssssuffer? Why sssshouldn't your children's children know nothing but sssstarvation, as mine did?"

There would be no reasoning with the centipede. Grief and isolation had long driven it mad with rage.

She tried anyway.

"There might be new centipedes in the world beyond," Ary pleaded. "Please, let us go. Let us help you. In the world beyond, we can start over. We can have a new beginning."

"I do not want a new beginning," the centipede screamed. "I want you to *die*!"

It came for her again, and this time, Ary was not fast enough.

Ary dove to the side, and a leg snagged her wing. She cried out as it tore right through the paper, cutting to the membrane beneath. The centipede's body slammed into the wall, sending a dozen terrible tremors through the earth. In the dark, Briar screamed her name, and then came a crash as one of the walls caved in. Cold air rushed in, and with it that sickly smell of mold.

"Ary," shouted Briar.

"*Run!*" cried Ary.

Ary couldn't see the centipede, but it didn't matter. She could feel it rearing over her. A leg pinned down her other wing; a second pressed to her throat. Mandibles clicked in front of her face, and Ary could *smell* the venom lurking in its fangs.

Ary kept her eyes open.

"I sssssshould have killed your wretched grandmother along with her friendssss," the centipede hissed. "You will never reach Atlasssss, little folk. You will never be free of thissss terrarium, and you will never be a hero. Today, you will *die*."

"Maybe," Ary whispered. "But she won't."

From behind them, the sound of running feet. Relief flooded Ary. Briar was making the smart choice that Ary couldn't. Briar was leaving her behind. Maybe she'd even find Owl and Shrimp. Maybe, together, they'd fix what Ary couldn't.

"Wait," said the centipede, and something in its voice didn't make sense. "Wait, my lord, *no*—there must be a misunderstanding—I am an enemy of the folk, like you—"

From the darkness came a spark and the smell of smoke. Fire lit up the world.

The weight on Ary vanished, leaving her on her back on the ground, her left wing bright with pain and surely bleeding. The earth trembled, and the walls shook, and suddenly Ary could *see*, because there was light, orange and bright and impossibly warm flooding the cavern. The centipede reared back, keening with fear, and the fire kept coming—but it never touched Ary. It danced over and around her in brilliant ribbons, until there was a fence, a wall, a *fortress* of inferno just out of reach. Ary's world spun, and when she looked up, she found herself meeting a pair of deep, black eyes.

"Hello, Ary," sighed Sootflank. "I see we've been making friends."

# FORTY-SIX

## *Who Comes Back*

Ary was dreaming. She had to be. Because in a thousand life-times, on a million different journeys, there was no future in which she'd ever thought Sootflank would come back. She'd been so certain the general had abandoned them for good. Who was Ary but a scared little fairy, unfit for this journey? She was certainly not worth protecting, certainly not worth *coming back for*.

But she wasn't dreaming, and Sootflank was here.

He was real.

Sootflank looked like a monster out of legends as he towered over her, weary and irritated as usual, his tail lashing behind him in quick, snaking patterns. Flames pressed in from all sides, but where Sootflank stood was a refuge of clean air, free of smoke and fire. On the other side of the fire, the centipede screamed with fury, twisting and turning, the earth trembling like mad as it drew as close as it dared to Sootflank's flames, then away again.

"How is it that I leave you alone for *two days*," Soot-flank asked slowly, "and you burn the place to the ground?" The newt paused, and for the first time seemed to notice

Briar, who had, in fact, not left Ary behind, and was instead cowering against the wall with her mouth hanging open. "Who . . . is that?"

Ary grasped for an explanation, then shook her head. "Later. Can you get us out of here?"

"Why else do you think I'm here?" Sootflank snapped. "To bring you tea? Ask how your day is going? Tell you a bedtime story?"

Ary felt a grin spreading over her face.

"Don't look at me like that. And stop smiling," the newt grumbled. "I didn't come back for *you*. I came back to save myself by sacrificing you to Atlas like a day-old turnip." He paused, and this time, his voice was softer. "Really, little folk. Did you think so poorly of me that you actually believed I'd leave you behind?"

Ary's eyes blurred, and as Sootflank lay down beside her with a grumble and told her to climb on, Ary was struck by just how much she had missed him.

"Wait," said Ary. "I thought you said you were poisonous to touch?"

"Oh." Sootflank actually had the grace to look awkward. "I lied."

With a swift movement, Sootflank wrapped his tail around Briar's waist and plopped her onto his back. Briar protested but immediately clicked her jaw shut when Soot-flank whipped his head around to level her with one of his trademark glares. He lifted Ary to his back with a grumble and pushed himself to his feet, and Ary wondered at how easily he'd picked them up, how effortlessly he seemed to carry their weight.

As if he'd done this before, for two other fairies, in a different time.

"Breathe as little as you can," Sootflank ordered. The gills on the sides of his neck flared, and his tongue flicked to his eyes, wetting them against the fumes. "And hold on."

"Wait," Ary gasped. "What about the centipede?"

"The fire should keep it busy," Sootflank said grimly. "And if not—well, let's just say news doesn't travel down very fast here. For now it thinks I'm allied with the newts, and that I'm keeping you *away* from Atlas. Let's not give it the chance to think otherwise. Now *hold on*."

"Wait," said Briar. "What is happening? Mossheart, who is this—what is he—*ahhhh!*"

And then they were running.

Sootflank did not run as smoothly as Shrimp—unlike the pill bug's even, skittering gait, Sootflank seemed to *bound*. Ary felt his muscles heaving beneath her as the newt raced across the cavern floor, his tail whirring as he directed the fire away from them. Heat built beneath his skin, and Ary winced. Though newts wielded fire, they had been creatures of water, once. Did the smoke hurt him, too? What was he risking, letting them weigh him down?

Why had he come back?

Sootflank swerved left, and Briar nearly toppled from

his back. Ary yelped, grabbing her before she could fall. The fairy made a terrified noise and snapped Ary's arms around her waist, clinging so tightly to her wrists it hurt.

Ary's head drooped. She was dizzy, and so very tired. There was an itching in her skin that she didn't understand, and her wings drooped, still aching from where they'd burned.

"Little folk," Sootflank rumbled beneath her. "Stay awake."

His even tone was the only indication that something must have been very wrong. Her grip on Briar's waist loosened.

"Little Mossheart," Sootflank pressed.

She was trying. But as Sootflank continued to run, as smoke crept in her lungs and heat wrapped her in its burning, dizzying embrace, the world began to blur. Sootflank kept speaking, and Gran's voice returned, and soon they were a blur, and she didn't know dream from reality, newt from fairy, grandmother from . . . whatever Sootflank had become.

Strange, to think he'd become anything at all.

"*Ary*," barked Sootflank.

*Canary*, echoed Gran in her mind.

"Stay with me."

Ary's eyes drooped, and then the dark took her, too.

# FORTY-SEVEN

## *The Granddaughter*

"Is she . . . dead?"

"What? Why would you ask that? What's wrong with you?"

Ary's eyes fluttered open.

She lay on her back in the dirt, in a small, carved-out cave. Her eyes were scratchy and achy, and every part of her hurt. And she was *itchy*. Ary tried to move and groaned as her entire body ached in response.

"Oh! She's alive! Oh, thank the Gardener."

A face appeared over Ary's—Owl, his cheeks stained with soot, his hair sticking up wildly. "I thought you were *dead*."

"*Owl?*"

He gave her a wide, toothy grin. "Shrimp and I escaped, and then we ran into Sootflank, and I felt something weird—"

Ary didn't know whether to laugh or cry. Of course he had found her. Something told her that she could have traveled to the end of this world or the next, and Owl Diggs would have found her, all the same.

"—And when he came back he said something about a

giant centipede and your wing was bleeding and we thought the centipede had *killed* you—"

Ary wrapped her arms around Owl and dragged him into a hug. The fairy boy squeaked, and then, after a moment's hesitation, hugged her back. He buried his face in her hair and went limp against her, and when Ary pulled away, both their cheeks were wet. Sootflank had asked her about family once. She'd said she only had Mama and Gran.

She had been wrong.

Ary's stomach heaved, and she barely had time to shove Owl off her before she rolled over and vomited. Bile splattered on the dirt. She heaved again, puking until her already-empty stomach ached. Tears dripped down her nose.

A familiar, cool weight settled beside her.

"Ary?" Shrimp whispered. "Okay?"

Ary threw her arms over him and pressed her cheek to his shell. "I'm okay. Are *you* okay?"

The pill bug whirred softly, and Ary thought of what a fool she'd been, to ever think of pill bugs as anything but brave.

Ary lifted her head and took in the strange crew assembled before her.

Owl hovered nervously in front of her, and the worry on his face made her heart ache. Shrimp supported her, quiet concern sparking his round eyes. Sootflank lounged farther back, chin resting on his feet as he pretended to ignore them. And behind him, slumped against the wall—

*Briar.*

Ary was moving before she could think twice. She lurched upright, half stumbling toward Briar, panic rising in her as she remembered how weak her pulse had been. There had been so much smoke, and so many fumes—

She was still breathing. She was safe.

Ary sank to her knees, and then to a seated position. Her head pounded something terrible, and she was so *thirsty*.

"Ary?" Owl asked anxiously. "Are you all right?"

Ary closed her eyes.

*The Ant Court in flames. Earwigs and ants alike curling up in the smoke. Quickspark in the pit, her eyes blazing with hatred, but with fear, too.*

*I will get out of this pit.*

*I will find you.*

*And when I do I will burn everything you love to ashes.*

"All right is generous," Ary said wearily. "But I'm alive."

"Ary," said Owl. "That. Was. Wild."

Ary gave him a tired smile—and then her stomach heaved again. She tipped sideways, retching, her entire body shivering. Sweat dripped off her and ran into her eyes. The world spun around her, her thoughts blurring. It was a long time before she could pick her head up.

"Ary—"

"Leave her be," Sootflank said in a surprisingly gentle tone. "She's lucky she's alive."

Owl and Shrimp shuffled back, though their eyes never

left her. Ary's head continued to pound, but it felt less like reality was ripping her in two. She drew her knees to her chest and huddled into a ball, the past day swirling like a confusing smog around her.

"Thank you," Ary said quietly. "Thank you, Sootflank, for coming back."

The newt rolled his eyes. "I told you I'm only—"

"Here to sacrifice me to Atlas like a day-old turnip," Ary finished. Now it was her turn to roll her eyes. "Sure. But thank you all the same. And thank you for saving her, too."

Every pair of eyes in the cavern went to Briar. She twitched, her eyes fluttering.

"Wait," said Owl. "Why *did* you save her? I thought she didn't want to come."

Now it was Sootflank's turn to look confused. "I assumed she was some insufferable Terra pup—is she not?"

Ary's face burned. "Not quite."

Owl's jaw dropped. "Ary, did you *kidnap* her?!"

"No!"

"Oh my gosh," Owl whispered. "That is so cool."

"I didn't kidnap her," Ary protested. "If I left her in the fires, she would have died—"

"Ah." Sootflank's tail lashed as he glanced around the cavern. "How touching that you developed a concern for the sanctity of life *after* you burned the Ant Court to the ground."

"Not on purpose!"

"Right," Sootflank snorted. "She just managed to be the exception—"

"She," a voice croaked, "has a name."

Briar did not look well—yet somehow, the fire in her eyes had already returned. She blinked furiously, coughed, and leveled Sootflank with a look that would have shriveled even the healthiest of mushrooms. "*Who* are *you?*"

Embers sparked around Sootflank's little tail. "I would watch your tone, folk pup—"

"Both of you, stop!" Ary snapped. Her head hurt so bad. If Briar and Sootflank started a bickering match, she'd walk right back into the fire. "Briar, this is—"

"Briar?" Sootflank grew very, very still. "Briar . . . Sunleaf?"

"Yes—wait." Briar's face fell. "How do you know my name?"

They stared at each other. Sootflank faltered. The embers sparked by his tail sputtered and flew off course. As quickly as his control had slipped, he regained it, but the shock on his face remained.

Brighter than the shock, though—*purer*—was grief.

"You're hers," he whispered. "The granddaughter."

Sootflank had never seen Wren Mossheart again after she betrayed them—not until Ary re-entered the Underground sixty years later. But that didn't mean he hadn't seen Dracaena. They had both lost their people, both lost their home. Ary would have thought it would have glued them together—but grief was a strange, muddy thing, and it had a way of driving wedges in even the tightest of bonds. Dracaena had found other folk, somehow—exiles, perhaps, folk who had existed on Terra's edges before drifting off, or maybe the few Seedlings who'd remained living Underground before the mold wiped them out. Maybe she hadn't wanted Sootflank in her life, a reminder of an ill-fated journey and the girl she'd lost.

And maybe she'd simply left him, as Wren Mossheart once had.

Ary looked at Sootflank, and she wondered, for the first time, which was worse—to mourn someone who was gone for good, or to mourn someone within reach, gone not by the cruel will of foul fates, but gone because they'd left you, simply because they wanted to.

Simply because they could.

"Yes," Briar said defensively. "Why? What's it to you?" When Sootflank said nothing, some of the fight drained out of her eyes, and her voice quieted. "You knew her, didn't you? My grandmother."

Sootflank cleared his throat once, twice, and Ary figured it was for the best that newts couldn't cry.

"I knew her very well," Sootflank said quietly. "We were . . . friends, a long, long time ago." He hesitated. "I looked for you when I heard what happened. I should have looked harder. I am sorry, little Sunleaf. You never should have had to endure the Underground alone."

Briar's bottom lip quivered, and suddenly Ary felt

embarrassed, as though this was something she had no business witnessing. Sootflank must have come to the same conclusion, because he rose to his feet with a grumble and looked at Briar with a softness Ary hadn't known he was capable of.

"We will need to keep moving soon. Quickspark and the earwigs will not waste a chance to stop us from reaching Atlas. But first, if you'll indulge an old newt, Briar—I'd like to talk to you alone."

Briar hesitated. She looked at Sootflank, hands bunched in her lap. She must have grown up as afraid of the newts as Ary. It was impossible to imagine how she must have felt, faced with one as terrifying as Sootflank, who looked at her with a gentle light and spoke of the grandmother she had lost. Briar sucked in a breath and glanced at Ary with a raised brow, her face oddly vulnerable.

Ary's heart did a strange little skip.

Briar was asking her if Sootflank was safe.

Briar was . . . trusting her?

Ary held her breath and nodded.

Briar looked at Sootflank with a lift of her chin as she hopped to her feet. "Fine, why not, seeing as I've been kidnapped and all."

Owl raised an eyebrow at Ary. "Told you."

Sootflank huffed out a laugh and flicked his tail behind him. "The rest of you get some sleep, if you can. I will wake you when it's time to leave." He inclined his head toward Briar. "Walk with me, little folk?"

"Okay," said Briar uncertainly.

Ary watched as Briar and Sootflank left, side by side, a fairy girl with her wings and the newt general turned ally. Both carrying wounds from Wren Mossheart and Dracaena alike. As they left, and silence crept into the space they occupied, a strange, unsteady feeling swept through Ary. They had, it seemed, accomplished the impossible.

They had their map to Atlas.

They had a day to reach it.

As Owl and Shrimp drifted to sleep, Ary sat awake in the dark, arms wrapped tightly around her knees as she realized that if everything went according to plan, tomorrow would be her last.

# FORTY-EIGHT

## *Down We Go*

It wasn't long before Sootflank roused them. For a bleary moment, Ary wondered why he'd woken them in the night—and then she remembered where she was. There was no day or night, not down here. After four days in the Underground, she had lost all sense of time.

"Wake up, Mossheart," Sootflank whispered. "Down we go."

Wordlessly, she came to her feet. Behind her, Owl and Shrimp were equally quiet. There was a finality to the air nobody wanted to speak of. They left quietly, not bothering to search for food. They'd long gone through all their rations, and the desperation of the ants had shown them everything they needed to know about their chances of finding anything else to eat. The five of them set off on foot, moving in single file.

There was a kind of rhythm to their strange group—for a while, Sootflank would lead, then Shrimp, then Owl, then Briar. The only one who was never the first to step into the dark was Ary. It felt wrong, but who was she to try to push them ahead? Sootflank and Shrimp had senses in the dark that no folk could hope for; Owl had whatever strange sense had propelled him here in the first place; Briar had Dracaena's knowledge.

Ary had nothing to offer, it seemed, but her life. Most loved, and freely given, if she could be brave enough.

Owl drifted ahead of their odd little caravan, head cocked as he listened to voices only he could hear, muttering to himself as he read. Briar had given him back the journals Ary had taken for her—to borrow, she said, since he seemed more interested in unraveling Dracaena's clues. It had thawed something between the two of them, this mutual desire to understand the secrets Dracaena had kept. And if she and Owl were amicable, Briar and Sootflank were almost *warm*. Ary had no idea what he had told her of Dracaena, but there was a light in Briar's eyes when she looked at the old newt.

From up ahead, Owl muttered the Gardener's Warning to himself.

"Spins . . . Dust . . . Key . . ."

Ary shivered. The words were like a prickle on the back of her neck, a rush of cold air reminding her of a door left open. There was *something* there, but she had no idea what.

Owl stopped. He turned back to them with an uneasy expression, his eyes stretched wide. Ary didn't understand until she drew closer.

All along, the tunnels of the Underground had forked and curved, splitting off in a dozen different directions. The map of the Underground had been an organic, wild thing, carved to the whims of the critters that scurried far, far beneath Terra.

Now there was only one.

Something strange lined the walls. Ary brushed her fingers against it, and was shocked to find it earthy, wet, and soft. It was moss, she realized—coating the ceiling, the tunnel walls, leaving only the dirt floor bare. There was a current to the air, a stir she didn't quite understand. Ary drew closer, and her heart sank.

The moss was shriveled at the edges; what had likely once been an endless tunnel of vibrant green was turning brown and dry as it, too, died.

They were almost out of time.

"We're close," Briar said from behind Ary. She looked beyond her with an almost dreamy expression and shuddered. "Grandmother always said . . . she always said that once I found the moss, I would know what to do. I don't know what lies beyond this."

Ary gulped. She felt the weight of their eyes on her—Briar, Owl, Sootflank, Shrimp. What an odd, ragtag band they had become, traveling with her to the very end of this world in hopes of finding a new one.

"Well, then," Ary said quietly. "Onward, I suppose."

Ary took a step into the moss tunnel—and the voices began.

*Spins . . . Dust . . . Key . . .*

It was like the voices of her dreams magnified tenfold, but instead of the angry howls that had blanketed Wren Mossheart, these voices were soft. Welcoming, even. They whispered in her blood, her bones, her breath. Hands touched her shoulders; they plucked at her hair, her wings, her clothes. Ary shivered. It felt so *real*. For the first time, she wondered about who else had come seeking Atlas. She recalled the Seedling shovels that had been scattered throughout the Gloom, relics of a pilgrimage long abandoned. Chives' knowledge of them, as though his father had known them well. The way Dracaena had slotted herself into the Underground so easily.

*Dust . . . Key . . . Spins . . .*

Beside Ary, Owl had gone white. Briar was rigid, her eyes shining with unease, her head craned to the side. Shock bolted Ary in place. She'd thought it was only her—that it had been some cruel trick of her imagination, a phantom conjured by her mind.

"You hear them, too," said Ary.

The three of them looked at each other uncertainly— the girl with wings, the boy without, the girl still waiting for hers. Briar's eyes flicked past Ary to the dark beyond, her brow knitting together, and Owl tucked his hands into his pockets and shuddered.

"Yes," Briar and Owl said faintly at the same time.

The hair on Ary's arms stood on end. How many others

had heard these voices when they'd drawn close to Atlas? How many had failed? They had felt so urgent, and Ary wondered if maybe some of these voices had belonged to other creatures and fairies long lost who had also come seeking a better world. If it wasn't just the living souls of the terrarium seeking a way out, but the ghosts of those who had failed, too.

*I'm trying*, Ary thought. *One way or another, this ends today.*

And perhaps it was just her nerves, or a trick of the breeze, but she could have sworn the voices grew softer, more content. Ary glanced at Owl and Briar, and saw from the unease on their faces they'd felt the shift, too.

Ary kept walking, drawn forward like a moth to a glow-shroom lamp. The dirt under her feet shifted. It wasn't until her steps began to echo that Ary realized they were walking on stone.

Just like that, the bug-carved tunnels of the Underground were gone; they were surrounded by only smooth rock and stray moss now, so perfectly cut it was if someone had used some massive tool to carve away a path.

Ary took one step forward, and then another. The path grew narrower with each step, until it was so small Sootflank could not fit comfortably.

Carved in perfect lines ahead of her, descending into the dark, were stairs. The moss did not extend beyond them, as though whatever magic that had allowed it to flourish down here in the endless shadows beneath their world had been cut short. There was only empty, cold stone, and a darkness filled with voices long lost.

"We found it," Ary said quietly, though her voice cracked like a shout in the echo of the stone hallway. "Atlas. Whatever it is—whoever it is—is ahead." She took a breath. "The rest of you should stay here."

"No," Owl said automatically with a worried frown.

"Absolutely not," said Briar with a roll of her eyes.

Emotion choked Ary. She looked at them and knew there was no arguing. Instead, she turned to Sootflank and Shrimp, her heart pounding in her chest. "The folk are the ones tied to Atlas. If there is danger ahead, I'll never forgive myself."

"Please," scoffed Sootflank. "I'm coming to—"

The corner of Ary's mouth tugged in a smile. "Sacrifice me like a day-old turnip, I know."

"No," said Sootflank, a rare roughness in his voice. "If there is danger ahead, you'll need me. I didn't come all this way to play the coward."

Ary nodded, doing her best to quell the burning in her eyes. She knew that if she cried now, Sootflank would never forgive her. She turned to the last of her group, her heart threatening to burst, because she already knew what he would say.

"Shrimp," Ary began.

The roly-poly quirked an antenna.

"You've already brought us so far. If you were hurt—"

"Ary," Shrimp said quietly. "We follow."

Ary's vision went blurry.

"We follow," echoed Owl, and he took Ary's hand.

"We follow," said Briar, taking Ary's other hand while adding with a dramatic sigh, "I guess."

That left only Sootflank. The old newt glared at them. "I'm not saying it."

Ary stifled a laugh, for fear it might warp into a sob. "It's okay. You don't have to say it."

"Well," Sootflank grumbled. "Now it's weird if I don't. Fine, *we follow*, happy? We're all pill bugs now. Great. Let's go die."

Ary was fully crying now. Sniffling, she wiped her nose on her shoulder and looked at the four of them. Maybe she had not been chosen for this—but they had chosen her. And in that, she had found everything that mattered.

"Okay," Ary said quietly. "We meet Atlas, then. Together."

Ary took a breath.

She turned to the dark.

And from behind them came a flare of heat, a scuttle of legs, and the snap of pincers.

"That's very sweet," a familiar voice sighed. "But I can't let you do that."

*No.*

Ary could only watch as Quickspark strode into the tunnel, a dozen earwigs behind her and a dozen more scuttling along the walls. The newt took one languid step forward, then another, her beady eyes bright with anger.

"You're too late, little folk," Quickspark crooned. "Atlas or not, we've won. Terra is gone."

# FORTY-NINE

## *At Last, Atlas.*

*No.*

Ary couldn't breathe. Couldn't think. The world threatened to tilt out from under her, and it was only Owl's and Briar's hands in hers that held her steady. Her head swam as Quickspark leered at them, as even more earwigs poured into the tunnels.

"Didn't you wonder why more newts were not pursuing you?" Quickspark crooned. "It's because they were *busy*, little Mossheart. While you wasted time in the Underground, your city burned. Your people are gone. Even if you break the terrarium, you will have no one to bring with you into the new world. *Nothing.*"

Ary swayed.

"No," she whispered.

"Yes," Quickspark sneered. "It's funny, really. For as mighty as you folk think yourselves—you die so easily."

Ary's head pounded. She wanted to scream; she wanted to *hurt* Quickspark, and the feeling startled her, because she'd never wanted to hurt anyone. The newt kept gloating, mocking their foolishness, the futility of their cause. Through it all, the voices that had been whispering to Ary murmured louder.

*Spins . . . Dust . . . Key . . .*

"Little folk," a voice said softly. "Get ready to run."

Ary looked up with a jolt. Sootflank was watching her with an almost . . . soft expression? There was a light of inevitability to the old newt's eyes. As though he were looking into a river and preparing to dive.

"Why don't you speak the truth, daughter," Sootflank said coolly. "Because if Terra is burning, why are you here to stall? Why don't you tell the Mossheart pup the *real* reason we fear Atlas?"

The smile slipped from Quickspark's face.

"You feel it, too, don't you?" Sootflank said faintly. "The weakening of the flames. How much harder they are to reach. Is that why you're talking, instead of attacking? Have you any heat left at all? Tell me—have you, like I, spent many a sleepless night wondering which flame you summon will be your last?"

"You fool," Quickspark whispered. "You *traitor*."

"The magic dying in this terrarium," Sootflank said with grim satisfaction. "The magic that has kept us alive, the magic that fails even now—is the magic that gives us our fire. I've long wondered what would happen if the terrarium failed. I suppose we'll find out soon enough."

Sootflank drew himself to his full height, his tail lashing through the air. Smoke stirred around them, and sparks flew in every direction. His fire wasn't nearly as strong as before—but Ary recalled the way he had withstood the ant venom, the mastery of fire he'd commanded with so little effort.

"Shrimp," Sootflank said calmly. "Take Ary, Owl, and Briar to Atlas."

"What?" Ary blurted. "Sootflank, *no!*"

The old newt looked back at her.

"Go," he said, and this time, it was not the voice of the tired, world-weary newt she had known. It was the voice of a general, as though Sootflank had stepped back through the years to reclaim the title that had been stripped from him with the betrayal of a different Mossheart. "Go, while you can, and let me do this one good thing. I have business to finish with my daughter."

In a breath, Shrimp was there. He scooped Ary, Briar, and Owl onto his back, grunting slightly at their weight. The earwigs behind them hissed, but none dared to step forward, not with Sootflank guarding the stairs, his tail impossibly ringed with the fire even Quickspark was now hard-pressed to summon.

"You left me," Quickspark hissed. "You helped the Mosshearts not once, but twice, and you *left me behind.*"

"I did," Sootflank said wearily. "I had hoped you would be better than me, Quickspark. I had hoped you'd be braver.

And I had hoped, more than anything, that if you did not grow up to be kind, you would at least grow up to be wise. I see I was wrong on all counts."

"Shrimp," whispered Ary. *"Run."*

"I'll kill you," Quickspark said. "I'm going to kill you, old newt. And then I'll kill the folk you love so dearly, too."

The smile that curled Sootflank's face turned Ary's blood to ice.

"First, child," said Sootflank, "you'll have to win."

Quickspark howled—and Shrimp leaped.

He flew down the stairs, Ary, Owl, and Briar clinging to his back, plunging into the darkness as behind them, Sootflank faced the daughter he had failed—and he fought.

*You die so easily.*

Quickspark's words rattled through Ary's mind as Shrimp ran. The staircase was a straight descent. Behind them, flashes of light lit up the tunnel. Roars came from above, but whether they came from Quickspark or Sootflank, Ary didn't know. She didn't tell Shrimp what they all knew—that, eventually, some earwigs would slip past. And strong as he was, Sootflank would not be able to hold his own forever.

They had one chance to reach Atlas, and they were running out of time.

*Terra is gone.*

Behind them came a scream, and the snap of pincers.

"Earwigs!" Owl wailed. "Shrimp, *go!*"

Shrimp ran faster.

*Dust, key, spins.*

The stairs grew wider. A pressure built in Ary's chest, in her lungs, her breath, her blood. There was *light* ahead, impossibly so, bright and pulsing and pastel and *alive*. So achingly familiar, it took her breath away.

*Spins! Dust! Key!*

They reached the bottom of the stairs. The pulsing, pastel light washed over them. Ary looked behind her, heart seizing as she watched earwigs scuttle down the walls.

She looked ahead, and the world stopped.

Glow-moths filled the sky.

Dozens of them, *hundreds*, not only in the pastel colors of the enchanted moths she'd known in Terra, but in vibrant, saturated neon, too. They bobbed through the air, rested on walls, fanned their wings in the currents. A cavern opened up before them, and the ceiling only went *up*. High, high above, tiny pinpricks of light flitted, wheeling in the currents over the Underground. Could the folk of Terra see them, too, shining like beacons of hope in an endless night?

Were the folk of Terra even still alive to hope for anything at all?

Was Mama?

*SPINS.*

*DUST.*

*KEY.*

Before Ary, carved in a perfect, immaculate circle, was a door. The impassive, blank face of the Gardener gazed down at them. Ary took in her wingless back, the strange roundness of her ears, the holy flower that bloomed in her outstretched hand, that familiar indent winking at its center. If Dracaena was to be believed, if Atlas was real—then the Gardener had not been a benevolent goddess, crafting this world perfectly from nothing. She'd been a guard, a prisoner, a person. She'd been *real*.

But had she been protecting them by sealing them away, or punishing them?

And if she was protecting them—what really lay in wait for them beyond the terrarium's walls?

Ary slipped from Shrimp's back and approached the stone door. Words circled the edges; it was both the Gardener's Promise and the Gardener's Warning, the lines etched in contrast to one another to show where the rhymes had broken. *Trust* replaced by *dust*, *eternity* replaced by *key*. Ary's heart pounded as her eyes skipped over the words. She still didn't understand.

And she was out of time.

Ary's fingers strayed to the Seedling shovel at her hip, twisted and bent from the journey through the Underground. Her fingers hovered over the metal, her hand shaking.

*Your life*, Chives' voice whispered. *You will have to pay with your life.*

*I'm too young*, Ary thought wildly. *I'm too young to save the world, let alone die for it, and I am not ready for any of this.*

Was this how Gran had felt? So small and unprepared and *angry*, faced with the demise of everyone against the ruin of her own life? Ary couldn't pretend to know exactly what had transpired here sixty years ago; she couldn't assume what Gran had felt or wanted.

But right now, with the clock of the world ticking down and monsters at her back, Ary could understand why someone might turn away.

*Mama*, Ary thought, her hand shaking.

*Terra*, she thought.

*But what about Ary?* a tiny voice whispered.

It wasn't right, it wasn't fair, and Ary thought she was beginning to understand why Gran had only ever looked upon the world's desire for a chosen one with bitterness. How easy to love a hero, when danger was merely a fun story to whisper at the dinner table, the monsters drawn away by the promise of young blood soon to be sacrificed. But she was just a child, just like Gran had been, and she was not ready, and this could not be love, that her home was so keen to see her life ended before it had begun.

Terra had never loved her. They had never loved Gran.

They had only loved having someone ready to die for them.

"Ary," Owl said, and though the earwigs were nearly upon him, he didn't sound scared. "Together, okay?"

Her eyes blurred.

"Together," echoed Briar.

Ary was finally understanding why some heroes could make terrible sacrifices. It didn't matter that she did not want this, that it was not right. It had not been rightness, honor, or the greater good that had driven her into the Underground. It had been Mama. It had been someone she loved. And when they faced Atlas, it would not be all of Terra she gave her life for.

It would be *them*—Mama, Shrimp, Owl, even Briar.

Their love made her brave. And their love made this worth it.

"Together," she whispered.

Ary placed the shovel within the indent.

Briar and Owl put their hands over hers.

And together they *pushed*.

The shovel clicked in—and with a massive groan, the stone door slid aside. The earwigs behind them howled as Owl, Ary, Briar, and Shrimp slipped through. As quickly as it had opened, the stone door slammed shut again, trapping them in the dark.

*Ary Mossheart*, a thousand voices whispered at one, and Ary remembered only a week ago, when a moth had come to her in the mushroom field and called her Wren. *Ary Mossheart*, they whispered as Shrimp, Owl, and Briar stood behind her. *Ary Mossheart, Atlas awaits.*

Three things happened at once.

Light flooded the cavern as dozens of glow-moths appeared, their brilliant wings painting everything in an incredible, ever-pulsing glow.

Briar, Owl, and Shrimp cried out as a netting of silk snapped around them, pinning them to the cavern wall.

And ahead of them, in the center of the cavern, a mountain began to move.

It woke with a groan. Dust filled the air, not the dust of the Underground or Terra, but the strange, sweet, silver-white dust that had filled her dreams. The mountain ahead of Ary heaved, and then it began to break apart. Where the dust flew into the air, patches of brown were revealed, as though something had been waiting here, long buried by time, and was only now beginning to break apart.

No—not breaking.

Uncoiling.

*Once,* Chives' voice whispered, *there was a god, cursed to hold up the world.*

Owl, Briar, and Shrimp cried out. A strange *thwick* sounded, but Ary was too focused on the thing uncoiling before her to afford a glance back. Silver-sweet dust filled the air, crackling where it touched her, filling her mouth with the same electric taste Gran's fairy dust had.

Ary took a step forward, and then another, as a massive, silver-dusted snake lifted its head—and met her eyes.

The voices in her head quieted. The moths stilled.

The snake leaned down, its wide yellow eyes flickering in the multicolored light of the glow-moth wings.

Ary took a breath and squared her shoulders. She was so close to the snake she could have reached out and touched it. It didn't move, watching her with an expectant gaze.

Ary Mossheart looked up.

"Hello, Atlas."

# FIFTY

## *A Life Most Loved, Freely Given*

Ary's wings itched like mad.

She swayed where she stood as Atlas looked down at her. He was *massive*—so big he nearly filled the cavern, so big he made Sootflank and the centipede look like tiny blips of life. And he was *old*; his scales were cracked, his fangs yellowing, and there was a heaviness to him that made her heart ache. Here was the exit plan the Gardener had left them, holding up the terrarium for the past two hundred years, and she had found him in his very last hours. Overhead, the glow-shrooms flickered and dimmed.

Atlas looked down at her, his tired eyes half closed as his tongue flickered in and out. She recalled the voice in her dreams, the way it picked through words with the careful grace of a dancer. A light entered his eyes, and when he spoke, his voice was so loud the cavern walls shook.

"At lasssst," said Atlas. "Little Mossssssheart."

"You called for me," said Ary. "Those voices, the dreams— it was always you."

The old snake tilted his head to the side with a groan,

his eyes sweeping the cavern and settling back on her. "You look like her."

The words knocked the wind out of her. Ary forced herself to stand tall and lifted her chin. Behind her, Owl, Briar, and Shrimp had gone still. Glow-moth caterpillars squirmed past them, spinning the silk that held them fast. They looked completely and utterly terrified—but Ary felt only calm.

She loved them, more than she had ever expected to. She loved them, and this terrarium, and the creatures in it—even the ones who had hurt her, even the ones who had taken more than they needed. They had all just been trying to survive, fighting for scraps in a world a hundred years past the day it had been destined to die. Maybe not all of them deserved a new world; maybe it didn't matter.

She would give them this second chance if she could.

"Okay," Ary said. "I'm ready. Free us from the terrarium. Take what you need."

Atlas looked down at her—and began to laugh.

It filled the cavern in great, sweeping booms. It shook the walls and sent more dust flying in silver-sweet clouds that coated Ary in a fine powder. Beneath the dust, brown scales covered the length of Atlas' body. He wasn't silver at all; it was only the strange dust that puffed off him now, flooding the air, flooding Ary with a strange, electric energy, that she had seen in her dreams. The snake laughed, and laughed, and laughed.

"Oh, little folk," he sighed. "If only it wassss that sssss-simple."

"What do you mean?" Ary frowned. "I'm here. I'm the Mossheart. I'm the life required. So cast the spell—"

"I cannot casssssst the sssssspell," Atlas sighed. "I only carry it. *You* musssst casssst the sssspell. Assss only a folk can."

"No," whispered Ary as finally she understood.

The warning that had haunted her.

The fury that Gran had felt.

Ary turned in one great circle, her eyes sweeping the cavern, the voices of Seedlings past swirling in her bones and the warning burning in her eyes.

"The flower from the myths," she said faintly. "It's here. It's the *dust*. It's *fairy dust*, oh Gardener help us, it's the fairy dust we need to cast the spell, and if I have to use it, that means—"

"The cassssster," Atlas confirmed, "musssst live to complete the sssssspell."

Ary's knees buckled.

*A life most loved, freely given.*

"No," she half begged. "No, that can't be how it works. You can't ask for the life of someone who loves me most." Who would that even be in this room? Owl? Shrimp? It wasn't right—it wasn't fair—

Ary sank to her knees. She swayed where she knelt, and

she understood now why the glow-moth worms had captured her friends. It wasn't to keep them from stopping her.

It was to prevent them from running.

"I can't," she whispered. "I won't. Let one of them use *me*, then. Let Owl cast the spell. I love him. He can take my life—"

"He cannot casssst," Atlas said calmly. "And you do not love the girl—not yet."

Ary could have screamed. "There has to be another way."

Atlas cocked his head to the side, his yellow eyes taking her in. "I have only an hour left, little Mosssssssheart. And it is one life, over all othersssss."

"No," Ary said vehemently. "No, I'm not doing that, okay? Don't give me that hero nonsense—don't tell me about chosen ones or prophecies. I am not *killing someone I love!*"

Overhead, glow-shrooms began to wink out. The cavern groaned as the magic in the terrarium began to collapse. Even Atlas seemed to sag. They had only minutes, but still Ary stalled. Suddenly it was sixty years ago. She was Wren Mossheart, a chosen hero, faced with an impossible choice— the girl she loved for the life of her people. One life for the world.

And in that moment, Ary understood.

*I do not want this.*

She had never wanted to be a hero. She had not wanted

*any* of this. Let them tarnish her name. Let them hate her as they'd hated Gran. If this was what it meant to be a hero, she wanted no part of it. And if her choice was wrong—so be it. Because it was far more wrong to ask a little girl to save the world. There were so many adults in Terra who had lived full lives, but it was not them who stood here before a great, tired snake, the fate of the world on her shoulders and the ones she loved behind her being asked to give their lives to save it.

It was just her. Just Ary, a girl whose wings had not yet unfurled.

And it was here that she drew the line.

Five more glow-shrooms winked out. The cavern dipped into a concerning dusk.

"Little Mosssssheart," said Atlas, and he sounded almost sorry. "It isss time."

Grief pounded through her. They had come all this way. She had betrayed Gran, burned the Ant Court, made mistakes and floundered and failed, but they had *gotten here*. There had to be another way. There had to be something she could do, something she could give up, that would still let her friends make it out alive. She'd wanted to make this worth it for them. She had wanted them to have a second chance, a new life; she had wanted anything better than what they had, anything at all.

She had wanted to find the sun.

"Ary," said a voice behind her.

"No," Ary said firmly.

"Canary."

"*No*," Ary shouted. "The answer is *no*, Owl. I am not letting you *die*, not for me, not for anyone."

"Um," said Owl. "That wasn't me."

Footsteps sounded behind her.

"I can pay the price," the voice said. "I couldn't, years ago. But I can now."

A shadow fell over Ary—too close to be Owl, too tall to be a glow-moth. A hand descended on her shoulder—familiar, soft, scarred, and wrinkled.

"My name is Wren," said Ary's gran. "And I have come to keep the Mossheart's promise."

# FIFTY-ONE

## *The Mossheart's Promise*

It wasn't possible. Not her, not *here*, not now—

"Gran?" whispered Ary.

Gran kept her gaze on Atlas, her hand firm on Ary's shoulder. Dark circles ringed her eyes, and flakes of ash clung to her wisp-white hair. But even now, even here, she had not lost the proud tilt to her chin, the stubborn gleam of her stare, the hard, almost-mocking set to her mouth. Her clothes were filthy, and scratches marred her arms, but she was alive, she was *here*.

Behind her, a glow-moth stirred, a coil of the rope the folk of Terra often used to bind the moths hanging from its midsection. The rope was tattered, as though the moth had spent the past few days dragging it through mud, snagging it on thorns or rolling it through the mold that filled the Gloom. And something about it was familiar—the pale blush of its wings, the crooked tilt of its antennae, though Ary couldn't quite place what.

"Wren Mossssheart," murmured Atlas. "Returned at lasssst."

Gran looked up at the snake.

"Sixty years ago, I made a promise on my honor, a promise on my name." She sucked in a breath, her narrow chest quivering. "But when I came to set the terrarium free, you asked not for my life—but the life of the one who loved me most. I would not—could not—let the girl who loved me pay that price. So I turned away. I went home and shouldered that failure. I've spent the last sixty years watching our world rot. I never saw her again. Sixty years ago, I saved Dracaena's life." Her voice faltered. "But I killed her in every way that mattered."

Atlas' head sank lower, as if the very effort of keeping it aloft was too much.

"You are out of time," Gran observed. "As am I. I can feel it in my bones, in the weakness of my breath, in the falter of my heart. I have lived, and loved, and suffered—and I am ready. So I will keep my promise, while I have this second chance." She turned, now, not to Atlas, but to Ary, and softened.

"Gran," Ary protested. "You *cannot*—"

"Canary." Gran's voice was firm but kind. When she looked at Ary, sadness and love shone equally in her eyes. "Look at me, little one. I wish I had more time—to explain, to apologize, to try to make right all my wrongs. But Atlas has only minutes left, and Sootflank cannot hold back Quickspark forever. The newts have attacked Terra. And we are out of time. I think a part of me always knew it would end like this—I think I knew from the moment you learned Dracaena's name."

Slowly Gran came to her knees, her posture a mirror image of Ary's as she cradled her granddaughter's face in her hands.

"You are so much braver than me," Gran whispered. "Kinder, too. And I am so, so proud of you. I'm sorry I didn't tell you that sooner. I let you shoulder too much, for too long. But I cannot let you shoulder this."

Tears leaked down Ary's face. "And I can't let you *die*."

"Please," Gran said wryly. "I'm the chosen one. What else are we good for?"

The ground was threatening to tip out beneath Ary. Above them, Atlas waited silently, and if the old snake was surprised, his eyes didn't show it. Briar, Owl, and Shrimp were entirely silent. Ary's chest heaved. This wasn't right—this wasn't how it was supposed to be. She had been angry at Gran, yes. She'd spent a lifetime in her shadow, chasing her love, resenting her legacy, and when Gran had left her behind in the Underground, she had vowed to be different.

But that didn't mean she wanted to lose her.

"Now chin up, little one." Gran quirked an eyebrow. "We've a big spell to cast."

Gran clasped Ary's hands in her own and tugged her to her feet. Ary clung to her grandmother's hands as if for dear life, her mind whirling with panic, her legs quivering.

Gran turned to Atlas.

"We're ready," she said. "Tell us the spell."

Atlas gave her a long look. "I do not know the sssspell."

Gran's face fell. "Excuse me?"

Atlas' coils lifted slightly in what Ary assumed was a shrug. "I do not know the sssspell. I guard the magic; I call the folk. But I am not the casssssster. When the Gardener warned the folk of Terra of their fate, it was they sssshe entrusted with the sssspell. Not I."

Ary's head began to pound.

"No," Gran said, the color draining from her face. "No, you must know it—I didn't come all this way—*she* didn't come all this way—"

The floor threatened to swallow her whole.

"I'm sssssorry, Wren," Atlas whispered. "It sssseems I have broken your heart again."

Ary was going to be sick.

They couldn't have traveled this far for nothing. Not after all they'd suffered, not with *Gran* here, just to stop because no one had thought to leave them with the Gardener-cursed spell.

"You're lying," Gran said, showing an old flash of temper. "You have it, you useless beast, so *tell* us."

Atlas regarded Gran with weary pity. Slowly, the snake lowered his head.

"At leasssst," he murmured, "thissss isss not ssso bad a place to die."

Ary's head pounded harder. There was something they were missing—something she had to know that Gran didn't—

Behind them, the stone door separating Atlas' cavern from the tunnels boomed and shook. Light flared beneath it, and something scuttled over the door. In front of her, Gran was pacing, her narrow shoulders shaking. "This can't be possible—there had to be something we missed, something I didn't know—"

Ary's head pounded harder. Every step through the Underground, the Seedlings who had once carried the knowledge of Atlas had left clues—their shovels in the dirt, their writings in the stone—

"Writings in stone," Ary whispered. *The carvings.*

Behind them, the stone door cracked as something heavy slammed against it.

"Ary," Owl cried. The boy thrashed against the wall, fighting the bonds of the glow-worm silk, and he raised his voice to shout. *"Ary, it's the warning! The spell is the warning! It has to be!"*

Of course.

It had been with them all along—etched in stone, scribbled in Dracaena's pages. They had puzzled over it, whispered it, dreamed it. They'd thought the warning was meant to lead them to Atlas.

But it was *for* Atlas.

"Gran," whispered Ary. "I know it."

Gran kept pacing, her fingers knotted in her hair.

"Gran," Ary said louder. "I know it. I know the spell."

Gran whirled to face her—and behind them, the stone sealing off Atlas' cavern shattered.

Earwigs poured through, Quickspark at their center. Sootflank was nowhere to be seen. They surged forward, and Atlas let loose a bellow, slamming the length of his tail down in front of the entrance, crushing the first line of bugs.

"Stop them," roared Quickspark.

"*Gran*," cried Ary.

They reached for each other, their hands clasping together.

Ary looked at Gran, her chest heaving. "What do I do? How does it work? I've never used fairy dust before. I don't know how to cast a spell, I don't—"

"Are you not a Mossheart?" Gran interrupted, a gleam in her eye. "Are you not my granddaughter?"

"I am," Ary whispered, tears streaming down her face.

And though Gran's hands shook, the old hero winked. "Then that's all you need."

The glow-shrooms began to wink out one by one.

Behind them, Briar, Owl, and Shrimp were shouting. Ary forced it all away—her friends, the earwigs, even Atlas, roaring and writhing before them. Fairy dust coated her skin, her lips, her hair, crackling with a power that was two hundred years waiting.

The words came all too easily.

*"What roots shall bloom, and what blooms must die, beneath this city to which we flee."*

Overhead, the ceiling cracked.

*"By the Gardener's hand . . ."*

Something cool brushed her back—Atlas, coiling around them, shielding them from the earwigs, lending them the magical dust that coated his scales and the life that burned beneath it.

*"A false world spins . . ."*

"Make me a new Mossheart's promise," Gran whispered, her own chest heaving, her eyes bright with fear and—something else. Joy, maybe? Relief? "When they try to rewrite what happened here, tell them how Wren Mossheart failed. Tell them I tried, and I made mistakes, and I was selfish, and cowardly, and cruel. Tell them it was wrong to ask a child to save the world, that it was wronger still that I let you try. Tell them every messy, imperfect part of my story that history will try to smooth away. And tell them, more than anything, even though I wasn't very good at it, even though I should have done so much better—tell them how much I loved my granddaughter."

Ary looked at the woman she'd known only a piece of her entire life. There was still so much she wanted to ask, so much she wanted to understand. But maybe that was what love was—never a full knowing, never a neat closure, but all the mess and mistakes wrapped together. Ary did not know if Gran was a good person. She did not know if she liked her.

But Ary did love her.

She had always loved Gran, and despite her scars, Gran had tried to love Ary back; she had *tried*, and it didn't fix anything, it didn't forgive, but maybe that could be enough, here at the very end of the world.

*I promise*, Ary mouthed, tears streaming down her face.

Beneath their feet, the earth heaved.

*"But in its dust . . ."*

*I love you*, mouthed Gran, over and over again, as though she were trying to fit a lifetime of love into only a moment. *I love you, Canary. I'm sorry, and I love you, I love you, I love you.*

Canary Mossheart flared her wings.

*"We find the key!"*

The magic swelled.

And the world went white.

# FIFTY-TWO

## *The Terrarium (Again)*

When the terrarium was fully rotted, the soil dry, the mushrooms molded, and the walls coated in slime, the fairies of Terra huddled beneath the Gardener statue and wailed as they lost their future.

It started in the ground: a bucking of earth, a bubbling of the soil. The newts and earwigs that had broken through the thorn wall faltered, and a howl went up as the newt flames flickered out one by one. The mushrooms shriveled to dust; the moss rotted black. Every crop, fungus, and fruit remaining in the terrarium withered in a blink, eaten up by the spell sweeping through. Terra's fountain ran dry; the mold faded. Tunnels crumbled, caverns collapsed, fences rotted. Beetles, pill bugs, ants, and even a centipede streamed from the earth in a panic. This was how a world died—inch by inch, life by life, and then all at once.

Deep in the Underground, an old hero held her granddaughter's hands and thought of love.

She held tight as the magic came for her and burned her up, as her granddaughter's wings burst into flame. Memories flashed of her as a girl, entering the Underground in a different era, a newt at her back and friends at her side—all lost now, all gone, save for her, who had survived despite it all. The old hero had spent her whole life fighting, and she was ready to be done. She was ready to rest. She held tight as everything went white, and she saw them—the ones she'd loved, the ones she'd failed.

The one she was trying to make it right for, even now.

The walls of the terrarium began to shake.

Cracks raced up the walls, splintering through years of mold and grime, sloughing it off in great sheets. Impossible pale light flooded the world, so bright it burned.

In her last moments, the old hero whispered one last promise.

"Dracaena," she sighed. "I'm coming home."

And finally, after two hundred years, the terrarium gave a great groan—and shattered.

# FIFTY-THREE

## *A Life for a Life*

Ary was on fire.

Everything burned—she felt nothing, could see nothing, except the burning in her skin and her arms and her *back*— oh, how her back *burned*. A pair of familiar hands slipped from hers; the shadow of a great beast shrank, the titan who'd once held the world settling down for his final rest. Someone was shouting, but Ary couldn't see, couldn't hear, couldn't think. There was so much *magic* in her, and it was too much for one girl to carry.

"Mossheart," a familiar voice said. "Don't you dare die on me now. Ary, *don't you dare die*."

"What's wrong with her?"

"I don't know! But the ceiling is breaking—we need to— *ack!*"

And then—familiar, cool legs closing around her. A scuttle of feet she'd come to know all too well, antennae brushing her shoulder as something lifted her up, and the voice of one that had followed her to the ends of the world.

"Ary," came a whisper. "Hold on."

A trill filled the air, followed by a flutter of wings, a pulse of light, and they were moving.

Her mind spun. Distantly, a part of her knew what had happened—what was still happening. Gran and Atlas were both gone, and maybe it was a blessing that her world was still a wash of burning white, and her last memory of Gran would be the look of love in her eyes that had burned a thousand times hotter than the magic crackling around them.

Gran's voice poured through her.

"They will try to make a hero of you," Gran had warned in the fragile moments as the spell took hold. "Do not let them. Everyone wants a martyr; everyone wants to be saved. When you reach the new world, Ary Mossheart, you write your own story. Nothing that comes next is promised or written in stone. Do what I could not and forge your own path, little one. And know, every step of the way, how proud I am of you."

Air rushed past Ary's cheeks as something powdery and soft brushed against her. And then they were moving *up*, currents of air swirling by. Earth rained down around them, echoed by the crash of boulders, the screech of stone cleaving in two as slowly, their world split apart.

The pain vanished. The world crashed back in, and Ary was the same, and yet everything had changed. She felt . . . lighter, somehow, and in the lightness was an ache, a grief not yet placed.

Ary gasped.

"She's alive!" Arms snaked around her, and tears wetted Ary's cheeks as Owl hugged her tight. Something *whirred* beneath them. "Sorry! You told me to stay still, didn't you? Sorry!"

Ary's eyes fluttered open, and she saw only air.

They were rising, quickly, the world a wash of moth powder and pale light. Owl and Briar hovered in front of her, knees dusted pink from the glow-moth whose back they knelt on. All around them, glow-moths rose with the currents, weaving effortlessly away from the rock that rained down around them. A few lengths away, two glow-moths flew patiently, their legs clutching a familiar, rocklike ball of anxious bug.

Ary twisted and saw that the moth was the same one who had brought Gran to the Underground. As if sensing her attention, its antennae twitched. The beast flapped its wings, and a whispery voice filled her mind.

*A life for a life*, the moth Ary had freed from the thorn fence whispered.

Ary could only watch as they rose into the Underground— and their world died.

# FIFTY-FOUR

## *Who We Find, at the End of the World*

Terra was gone.

When they landed in the village what felt like a mere hour later, they were greeted with only ruin. Not a folk was in sight, and there was no mold to be found—only dust blanketing the wreckage of crumbled homes and nestling in cracks cleaving the roads. The folk of Terra had left in a hurry. Clothes hung fresh on clotheslines, and blankets stretched forlornly on dead-moss lawns. Not a whisper of life greeted them when they landed, only the groan of the earth beneath their feet, the rumble of stones still settling, and a strange, pulsing whistle as air swept around them and plucked at their hair. Since when did air *move*?

"Hello?" Ary called. Her voice echoed through the village, warping oddly against the broken homes. Shrimp trilled nervously behind her, hovering close to Owl as he took in Terra with eyes the size of moth wings. Only Briar remained still. She stood alone, her shoulders hunched, brow furrowed, and a part of Ary was glad the Terra she'd known was gone. This was Ary's home, but it was a home that had cast children into a creature-filled dark to fix the problems they couldn't be bothered to face. This was a home that had demanded sacrifice, and pain, and given little in return.

And Ary found she was a little glad to see it broken.

"Come on," Ary said. "They have to be here somewhere."

She didn't look back to see if her friends followed.

Everywhere carried evidence of Terra's ruin, first at the tails of the newts, and then the spell itself. Scorch marks warped mushroom-tree husks; dust filled fields where produce had burst. All the mold, it seemed, had burned up with the spell, leaving behind only ash, a whisper of the rot, an echo of ruin not fully escaped. The dust muffled her footsteps, adding a strange, blurred quality to the world, and Ary found that as they drew closer to the fountain, for the first time in a long time there was no fear pulsing through her. Only exhaustion and calm. They had done it—the terrarium was fully broken, if the golden light and wind slipping past were any indication.

The outside world awaited.

But first there was something she needed to see.

They entered the market, and her heart skipped.

The statues of Terra's three great heroes had been reduced to rubble. The fountain itself had cracked, the water that had spilled free long dried. Ary crept closer, Briar and Owl on her heels, surveying the pile of stone where Gran's statue had once stood. There was no telling which one had been hers. For all their adventure, for all their conquest, Terra's heroes were like the dust at her feet or the mold now burned—gone in a flicker, a flash, left only to memory. And someday even that would fade, too.

Ary liked to think Gran would have preferred it that way.

"Hello?" Ary called. "Is anyone there?"

A ruined Terra looked back at her. Only the whistle of the newly swirling air answered, raising a chill on Ary's skin. There was no movement, no life. Despair wrapped claws around her throat. Were they too late? Had the folk of Terra already gone? Or worse, had the newts been successful? Had they . . . ?

"Ary," Briar said gently. "No one is here."

*No.* She had lost too much already.

Ary cupped her hands around her mouth.

"*Hello!*" she shouted. Her voice echoed back to her, warped and tinny.

*Hello . . . hello . . . hello . . .*

"Ary," Owl began.

And then behind them, a rumble.

A stone plinked to the ground—and then came a *whoosh* of dust as a door flush against the ground popped open, and a fairy head with it, dusted completely white. The fairy looked around, wincing against the unusually bright light, and gasped. "*Ary?*"

"*Tulip?*" Ary blurted.

Tulip staggered from the hole in the ground, Basil on her heels. Another fairy followed, and then another, until almost all of Terra poured out. Ary watched them with an increasingly frantic heart, a sick feeling stirring in her stomach. She recognized face after face, folk after folk. They drifted toward her, clamoring with questions, but Ary ignored them, her eyes searching the crowd, her heart pounding harder as she sought the only fairy that mattered. The line thinned. Only a few folk were emerging now.

*Please*, Ary willed. *Please.*

A new head poked out—mouse-brown hair, tired eyes, and a weary smile.

And then Ary was running.

Every ache, scrape, and worry of the past five days left as she sprinted across the ruins of Terra's market. Mama stood tall—taller than Ary had seen her in years—and there was a weariness in her still, but there was a weariness in Ary now, too.

Mama was real, Mama was *here*, and Mama was free of mold.

At the sound of her footsteps, Mama turned and held out her hands.

Ary threw herself into Mama's arms, and together they fell to the ground, laughing and crying and kissing each other's faces, marveling in the joy of what it was to still be here, breathing and laughing and alive at the end of the world.

Marveling that they had found each other at all.

They waited for Ary in the market.

Whispers wound through the folk, that the young

Mossheart child had done something remarkable in the Underground. In the bright light of the outer world, the folk of Terra looked small and wan, huddled together among the dust, wing stubs shivering and veiny hands clutching what meager belongings they could carry. Beyond them, others approached—beetles, a few ants, and even the odd newt. More creatures filtered in, following the pulse of the glow-moths, though some scattered, opting to scuttle their own path into the world beyond. A pill bug crept forward and gave an odd little trill; Shrimp stiffened, antennae cocked, and then practically sprinted forward. Another pill bug appeared from the terrarium, and another, and another, soon outnumbering the folk. Shrimp turned to Ary, his eyes alight, and he didn't need to speak for her to know what he would say.

Ary watched as the size of the crowd swelled, scanning it with a nervous skip to her heart, searching for a familiar face, that telltale whisper of smoke—

"Well," someone snapped. "What are you waiting for? I didn't survive the apocalypse to stand around *chatting*."

Ary's heart soared, and before Sootflank could protest, she flung her arms around his neck and hugged him tight.

The old newt grunted against her weight. There was a limp in his gait, and gash marks marred his flanks. He grumbled as Ary hugged him, and when her shoulders shook from the effort of holding back tears, Sootflank patted her head with the tip of his tail.

"Now, now, little folk," he sighed. "People are staring."

Ary said nothing and squeezed tighter.

After a long pause, Sootflank murmured, "Good work, Ary. She would be proud."

Ary wiped furiously at her eyes and stepped away. She could feel the bewildered stares of the folk of Terra on her—some colder than others. Mayor Nightingale's eyes narrowed a fraction as she took in Ary standing so close to a newt, her harsh mouth flattened to a grim line, but Ary didn't have it in her to care. Let them try to punish her. Let them try to tell her she had done wrong by trusting Sootflank, by trusting anyone in the Underground, and saving them all.

Ary stepped back and cleared her throat. "I'm sure many of you are wondering what happened," she said slowly. "The truth is—well, the truth is that many of us were not told the truth for many years. We—"

"Are very overwhelmed," Mayor Nightingale cut in with a humorless laugh. She swept forward, her white sleeves stained with ash. "And now we must rebuild."

Ary spun to look at her, incredulous. "What?"

The mayor put a hand on Ary's shoulder. From the distance, it might have been a motherly gesture. Instead, Ary felt the warning pressure of the mayor's hand pushing down. *Be silent*, the sharp bite of Nightingale's nails demanded. *And play along.*

"Terra has suffered before," Nightingale said. "But we are a strong people, and—"

"What is that light?" someone called, pointing at the golden rays spilling across the wreckage of their town.

"Our homes are *gone*! What are we to do?"

"Why are the ants here? What happened to our fence?"

Though Nightingale stood slightly ahead of her, the folk of Terra were looking to Ary. Her head spun in a dizzy whirl. This was not what she had wanted—she did not want to lead anyone, she did not want to *decide*.

And she did not want Terra to try to make a hero out of her, so soon after they had lost their last one.

Ary lifted her chin.

"Terra is gone," she said. "And it's not coming back. There is a whole world beyond ours. I can't tell you where to go, or what to do. But you are welcome to come with me into the new world, if you wish—"

"New world," Mayor Nightingale sputtered. "The child is clearly unwell—still a wingling, truly, and allied with a *newt*, at that." Her nails dug in harder, and Mayor Nightingale made a great show of turning to Ary, looking down her nose at her with a cold, flat gaze. "I would speak with Wren. Where *is* your grandmother, little Mossheart? Where is Terra's hero?"

Ary drew back, her heart threatening to collapse.

*Make me a promise*, Gran had said.

How was she to explain what Gran had done? How was she to explain Dracaena, the journals, the world beyond? Ary opened her mouth to speak but found herself without a voice. For all she'd done, all she'd saved, she was still a child, and Nightingale was an adult, keen to make an example out of Ary in a bid to retain her already fracturing power.

"Gran," Ary began weakly. "She . . . well, you see . . . the thing is . . ."

"Where is she?" Nightingale demanded, an edge of meanness to her voice, and Ary recalled their conversation in the dark, the way the mayor had tried to bribe Gran with food and security if only she would spin lies of comfort to a people slowly dying.

*Everyone wants a martyr; everyone wants to be saved.*

How furious Nightingale must have been, to have never been able to make Gran her pawn.

How furious she must be now, to realize Ary would not play along in her twisted game, either.

"Gran," Ary tried again, her voice shaking. "Gran is—"

"Gone," Mama said calmly. She stepped forward to thread her arm around Ary's shoulders, prying Nightingale's hand from Ary with an easy flip of her wrist. Mama looked out at the crowd with a half-lidded gaze, and the tightness of her arm around Ary was more comforting than a thousand Seedling shovels wielded in the dark. "My mother, Wren Mossheart, is dead."

A gasp went up, followed by a wail. Bitterness flooded Ary. They cried as though they'd loved her gran. But they had never truly known her; they had never cared.

"Terra's last hero has seen the end of her story," Mama continued, her voice steady in the upheaval of the market.

"And it is not up to Ary to tell you where you take your lives next. She is a brave child—but a child, nonetheless. And she has done enough." She paused, cutting a look at the mayor that would have shriveled moss. "You would be wise, Iris, to mind how you speak to my daughter."

"I am the *mayor*—"

"Of what?" Sootflank drawled, drawing forward to loom ominously behind Mama. At the sight of him, Mayor Nightingale went white. "Your village is gone. Your *world* is gone. You are mayor of the rubble, from what I can see." He paused and looked flippantly at the rest of the folk. "For what it's worth—I knew Wren well. None of you were worth her sacrifice."

Ary had a feeling that the outraged cries of the folk were the sweetest thing Sootflank had heard in years.

Mama turned her away from the villagers, her arm still wound tight in a protective embrace. The scent of her was all around Ary—warm and sweet, the musk of new earth and freshly sprouted toadstools. Warm, solid, and *alive*.

"Come, little one," Mama murmured. "Tell us where to go."

Ary's heart wobbled. For a second, she feared Mayor Nightingale would shout after them—but Sootflank was at her back, Shrimp at her left, bearing Owl and Briar atop his shell. They were a shield around her, a protective curtain from the folk of Terra and the world she was leaving behind.

Funny, how love could take so many different forms.

"The cliffs," Ary said quietly. "We go to the cliffs, and beyond."

# FIFTY-FIVE

## *Sunlight*

The walls that had once cradled Terra's world were in ruin. All her life, Ary had gazed upon the formidable cliffs, wondering at the meager patches of light that snuck through. Now they were shattered, clustered like great, sharp boulders. As they drew closer, a strange sweetness entered the world—not the sickly threat of mold, but something fresh, something new. The cliffs rose above her in great, broken pieces, glinting clear in the midday light—and it *was* midday, the light so much brighter than anything she'd dared to hope for.

It almost smelled . . . green.

Mama dropped her arm from Ary's shoulder, and Ary let her. She led the way forward, her head pounding as she walked faster, squinting against the golden light that was so richly bright it was almost painful. A crowd had formed behind her—creatures that had opted to follow the Moss-heart child, and folk of Terra as well. Mayor Nightingale and at least half the village were nowhere to be found. And though the thought of them trying to rebuild among an empty ruin worried Ary, she did not feel guilty. She did not feel like it was her job to turn around.

After all, she was only twelve years old, and it was not up to her to save them.

The wind grew stronger, and so did the green scent, the whisper of something alive, something bright, something *more*. Ary shuddered, picking her way across shards of glass. Her reflection flashed back at her, and for a second she froze. She recalled the way her friends had stared at her, the fire at her back.

Atlas had spoken of a sacrifice—and though she had kept her life, it seemed that Gran was not all she'd lost.

Her wings were gone.

The papery covering that had plagued her for years had burned up with the magic, and so had her wings. But instead of a smooth back like Owl, or the painful stubs of fairy folk, a skeleton had been left in their place. Thin, flightless membranes fanned out behind Ary, forming an eerie outline of where her wings had been. She twitched them experimentally, and though they moved, they could catch no air, stir no breeze. Were it not for her reflection in the glass, Ary wouldn't have known they were there at all. *Ghost wings*, she thought. That was what she carried now—not full wings or the stubs of wings long lost, but ghosts, one last testament to what she had lost in the Underground.

The wind stirred, and with her breath held, Ary stepped clear of the glass and out of the terrarium.

She waited for a crack, a shock, some sense of *wrongness* in her body. But she felt . . . the same. Though the world before her was utterly unfamiliar, there was no protest of her very being to leave her world behind. It was as if the terrarium had never mattered at all.

Ary looked up, and her mind ground to a halt.

They were . . . in a house?

A very, *very* large house.

Mama, Sootflank, Briar, and Owl filtered in behind her, taking in their surroundings with mouths agape. It was as though someone had taken the furnishings of a fairy home and blown them up to a thousand times beyond their size— chairs big as mountains, long covered in dust, sat against the wall. Was this the Gardener's kingdom, then? Or some warning of what lay beyond?

Ary took one nervous step forward, then another. A familiar glint caught her eye, and her blood ran cold.

Their terrarium had been left on a massive table, half basking in rays of golden light.

And it had not been alone.

Beside it, another pile of shattered glass and earth rested, long covered by dust and bleached by time. Whoever had been in that terrarium had left it behind long ago.

Beside it, the glass walls nearly black with grime, was a third, sealed terrarium.

The hair on Ary's arms stood on end. Something in her called her toward it; something else pulled her away. The terrarium had a sense of foreboding, like a centipede curled in the dark. No light permeated the glass. Not a flicker of movement stirred beyond.

Ary knew it wasn't possible, but for some reason it felt like the third terrarium was . . . watching her.

"Young Mossheart?"

Ary turned, her thoughts torn away from the terrarium as she surveyed the strange, ragtag band that had accumulated behind her. Only a smattering of folk had followed her beyond the terrarium's walls. Ary watched as more creatures streamed from the terrarium—beetles, ants, the stray spider.

Behind her, the wind stirred.

Golden light filtered through the window, more radiant than anything she'd ever dreamed. Beyond it, the sky was an endless expanse of burning, impossible blue. The wind rushed in, bringing the scent of things green and growing, of fast water and wet earth. But beneath it was something Ary didn't understand—a chemical reek, an artificial rotting, slick and new and burning. It smelled out of place.

*Ghostwing*, the wind seemed to whisper, *find us*.

Ary twisted to look at her friends, but their faces were blank. They had heard nothing. Ary pushed her worry aside. They had left their dying world behind to find this one, and they were ready for whatever it held. She hovered before the window, her eyes on that ever-blue sky, on the impossible, golden light that draped them in soft rays. This world was so bright, so beautiful, it almost hurt to look. To think she had been impressed by the weak fragments of light that made it through the terrarium's walls. To think she'd ever considered it real light at all.

They had done it.

The former inhabitants of Terra waited behind her, waiting to see what she would say, ants mingling among folk, pill bugs clustered together in a nervous little pod with Shrimp at their center. She felt their attention like a heavy cloak. Shedding the mantle of ill-fated hero would not be as simple as walking away from Mayor Nightingale. But that was a problem for tomorrow.

"All right," Ary said, her eyes still trained ahead. "Everyone stay close to me. We don't know who or what is out there."

Mama brushed an affectionate hand over her hair. Sootflank drew closer with a rumble and a roll of his eyes, as though the concept that he wasn't ready for any and everything was an affront against his very being. But even he looked a little nervous. And here, before that warm yellow light, standing atop what seemed to be a giant's table, he looked . . . small.

They were all so, so laughably small.

And maybe that wasn't such a bad thing.

Ary looked back at her family and smiled. "Ready?"

They did not look ready; they looked scared. But they nodded all the same, inching closer behind her, none of them willing to move past wherever Ary first stepped. The light was so beautiful it felt like something out of a dream. Ary dipped her toe into the closest golden ray, half expecting it to sting her, but it was *warm*. Like the embrace of Mama's arms, but richer, the very heat sinking to her bones.

Ary had never realized how much of her life she'd spent in the cold.

*We made it, Gran.*

"That light," Briar asked, a look of awe on her face. "What is that?"

"Sunlight," said Ary.

Owl's brow furrowed. "What is *sunlight?*"

"I don't know," said Ary. "But we're going to find out."

Ary took Mama's hand, and together they stepped into the sun.

# Acknowledgments

I began working on this book in 2020, about six months after I sustained a brain injury that uprooted my entire life. There was a time where I wasn't sure if I would ever be able to read properly again. Words blurred together; reading just a few lines rendered me so dizzy I couldn't speak. Suddenly the thing I loved most had become an impossible task. So I went back to the basics: in an attempt to relearn how to read, I reread a lot of the middle grade books I had devoured as a kid, relying on memory, accessibility, and wonder to push me through walls of blurry words. And then one day, like a lightning strike, as I was staring at a miniature terrarium sitting on my desk, Ary Mossheart appeared. I didn't know if I could ever write another book. Ary made it clear I needed to try and do it anyway.

I owe such a debt of gratitude to my agent, Jim McCarthy, who believed in this book from the beginning, and whose kind counsel has kept me sane through a very rocky few years. Jim, you are just the absolute best. My books are only going to keep getting weirder. Sorry!

My editor, Kristin Rens, has been an absolute gift and an

incredible partner in bringing this story to life. Thank you for enduring three-hour phone calls and for not even blinking when, on our offer call, I had genuinely forgotten several parts of the book I'd written thanks to my TBI. Thank you for believing in this book, for believing in Ary—and for making it clear I was not allowed to kill off Shrimp. I'm so excited to create more stories with you.

A special thanks to Dr. Michael Collins, Dr. Anne Mucha, Dr. Cara Troutman-Enseki, and the rest of the staff at UPMC in Pittsburgh. I'd started to lose hope I'd ever make a full recovery before we made the six-hour drive to your clinic, and it's felt a little bit like a miracle to finally have so much of my life back. I can never express the depths of my gratitude.

Now, I am going to attempt to thank everyone else who has helped this book come to life, but even before the injury, I have always had a very bad memory. I am going to do my best!

First, a huge thank-you to the wonderful team behind this book, because it really does take a village—particularly Molly Fehr, for designing the cover of my dreams and for illustrating the gorgeous map, Cathleen McAllister for creating a cover so stunning I want to frame it, my copyeditor, Jessica Berg, for catching the typos of my nightmares, and everyone on the B&B team, including Emily Mannon and Robby Imfeld in marketing, Taylan Salvati in publicity, Patty Rosati and her team in school & library marketing, Amy

Ryan in design, Sean Cavanagh in production, and Kerry Moynagh, Kathy Faber, and the rest of the sales team.

Amelie Wen Zhao, Katie Zhao, Alyssa Eatherly, and Grace Li read very, very early drafts of this book and gave me the encouragement I needed when writing felt impossible. I am so grateful to you all. Thank you also to Andrea Hannah, Kristin Lord, Aimee Carter, Ayana Gray, Meriam Metoui, Laura Steven, Layla Noor, Kyla Zhao, Isabel Ibanez, Jamie Pacton, Adrienne Tooley, Andrea Tang, Sheyla Knigge, Peter Lopez, Skye, Sarah Underwood, Beth Revis, and Brittany Davis for your kindness, friendship, advice, and commiseration. This industry is wild. Author friends make it a little more bearable. A huge thank-you to my Patreon patrons and everyone in the Story Grove for your friendship and support, with special thanks to Krista. Thank you also to Sofiya Pasternack and Katie Zhao for saying such lovely things about my weird, moldy book. You guys are so nice.

I'm very lucky to be loved by people who do not really understand That Weird Book Stuff Becca Does, and who unconditionally support me anyway—special thanks to Meagan Cotter, Melissa O'Keefe, Sabrina Cottrell, Natalie Noland, Mara Bouvier-Schatz, and Franklin Tibbits (I guess). Thank you, Hannah, Mom, Dad, and the Lorias for being so wonderful about my very weird job, and to Aunt Diane and Uncle Dusty for being my very first readers all those years ago. A very appreciative thanks to my therapist, Kelly, for . . . literally everything. Thank you as well, forever, to

Vicky Stringer and Kristen Remenar, for helping a dorky kid believe she had a story worth telling long before she actually did. (We got there eventually! Depending on who you ask.) Thank you also to Annie Gilson, Peter Markus, and the English and creative writing departments at Oakland University for all your support. Go, Grizzlies!

Shout out to my fourth grade nemesis for calling me stupid when I said I didn't like to read, which kickstarted my villain arc to destroy you in our school's reading contest. I am still annoyed that you didn't care when I beat you. I had to read, like, forty books that year, man. That's a lot for a ten-year-old! Anyways, you're probably living a normal life now and I write kids books for "fun," so you won in the end. Jerk.

I read and reread a lot of books when I was in recovery, but there are a few in particular I want to mention—the Gregor the Overlander series by Suzanne Collins, *The City of Ember* by Jeanne DuPrau, *The Tale of Despereaux* by Kate DiCamillo, the Ranger's Apprentice series by John Flanagan, *Howl's Moving Castle* by Dianna Wynne Jones, and *The Girl Who Drank the Moon* by Kelly Barnhill all fed into the fabric of this book, and helped me rebuild my ability to read when I thought one of the things most precious to me was gone for good. I don't know who I would be without books. I feel very lucky I didn't have to find out.

I'm sure it's weird to thank a coffee shop, but I'm going to do it anyways. Atomic Coffee & Dessert Oasis are where most of this book was written. Thanks to the staff for letting me camp out every day for months on end to finish this book. Sorry for disappearing without a warning the moment I turned the book in and leading you to think I had moved or died. I'll be living there again for the sequel.

A huge, special thank-you to the readers, librarians, and booksellers that have enthusiastically supported my books and my career; it truly, truly means the world, and it makes all the difference. I take none of it for granted. Thank you in particular to Jen, Jenny, Alyssa, and Megan, and the entire staff at Sidetrack Bookshop. I am so lucky to have a fantastic local indie run by the absolute best people. If the person reading these acknowledgments is ever in Michigan, please give Sidetrack a visit! You won't be disappointed. And if you are, well, you're wrong.

And lastly, but never least, thank you to David, my best friend, my biggest cheerleader, and the world's best cat dad. I don't know how I'd do any of this without you. When I write about all the ways love can make us brave, I'm writing about you.